MAGIC AND MYSTICISM
OF THE THIRD MILLENNIUM

BOOK 10

EMIL STEJNAR

ANDY MO

The Son of the Gnome King in the Human Realm

STEJNAR VERLAG

This book is part of a unique course of learning in magic and mysticism. In his books, Emil Stejnar has brought magic and mysticism from the world of medieval miracles into the modern world of scientific study. His ideas and discoveries are also recognised in academic circles.

© Copyright 2023 by Emil Stejnar
2nd Edition

All rights reserved, including reproduction
of excerpts in print or via electronic systems and media.
Cover & Layout: Rittberger+Knapp, www.rittbergerknapp.com
Cover montage from: ©AdobeStock/Kanea Romolo &
©AdobeStock/Tavani, JineKnapp
Translation: Hereward Tilton

ISBN 978-3-900721-27-5

www.stejnar-verlag.com

The books of *Magic and Mysticism of the Third Millennium* provide a reliable, comprehensive introduction to the entire field of esoteric and spiritual scholarship. Previously accessible only to a select few, the instructions and insights are now available to a wide and fascinated readership through the publication of these 13 volumes. Stejnar shows that the esoteric can be exciting, intelligent, and extremely helpful in everyday life.

The books of *Magic and Mysticism of the Third Millennium* comprise 13 volumes. Every volume is complete in itself and addresses an important subject.

BOOK 1: The Book of the Master and His Heirs.
BOOK 2: Spiritual Exercises for Freemasons.
BOOK 3: The Four Elements.
BOOK 4: Out-of-Body Experiences.
BOOK 5: Astrology.
BOOK 6: The Adept Franz Bardon.
BOOK 7: The Book of Guardian Angels.
BOOK 8: The Theban Calendar.
BOOK 9: Diet-Yoga.
BOOK 10: Andy Mo.
BOOK 11: At the Portal to the Final Lantern.
BOOK 12: Dreaming Can Be Dangerous.
BOOK 13: Gnosis Tantra Kabbalah.

WHAT IS THIS BOOK FOR?

This book is intended to introduce children and young people to the world of magic and mysticism in a way that's easy to understand. Or rather, to lead them away from that world again. For we have every reason to fear that millions of young Harry Potter readers – unless they are educated – will try out the dangerous practices of an Aleister Crowley, or will end up with one of the many 'magical' groups and occult sects. Only education can prevent this.

A serious realm of esotericism also exists. Magic isn't a spell to make your life easier or conjure up spirits. Magic is the systematic training of spirit and soul.

A true magician doesn't engage in magic and mysticism to change the world with magical powers or summon spirits. The sole purpose of spiritual training is to change yourself in such a way that the spirits and the world can no longer change and control you according to their will. You don't need any magic formulas or rituals to do this. People who apply the rules of positive thinking are already magicians who can mysteriously shape their future in accordance with their own ideas.

Every thought can serve as a helpful spirit. But thoughts can also degenerate into demons. That's why it's important to master your thoughts. And that is precisely the goal of any true magical training.

The earlier children learn this, the less danger they will later sink into the swamp of pseudo-magic.

So I hope that Andy Mo's message will find its way into the hearts of readers young and old.

Emil Stejnar

CONTENTS

What is this book for? 5
Prologue 9
In the Borderlands 12
Baphomet 20
At the Threshold 26
The Book of the Master 29
The friends and the magic circle 36
The breakthrough 44
Gnomes, magic, and spaghetti 47
An earth spirit is summoned 65
Welcome to the wizards' club 67
Humans, big city, underworlds 78
Einstein and the question of spirits 97
The raven Yks 121
Goldstein 132
The liberation of the raven Yks 144
Only children can defeat Baphomet 154
The first lesson in magic 163
The passage through the darkness 177
Shadow worlds 186
August Kleindienst's circus act 191
The gardener, Christ, and Baphomet 201
Good and evil 206
The baptism of fire 212
The Formula of Nothingness 217
Every book has a soul 221
The emerald 233
The secret of a pact and a good salad 240
Thoughts are spirits 255
The conjuration at the cemetery 258
Magic is working with the spirit 268
The school trip 273

Humans are the next spirits 281
The magic of the attracting power of thoughts and wishes 289
Astrology: Tides of power and life 301
Karma and rebirth 308
The Shadow 313
Amue 314
The alchemist 318
Incarnation 325
I am 331
The body is a prison for a spirit 337
Spirit times spirit equals human 342
Learning to fly 345
Spiritual training - The power of imagination 348
Concerning the beyond and life after death 358
The secret society of 'the scales' 368
The rescue mission 384
Farewell 398
Shaping this world and the next with the Formula of Nothingness ... 399
Epilogue 412
The Books of *Magic and Mysticism of the Third Millennium*
in 13 Volumes 414
About Emil Stejnar 447

PROLOGUE

*Archival extract. Department Element Earth File AE! 10 N 9
Solar 20.7S9, time calculation according to humankind new I7S9*

Dark clouds are gathering on the surface of the Earth. They call it enlightenment. Technology and science, but the new spirit obscures more than it illuminates.

*Annotation. Addendum 1:
Solar 20.959, time calculation in new human terms 1959*

Conditions on the surface of the Earth have deteriorated dramatically in the last two hundred solar years. Due to the increasing pollution of nature and the clouding of the spirit which provides perspective, we no longer have a basis for existence in the regions humans inhabit. We have been forced to retreat.

In the past there was a nixie living in every lake; the sea was populated by water sprites and undines, and there wasn't a waterfall or a river that didn't hide a water spirit. The mountains and fields were teeming with gnomes. The sylphs were carried by the winds through the human realm and regulated the weather patterns. A tree spirit lived in almost every tree, a troll in every boulder. Together with elves and fairies, the elemental spirits made sure that nature unfolded properly and that the blind forces of the elements didn't cause too many natural disasters. Thanks to the many fireplaces in houses, even the fire spirits were close to the people and could serve them; now they are banished to the confines of the volcanoes. Instead of asking a water sprite for a good catch, people fish with dynamite and oversized nets; rather than making the work of us gnomes easier by preparing compost, they spread artificial fertiliser, driving away the last of us.

Humans are becoming more and more distant from the beings of the spirit world. They only concentrate on the gross material plane. They explore the molecular structures of matter and neglect their own spirit and soul. While science and technology are making enormous progress, humans' mental abilities are atrophying. They're no longer able to perceive ethereal beings. As a result they have lost faith in the spirit world. Not only their ability to perceive us, but also their sense of morality has withered away along with their faith in spirit and the spirits. People have become ever more devoid of conscience, and the few spirits who are still able to exist near them correspond completely to their nature. Thus grows the power of the Shadow – they call him Baphomet. From their egoism, their lack of compassion, and their greed he mixes the mortar of evil and builds that wall which separates not only one living being from another, but also this world from the beyond. Now it is only permeable in a few places. So far, two expeditions aiming to advance as far as these places and locate them have failed. If we fail to enlighten the inhabitants of the Earth so that they tear down and overcome this wall, humanity will perish.

Annotation. Addendum 2: Solar 21000, time calculation in new human terms 2000
The Gnome King Andimo set forth on another expedition. To this day he has not returned.

Annotation. Addendum 3:
Now his son Andy Mo Junior has also disappeared. The search for him was fruitless and has been called off.
The king's brother is preparing to take office. Has Baphomet, the prince of the Shadow, triumphed?

The seal of the Gnome King Andimo.

IN THE BORDERLANDS

"Andy Mo!" cried Mrs Mo. "Andy Mo Junior, come back! Don't look for the gate – you'll get mired in the Borderlands between worlds, just like your father did."

But Andy Mo had already left. He knew his mother's fears were justified, and he took her concerns very seriously. But he had to do it. Fortunately she had no idea how close he already was to his goal. What he was planning to do today was really dangerous. He would have loved to embrace her one more time, as he didn't know when – or even if – they would ever see each other again. But that would have aroused her suspicion, and the parting would have been even more difficult.

So far, all attempts to find his missing father had ended in failure. The last expedition hadn't returned home at all. That's when they had stopped searching. He was the only one who never gave up. Most other young earth spirits were working underground from dawn to dusk, stratifying ores, grafting crystals, and arranging the soil for the tree roots so that the humans above could survive. But he had been roaming through the dangerous Borderlands, and now he had in fact discovered a trail. Soon he would know if it really led to the human realm.

Andy Mo had always been different from his peers. He always had other matters on his mind. He liked humans a lot, but he wanted to help them in a different way. He knew from his father that they were constantly struggling with problems and worries which didn't exist in the spirit world.

"That's because they've fallen completely under the spell of Baphomet, the lord of matter and its shadow beings", his father had explained to him once. "Now they don't believe in the spirit realm any longer, only in the world they can see and touch. This has distanced them from us, and we can no longer stand by them as we once did. Most humans have even forgotten that they themselves are spiritual beings, and now they only identify themselves with their bodies."

Andy Mo was shocked when he first heard this. He found it hard to imagine how anyone could forget that they were a spirit. What else could you be? True, he thought to himself, thoughts and feelings can't be touched – but these fleeting spiritual entities, this stuff of which dreams are made, is also the stuff which comprises all rational beings. What would be left of you if you didn't have thoughts, feelings, and desires? You can't see your 'I'.

From that point on, Andy Mo wanted to learn more about humans. He studied everything there was to read about them. Now he knew who they were, how they felt, what they thought, and he wondered why they used so few of their spiritual faculties. He realised that humans couldn't even perform magic, even though they could be like gods if they did. All they needed to do was integrate the invisible into their lives, he thought. He wanted to help them rediscover the spirit realm.

That had been his father's goal too. The Gnome King Andimo had also been more interested in the world of human spirits than in the world of earth spirits. In fact he felt so close to humans that once he even confessed he wanted to be like them. This was despite the fact he knew very well that humans are sad much more often, and that they have many more desires than other beings and spirits who aren't stuck in a gross material body. But none of that seemed to bother his father. Once he stated that humans are superior to earth spirits, although he didn't tell Andy Mo why. There had to be something in the human realm that they didn't have in the spirit world, Andy Mo reasoned, and he was steadfastly determined to find out what it was. But to find out, he had to be closer to them. You can't learn everything from books.

In the meantime his father had disappeared. Because he was his immediate successor, he had been given the best possible education. As a future king he was instructed in all the sciences, and he knew more than some intelligences of the higher spheres. He had also received and studied texts from his father on secret knowledge – writings which were otherwise only accessible to kings and princes of the realms. Within them he had discovered many matters which no one else could even dream of. But the path to the humans was not recorded anywhere. His father had told him many things, but he had never revealed to Andy Mo the hidden place leading directly to the human realm. He had always put him off with the words: "Perhaps in a few years when you're older..." But now it was too late. The king hadn't returned home from the Borderlands, and anyone who had dared to venture too close to the last open gate had disappeared.

That happened two and a half years ago, Andy Mo recalled sadly. Everyone else thought his father was no longer alive, as no one had ever returned from the Borderlands – let alone the human realm – after such a lengthy absence. Yet he was convinced that they would see each other again. There was no doubt in his mind that his father had passed through the gate and was now living with the humans. He wondered if perhaps Baphomet, the Lord of Shadows, had tracked him down there and was holding him captive somewhere.

That was Han Mun Ton's opinion as well. He had often spoken to him about his father's disappearance. Han Mun Ton was the oldest of them all, older than father or grandfather or the Old Man of the Mountain.

"It's time", Andy Mo said after entering the sage's simple hut. "I'm leaving today."

The old man nodded.

"If your father is among the humans, there isn't much time left to save him. None of us have been away for more than three years. Those who stay longer don't come back. On the surface of the Earth, a spirit without a body loses its orientation after only two years. You forget who you are, gradually lose consciousness, and die." After keeping silent for a while, he added: "That's what has happened to everyone so far. Are you really willing to put your life on the line, Andy Mo? The chances of you succeeding are very slim."

"I am ready", Andy Mo said, and for the first time he was overcome by fear.

Again the old man nodded. Then he got up and walked to a chest at the back of the room. When he returned, he was holding a small glass vial in which a mysterious red liquid was shimmering.

"You must find the king, Andy Mo. And when you have found him, provide him with some of this elixir: it is the only way he will survive. You can also partake of some yourself when you realise you are reaching the end of your tether. But be careful with it", he added seriously. "You may only open the bottle four times. Each time, some of the power will escape."

Andy Mo carefully stowed the precious vial in his backpack. Then the old man blessed him, and he set forth on the path.

*

Andy Mo knew he had only six months left to bring the life-saving medicine to his father. He had already uncovered his first lead, and he wanted to follow it up. It began in the green cave in front of the large lake where the silver waterfall flowed; beneath it lived Amue, the nixie. The entrance to the realm of the water spirits lay in the north. He had to cross the darkest region of the Borderlands to get there, but he knew the way.

It began behind a cliff face that was impenetrable, even for earth spirits. The rock was so slippery that it was impossible to climb over it. But Andy Mo had discovered the secret passage. It lay in the remains of the ruined castle that had been built at the foot of the cliff. No earth spirit dared enter this ruin, for it was said you would never make it out again. Indeed, nobody would even approach it, as it would spell your doom.

So Andy Mo was all the more surprised when he saw somebody standing in front of the walls. It was his cousin Zoton Luz, the son of his uncle, who deeply despised Andy Mo because he came after him in the line of succession, and he wanted to become king himself. He was just as tall as Andy Mo, but broader and more sturdily built. On a purely physical level he was far superior to him. Grinning scornfully, he blocked his path.

"Is the little prince on the road again? I've been watching you for some weeks now. You go into the ruins and you disappear; you're simply gone. And yet later you come back out. So you've found a way through. You're going to show it to me now, then I'll let you go."

But Andy Mo shook his head. He loathed his cousin, who was detested by everyone else as well. Yet he was also afraid of him. Zoton Luz was brutal and unpredictable.

"Come on mister, get lost", he said calmly, trying to keep his cool. "There's no demand for types like you on the other side." He tried to distract him and jump over him with a mental leap, but his adversary saw through his plan and blocked his path again.

"So you want to go up to the human realm. You want to play the hero. You want to free the humans and your father from the power of the Shadow. Go ahead – I won't stop you. You won't have any more success than he did. You won't be coming back either. Then you'll both be gone, and my father will be king." As he spoke, Zoton Luz was slowly getting closer. The sly look from his slanting black eyes scanned Andy Mo, fixed on him – and then suddenly, abruptly, he grabbed him by the neck with both hands. "Where is the passage?" he hissed, and Andy Mo could smell his cousin's bad breath. "Show me how to get to the plane of the other elements, or I'll kill you."

Andy Mo felt completely caught off guard. His opponent was stronger than him – but he had more magical power. Now he put it to use. Rather than using his hands, he fastened tighter and tighter around his opponent's windpipe with his concentrated thought power, and eventually Zoton Luz couldn't breathe either and clutched at his throat.

And so Andy Mo was free. He wasn't a coward, but now wasn't the time for a pointless fight. He grabbed his backpack and his lamp and ran towards the safety of the walls. But he didn't get far. His cousin also knew how to paralyse an opponent with concentrated thoughts. Using his imagination, he pumped ever more weight into Andy Mo's legs. His feet became as heavy as lead, and his steps became slower until he could go no further. It felt as if his legs were stuck in a swamp. His adversary came up behind him. Zoton Luz had the upper hand again.

"Even if you make it to the surface of the Earth and find the king, it's too late", he sneered. "He's long since lost consciousness. Neither of you will ever make it back. Then my father will take charge of the affairs of state. We represent the interests of the gnomes, the spirits, the beings of the spirit realm. What do we care about humans? We'll negotiate with Baphomet and then rule over the other elements – perhaps even the attendant spirits of the solar realm."

Andy Mo shuddered. He knew this is what would happen if he failed. Since the humans had stopped caring about the gnomes, they too were losing interest in the human realm. Many gnomes already thought like his uncle. A revolution was brewing that only his father could prevent. And it had to be prevented – for without the help of the spirits, the humans would perish. He couldn't admit defeat. He had a mission to fulfil and he possessed the elixir.

"What elixir?" asked Zoton Luz, who had been reading Andy Mo's mind. "What aren't you telling me?" He was furious and was about to pounce on Andy Mo. Taking advantage of his angry opponent's brief moment of inattention, Andy Mo managed to escape from his sphere of influence. With a few steps he was at the entrance to the ruins, and with one daring mental leap he transported himself to the other side of the ravine which gaped immediately behind the walls. He disappeared before the eyes of his bewildered cousin.

There was no special passage to the other world among the ruins. The secret was this: all you need to know is where you want to land, and then you simply plunge into the void. At first you land in no-man's land. From there, the path leads to the next plane.

*

With great difficulty he fought his way through dense thorny undergrowth. It had grown out of the confused human ideas which had gone astray there. He waded through the swamp of their turgid feelings, and he was exposed to their unrestrained emotions of anger and hatred – here between the worlds they manifested themselves in the form of exploding projectiles. In no-man's land their material greed and ice-cold human egoism crystallised into rocks which were impenetrable even for earth spirits.

During his previous forays through the Borderlands, Andy Mo had learnt to avoid the various threats there. He was familiar with the places which were particularly dangerous, and he knew how to avoid them. He also knew very well that actually entering the human realm was even more dangerous. Han Mun Ton had warned him emphatically: no one had returned in recent years. Nevertheless, he was determined to continue searching for the passage and to brave the last step. There was no turning back.

Sometimes positive thoughts and feelings from the human realm also shone out, lending him confidence and courage. He certainly wouldn't have made it this far without this revitalising and guiding glimmer of hope.

But today was different. A lifeless, paralysing silence lay over the last stretch of desert he had yet to cross. It was frighteningly lonely here, as always, but today he was not alone. He could clearly sense that something ghastly was lurking somewhere. He felt the abysmal hatred this being had for him, as well as its desire to attack him and annihilate his existence. He realised that it wasn't the shadows of the humans which were threatening him here; rather, it was Baphomet, the Shadow of the world. He had tracked him down, and now he would stalk him, just as he had stalked his father. If Andy Mo had known what was lying ahead for him in the coming months, he would have turned back.

An oppressive gloom ousted the last glow of dawn and darkened his soul. Like a grey mist, the ghostly light seemed to smother everything; it took his breath away and covered the rock like fine, greasy soot. Everything was grey for as far as he could see. It even overwhelmed the light of his lamp, which would normally illuminate the hardest rock with crystal-clear clarity. The palpable darkness penetrated his bones like icy cold and paralysed all his life force. The silence thundered painfully in his ears; it was harder to bear than the terrible din of war earlier in the Borderlands. Andy Mo was seized by the fear of death.

Never in his life had he felt so lonely, so abandoned, and so menaced as in this grave hour. But the Shadow's misty breath of death grew thicker, and soon it enveloped him like a shroud. The darkness filled the room with a merciless impenetrability which wrapped itself around him like shackles, depriving him of his last freedom.

Andy Mo had long since lost his bearings. He could only guess where the safety of the cave entrance lay, yet he lacked the strength to move. And although he could no longer see anything himself, he knew very well that his enemy was constantly watching him. The darker the world became, the more clearly his adversary could see him. He knew it was only a matter of time before Baphomet captured him completely and dragged him into his Shadow Realm once and for all.

An inner voice urged him to turn back: "Save your life – it won't help your father if you're dead, and you'll be chosen as his successor." Spectral phantoms conjured up images of his mother crying and fretting about him. Amue, the nixie who was like a fairy godmother to him, appeared and beckoned.

Exhausted, he dropped down and cowered in the hollow of a large stone. He thought longingly of his father and felt for the elixir he wished to bring him. As cool as a jewel, the bottle lay in his hand, and he wondered whether he should drink from it. But the touch alone lent him confidence. He recognised that it was the images of his own shadow which were tempting him to turn back. He realised that he was about to give up, and then all would be lost for his father as well. That must not happen. He had completed every undertaking up until now. Resolute, he pulled himself together once more and tried to penetrate the paralysing lack of light with his gaze. And then a miracle happened. Was it the recollection of his goal or the touch of the elixir that had filled him with a new-found courage to live? In any case, the shadows faded as quickly as his determination grew. The dark force that sought to prevent him from venturing onward lost its power and retreated.

Immediately in front of him there was a flash of light. A brilliant radiance broke through the darkness, showing him the path. Andy Mo joyfully recognised the passage to safety he was seeking. With the last of his strength, he squeezed himself into the rock jutting out of the desert before him, and immediately he felt relief. His lamp cast its familiar light forth once more, and his powers returned with the light. The Shadow had lost its power.

Little did Andy Mo then know that the real battle was about to begin.

BAPHOMET

Baphomet, the Prince of Shadows, froze. He knew he'd made a mistake when he had the Gnome King captured, but only now did he see through his plan: it was not the king, but rather his son Andy Mo Junior, who would be his adversary. He would finish what his father had begun. He would help the humans break through the wall he had built between the worlds.

That means the old man knows his secret: the mystery of the Shadow. It means he knows what is written in the Revelation. It means he knows what no one else knows: only children's souls can deprive him of power. Young humans don't cast shadows. And if they learn to use their inner lights in time, they can prevent the shadows emerging later.

"If the boy is as clever as his father", Baphomet thought to himself, "then my kingdom is in danger." He had just proved that he was brave. Only he and his father had managed to resist him for so long. He too had evaded capture in the Borderlands where Baphomet's Shadow Realm began.

Furious, he was now forced to accept that the king had allowed himself to be captured; it had been part of his plan. In this way he had prepared the path for his son. He will search for his father, find him, and free him, since he possesses the elixir. Then he will learn the secret from him. And if he subsequently succeeds in spreading this knowledge among the adolescents of the humans, his power will be finished.

For thousands of years, the Gnome King had been his most dangerous opponent. Of all the spirits, he was the closest to the humans. That is why the ONE – they call him 'God' – also chose him, entrusting him with the mission of helping humans develop. He not only rules over the gold of the earth; he also knows how to mine the gold of the spirit.

First he taught humans how to extract material wealth from the dark interior of the earth. Then he showed them how to draw true spiritual values from the hidden interior of their own being. Previously this spiritual gold had been reserved only for the gods. But the old gnome had let some humans in on the secret. He revealed to them how they could become as powerful as the gods by training their spirits. He taught them how to master their four essential limbs of thinking, feeling, willing, and consciousness using the power of the four elements, and thus he introduced them to the lesser mysteries. He also initiated some of their priests into the greater mysteries. To these priests he revealed the way in which the gods bind human spirits to their realms, and so drain them of the spiritual power they've gained.

Then he inspired one of them to write the Book of the Master, and so he made the mysteries accessible to all. Although the Gnome King only used to initiate priests and alchemists into the science of spiritual transformation and gold-making, soon everybody will be taking an interest in these matters. And so humans will come to understand that spiritual values are more enduring than earthly treasures, and they will strive to attain this spiritual wealth. If they seriously study the laws of Hermetics and learn how they themselves can use their inner fortune, they'll soon disempower the gods and their shadows. Up until now he has been able to prevent this from happening. True knowledge is still limited to a few initiates, and he, Baphomet, has been able to distract and seduce them. But all this will change if the Gnome King manages to win over the children as well.

Ever more young humans are already beginning to take an interest in the science of magic and the world of spirits. If this interest is purposefully promoted, Baphomet's power will soon be finished, and clearly Andy Mo Junior is set to take on this mission. For once the children are initiated into the lesser and greater mysteries, it's only a matter of time before they also unlock the last secret of this planet: the true mystery of the void of infinite space. Nobody knows the one true revelation yet.

Baphomet rejoiced that they had not yet found the document of the Formula of Nothingness, which holds the key to the knowledge of true action and the knowledge of life and death. He was keeping it in the human realm. That's why it has not yet been discovered by any of their seers. Even the old man hasn't discovered where it's hidden yet. They're all searching for it in the 'beyond'. In doing so, they equate the realms which form out of their fantasies with the spiritual world. They don't realise that they're blocking their own perspective – they believe they can find the truth in their own dreams, which form the planes with their shadows. Rather than seeing through and making use of this fact, they constantly deceive themselves.

Only those who possess the document would be able to overcome the realm of spectres they name the 'beyond'. They could even ascend above the worlds of the gods upon which they all cast their shadows. Not even the gods know how to truly grasp the void which contains everything. Only one of them – the ONE – actually resides in the sphere of timeless eternity. All the others rely on the shadows of humans for their orientation.

But it hasn't come to that point yet, Baphomet knew. He will prevent the son from completing his father's work. Without knowing it, gods and humans alike are all still banished to their own space in the realm of their shadows. But they don't realise it, because the Shadow – like the ONE – casts no shadow itself. They grope about in the darkness and believe it is the light.

"The old man knows a great deal", Baphomet thought to himself, "but he doesn't know everything." He didn't know that Baphomet knew what he knew – that he saw through his plans, and that had given him an edge again. He had no idea that his son was about to fall into his trap. Into the human trap. For if he succeeded in infiltrating their world, he would soon think and feel and act like them. He was already behaving like one of them. He was much taller than all the other earth spirits; he was multifaceted, inquisitive, and displayed compassion and courage. His pleasant appearance, his proportions, and his confident, cheerful nature were also more like those of the young humans than the spirits. Once he was among them, he would soon want to be exactly like them. That wish would occupy him, distract him, bind him, and – like every wish you cherish for too long – would become a prison from which he could no longer free himself. The spirit of the gnomes consists of only one element, not four like the human spirit. He could let the boy go: he would fall into the trap all by himself.

*

Andy Mo breathed a sigh of relief. He was back in his element and he felt safe. After a short rest, he followed the unusually rich vein of gold which began under the rock at the North Cape of the Borderlands and led straight to the nixie's cave. For earth spirits, such veins of ore are like well-lit roads. On the other hand, earth spirits find it impossible to move in open space. Just as birds need air and fish need water, they need the density and heaviness that the element of earth grants them.

The blue-green lake glittered mysteriously before him, bathing the cave in a magical light. Relieved, Andy Mo realised that Amue was already standing on the shore, waiting for him. He never knew if he was going to come across her. There was no sure way for gnomes and nixies to meet up.

Silently they gazed at the water; its unfathomable depths could only be guessed at. The far shore was not visible, and the steep, inaccessible rock walls of the cave were lost in the ever-surging mist of another world. There was no way forward here for earth spirits.

"The river that connects the living with the dead also flows through this lake, and that makes it dangerous even for us water beings", the nixie explained. "You must be careful, Andy Mo."

Normally gnomes and nixies can only survive in their own element. Without Amue's help he knew he would never be able to cross the water; yet the friendship which bound them together allowed them to overcome the limits set by their nature. And she encouraged him to venture into the element of water, despite the danger.

"It's definitely the right way", she said. Besides Han Mun Ton, she was the only one who was encouraging him to continue the search. "Your father must have come this way too, otherwise his invisible trail wouldn't have led you to me. If you concentrate upon him and his thoughts, you'll be able to follow his path further as well."

Amue was also the one who had told him about the strange light oozing from the hidden crack. Today he wanted to investigate this strange glimmer in the world of earth and water spirits. If it was the right trail, it would continue on the far shore – of that they were both convinced.

Once again, Amue explained to him how to live and move in water, an element that was unfamiliar to Andy Mo.

"If you think you're losing yourself, don't fight it. At first the cold will paralyse you and give you the impression you're being numbed and swallowed up by the silence surrounding you. Then you'll feel the damp. You'll believe you're dissolving in the infinite sea. Let it happen, but pay attention to your feelings. Instead of allowing fear, maintain hope and love. These feelings will carry you to the far shore. Think of your father, for whom you're daring all this and for whom you're ready to sacrifice your life; think of the people you want to help. The secret of our element is selflessness and compassion. We can protect anyone who has these forms of love within them."

Tenderly, she embraced him one last time. "I can only accompany you a little way", she said sadly. "Even we cannot survive in the River of the Dead which crosses our realm." Then they both dived resolutely into the floods.

But it was much worse than he had feared. The initial shock froze him; once he had recovered, Andy Mo felt like a piece of ice dissolving and disappearing forever into its element of damp cold. That frightened him. There was nothing solid left for him to support himself. Everything was dissolving, melting away, dispersing in billowing waves like seaweed in the ocean. Andy Mo could feel himself detaching from himself; layer after layer of his being was disappearing. Losing more and more of his identity, he felt himself merging with his surroundings. "So this is what dying is like", he thought to himself, and he fought in vain against the temptation to surrender completely. Only Amue's selfless proximity lent him buoyancy and security.

But then it happened: Amue disappeared. She had been caught up in a current and swept away. He suspected they had fallen into the current of oblivion, and he felt there was no escape from its deadly undertow. All the same, he didn't think twice and tried to follow her. His entire consciousness was filled with the desire to save her. He remembered her last words: "Our element is self-sacrifice and love." Despite the raging forces, it was eerily quiet. The grey spectres of cold souls drifted by – the compassionless dead, the lonely shadows of their former selves. And suddenly she appeared before him. Like a veil, he saw her long golden-green hair and managed to catch hold of it. He just managed to push her into calmer waters behind a rock which was jutting out of the water; then he was swept away again by the current.

I'll gladly sacrifice myself for you", he thought to himself, and he felt his senses fading away. He was at the mercy of the negative powers of water; but once they felt that he had also mastered fear, the dark side of their element, they lost their power over him. They let him go, and a gentler current carried him safely to the far side of the lake.

Soon Andy Mo also found the trail on the far shore; it had been left by the strange radiance seeping from the solar realm of the humans. With some difficulty he managed to squeeze through the crevices in the rock, and he followed the glow along. Just as he had followed the vein of gold like a stream bed before, so now he was moving between the various mineral formations until they too dried up. The layers of rock became ever more devoid of content. The sandier and looser the earth around him became, the more difficult it was for him to make progress. The path became more arduous, but the light which oriented him simultaneously intensified, and he felt the closeness of the humans ever more clearly.

Combined with the overwhelming desire to help his father, the gentle glimmer from the human realm formed a solid ground of confidence upon which he ventured forward. Through this feeling of selflessness he overcame the law which separates the worlds. The path suddenly and seamlessly ended in the wood of a thick, gnarled root from the trunk of an ancient elder tree. Birds chirped in its branching canopy, and from a large knothole Andy Mo, for the first time in his life, could look directly into the human realm.

AT THE THRESHOLD

"There you are, finally!" A creaky voice came from behind Andy Mo. "I've been expecting you for a long time. Your father also passed by here. His lantern is still standing there – he doesn't need it in the human realm. I'm Krux. I live here in this tree."

The tree stood in a schoolyard just outside the open window of a classroom. The asphalt square was empty, and there was no one in the class either. The lesson had not yet begun.

Andy Mo was exhausted and confused, but happy. He had achieved his first goal. Although there were many questions, the battle with the dark forces and the arduous climb to the light of the solar realm had tired him so much that he just wanted to sleep. The friendly tree spirit with the kind eyes and the funny bulbous nose fully understood this.

"You can stay in the room your father used when he was with me", he suggested, and made up his bed in a cosy chamber.

But then Andy Mo spotted the boy and was immediately wide

awake again. Just below his lookout, leaning against the trunk of the elder tree, a student was sitting and clearly enjoying the first rays of the mild morning sun. A thick book lay on his lap, but he wasn't reading – he was gazing pensively into the distance. His clear eyes were as blue as the sky in which his thoughtful gaze was lost. The fact his blond, slightly wavy hair was difficult to tame was shown by the natural curls which framed his tanned face and softened his serious, disciplined features. The trained muscles of a lean body were visible through his white T-shirt, and although he was sitting you could tell he was tall. Everything about him looked confident, athletic, and fresh.

Andy Mo was immediately impressed by the first human he saw. He had only known them from illustrations in books and had imagined these beings differently. In reality, their charisma far exceeded his expectations.

Are they all so tall and beautiful?" he asked Krux. "Even our kings don't look like that. He looks like he could accomplish anything! Is it really the case that he can't perform magic?"

That's Michael Freiwald", replied Krux, who knew almost all the pupils and teachers at the school. "A completely normal human child your age. He really can't perform magic – not yet – but he's a medium and might learn."

"What is he doing here all alone", Andy Mo wondered, "and where are the others? I thought humans weren't loners and preferred to live in groups."

"He often comes this early – when he comes", Krux chuckled, "because sometimes he skips school. The handsome lad is friends with the headmaster's daughter and they usually have breakfast together under this tree. Kathi brings breakfast from the canteen, but today she seems to have overslept. Michael has no parents, incidentally. Or rather, he lives alone. His father is somewhere in South America looking for emeralds, and his mother died three years ago."

Andy Mo immediately felt sorry for him. Ever since his father had gone missing, he knew how much he missed him. But at least he still had his mother; the other lad was all on his own. He had immediately liked the boy, but now he felt even more connected to him. He felt that a friendship was developing within him. It couldn't be a coincidence that he, of all people, should be the first human he met.

Andy Mo waved through the tree window and called out "Hello!", but the lad took no notice of him. He obviously couldn't hear him.

"Why doesn't he notice me?" he asked. He wanted to get close to him by using a mental leap to transport himself through the open window. But to his surprise, he bumped into the hole in the bough as if it were an impenetrable pane. The entire world outside seemed to him as if it were cast in glass. Try as he might, he couldn't even reach his hand through the opening.

"Different laws prevail up here", Krux explained. "Just as humans can't walk through our earth and rocks like we can, so their thin air is like a solid wall to us. Your father didn't manage it right away either. He couldn't tell me how he eventually made it across, as he never came back. Later I'll tell you everything I know about him in detail. Rest now, nothing will happen here for an hour. I'll prepare something to eat in the meantime."

But Andy Mo tried again and collided hard against the invisible wall once more. He couldn't penetrate the solar realm of the humans. Had it all been for nothing? He was deeply disappointed and looked sadly over at Michael. And that was when it happened. Somehow Michael must have sensed his feelings, because suddenly he looked up as if someone had called to him. His gaze scanned the branches attentively, but he couldn't see Andy Mo in his perch.

All the same, Andy Mo was happy. He had succeeded in making his first contact with the human realm. With this feeling of satisfaction he fell asleep.

THE BOOK OF THE MASTER

"Christian, get up, you've overslept again!" his mother called, but Christian didn't hear her. It wasn't until she came into his room and shook him awake that he came to.

"Damn!" he groaned. "Not again – and the first lesson is maths. Will you drive me to school, Mum?"

While Andy Mo was lost in the dream worlds, Christian was trying to return to the real world. After an exciting night in a world of wild dreams, he felt exhausted and was struggling to wake up.

"No wonder you're tired", his mother called out from the kitchen. "Your light was on until two o'clock. Were you on the internet or reading something exciting?"

"I found something really cool in dad's shop", Christian replied a little later as he slurped his cocoa, which was already waiting for him. "A book about magic, demons, gnomes, and spirits – it's called The Book of the Master and His Heirs."

"A fairy-tale book", his mother observed with amusement. "When did you start reading children's stories again?"

But Christian protested.

"It's a book for adults. Actually, it's a kind of diary – a private manuscript. It contains a doctor's description of how he was admitted into a Freemasonic Lodge. During the initiation ceremony he is symbolically killed, and he suddenly experiences himself as a spirit without his body."

"An out-of-body experience", interrupted his mother, who was a doctor herself and was becoming curious. "Such things do occur. Patients who've experienced similar events during anaesthesia have told me about it."

"It gets even better", replied Christian, who was pleased that his mother was taking the story seriously. "Not only does he leave his body, but immediately afterwards he lands in another mortal shell in another time, and he experiences scenes from a past life. He's a monk in the Middle Ages. Back then he was in possession of a book of spells which described exactly how to enter the realm of spirits, and he owned magical items which lent him power over demons. He fights Baphomet, the demon who tempts people to do evil things, but before he can defeat him he's burned at the stake by the Inquisition for witchcraft. Rather than dying, however, he reawakens as a doctor in our time and experiences the continuation of the ceremony in the Freemasonic Lodge.

"And here's the great part", Christian added, reaching for some toast. "The doctor was so convinced by his vision that he went off to investigate the whole matter. And sure enough, he found the chest with the Book of the Master and the magical items he had hidden in a cave back before they executed him. Now he has his magical power back again, and he's continuing to fight against the evil which keeps people under its spell."

What Christian didn't tell his mother was that he, too, had found the book in a most mysterious fashion. He didn't know what to make of it himself, nor did he wish to make a fool of himself. All he knew was that either the house was haunted or he was a sleepwalker. Because it was actually a strange gnome who had appeared to him in a dream and had led him to the chest in his father's shop. He resolved to investigate this matter further.

Christian didn't mention anything about his plans either. It all seemed so unbelievable that he thought he was still dreaming. All the same, he was convinced that this being which had gotten him out of bed really existed. The world of spirits fascinated him, and he wanted to make contact with them, just like the monk and the doctor had. He had to get to know these invisible worlds.

There was a lot of underlining and many notes in the book, which was actually a poorly bound manuscript with many loose pages. For example, it said: "See Book 2, *Spiritual Exercises for Freemasons*", or: "See Book 4, *The Four Elements*". From this you could infer there were further volumes. It was also clear from these textual references that the other volumes described the exact process of how to contact the invisible intelligences. The doctor had obviously rewritten the manuscript from the Middle Ages which he had found in the cave's shrine, adding his own experiences.

For Christian, it was clear that he had to get hold of the missing instructions. He had the feeling that even what he had already read would fundamentally change his life. This was confirmed on the last page of the book, which ended with a kind of testament the monk had already written. The doctor had also concluded his new version of the Book of the Master with it:

"To the person who finds this legacy, whoever you may be: when you have read my testament, you will become another person. Whatever has hitherto been for you no longer counts. From this point forward you are a link in the long chain of a spiritual community fighting for the survival of human souls. Knowledge of the battle raging in the invisible realms for the spiritual power of the born and the unborn will henceforth rob you of your peace. You are an initiate, and as a knower you bear responsibility. Preserve your freedom and tranquillity by tolerating no evil within you. Be wakeful and follow your conscience. Be a fighter for truth, justice, and charity. All hail to you, and welcome to our venerable circle of Masters."

Christian felt exactly the same way. He had become a different person that night. A new phase of life had begun for him. But he didn't mention anything about that either – he only said that it was the most exciting book he had ever read.

"Sounds great", interrupted his mother, who had been listening attentively to him. "Many people believe in reincarnation. Let's talk more about it in the evening – we have to go, you're already running really late." They lived in a renovated Biedermeier-era carriage house, which was a heritage-listed building. It had two floors. The living quarters were upstairs, and the shop and gallery were downstairs. Christian lived in a cosy room in the attic. The house was located in the pedestrian zone of Vienna's posh Hietzing district, so the car was parked two streets away. It was a clear morning in early June, and already remarkably warm for that time of year.

As calm as a taxi driver, Ms Baumann steered the Volvo through the dense, hectic morning traffic.

"You drive just as safely as Dad", Christian remarked appreciatively. "He seems different to me since the theft, by the way. He's suddenly so taciturn; I think he has other problems."

"I'm afraid you're right", his mother confirmed. "But it's no wonder he's worried. I should probably tell you: if the paintings which didn't belong to him and which he only took on commission don't turn up again, he'll have to declare bankruptcy. The paintings in question are two previously unknown winter landscapes by Dombrowsky. Leopold Ludwig, the director of the Ludwig Foundation in the Museum Quarter, paid 700,000 euros for them."

"Weren't the paintings insured?" Christian asked.

"Yes, but since your father personally handed them over to the thief posing as the museum courier, the insurance company is refusing to cover the loss. Now the buyer is demanding his money back. The old owner has already cashed the cheque, of course. It could result in a lengthy legal battle. But the next instalments for the renovation are due. We only have one month left, then the house and the shop will be auctioned off."

"Oh my God!" exclaimed Christian, visibly shocked by the news. "Why didn't anyone tell me? I'm not a child anymore. You have to help Dad, don't you?"

"I see it the same way, that's why I just told you. But he only told me yesterday. You know him – he always wants to keep problems away from us. Still, we won't be able to help him. My salary as a doctor in the hospital is just enough for our current expenses. Unless a miracle happens, we'll be broke. But where are miracles these days?" she added resignedly, pulling into the car park in front of the school. However, Christian didn't get out.

"How could this have happened?" he asked, speaking more to himself than to his mother. "Dad is always so conscientious – he doesn't make mistakes."

"He didn't", his mother confirmed. "But for him to fall in with two scammers at the same time is more than just an unfortunate coincidence. Now get to class. If I know Professor Kleindienst, the punctuality fanatic will grill you for being late again."

"He can go to hell – he's such an idiot. We have other problems to solve now. Thanks for the taxi, Mum – and don't worry, I believe miracles still exist today."

*

"It feels like a miracle to me", Andy Mo said to Krux after he had rested a little. "I'm on my father's trail and I'm looking into the human realm – I can hardly believe it." Together they followed the lesson, which had already started. The tree spirit thought this would be the quickest way for Andy Mo to get to know humans better.

But the first glimpse into the human realm was sobering for Andy Mo. Even though it was a school class and a certain amount of order was necessary, he was surprised by the strict way humans treated each other. His teachers were quite different.

"Good morning, Baumann. Late as usual", the professor greeted Christian sarcastically as he burst breathlessly into the silence of the class. "Nice to see you finally found us. Can you tell us what time it is? You're late again. You're always late. Step up to the blackboard right now and enlighten us, please – find the square root of four hundred and forty-three thousand, five hundred and fifty-six." Christian's face turned red. He knew what was coming now. Finding roots and squaring had never been his strong point. He was lost in thought and he didn't even hear someone whispering the solution to him. But Kleindienst heard it.

"Freiwald, of course. The Robin Hood. The fighter for the weak and poor in spirit. The saviour in times of need. Since you like arithmetic so much, come to my room after class and create two pyramids for me."

It was a punishment paper from the lower grades of the grammar school where Professor Kleindienst had previously taught. You have to multiply a three-digit number first by 2, then by 3, then by 4, etc. up to 9 and then divide it inversely by 2, 3, 4, etc. – an excruciatingly boring procedure. And if you haven't miscalculated, the first number comes out again at the end. But of course you miscalculate, because

Kleindienst made sure you didn't use your calculator.

Then the professor turned back to Christian. But he was still no closer to the solution.

"He doesn't know", he declared triumphantly, and you could see how he enjoyed humiliating Christian. He drummed hard on the table with his pencil, which sounded uncomfortably like gunshots. "So, something simple. Two unknowns." Kleindienst went to the blackboard and wrote: $x + y = 62$. "What numbers are we looking for?" Christian didn't understand the simple example. He was just thinking about his father and staring straight ahead.

Kleindienst shook his head. "He can't even grasp that. This demand is indefinite and ambiguous. That's what the art of pure reason tells us. Something is missing. So we add: $x - y = 2$. Now it can be calculated."

Christian still didn't understand and began to sweat. But Kleindienst suddenly became hot as well.

*

"I don't believe this", Andy Mo exclaimed indignantly, looking at Krux with wide eyes. "Isn't there anyone to put that impudent human in his place? He's making the poor boy's life miserable. Why does the lad put up with all this?" But then he remembered what his father had already told him: humans can't perform magic. Krux, who could read his thoughts, confirmed that fact:

"Very few humans know anything about magic. They only learn how to defend themselves with their hands and feet; they know nothing about defending themselves with the help of their spiritual power. Since they have no control over their impulses, thoughts, or feelings, they're unable to transmit them outwards. Only what you master within yourself can also be directed outside of yourself. That's why they have no power over space and time." Then he chortled: "Maybe we can help him a little?" Andy Mo was immediately enthusiastic at the thought.

"I'll tighten his tie until he can't talk so stupidly", he suggested, and he tried to transport his way into the classroom through the open window with a mental leap, as he had done before. But he couldn't get through, of course.

"We'll have to do it differently", said Krux. "Christian is already desperate. Try it with your thoughts. As a tree spirit, I can't leave here at all, but my imaginings carry quite far; you try with your mental images as well."

Together they imagined pulling the professor's blue tie tighter and tighter. Earth spirits learn to concentrate their thoughts in the first grade. They succeeded effortlessly. Kleindienst grabbed at his collar and desperately tried to loosen the knot of his tie. His face turned red.

While the professor was gasping for breath, Andy Mo gave Christian the solution to the problem. It really was quite simple. He thought of the correct numbers and imagined them landing in Christian's consciousness through the wish 'send to'. Andy Mo could literally feel Christian's relief as he remembered the correct calculations and rapidly wrote the numbers down on the blackboard as if he were the professor himself. There was a murmur of approval from the class.

Andy Mo was thrilled as well. His success gave him the courage to try reaching the other world again. But once more he failed.

"Concentration alone is not enough", explained Krux, who had been watching everything. "Wanting to cross over isn't enough – there has to be someone waiting for you on the other side. The first time you do it, you need a friend among the humans. It's best if a magician who knows your name and sign calls you. Your father was probably helped by one of the initiates who know about our spirit world. They say it's possible to enter the human realm with their help."

"My father had many friends over there, but nobody knows me", Andy Mo replied despondently. "Nor do I know any initiate who would call me." Andy Mo became sad. "And since I can't get out, I'll never know one. I'll never find my father."

Krux knew a lot about humans because he had lived near them

for a long time, and he comforted Andy Mo: "It doesn't have to be a great magician – it's enough if they simply believe in the world of spirits. It can also be a boy or a girl from over there. If somebody believes in us, we can even appear to them in their dreams under certain circumstances. And once someone has seen one of us, even if it's only in a dream, we can make contact with them again later. We can take their hand." Krux noticed that Andy Mo was regaining hope, and he continued with relief. "Once you've been outside one time, it gets easier and easier. I've read that you get used to the special circumstances. It's just the first time that's difficult."

Then the bells in the building rang shrilly, and the students rushed into the courtyard.

THE FRIENDS AND THE MAGIC CIRCLE

To Andy Mo's delight, Christian Baumann and Michael Freiwald – who were obviously good friends – came to the elder tree. They climbed up onto the thick bough where he and Krux were watching, so the two earth spirits could hear everything the pair of friends were talking about. However, to their surprise they weren't discussing the annoying incident with Kleindienst. Rather, Christian was talking at length about the magic book he had found in his father's shop.

Andy Mo was astonished. The secrets of magic and the invisible world of spirits were reported quite openly in this Book of the Master, and from their remarks he could tell that the two friends were convinced these spirits existed.

"Humans know a lot more about us than we thought", he said to Krux, who was also pleased with the understanding of the spirit world the two friends displayed.

Eventually Christian recounted how he had come into possession of this book:

"I had a strange dream. Now that I think about it, the whole thing seems most mysterious to me. Actually, I dreamt that I had woken up and there was a friendly gnome standing in front of my bed. Not like the funny garden gnomes, but kind, serious, and dignified. Somehow I felt that the spirit was urging me to follow him. So I followed, and he led me straight down to my father's shop; there was an old box there, and within it was a chest. The little fellow pointed to this chest and I wanted to open it, but I stumbled and lost a slipper. At the same time, I really woke up. The dream had been so clear, and I was wide awake – and when I couldn't find my slipper, I went back down again to look. And what do you know: in front of the box was the slipper! So naturally I became curious and looked for the chest. And when I found that as well, I looked inside and there was the book."

Michael Freiwald, who had listened attentively to his friend, was deeply impressed by what he heard.

"That's absolutely unbelievable!" he said with conviction. "It's mind-blowing. We're on the track of something sensational – you do realise that?" He was visibly riveted. "You must copy this for me. This is a true story, not a fairy tale. I can feel it in my gut, this is revealing something more than religion, philosophy, or one of the usual global conspiracy theories. It's about the future of humanity. The secret superiors who rule the destiny of the world aren't the bankers and the corrupt politicians. Those are just the lackeys of this Baphomet and his spirits. We're ruled by gods and demons. We are being challenged, my friend. This knowledge places a burden of responsibility on us. We have to do something. But first we absolutely must find the missing volumes with the secret instructions. Only then can we penetrate the spirit world and thwart their plans."

"We can't do it alone", Christian agreed. "We need allies. Who else can we bring into this?"

They thought long and hard about who they could really count on – and above all, who they could trust with this knowledge. Christian would have preferred to have all his friends with him. But Michael Freiwald believed that until they knew something concrete, only a few people should know. None of the adults were suitable, in any case. So they agreed only to confide the secret to Kathi and her friend Miri Li for now.

"The four of us will be a strong team", Michael predicted. "We'll form a secret magic circle." And they decided they would meet at his place next Sunday. "I'll bring something delicious to munch on, as usual", he announced. He knew how much everyone appreciated his cooking.

Then Christian told the story about the fraudsters and the embezzled painting, and how his father was in danger of going to prison and they would lose their house. Michael Freiwald was outraged.

"That's unbelievable", he said angrily. "Those rats! This sort of thing only happens in the movies. We must stop them. But if things really go wrong, you can all come and stay with me – I'm only really using the kitchen and one room. I hope we'll find the missing magic books soon, then maybe the spirits will help us to catch these crooks. After all, what's magic for? But right now I have to pee – the milk's pressing on my bladder."

"I have to go as well", Christian said, and he swung down from the tree. And that's when it happened. The bough was rotten and couldn't withstand the force. It broke right behind where Andy Mo was. While Christian landed flexibly at the bottom, there were far-reaching consequences for the others.

Not only did Michael fall to the ground with a cry, but Andy Mo also whirled through the air like a leaf in the wind. Without thinking twice, he had tried to save Michael from falling; in doing so, he had lost his own footing. For him, the loss of the solid support offered by the tree's wood was a catastrophe. He felt completely unprotected in mid-air. At the same time, he didn't feel like he was falling to the ground; rather, he felt himself falling in all directions. His being dissipated like smoke in the wind. In this element he knew he would lose all the components of his being and disintegrate into millions of spirit molecules. All the same, he experienced the lightness of his free fall as a pleasant numbness. It seemed to take place in slow motion. Long before he landed on the ground, dizziness confused his thoughts, and he felt his consciousness fading away. It was even worse than in the water. There, at least, there had been something to absorb him as soon as he dissolved and melted into it. But he knew he would disappear completely in the air. This element was alien to him. The mobile, loose, light fluid was deadly for him, as he was used to supporting himself on all sides in the dense, solid, heavy matter of the earth. This unusual freedom offered him no support. He felt like a thought that was being forgotten. Yet he was still more concerned about Michael than himself: how would the boy survive the fall? This compassion preserved his consciousness for a moment longer, as it had done earlier in the element of water, but then everything went grey before his eyes again.

"You must think too, Andy Mo", he heard Krux's unmistakable voice as if from far away. "Concentrate on your goal: you want to enter the human realm to find your father. Let your thoughts carry you, and you won't lose yourself in the element of air."

Of course! That was why he was there, he reminded himself, and he focused all his imagination on that one thought. Concentration is one of the gnomes' favourite games, and it's the first thing – after order – that they must learn to navigate their world. He concentrated on his father and suddenly knew he was closer to him than ever before. Andy Mo felt himself gathering together again, despite the unfamiliar state of lightness, and he landed surprisingly softly on the ground as if it were moss. For the first time in his life, he found himself in the human realm. He was standing on solid ground, and yet he simultaneously had the unrestricted freedom of the sky and the illuminating, warming sunlight above him. It was a completely new feeling of being alive. Andy Mo felt as if he had been reborn. But the joy didn't last long. His body wasn't dense enough yet, and the schoolyard was becoming a soft swamp in which he was slowly sinking. However, before he sank he managed to take a few squelching steps towards Michael; it didn't seem the fall had ended so smoothly for him.

Michael had already hit his head hard on the asphalt, and he could see a thousand stars. For a few seconds he lost consciousness, and when he regained it, he could see Andy Mo in front of him as if through a veil. For the first time in his life, he saw a spirit. The spirit looked at him with equal interest and seemed even more fascinated by the encounter than Michael was.

"He's really hurt", thought Andy Mo. Blood was pouring out of a bad wound on his forehead. Andy Mo gently touched the spot and closed the open vessels with his thoughts. It stopped bleeding immediately. Michael watched the scene in a daze, as if he were in a delirious dream. He couldn't believe his eyes when he saw the earth spirit in front of him, and he clearly felt the caring warmth emanating from Andy Mo as he compassionately stroked the wound. Later, he would doubt that he had really experienced it at all.

But then Andy Mo finally lost the solid ground beneath him and sank ever deeper into his underworld. He only managed to find his footing again in the roots of the elder tree. Krux had been watching the accident; he was waiting for him, and helped him back into the protective tree.

"Well, that worked out well once again", he remarked with relief. "Are you hurt?"

"No, I think I'm okay", Andy Mo replied, tenderly touching his limbs. "I just feel a little woozy." In retrospect, he didn't find it so terrible anymore. Until now, his existence had been entirely focused on the ability to concentrate and hold himself together. But the experience of loosening and expanding in the air had immensely extended his existence, now that he had learnt you could expand without losing yourself.

"You can dissolve and still not lose yourself!" he said, enthusiastically describing his experience to Krux. "I didn't die in the water when I surrendered and merged with the element, and I survived in the air even though I completely detached myself from everything which had held me together before. The water softens you and lets you feel what others feel because it connects. And the air offers you insight into regions which are otherwise hidden. When you're flexible, expand yourself, and open yourself up, you gain a greater overview and can gather new insights."

"Not many of us have managed to do what you have just achieved. You have passed through alien elements. Besides the lightless underworld at the Borderlands of the earth, you have experienced the principles of water and air. And you have been to the human realm and returned unscathed. Only human beings can master the four elements: earth, water, air, and fire. A magician can master five. It's a miracle you survived all of this. Beware of fire; you will not survive it. But what you have experienced has brought you a great step forward. Now you need some refreshment. A hot elf chocolate will get you back on your feet."

While Krux was busy at the stove, Andy Mo watched through the tree window as a gorgeous girl lovingly tended to Michael. It had to be Kathi. Then a teacher and the school doctor arrived to give him expert care.

"I don't think he's been hurt too badly", Andy Mo noted with relief, not realising that as he leant out, his head and arms were able to enter the solar realm. His brief stay with the humans had changed something about him.

But Krux noticed it right away.

"Watch you don't fall out of the window!" he called out to him. "You've grown denser, Andy Mo." But at first Andy Mo didn't seem to hear him. Only slowly did he realise what he meant. He repeatedly stuck his head into the other world and splashed his hands in the air like a child in water. Although he could only come out up to his shoulders, he knew that this was just the beginning.

"How did my father actually get across?" asked Andy Mo.

"I don't know exactly", replied Krux. "He seemed to be waiting for something. A magician – or perhaps there were several – were supposed to help him lay the necessary groundwork for the encounter. You know, when it's midsummer in the solar realm, the walls that separate us become much more permeable, and more light and barakat get through to us." Then he thought of something else. "Maybe you should try something different. Your father learnt to walk on the underside of the Earth's surface. Eventually he could move there almost as surely as along a vein of ore. He would sometimes find rocks and trees inhabited by nature spirits, but also other places near certain humans where he could see through, like here. He was convinced that, with just a little more barakat, he would be able to walk on the surface of the Earth."

"Barakat – what's that?" asked Andy Mo in wonder. "I've never heard of it before."

"Barakat is many things; it changes its quality depending on where you are. In the realm of gnomes it's gravity, the force which holds things together. In your spirit it produces your ability to concentrate and master things. For the sylphs in the air element, barakat is the opposite: looseness, lightness, joyfulness. For the nixies it is the calmness and stillness, the kindness and compassion, the patient waiting, and the unifying love which also unites opposites. On the other hand, the fire spirits experience themselves in fiery barakat – in movement, action, courage, and everything which strives to separate."

"And for humans?" Andy Mo wanted to know. "What is the barakat which sustains humans?"

"I think they call it spiritual energy and life force. In any case, it's a kind of fuel for their existence, and it's the light which illuminates their field of consciousness. Just as they need money to survive, so they need barakat to exist. Those who have a lot of barakat have vitality, intelligence, and willpower. Together gold and barakat ensure survival and power in the human realm."

"So if I understand correctly", Andy Mo pondered, "we can't stay in the human realm because the foundation of our life is missing there. Everyone needs a different life element. The density and heaviness which we earth spirits need are simply under the earth rather than in the air. But couldn't we send our barakat over, just like thoughts, and use this elemental package as a vehicle?"

"That might be possible", Krux murmured. "Now that you mention it, I recall your father had the same idea before he disappeared. Previously he had tried it through the world of dreams. We may not be able to enter the human realm, but there's still a way to appear to them – namely, through the dreams we design for them.

The dream realms reach into the Borderlands of the spirits, where we can communicate with humans under certain circumstances."

"My God!" exclaimed Andy Mo. "Then maybe it wasn't a dream at all when Christian saw the gnome standing next to his bed. Maybe that was my father! He led him to the book so he could learn how to summon us. I'm sure they'll find the missing volumes as well, and soon they'll know how to do it. Michael saw me when he was half unconscious – he'll summon me. Then I can cross over." Andy Mo was very excited, but Krux dampened his joyful expectations.

"It's not that simple, unfortunately. I'm afraid I must disappoint you. What people dream takes place in the Borderlands or in their imagination, not in their real, gross material dimensions. The apparition that led Christian to the cellar was probably just a reflection of a concentrated thought, you see. A phantom at best, and not a real being who…"

But Andy Mo vehemently disagreed, insisting: "It must have been my father. Who else would have an interest in initiating a young person into the mysteries here, of all places? Only he could have known that I would come looking for him here, and that I would need a friend from the other side among the humans to meet me halfway."

"You're quite right, Andy Mo", Krux concurred. "I completely agree with you. It was surely your father who orchestrated that dream. But he wasn't inside the thought projection. Think about it: if he could move freely, he would be here and wouldn't have us looking for him. I'm convinced he's being held captive somewhere."

Andy Mo understood and became gloomy again. He was also thinking of his mother, who would soon start to worry if he didn't come home.

Then he decided: "Tomorrow I'm going to try to walk on the underside of the Earth's surface." Krux thought it was a good idea.

In the meantime the milk was almost boiling over, and the old tree spirit quickly took the pot off the stove. He mixed the cocoa powder, brown cane sugar, a little vanilla sugar, and a pinch of cinnamon in a large jug and poured a little hot water over it. He only added the milk once everything had dissolved. Finally, he put a piece of cooking chocolate into the jug and stirred until it too had melted. It smelt like Christmas and tasted like liquid gingerbread. Andy Mo was thrilled.

The two of them talked for a long time. Krux told him all about his father, and he also had a lot of other things to say. He was much older than Andy Mo, so he had gained more experience. In addition, his closeness to the humans lent him insights into their world that an earth spirit living deeper down would never gain.

THE BREAKTHROUGH

The next morning Andy Mo went on his first excursion. He didn't even try to leave his safe, familiar surroundings in the element of earth, but did as his father had done: he simply turned himself around and used the impenetrable skin of the solar realm as solid ground. For earth spirits, there is no gravity to pull them in one direction. Each and every spirit is a centre of gravity in their own right. Density and solidity are the same for them as air is for humans. There is no beneath or above for them: they live in the earth just like astronauts live in space.

So he walked on the underside of the Earth's surface, and it went much more easily than he had expected. He understood how it worked after only a few attempts. The solar realm supported him like the icy cover of the blue lake which formed the border to the land of the nixies.

"You still have to be careful", Krux had warned him. "There are some places which are thinner, and on certain days they are even wide open. If you fall out there and the hole closes back up, you can get lost and never find your way back."

Andy Mo quickly realised what he meant. Sometimes the strange ground of the human realm swayed like a hammock, and in these places it was also somewhat transparent. That's where he was particularly careful. However, he remembered the places and used them as landmarks for improved orientation during his wandering. He had discovered that these places possessed different qualities. Just as some rocks are permeated with gold or silver or iron, so he felt different emotions where they were more transparent – awe and peace, for instance, but also fear or hatred. Krux had also explained this phenomenon to him.

"Once upon a time, these were meeting places for the various beings of this world. Our kings met there with the priests of the humans and established the connection between spirits and human beings. But when more and more humans lost faith in us through Baphomet's work, these places fell into oblivion. There are only a few priests and shamans left over there who use the old power places to access the energies of our elements. But some places are also abused by the Shadow's minions for their dark purposes."

So besides modest little chapels and the magnificent cathedrals and temples of various religions, in these places Andy Mo also found dark burial places and mysterious ruins. Often, however, there was only a large granite stone or an ancient tree on the human side. Some of these natural dwellings were still inhabited by a rock spirit or a tree spirit.

On the very first day of his explorations, he got to know two of them better. They were as friendly as Krux, but neither of them could tell him where to find the king. They only knew that he was missing, and they believed that Baphomet or a human magician was holding him captive somewhere.

After two days, Andy Mo had gotten used to the special circumstances and the new way of getting around. The walks no longer presented any difficulties for him. Now he was moving along the Earth's undersurface like a diver under the ice. He clearly felt that some places were thinner and allowed more light from the solar realm to pass through, while the solar realm receded into the far distance in other places. He also noticed a kind of current which caused him to give preference to certain directions. He realised that it was thoughts, ideas, and images which were guiding him, and he allowed himself to be led by them. He thought of Michael; he had felt a special connection with him as soon as he had seen him, and he wanted to be near him. He wanted to check on his injury and give him vitality so the wound on his head would heal more quickly. Michael hadn't attended class since his fall; presumably he was still weakened.

In the gnome realm, Andy Mo could instantly transport himself to any location if he had a destination in mind. But he didn't know what Michael's surroundings looked like. Nevertheless, when he thought of Michael he felt nudged in a certain direction, and he followed this gentle pull. As he did so, images emerged as if from fog: he saw a huge park-like garden, a cosy brick house with a wooden veranda painted yellow, and then he spotted Michael as well. At first everything appeared blurry, but the vision became ever clearer as he concentrated on it, and he zoomed in faster and faster.

Just like when he had landed in Krux's tree house, this path also ended above the ground without any transition. Only this time it wasn't a tree – it was a huge, polished granite boulder. The rock was spacious, and you could sense that it had been furnished by benevolent beings. It housed three cosy rooms inside, much like Krux's tree house, and Andy Mo immediately felt at home. The tip of the boulder jutted about five metres above the meadow, and he could see out from a window-sized round hollow which was filled with rainwater like a bowl. The water was like a protective disk which reflected the surroundings and provided him with a panoramic view. He could see the outside world as if it were on a television screen, and he didn't even need to leave his position to do so. It sufficed for him to concentrate on an object outside, and it immediately appeared more clearly on the magical screen.

Then when he tried to stick his head through this natural opening, he also succeeded immediately. To his great delight, he found himself exactly in front of the house he had previously targeted in his vision. Although he couldn't see Michael, he could hear his voice through the open windows. "This must be one of those old cult sites", Andy Mo rejoiced, knowing that he had come a great deal closer to his goal. From here, following the old tradition, he wanted to re-establish contact between the human realm and the spirits. He didn't manage to get through with his whole body, but he felt there was a gate here – it just had to be opened from both sides.

GNOMES, MAGIC, AND SPAGHETTI

Michael lived all alone in an old, romantic brick house hidden behind a thick hedge on a completely overgrown plot of land. The servants had been housed there in the past. The main building was at the front, and it looked like a haunted castle with its many pointed towers and oriels – there were even supposed to be secret passages somewhere. But the large villa remained uninhabited. The estate had belonged to his grandfather and still possessed the spirit of the last century. They had started to renovate the house, but then they had run out of money. Since he was alone, he preferred to live in the small annex. He found it much cosier there. He had furnished the sunny rooms to his own taste with IKEA furniture, and he felt more comfortable there than in the old, stately building.

They had moved to Austria only three years ago, when his mother fell ill with a dangerous liver infection. They said she had a better chance of surviving there. But the doctors couldn't save her.

They used to live in Colombia, where his father searched for precious stones in the mountains. Michael was often allowed to accompany him, despite the danger of bandits. Now he missed the adventures in the wilderness. But he had ended up staying in Vienna because of school and his friends – and especially because of Kathi, who comforted him lovingly in the period of mourning following his mother's death. His father flew back alone. Initially he only wanted to settle some business matters, but he stayed in the mountains when he saw that Michael could manage well on his own. Whenever he found some gems, he sent him money; often he would only send photos and letters, but they would be twenty pages long.

47

Still, everyone envied him because he lived in absolute freedom like Huckleberry Finn or Pippi Longstocking. Nowadays that didn't even exist in novels.

So Michael had learnt to live completely on his own. He cooked fantastically, took care of the household, and loved the quiet solitude which the huge estate provided him. Far from being a loner, however, he was very popular with everyone, and he often invited friends over for dinner.

Today's occasion, however, was a special one. It concerned the Book of the Master and the spirits.

*

They sat around the large round table like the Knights of the Round Table. However, there were only five of them, and instead of swords, a copy of the mysterious book lay in front of each of them. Christian had given them the manuscript two days earlier so they could study it at their leisure. Only Leif Andersson received his copy now. He had turned up at Michael Freiwald's by chance and was spontaneously accepted into the circle of those already initiated.

Leif was a good year older than the others, and his serious features revealed he was also more experienced than they were. His inquisitive gaze sometimes had something challenging about it, and you had the feeling that nothing escaped his dark, alert eyes. He wasn't tall, but he was slim and dressed trendily. His closely trimmed hair lent him a daring look.

Andy Mo could see the three boys clearly from his vantage point. But he could only see the two girls – Kathi and Miri Li – from behind, as they were sitting with their backs towards the window. He could hear everything they were saying, however, and he was able to follow the whole scene.

Michael lit a candle and said nothing for quite a while. It seemed as if he was praying, and a solemn mood filled the room. Eventually he cleared his throat and began:

"Before we get down to business and talk about the book, I would like us to briefly inform Leif about its contents. We can summarise what we know and then discuss what we want to do next. To conclude we'll have something nice to eat – I've already taken care of that. Is that okay, or does anyone have any other suggestions?"

They all agreed. Michael had a gift for calling the shots without being domineering or pushy. They were happy to let him lead because they all knew they could rely on him. He was yet to disappoint any of them.

First, he asked Christian to explain how he had come to possess the book, and Christian told them about the dream, the spirit next to his bed, and the lost shoe. Nobody had known about that except for Michael Freiwald. They were all very impressed, but there were no further questions. They were convinced that the gnome had specifically led him to the book. Then Michael briefly summarised the plot of the story, and finally he got to the heart of the spiritual content:

"The Book of the Master is a private manuscript, presumably a secret document for Freemasons, and unavailable in bookshops.

"It claims that humans – without being aware of it – are the slaves of demons. They are kept like dairy cows by these invisible spiritual beings and are seduced by them to do evil. The gratified urges, the fears, and the unrestrained emotions of humans are the lifeblood of these invisible powers. Their overlord is called Baphomet.

"If people were to spiritually perfect themselves in accordance with their divine destiny, Baphomet and his twelve princes would be deprived of power and would have to perish. That's why they're trying to prevent this from becoming known by all means possible.

"To learn more about these secret connections, the author ventures into the invisible Temple of Might. There he gains insight into the various plans the demon princes have concocted to prevent humans from freeing themselves from their sphere of influence.

"He uncovers two monstrous plots: one involves the destruction of a large part of the Earth – and with it the basis of human life – before the more advanced humans reach their goal and can enlighten and save the others. Then evolution would have to start all over again, and the demons would remain the superior beings on this planet.

"The second scenario envisages the opposite. Technology perfected to the highest level will provide humans with luxury and pleasure without any effort. This will remove any need for self-discipline and compassion, which will inevitably lead to a degeneration of human mental and spiritual abilities. Both variations are already being tested.

"Baphomet and the Princes of Power have minions among the humans for this purpose, but exposing and fighting them alone will not save the world. The real battle takes place within each individual. Humans must also defeat the evil within themselves: only then will the Shadow which dominates the world be defeated and starved.

"That's why the author calls upon every reader not to tolerate any negative qualities, unpleasant thoughts, or feelings within themselves, as these connect you with the corresponding dark cosmic forces. Without realising it, you strengthen their power while losing control over yourself.

"He suggests that, just by knowing these connections, you have already become a chosen one. This is the first step on the path to magic. Whoever knows the secret automatically becomes a link in a chain of initiates. You can recognise them by the fact that they're not easily tempted; they attempt to control and master themselves and their impulses because they don't want to be dominated by the demons. They stand up for truth, justice, and compassion. Once you have recognised the powers behind your urges, fears, and desires, and believe in the world of spirits, you are not the same as before."

"That's true", Christian interrupted him spontaneously. "I've become a different person since the apparition in the night, and since I've been studying the Book of the Master."

"I'm not the same either", Kathi declared. "I've already read everything twice and since I became aware that I'm a spirit being, I want to get to know the world of spirits better and meet one of the invisible beings like Christian did."

"I feel the same way", Michael stated in conclusion to his introductory report. "When I fell from the tree last week, I even had the impression that this gnome from the book was standing in front of me. Since I've come to know all this, I feel different – somehow involved in something unknown, like before a great journey or something. I think something's going to happen soon." Even Leif Andersson, who was always sceptical, announced that he would immediately study the manuscript, and he confessed that he was eager to read the other volumes as well in order to learn more about the world of spirits.

*

"I think we all want that", Christian said as he took the floor again. "In fact that's also the reason for our meeting today. I had hoped you would be interested, and you haven't disappointed me. We will search for the books and we will find them. Actually, there's enough in the volume we already possess to not only change ourselves but the whole world as well. I suggest we meet twice a week and work through everything together. But before we discuss how we wish to proceed, I have something to read to you.

"I found another loose sheet in the chest. It bears the same handwriting as the many notes and references which can be found on almost every page of the book. To be precise, it's a warning about reading this book."

"Consult your doctor or pharmacist about risks and side effects", jested Leif Andersson, who always had to crack jokes, even in the most serious situations. But Christian didn't let him interrupt.

"Please listen:
'Keep your hands off magic and any form of sorcery if you are not conscientious, honest, and brave. Only those who are full of compassion and without any desires may dare to do it. If

you still can't help yourself, be it out of curiosity or other desires, and wish to occupy yourself with the science of Hermetics, then try to attain at least some of these virtues.

'You are a spirit in a body, which serves you as a support in this world. In the spirit world you lack this protective shell. There it is only the qualities of the spirit which carry you: conscientiousness and the ability to concentrate, self-control and courage, openness and kindness. These are your bones and muscles which lend you support and security in the hereafter. If you lack these qualities, the spirits have contempt for you. If you still venture into their worlds, they will turn you into their servant without you even realising it.'"

"Well, bravo!" Leif scoffed. "A pious raised forefinger. Why do I need magic if I have no desires?"

"Perhaps to help others, you egotist", Miri Li replied, looking at him sharply. "All you ever think about is yourself."

"Now, now, don't argue", Michael Freiwald interjected, trying to nip an argument in the bud. "Let's think about the best way to proceed instead. Actually, we're already a proper secret society, and I think Christian's idea of meeting every week to study the science of magic together is great."

"It all reminds me of Harry Potter's school of magic", said Kathi, who had read all the books. "We also want to learn magic, and..."

But Christian protested: "Harry Potter is a fairy tale – it's a story that Miss Rowling made up. What's written in the Book of the Master is reality."

"You can't possibly know that", Leif Andersson objected again. "Just because it's written for adults, that doesn't mean what's claimed there is true."

"Leif is right", Christian admitted. "But if the book is real and what's written there really is true, then it's sensational. These aren't children's stories with flying brooms and magic wands from the occult supermarket. It describes how you can leave your body and learn to fly on your own. I'm convinced that if you follow the instructions and exercises, you can truly acquire magical abilities. However, we also need the other volumes."

"We'll have a hard time getting our hands on those", Michael feared, lifting up one of the loose pages. "This is a secret manuscript. It says so in black and white: only for personal friends, limited edition of 99 copies. The first page, where it usually lists the publisher, is missing. It starts on page three."

"Perhaps we can find the author who wrote all this", Leif suggested, showing some serious interest again. "Then we'd know right away what to make of it all."

"That would be one possibility", Christian replied, taking up his suggestion. "It's clear from the contents that he must be one of the people involved. It's a diary, after all."

"Why don't we investigate all the people who are mentioned by name?" asked Kathi. "I have a feeling the names are real. The streets and squares match reality, at least, and so do many of the events."

"Did you notice the dedication on page three?" asked Miri Li, and everyone searched for the page. In barely legible handwriting which was obviously written in ink and somewhat smudged, it said: "May this book be a guide for you on your path to the light", and underneath that: "For Prof. Dr Adolf Hemberger, trvb.: Your brother", as well as an illegible signature which couldn't be deciphered.

"That would be something absolutely concrete we could follow up", Kathi said. "There can't be that many academic Hembergers. That gives us eleven people and the professor." Kathi was known for her phenomenal memory; she had all the names in her head. "We can forget about five right away, as they certainly can't be the author of the book", she went on. "That leaves six: Dr Michael Stein, Martin Schuh, Berny Specht, Emil Stejnar, Horst Krbec, and this Professor Hemberger. Three of them live in Vienna, where most of the action takes place."

"There's something else", Leif spoke up, and you could tell he wasn't sure if he should say it. "Actually, I shouldn't tell you, but if I've understood the matter correctly, this story is also concerned with Freemasonry. My father is a member of a Lodge."

The others stared at him in amazement.

"Wow, that really is incredible", said Christian in surprise. "You're standing directly at the source. It was no coincidence that you wanted to visit Michael today. What kind of spirit summoned you?"

Michael was also visibly pleased.

"This makes everything much easier", he noted. "Now we can pursue three leads: the Freemasons, the names of the people involved, and the owner of the book – this Professor Hemberger. Leif will ask around among the Freemasons; we simply must use that access he has. I'll take all the address books and you can look for the names in the telephone directories, Christian."

"I'll go to the National Library", Kathi announced. "In case you didn't know, in German-speaking countries anyone who writes something which is made available to others is obliged to send a copy to the National Library. The idea is to prevent any secret organisations from overthrowing the state", she said, turning to Leif, who looked at her incredulously. "That way the politicians think they can stay well-informed."

"Why don't you just look it up on the internet", Miri Li remarked. Yet she was the only one who still wasn't online. She also didn't use a mobile phone, a credit card, or lipstick.

They all looked at each other in dismay. None of them had thought of that.

"Of course", said Leif, "the girls are always smarter. Let's just Google the names. Where's your computer?"

"The connection is upstairs", Michael said, grinning. "I'll see to the food in the meantime. I think we deserve a snack."

Everyone enthusiastically agreed. They could sit outside because it wasn't cold, so the girls set the table in the garden. The sun's rays had warmed up the terracotta tiles covering the terrace floor. The sky was almost cloudless; only the two contrails of a vanished plane cut diagonally through the deep blue before silently dissolving. The balmy air was filled with the mysterious scent of lilac; there was a bird somewhere, otherwise just peaceful silence.

*

Andy Mo was also enjoying the unfamiliar view of the human realm, and he already felt at home in his stone house and in Michael's garden. The quiet atmosphere was familiar to him despite the strange Earthly surroundings; peace reigned here. He was glad that the friends would be sitting outside and that he could now have a better view of the group. Kathi cleaned the table and the two benches, called out to someone in the house, and then Miri Li arrived.

With a graceful movement of her slender hips, she deftly pushed the half-open door aside and placed the overloaded tray on the table.

"What a splendid day", she said to Kathi. "If the weather stays like this, we can go swimming soon." With that, she slipped out of her jumper; she was wearing a white T-shirt underneath, and she stretched her arms above her head towards the sun, looking like a prima ballerina.

When Andy Mo saw the girl in her full form, it hit him like a thunderbolt. He felt something that made all the feelings he had ever experienced explode – first in his stomach, then in his throat, and finally in his head. Miri Li possessed a truly unearthly beauty. She was smaller than the others and moved her slender, delicate body with a bewitching but gentle, natural grace that reminded him of his nixie siblings. She even set the plates and cutlery as if they were flowers or living beings. Her big, dark eyes seemed dreamy and serious. It was the same kind look as the fairy who had always comforted him when he was sad as a child. Lost in thought, she brushed her long black hair out of her face; it had fallen over her forehead while she was setting the table. When she happened to glance in his direction without recognising him, he felt a pain in his chest unlike any he had ever experienced before. With a jolt he realised that he wasn't human, and so he would never experience the fulfilment of the love he felt for this being.

At first he wanted to retreat into his boulder, deeply hurt. But he couldn't take his eyes off her. The desire to be close to the girl, to reveal himself to her, to touch her, was overwhelming. He was drawn to her with every fibre of his being. He couldn't help it. He had to try to leave his rock house without human help. Who knows when they will be able to summon him into their world according to the rules of the magical art, he thought to himself.

He already knew that he wouldn't be able to do it with a mental leap. So he tried concentration. Miri Li in his heart. Miri Li in his thoughts. Miri Li was his goal. With Miri Li in his mind's eye, he imagined himself rising from his spirit world, possessing a solid body like humans, and walking towards her across the meadow. And he succeeded. The irrepressible power of longing, of affection, of love for Miri Li gave him the strength to overcome even the last obstacle on the way to the solar realm. Andy Mo freed himself from his element. He rose from the boulder and could actually walk on the surface of the Earth.

But then he was overcome by dizziness, and he felt as if he would sink again after all. A force he couldn't resist pulled him back into his sphere. Andy Mo understood that it wasn't the quality of the ground but his own constitution that was causing him to merge with the earth. As a spirit he was much more volatile than the air, and in the open he felt like he was dissolving; nevertheless, a heaviness weighed on him, pulling him downwards. He had to try to balance these two opposing forces. Andy Mo realised that he had to create a shell for himself which surrounded him just as tightly as the dense matter of the rock and ores in his own world. He had to ensure the cohesion of the components of his being himself.

In his mind he imagined he was as stable as a crystal and had no need of pressure from outside. For a few seconds he managed to imagine the support which the protective ores and minerals usually provided him. It was a completely new living sensation. He suddenly felt the ground beneath his feet and could detach himself from it – that was a below. And he also felt the open air, the vastness of space, an above that kept him upright.

With unsteady steps he walked towards Miri Li. She was standing in front of the house, looking in his direction. She must have seen him – yet she didn't notice him. He waved to her, but she turned and disappeared before he reached her.

Exhausted and resigned, he decided to turn back. He felt he couldn't hold on much longer. Now he knew he wouldn't make it without human help. He needed their thoughts as a shell for his spirit. He had to inspire them to summon him. Because if they tuned in to him and expected him, if they thought of him and believed in him, then their imagination would serve as the basis for a solid shell into which he could slip, and then they would see him. And once they saw him and formed a concrete image of him, he could appear to them more easily and remain among the humans longer. But how could he get them to summon him when they had no idea he even existed? Only Michael had hazily perceived him while he was unconscious.

But then he remembered the Book of the Master. His father was mentioned in the first volume, so they had all read about him. Christian had even seen him in a dream vision. If they summoned the Gnome King, he could appear in his place. After all, they had the same name. He tried to concentrate on Michael and Christian, tuning in to the two friends and forcing himself on them in his thoughts. He forced them to think of Andy Mo. Andy Mo, Andy Mo. Andy Mo.

*

While Michael prepared his spaghetti à la Freiwald, Leif and Christian were already working on the computer.

"Try the names first", Christian suggested. "Everyone has a homepage these days." But they didn't find anything. They had already entered the third name into the search engine without any results.

"The people from the Book of the Master seem to be from yesterday", Leif realised after half an hour. He was disappointed and wanted to switch off the computer. But then the girls came to fetch them for lunch. Kathi was looking over his shoulder at the screen, and she immediately spotted the mistake.

"If I remember correctly, the professor's name is Hemberger, not

Hamburger – and Stejnar is spelt with a 'j', but you used an 'i'."

"I'd love to have your memory", Leif murmured appreciatively, and then the first information arrived. They hadn't expected such a wealth of data: The Freemasonic Museum, Bayreuth Library, Who's Who: Stejnar, Abramelin and Co., Alpha Astron and Omega, St. Gallen Cantonal Library, Guardian Angel Forum, German National Library Leipzig, Austrian National Library Vienna, Zurich Central Library.

"Clearly magic is no longer a secret science", Christian remarked with surprise. "Now nothing stands in the way of our excursion into the spirit world. We'll find the books." Everyone crowded around the monitor excitedly.

But Miri Li reminded them about the food. "Come now, please – the spaghetti will get cold otherwise. You can continue later." Then Michael called from the garden, and they went downstairs.

RECIPE

SPAGHETTI
For about 4 people

Ingredients:
500 grams of spaghetti
500 grams of minced beef
4 tablespoons of olive oil
4 cloves of garlic
1 onion
1 slice of ham – about 50-100 grams (optional)
1 carrot
1 stick of celery (optional)
1 can of peeled tomatoes
2 tablespoons of tomato paste
100 grams of Parmesan cheese
Parsley (optional)

Preparing the sauce:
Heat the olive oil in a large pan. Add the finely chopped onion (plus the carrot and celery) to the pan and sauté lightly. Add the minced beef. Break it apart and crush it with a fork, then keep turning and mixing with a wooden spoon. Brown it on all sides until its crumbly and crispy. Season with the crushed garlic, salt, and pepper. Add the tomatoes and tomato paste (plus the diced ham) and simmer for about 15 minutes. Stir frequently. Sprinkle with finely chopped parsley and serve.

Preparing the pasta:
Bring a large pot with plenty of water to the boil. Add a tablespoon of salt and a little olive oil. Then add the spaghetti. Cooking time is indicated on the package (about 9 minutes). Taste it in between so that it doesn't get too soft. Stir occasionally. The pasta is ready when it's soft on the outside and firm to the bite on the inside – this is called 'al dente'. Strain it, put it in a bowl, and mix well with a little olive oil or butter. Divide it among the plates. Pour the meat sauce over the top and sprinkle with grated Parmesan.

CHOCOLATE PUDDING
The recipe is usually on the packet – but you can improve the taste.
For about 4 people

Ingredients
500 ml of milk
125 ml of cream
1 sachet of Flana or another pudding
4 tablespoons of sugar
1 packet of vanilla sugar
1 tablespoon of cocoa
About 50 grams of cooking chocolate
1 tablespoon of butter
Meringue cookies

Preparation:
Mix the pudding powder with the sugar, cocoa, and vanilla sugar. Add 2 tablespoons of cream and 3 tablespoons of milk and stir until smooth. Bring the remaining milk to the boil with the butter and remove from the heat. Slowly stir in the prepared mixture. Put it back on the heat and simmer on a low temperature for 1 minute, stirring constantly. (If you use regular custard powder, follow the cooking time indicated on the packet. However, use a little more milk than it says, as the pudding won't be turned out and should be creamy). Pour it into a large bowl. Leave to cool. Whip the cream and fold it loosely into the pudding with the chopped chocolate and broken meringue cookies. Serve.

*

To be closer to his friends, Andy Mo had slipped into the elder tree which grew out of his rock house. Its branches covered the entire terrace, and he could see everything better from the branch where he had made himself comfortable. It was as if he was sitting at the table with them. But he still felt left out. The fact that they couldn't see him hurt him more than the fact he couldn't move around in their world as he wished to. He hoped his mental signals had been picked up and they would soon summon him into their world. Then he would find out whether he was able to condense enough for them to perceive him as well.

After eating the spaghetti, the girls cleared the table and fetched the pudding. While they prepared the whipped cream, Michael went upstairs to print out the information. Everyone received a sheet and took up the task of investigating one of the addresses. Then Michael disappeared briefly into the cellar and returned with a small saw.

"We should deal with the science of magic not only theoretically, but also practically", he explained, placing the tool on the table. "For that we need a magic wand, among other things."

"That's a great idea!" Leif exclaimed. "Theorising is useless.

Only practice will show if there is any truth to the whole thing. Let's make ourselves a magic wand and summon a spirit." But Michael tempered his expectations.

"I'm afraid it's not that simple. You haven't read the manuscript yet, but it explains that you need more than just magical devices. You must first develop magical skills before you can use these tools. Unfortunately, there are no magic wands or magic formulas which work on their own. At least that's what the author of this book claims."

"What kind of abilities are those?" asked Leif with interest.

"The power of faith, the power of imagination, and an indomitable will."

"I'm getting a little spooked by it all now", Miri Li declared. "When something's bothering me, I pray or ask my angel to help me, and usually the problem resolves itself in some way. I think we should be careful – who knows what we're getting ourselves into." But Kathi reassured her friend.

"We don't want to cast spells or summon spirits to ask for anything. I think our primary concern is knowledge and insight. We want to learn more about the spiritual world and its inhabitants. This will also teach us something about ourselves. After all, once we die, we're just spirits as well."

"That's how I see it too", Christian agreed. "Although I must admit I'd be very happy if this gnome who led me to the book in the cellar could also lead me to the stolen paintings. If they're not found, my father will go to prison. There are charges of attempted insurance fraud pending. And since we're broke, we can't pay the damages incurred. My father is at the end of his tether, and my mother is totally devastated as well."

"What a mess", Michael fumed. "I don't know anyone as law-abiding as your father. We must help your folks, and I think this gnome is just what we need. I've already thought of asking him for help, by the way. Apart from wisdom and insight, this earth spirit is also responsible for all the treasures lying beneath the earth. In fact I wanted to ask him to help my father find a valuable gemstone, because I'm broke as well. He hasn't sent any money for three months. There's a mortgage on the property. The payments for the television and the computer are due, and I can't overdraw my account anymore. I'm facing repossession. But if this earth spirit knows where gold and gems are located, I'm convinced he'll also be able to track down where the paintings are hidden."

Christian searched the book for the passage describing how Dr Stein was introduced to the secrets of the spirit world by this being.

"His name's Andimo. There's also a picture of his sigil, which you can use to summon him." Curious, they all bent over the manuscript and examined the strange sign of the spirit.

"It looks like a mountain", Miri Li commented. "Inside there are three layers, and the loop could be a winding mountain path or a hidden cave."

"It might even be the same spirit which led me to the Book of the Master in my dream."

"That would be logical", Kathi said, who always thought over everything twice. "Then the whole thing would make sense. He wanted you to find the book – that much is obvious – so he also won't mind if we ask him for help."

"Or me", Andy Mo said happily, although naturally they couldn't hear him. His plan had worked; his thoughts had reached their goal. He also saw it as further proof that his father was alive. In anticipation, he had wisely prepared the friends' meeting by leading them to the Book of the Master. They both bore the same name. When the friends summoned the Gnome King, he could appear in his place. And since they were expecting an earth spirit, they would be able to see him just as well.

"Isn't it strange that we all suddenly have these problems?" Miri Li observed thoughtfully, explaining what was worrying her. "My parents are also under financial pressure. They're being blackmailed by the Chinese mafia. They have to buy meat at greatly inflated prices from the Russians, and they're forced to hire a certain outrageously expensive security service which only collects money rather than providing security. They've just about managed that.

But now the criminals are demanding an additional two thousand euros in protection money for each of the two restaurants. My father assured them that they can't afford it, but they're insisting."

"You must bring in the police", Leif said, appalled. "You can't put up with this."

But Miri Li disagreed. "You can't", she replied. "They'll set fire to one of the restaurants. They'll do it. And if that doesn't work, yesterday they threatened to kidnap me or kill one of us."

When he heard this, Andy Mo was shocked. He had no idea how he could protect the girl. The fact that three of his friends were simultaneously being put under pressure couldn't be a coincidence. He suspected that Baphomet was behind it. Now he was using any and all means possible to prevent anyone from supporting him in the search for his father. The Prince of Shadows also had minions among the human beings, and he was deliberately using these henchmen from the underworld against his opponents. Now it was up to Andy Mo to help his friends. But how? So long as he was unable to move in their world, there wasn't much he could do for them. He had to get them to summon him immediately. There was no time to lose – if they waited until Midsummer, it might be too late.

Once again, he concentrated upon Michael and sent a thought packet to his consciousness: "Remember, you have seen me, I can appear to you again – summon me, do it!" And it got through.

"Perhaps we should try an experiment straight away", Michael pondered. "Time is running short and we've got nothing to lose."

"I think that would be a spell we could justify", Kathi agreed, and everyone approved.

"So we'll make the wand", Michael said. "It should be made from the wood of an elder tree, and we have one right in front of us." He climbed onto the bench and pointed to a branch. "That one would be suitable", he stated. "Pass me the saw, please."

"Why elder wood, of all things?" Leif wanted to know. "How do the shamans cast spells where elder trees don't grow?"

"I've got no idea", Michael replied, slightly irritated. "I think elder trees grow everywhere. I cut this tree above us back down to two metres every year, otherwise we couldn't sit here, and by autumn it has grown back completely. It's so robust that you can even plant a sapling upside down."

"What? Then the roots become branches?" asked Miri Li incredulously.

"Yes. What was previously growing in the ground strives up towards the sky, while the branches turn into roots. I think that makes its wood a special conductor for earthly and heavenly forces."

"'As above, so below' is an important tenet of Hermetics", Kathi explained. "That's in our Book of the Master, after all."

Michael expertly eyed the tree once again.

Andy Mo, who was following everything closely, recognised the opportunity that was presenting itself. As quick as a flash, he spread himself thin and squeezed into the branch Michael had his eye on. This branch had grown straight, was as thick as someone's thumb, and would be perfect for a wand. He was aware that it could be dangerous for him, and that he would be trapped as soon as the branch was cut from the tree. He had no idea how he would get back or what would happen next. But he took the risk.

And indeed, Michael did saw this very long, straight branch which Andy Mo was hiding in from the trunk. Then he shortened it to about 35 centimetres and carefully scraped off the green bark with a knife. Finally, he carefully smoothed the white wood underneath with fine sandpaper.

"Finished!" he announced proudly, looking at his work with satisfaction. "This is sacred to us from now on." He placed the wand on a purple silk cloth he had laid out ready, and everyone was allowed to examine it closely.

Miri Li was the last to take the magical instrument in her hands. She gently stroked her delicate fingers over the shiny, silky-smooth wood, which was still damp.

"It feels nice", she mused. "Like cool skin. It's as if you're really touching a living being." Andy Mo shuddered at her touch. He felt as if she was addressing him personally, and he didn't know whether he should be happy or cry.

AN EARTH SPIRIT IS SUMMONED

"I think we should perform the summoning within the old walls of my grandfather's villa", Michael suggested. "We'd have the appropriate mystical atmosphere there. Besides, it's starting to get cold."

Sure enough, the wind had picked up and clouds were gathering. Christian helped the girls clear the table while Michael and Leif went ahead to unlock the building. It took a while before they could open the old-fashioned lock, which was jammed. Then the others arrived. Miri Li was wearing her dark blue jumper again, but the chilly air made her shiver as she stepped into the huge reception hall.

"I can understand why you moved out of here", she said. "I'd be afraid to live in this house alone." But Christian disagreed.

"Well, I think it's great", he said enthusiastically, looking at the chandeliers and the huge paintings on the wall of the drawing room.

"It's like my father's antique shop, but it's living. It's like being transported back to times long past. Why don't you sell these things?"

"Because everything is already mortgaged", Michael confessed. "Except for a few pieces, nothing belongs to us anymore. Even the library has been put up as collateral. Every book has been catalogued for auction. My grandfather was in debt, and treating my mother's illness cost a lot of money." The friends fell silent, concerned.

"The earth spirit will help us all", Christian said confidently. "However, I'm not sure if we should really summon him here, or if it wouldn't be better outside." They had ventured further and were looking reverently at the many books on the shelves of the next room, which was enormous. Three of the wood-panelled walls were crammed from floor to ceiling with leather-bound works, most of which were old. On the opposite side of the room was an open fireplace.

Although the house had been unoccupied for a long time, it wasn't musty, but smelled of leather, wood, and the past. The last rays of the evening sun filtered through the high windows, bathing the room in a mysterious light. There was a strange mystical atmosphere. It wasn't unpleasant, but you could feel there was something in the air.

"I think Christian's right", Miri Li said, looking around intently. "We could have our planned conversations in this room, which provides us with a stately setting, but we should wait for Andimo out in the open. He would feel more comfortable at the granite boulder in front of the house."

"It's more romantic outside", Kathi agreed, and so they went back out into the garden to inspect the stone Miri Li had mentioned. The wind had died down in the meantime. It wasn't as cold as before either, so they decided to perform the invocation in the open air after all.

The peaceful evening ambience put them in a state of mind which connected them with the spiritual atmosphere permeating nature. Michael searched for something warm for everyone to wear, as he wanted to be sure that no one was cold. For Andimo he brought a huge quartz druse and placed it on the stone in front of him. Five large, clear rock crystals were protruding from the mineral like antennae.

I think he'll like this", he said. "I found this rock myself, and I spent five hours dragging it down the mountain. Earth spirits love crystals." Then he drew the sigil on the rock with a piece of chalk and became serious.

"Now we're going to focus on this Andimo. Everyone in their own way. Christian has probably already seen him and can conjure up an image of him; I'm picturing the friendly chap I saw when I was half unconscious. Everyone else can simply wish he hears us and appears."

Wand in hand, Michael stood on the crest of the boulder while the other four silently formed a circle around him. The sun was sinking, and the red glow of the evening sky was reflected in the round puddle on the boulder. Suddenly they all sensed that the world around them was changing. An eerie silence descended over them like a huge bell, transporting them to another world. Michael's voice sounded as if it came from far away.

"Andimo, King of the Gnomes, we call upon you and ask you to make yourself visible before us. We need your help. Come, appear." Michael repeated this formula three times, but the second time they could all see it already. Something flashed, and the crystals began to glitter in the twilight as Michael drew the sigil of the earth spirit Andimo – which was also Andy Mo's sigil – in the air with the wand. The crystals shone as if they were lit from within. The air above them shimmered as if it was electrically charged. Michael almost dropped the wand in shock, Miri Li groaned, but in the end they all maintained their composure and waited anxiously to see what would happen next.

Andy Mo was excited too. He felt himself being addressed. He felt a new world opening up to him. Finally, the time had come. Even if he hadn't wanted to, he would have complied with their request. Bundled together, the hopeful thoughts of the five were like an obligation for him, urging him to comply with their desire. They prepared the way for him and created a space in which he could manifest himself. Their desire to see him seized him like the current in the realm of the nixies, and their faith opened a portal into their world. Their thoughts of him touched him like hands stretched out towards him – hands which he could grasp so their spirits connected with his. All by himself, he managed to grow into their ideas and clothe himself with the image they had of him. Suddenly everything was happening almost effortlessly. He stood before them, condensed, and from their stunned faces he could tell that they saw him.

WELCOME TO THE WIZARDS' CLUB

"Hello!" he greeted them, smiling hesitantly and waving. "Here I am. It took quite a while, but it worked out in the end."

The five friends stared at him, flabbergasted. Michael was the first to pull himself together, but he didn't know what to say. So he also said: "Hello!", and then: "Welcome to the club!"

"He's cute", Kathi remarked, and Christian realised that it wasn't the old gnome who had led him to the book.

"That was my father", Andy Mo explained. "He set up this encounter when he let you find the book. He's being held captive somewhere in this world and he needs my help. But I wouldn't be here without you."

"Another one who needs help", Christian observed. "What on Earth is wrong with our fathers?"

Kathi tried to explain to Andy Mo what Christian meant, but he gestured to her that it was okay.

"I'm in the picture. I know your problems. I've been watching you for days. Besides, I can read your minds. Miri Li and Leif are in the greatest danger."

"Why me?" asked Leif in surprise. "Other than Kathi, I'm the only one who doesn't have any problems."

"Yes, you do – you just don't know it yet. You've got the wrong friends and hashish in your back pocket. If you keep going like this, you'll go downhill. You're too radical for the underworld. Boundaries are a challenge for you – including the boundaries with evil. A lad like you won't get back out of there."

The others were concerned. None of them smoked. But it was true – lately Leif had been closing himself off and was going his own way.

Michael interrupted the awkward silence: "We should go into the house." Night had fallen, filling the garden with its shadows.

"Please take the crystal with you", Andy Mo asked. "We'll need it." Then he led the others towards the old villa. Relieved, he found he could still hold himself up without sinking. It wasn't difficult in the slightest – and when he turned and saw the others following him, he knew that he was still visible to them, and that they could even see him in the darkness.

"The gate's locked", Michael shouted, but Andy Mo walked through the wall as if it wasn't even there. "Thank God," he thought, "I can still do that too" – for he'd heard he would lose that ability in the human realm. Then he went straight to the library and waited for his friends there. He had quickly become accustomed to the special conditions in the human realm, and he walked up and down the large room with sure steps, repeatedly touching objects, lifting vases and sculptures, and taking books from the shelves to leaf through them.

The others joined him in the meantime, and the host gestured silently for them to take their seats. Everyone sank into one of the old leather armchairs and waited anxiously to see what would happen next; they were still completely bewildered by what they'd just experienced. No one said a word. Miri Li began to feel cold again; noticing, Michael fetched her a blanket from the cupboard. Then he lit a fire in the fireplace. The old logs ignited immediately, and the comforting warmth and flickering light soon created a cosy atmosphere.

Andy Mo, who had been watching everything closely, stood in front of the fireplace for a long time and gazed into the flames, entranced. Then he finally turned to his friends.

"First of all, I would like to apologise to you", he said, turning to Leif. "I had good reasons for revealing your personal affairs in front of the others. Drug use is a life-threatening matter for us spirits. In our land, these consciousness dilutants are only used by priests and kings, and exclusively with the aim of communicating with beings in other spheres. Anyone who uses them without preparatory training will lose themselves in the Borderlands and become their own shadow before they reach their goal. It's no different for you humans. No one can free themselves alone. That's why I told the others. In our land nobody would remain silent if their friend was taking drugs. 'Watch them', we would say. 'They're in danger. I can't help them alone.'"

"For us it's the opposite", Christian explained. "For us, it's a point of honour not to tell anyone. Everyone who knows promises to keep it secret. You just look on – or rather, you look away. Who wants to betray a friend? And besides, someone who takes drugs can't be helped anyway."

"Yes they can!" Kathi objected. "Do you think Tommy's parents would have given him those student pads and reams of cash if they'd known he was smoking weed? Now he's hooked on the syringe. Once it gets to that point, it's too late – at the beginning, you might still be able to do something."

Leif had been silent until then, but now he became angry.

"Wouldn't we rather talk about something else", he said irritably. "I don't take drugs. I don't need help. I don't have a problem. Is that clear? Okay, I bought this stuff. It just happened – I was thinking about expanding my consciousness, but that's about it. Damn, we've got a real spirit in our midst, and we're talking such silly crap. Come on, Andy Mo, tell us about yourself and your father. Show us how to do magic."

After listening to the torrent of talk with closed eyes, Andy Mo shook his head imperceptibly, as if talking to himself. Then he looked everybody in the eye in turn.

*

"You want to learn magic. Okay. My father probably brought us together for that reason. So I'm going to teach you a few things. But without drugs – is that clear? And you still have to find the missing Master Books. I'm sure they describe a lot of things which even I don't know." Then he walked over to the large black chest where Michael had placed the crystal druse and the wand.

"What you did with the crystal was a great idea. It helped me a lot. May I keep it?"

"Yes, of course – it's yours", said Michael, happy that he could bring Andy Mo some pleasure. But Andy Mo had something special in mind for the gift.

"Please remain calm", he asked those present. "No matter what happens, nobody is to move from their seat. This is not entirely safe, at least not for me, and I must concentrate completely."

First he unwrapped the wand from the cloth, bowed to it, and held it against his forehead for a few seconds. Then he breathed on it and stroked it a few times with the palm of his hand while concentrating, as if to magnetise it. Finally, he tapped it three times in a strange rhythm. The echo reverberated eerily through the room, as if it came from another world, and Andy Mo commandingly muttered a few unintelligible words.

The friends silently and excitedly watched what he was doing. When he raised his wand and drew some lines in the air, it began to flicker around him again. Then he touched the tips of the five crystals in turn. Each time, as if projected by a laser, his sigil appeared and burned itself onto their smooth surface. Now Andy Mo broke the thumb-thick crystals out of the rock, which came loose from the druse like ripe fruit.

The whole procedure seemed to have strained him, for he was swaying, even though he didn't let on to the friends. He carefully placed the wand back on the table, bowed again as if it was a sacred object on an altar, and wrapped it up again with the cloth. Then, with the solemnity and dignity of a priest, he handed each of those present one of the five glittering stones he had prepared.

"You shouldn't use the wand again for the time being", he explained to the friends. "Incidentally, it only worked because I was already in the wood before Michael carved it. I was waiting to be summoned by you. Now, however, it has been initiated and is effective. Because it has been worked with successfully, it has become a real magical tool. Make sure that the wand doesn't fall into the hands of strangers, and beware of misusing it. Use your crystal instead. You can use that to summon me – that's enough for starters."

Andy Mo's voice grew quieter and quieter. He seemed uncomfortable as he touched his forehead several times. Miri Li was the first to notice and wanted to get him something to drink, but he waved her off.

"Unfortunately I'm a spirit, not flesh and blood", he explained. "What you see of me is made of light and shadow." Suddenly he staggered, and when Miri Li tried to support him, she actually reached straight through him. "You'll have to excuse me now", he said in a weak voice, and you could see he was struggling to keep himself upright. "That was a first for me too."

"Is there anything we can do to help you?" asked Kathi, stepping up to her friend's side. "There must be something to keep spirits alive too."

"There is", Andy Mo confirmed, but his words were barely audible. "I'll explain later – don't worry, I'm not dying. I'm just having a hard time condensing myself so you can hear and see me. I'll definitely be back, though."

As he spoke these last words, a change was coming over him. He began to flicker again and became glassy like a lifeless sculpture. His contours melted away like ice crystals in the sun, and then he dissolved completely and disappeared.

For a while it was absolutely quiet.

"Wow!" said Leif, who was the first to regain his composure. "That was awesome. Nobody's going to believe that – I can't believe it myself. I won't be forgetting today anytime soon."

Christian, who was still staring at the spot where Andy Mo had just been standing, agreed with him. Shaking his head, he looked at the crystal in his hand. "If I wasn't holding this stone, I'd think it had been a dream."

Kathi also shook her head. "He was just like us", she observed. "There was nothing spooky about him. I'm not going to be afraid of spirits from now on."

"I could even fall in love with this one", Miri Li said, caressing her crystal lovingly. "There was something so soothing about him, and beautiful too. I'm looking forward to seeing him again." Leif looked at her out of the corner of his eye, startled, but nobody noticed.

"We must keep what happened here – and whatever else happens – a secret", Michael demanded. "You must promise me that. Firstly, because no one will believe us anyway; and secondly, if anyone finds out what we're doing, we'll have the cult-hunters on our backs straight away."

"Michael's right", Christian agreed. "Those fanatics smell Lucifer everywhere. Drugs and blood. Last year they reported my dad for having a voodoo doll in his shop window. He didn't even know what the doll was actually for, and since then they've been snooping around the shop and spreading wild rumours. Of course, they always find something: a skull, a mask, a picture with a pentagram. In their eyes everything is the work of the devil, used to conjure up evil at black masses."

"Maybe those idiots are behind the theft of the paintings as well", Michael suggested. "They were trying to ruin your father that way. Last year, members of Opus Angelorum set fire to a nightclub to drive out the devil there. A prostitute was burned alive."

"We should protect ourselves", said Christian. "So we're not tempted to blurt things out carelessly, I suggest we take an oath of secrecy like the Freemasons. After all, what we've just experienced has turned us into a special chosen community. Who knows what else we're going to experience in the future? I think there's still a lot in store for us."

They had no idea how right he was.

Since no one objected to the voluntary obligation to maintain silence, Michael immediately prepared the ceremony. He fetched a three-armed candlestick from the mantelpiece and placed it on the old chest which had also served as an altar for Andy Mo's spell. Then he asked them to place their crystals on the shrine and solemnly lit the candles.

"Please repeat after me: *I vow…*"

"I vow…"

"*…not to disclose anything we discuss, experience, plan, or do in our circle…*"

"…not to disclose anything we discuss, experience, plan, or do in our circle…"

"*…to other people without prior consultation.*"

"…to other people without prior consultation."

"*So help me God.*"

"So help me God."

"Amen", added Leif, avoiding the sharp looks the two girls were giving him.

But Michael smirked. "This matter is so serious that a joke in between won't do any harm", he said. Then he returned everyone's magic crystals. Only now did they notice that their initials were also carved into them. "The crystals not only connect us with Andy Mo and the spirit world – they will also remind us of our fellowship and our vow." Without skipping a beat, he added: "I'm thirsty. Let's break off, I could do with a good drink."

Christian looked at his watch. "Okay, it's nine – we'll catch the bus at ten then, that'll be fine." The others were also thirsty and agreed to the proposal.

"Please go ahead", Michael said. "I'll join you in a minute – I want to tidy up a bit more." Kathi wanted to help him, but he asked her to fetch a bottle of elderflower juice from the cellar, and they all went off together.

The fire in the hearth had burnt down to the embers. He gathered the ashes together and a few red and bluish flames flickered up, only to go out again immediately. Shadows flitted around the room.

As Michael locked the wand in the chest, a strange feeling gripped him. Andy Mo's warning came to mind. He would soon find out how justified it was. If he'd known what would be done with the wand, he would have burned it immediately.

The mood among the friends was also subdued. No real conversation emerged; everyone was too preoccupied with their own thoughts. There were creeping doubts as to whether what they were doing was right, but no one voiced them openly. It was a fully justified fear of the unknown. They had opened a portal into a world they didn't know, and they weren't sure what lay within it. What other powers had they paved the way for?

*

Andy Mo had quickly recovered and consolidated himself in his subterranean element. Relaxed, he lay on the soft bearskin in his new rock house and went over the experience in his mind. Thanks to the help of his friends, he'd managed to gain a foothold in the human realm. Nevertheless, new obstacles had appeared, and he hadn't expected them. Now his friends needed his support in turn, and it was clear to him that he had to help them first. Yet he suspected that this was only the beginning. Baphomet was making it really difficult for them. Miri Li seemed to be in the greatest danger, and Leif Andersson was also at risk. The art thieves had to be caught too. Finding a valuable gemstone for Mr Freiwald was the least of his problems, although he wasn't allowed to simply place the stone at his feet. That would violate the law of Divine Providence. He had to inspire him to dig in the right place on his own, and that would be time-consuming.

But Baphomet also had to abide by these laws. He, too, could not directly intervene in Earthly events and could only act through humans. But who were his Earthly minions? Who would be his concrete opponents?

There was a great deal to be done, but he didn't know where to start. And he had absolutely no idea where to look for his father – he didn't even know whether he'd be able to enter the human realm without outside help from now on, or how long he could stay there. Despite the success he had just had, Andy Mo was desperate and dejected.

But then it occurred to him that perhaps he could find a clue to the king's whereabouts in the Book of the Master. He couldn't imagine that his father had led his friends to the book just so they could learn magic from him. He had explained to Andy Mo often enough that humans didn't need formulas and rituals – they could determine their lives solely by the power of their thoughts.

This realisation made him optimistic again. Tomorrow he would ask Michael for a copy of the manuscript. He was sure to meet him in the schoolyard, he thought. Then it would also become clear how he could move around in the human realm now. He was looking forward to meeting Krux again, too. He would be amazed by everything he had experienced. Although he had only been away for a day, it seemed to him as if it had been years. Time in the human realm obviously followed different laws: this new reality was far more stable in every respect than the spiritual worlds. Even thoughts here seemed to have a life of their own and kept intruding into his consciousness against his will. Images of his mother and his home appeared, warming his soul like lights from a distant past. But then they turned into shadows, and he pushed them away. Miri Li came to his mind. He should have asked her where she lived and remained close to her, as that was the only way he could protect her. Where had he kept the elixir? Like waves on the beach which disappeared without a trace in the sand, feelings and thoughts flooded over him and took parts of his consciousness with them. Andy Mo fell into a restless sleep.

*

Baphomet was satisfied. He had summoned his two most trusted underlings to discuss the next steps.

"Everything is going according to plan", he announced emotionlessly. "But we must still alter events." They gazed silently at the magical carpet of light and shadow on which they could watch events in the world. Then he continued: "Our man is weaving the pattern of his villainy. He doesn't realise that we're pulling the strings. He wants power, and we want the souls. Andy Mo will soon be alone again. Christian's father has been arrested and must sell his shop – that eliminates Christian. Michael must move away as well, as he can't pay the mortgage on the house. His father is ill with malaria and can't go into the mountains for the next few weeks. Leif is becoming one of our people – he has already taken the first step. Only Miri Li is a problem."

The others looked at him questioningly.

"Andy Mo has fallen in love with her, as planned", one underling said. "She will love him in return. The feelings will bind him."

"Or inspire him", the other underling realised, agreeing with Baphomet. "The boy has progressed much more rapidly than we thought. With her help he can fulfil his mission."

Silent and motionless, erect as mighty pillars, they stand around the carpet of opalescent light. They bear the roof of infinity: eternal darkness, with stars and galaxies twinkling through the fissures.

But their heads are lowered and their concentrated gaze plunges into the seething mass in the square at their feet. Soul sperm, the mental semen cells of unborn thoughts, like glass tadpoles born from the toad spawn of human desires; living building blocks lacking only the sense to act. Twitching shapes, writhing blindly like eels. Snake-like, their blinded heads poke out of the seething slime and Baphomet harvests them. He cuts them like ripe fruit with his axe: srrt, srrt, srrt. Like a chorus of crickets, a penetrating shrillness resounds, metallic and eerie. Whatever he harvests freezes, only to immediately awaken back to life in accordance with his will: formed into inspirations, fertilising fantasies, consciousness-impregnating thought-maggots which sink into time and space and latch tightly onto the receptive brains of willing minions, reborn as the first impulse to action.

Silent and motionless, erect as mighty pillars, they stand around the pool of opalescent light, binding shadow-seeds together and directing the twitching, flaming arrows towards the target. Satisfied, they gaze upon a house and know that it will burn.

"She will die", Baphomet decrees, "and he will not wish to live without her. He will follow her. He will want to help her in the realm of the dead. He will return to the spirit realm and forget his mission."

*

Andy Mo jerked awake. It took him some time to get his bearings. The dream he had dreamt held him captive. Only slowly did he come to, recognising the magical window above him in which the cold darkness of the night and the twinkling stars were reflected.

It had just been a dream. But the flames were real. Only predetermined events from the future glimmered like that, and Miri Li was in the burning house. But where was the house? He had to find her and warn her – but how?

Andy Mo concentrated on the girl, trying to locate her, but there was no trace of her. Miri Li was asleep. And he received no signal when he tuned in to the other friends – they obviously weren't awake either. He couldn't even locate the crystals with his sigil on them; his clairvoyant ability had been disrupted. His first stay in the human realm may well have weakened him more than he imagined. Nevertheless, he wanted to go up again. He saw no other option but to look for Miri Li directly in her world. Then he remembered Michael. He lived right above him – he could wake him up. Resolute, he ascended.

HUMANS, BIG CITY, UNDERWORLDS

The night received him as the sea receives the diver – repellently alien and threatening. At the same time, he felt the tingling, seductive allure of the unknown. He stood on the boulder and listened to the sounds that formed themselves into inner images: a bird whistling a tired tune in its sleep, the soft swishing of branches, a rustling in the bushes. Even gravity posed no problems for him. He felt safe again after just a few steps. Purposefully he approached Michael's house and stepped through the wall.

But Michael wasn't there. His bed was untouched. Andy Mo searched all the rooms in vain. He wondered if Michael was spending the night at the home of one of his friends. He was at a loss, and he had no idea how to find Miri Li.

Feeling resigned, he squatted down on the bench in front of the house – exactly where she had been sitting – and thought over how he should go about things. Then he had an idea. He could try something he used to do in the land of spirits. Hide and seek is a popular game among gnomes: one gnome makes themselves invisible while the others search for them. Finding someone can only be done with a very specific technique, but he had mastered it perfectly.

First of all, he imagined Miri Li's body with every fibre of his being while simultaneously trying to forget his own body. He formed the delicate features of her face, imitated her graceful movements in his mind, and tried to think and feel like her. In his spirit he merged with her being until he had the sensation that he *was* her. Then he let go of her, and it worked: he sensed a target, as if he were a pendulum swinging towards her. He had tracked her down and found her. He couldn't see her, so he couldn't mentally leap his way into her proximity, but he knew which direction to go. And without thinking twice, he set off.

Since the material world presented no obstacle to him, he made good progress. He didn't have to pay any attention to anything which stood in his way and went straight through trees, bushes, and fences. As he did so he developed a technique which allowed him to take larger steps, as if he were an astronaut on the moon, without losing sight of his goal. So he quickly crossed some properties which resembled parks with magnificent villas; then both the gardens and the houses became smaller, and at the end of the estate the usual big-city apartment blocks rose up. They were lifeless canyons of asphalt and concrete – devoid of humans, desolate, like a prison even under the wide starry sky of the night. This was another world.

Andy Mo continued on quickly. While a dog he had frightened was still barking at him from a quiet corner, soon another unfamiliar noise boomed ahead of him. Like a living avalanche of rubble, the urban traffic rolled noisily past him. Although there wasn't much going on at this late hour, he was still startled every time the cars roared by. There was something threatening about them. He sensed he couldn't pass through these vibrating machines as he did through a wall, and he instinctively avoided them. He was also irritated by the bright lights of the neon signs, which blinked ever more obtrusively and frantically the further he penetrated into the centre. Several times they caused him to deviate from the direction he was aiming for.

To avoid getting lost, Andy Mo moved along the streets like the humans on the pavement rather than going through walls. These pavements soon became wider, the traffic increased, and ever more humans appeared despite the late hour. Yet they took no notice of him. They didn't seem to see him at all, because when he failed to avoid them, they walked straight through him as if he wasn't even there. Although Andy Mo had known that he would only be visible in the human realm under special circumstances, and only to certain people, this fact now affected him greatly.

An indescribable loneliness overcame him. He became acutely aware that he was completely alone and on his own in a strange, unknown world. Like a choking force, a deep longing for his friends seized him and drove him forward. He felt that he couldn't make it much longer on his own. He was tired, and he had to stop increasingly often to get his bearings. He found it difficult to concentrate in the hustle and bustle around him, and now he understood why humans couldn't perform magic: their world was too shrill.

He urgently needed a quiet place to gather himself together again. For a split moment, he wanted to return to his element. And when he located a cave beneath him, he switched off and simply let himself sink into the earth. But he shouldn't have done that; it was his undoing. The cave he landed in was an underground train tunnel. He immediately knew that it was no place to relax, but he realised too late the real danger he was in. All he felt was the high-voltage line nearby, a materialised form of fire like the penetrating sound of a dentist's drill. He didn't notice the train approaching at breakneck speed behind a curve. By the time the beam of light hit him, it was too late. The wagons roared over the top of him before he could dodge the howling metal colossus.

The impact shouldn't have hurt him that much. But the frequencies of the gigantic electric motor whirled him around like a blender, hurling parts of him in all directions and threatening to break all the thoughts in his body (it is well-known that thoughts are the bones of spirits). Andy Mo lost consciousness several times. Fire is hell for earth spirits, and electricity means certain death. What saved him was the fact that he'd already passed through the elements of water and air and could also live on the surface of the Earth. He knew how to cling to a thought so as not to lose himself, and he thought specifically of his friends. Of Michael and Kathi. Of Christian. Of Leif. And of Miri Li. And slowly he gathered himself together. He gradually felt whole again, and his senses awoke to new life.

But he had no idea where he was. Blinding flashes and pounding noise were still swirling him around in circles and threatening to deprive him of his consciousness again. But in a different, seductive way. True, the invisible roaring tides swept him along, but they also held him firmly, they carried him, even though he was sinking into them. It was a pull upwards, a chaos with a system. The power of the rhythms of light and noise seized him, moved him, relieved him of worry and drove away everything that oppressed him. He had landed in the nightclub above the underground railway station.

He was one among many. The pounding rhythm amidst the inferno acted like a magnet, drawing them all in. Every person for themselves. Mindless puppets on beaming strings of artificial light. Demon fingers slipped into the soulless shells and moved the puppets from within, making them dance, lonely and yet all the same, like numbed soldiers of nothingness.

Andy Mo didn't know how to free himself, nor did he wish to. But then he saw Leif and came to his senses with a jolt.

With twitching limbs and an expressionless look, his friend stomped through the crowd without noticing him. Nor did he notice the two other people at his side who hooked under his armpits and gently but firmly pushed him off the dance floor. Only when they forcefully dragged him towards the exit did he start to resist. But the two guys were stronger. Nobody was taking any notice of what was happening; it all happened very quickly. Andy Mo managed to follow them into the street and saw them dragging Leif into an unlit archway – then they started beating him up. Leif didn't stand a chance.

Andy Mo grasped the situation in a flash. The only way to take out the attackers was to paralyse them. He concentrated, made a hand gesture in their direction, and placed a cube of his element over them. Almost instantly, the three froze. As motionless as insects in amber, they were stuck in the strangely shimmering cage. Andy Mo looked pleased with his handiwork – he was glad that it also worked in the human realm. This was how gnomes fixed molecules in rock. He made a note of the fact it could also be used to hold hooligans in place. Then he grabbed Leif's hand and pulled him out of the artificial gravitational field with a strong jerk. It made a smacking sound, like pulling a cork out of a bottle.

Leif stared at Andy Mo as if he were a ghost. Then he looked at the two motionless figures and grinned.

"Man, that was awesome. You really can do magic. Thanks, by the way. You arrived just in the nick of time. How did you know I needed help, and how did you find me?"

"By pure chance", explained Andy Mo. "I was looking for Miri Li." And while he hastily tended to the gash on Leif's forehead, he briefly recounted his dream and his accident in the underground train tunnel. Leif's left eye was also swollen shut, and he winced when Andy Mo touched his chin. "They really did a number on you – what do they want from you? And what was that horrible hellish temple we ended up in?"

"I owe them money", Leif confessed, spitting blood in their direction. "And that temple is not a temple – it's a nightclub. You won't find Miri Li here, but she doesn't live far away." He glanced at his watch. "We can get to her place in five minutes by night bus. We'd better hurry, though." Then he pointed to the entrance of the building. "What's going to happen to those two?"

"Don't worry about them", said Andy Mo, drawing strange lines in the air as he had before. In the same instant, life returned to the figures. They began to move grotesquely as if in slow motion, like dancing bears stuck to the ground. But they couldn't really get going. It was as if they were up to their necks in an invisible swamp. Andy Mo nodded in satisfaction. "It'll take a few more minutes – let's get out of here before they fully recover. They still think they're dreaming."

*

The bus appeared around the corner, and they just managed to catch it. Out of breath, they got on. Leif asked for two tickets, but the driver tilted his head and raised an eyebrow.

"Where's the second person?" Andy Mo grinned while Leif blushed.

"Of course", Leif said, realising that the driver couldn't see Andy Mo.

"Just one ticket."

They were the only passengers, and they sat down right at the front. It was the first time Andy Mo had been in a motor vehicle. At first he worried he couldn't handle being near the engine, but it went much better than he feared. He looked attentively out of the window and was fascinated by this way of travelling.

"It's fast, yet you can still see how you're progressing", he enthused. "It's different with us in our spirit realm. There's no space in between things: you focus on your destination, and if you succeed, you're there instantly."

"And what if you don't succeed?" asked Leif.

"Then you didn't really know your destination well enough, and you end up somewhere else or nowhere. You try again or find better information."

"But that would mean you're a prisoner of your experiences. How are you supposed to get anywhere if you have to know it first?"

"In fact that can be a problem sometimes", Andy Mo admitted. "But you always have some idea of a destination, otherwise you wouldn't want to go there. The harder part is to visualize it clearly. You won't achieve something if you don't have it unshakeable in your mind."

"That's like us with life goals", remarked Leif. "Our philosophy professor always preaches that: set yourself a goal, he says, and you'll reach it."

"And do you have a life goal in mind?" asked Andy Mo. "What do you wish for? What are you striving for?"

"Until yesterday, all I really wanted was to have fun and a cool car. But now I want to explore the spiritual realms and magical power. You can achieve anything with that, right?"

"No, definitely not everything. But we'll talk about that once we start working together in Michael's library."

"Just tell me one thing", Leif demanded. "Could you conjure up money?"

"Not in the way you imagine, with 'hocus pocus' and the banknotes suddenly appearing. I assume you're thinking about your debts?"

"Yes, but I'll be getting the money anyway. Some friends were going to bring it to the nightclub tonight, but the others came too early. And then you arrived. But I'll take care of it – Miri Li is more important. The crooks won't get me a second time."

The bus driver turned around briefly and looked curiously at Leif, whose face was badly battered from the brawl – first he asks for two tickets, and then he starts talking to himself. But this time Leif didn't mind if someone thought he was crazy. He squinted his eyes, made some unintelligible sounds, and bared his teeth like a monkey. Andy Mo was watching the scene with amusement, and he joined in the fun. He went to the front, tapped the driver lightly on the shoulder – first on the left, and then on the right – and then honked the horn twice. The shocked driver's head rotated. Then he went as stiff as a board, straightened up, and just looked straight ahead.

They got off at the next stop. Although they were already in the city precinct, it was a quiet, upscale neighbourhood. The street was lined with lovingly maintained Biedermeier houses and villas surrounded by tall, ancient trees.

"Two hundred years ago this was on the outskirts of Vienna", Leif explained to his friend, "but now it's a posh district. Embassies, consulates, and rich people have moved in."

Andy Mo looked around attentively. There were almost no humans to be seen – the area was deserted at this time of day. There wasn't any traffic either, as it was a pedestrian zone. Their footsteps echoed on the asphalt as they crossed the small square.

"That's Christian's parents' shop", said Leif, pointing. "And right next to it is the Li family restaurant." Although it was already closed, there was still a light on at the back of the restaurant – Miri Li's parents were obviously tidying up the kitchen. After fifty metres, they turned the corner and followed a steep, narrow street. The area suddenly looked poor; the houses were close together, and they no longer seemed as well-kept as the villas before. Leif pointed to an older building. "Here it is – this is where Miri Li lives. She's asleep, everything's quiet."

Andy Mo looked at the two-storey detached house with relief. But then he took a closer look and was startled: it was exactly the same place he had seen in his nocturnal vision. The narrow, high windows, the crumbling plasterwork, and the green front door. He recognised everything.

"Miri Li's room is upstairs", Leif explained. "The ground floor is more of a storage area." They followed a gravel path to the back of the house, but everything was peaceful and quiet there as well. They couldn't see anything suspicious. "What should we do now?"

Andy Mo wondered if he should wake Miri Li and warn her. But suddenly his fear seemed exaggerated and ridiculous – perhaps it had been just a dream after all, and he didn't want to worry her about it. Besides, he was infinitely tired. He sensed that he wouldn't be able to keep himself awake much longer.

"I don't think she's in any danger for now", he said. "Let's go home. I know where she lives now, and I can transport myself here at any time." For good measure, he carved his seal on the door.

Suddenly a window opened upstairs; it was Miri Li. She was very surprised when she recognised them in the shade of the trees, and she immediately came down.

"My God, what happened to you?!" she exclaimed in horror before greeting her friends. "Come on in. Who beat you up like this?"

Leif's face really didn't look so good. Dried blood was crusted over his upper lip, which was split and swollen, while his left eye was reddish-purple and almost swollen shut. Miri Li disappeared into the bathroom and returned with a first-aid kit. She carefully and skilfully tended to the wound, which had begun to bleed again. Like a nurse, she gently but resolutely overruled Leif's initial protests so that he sat still and endured everything patiently.

Andy Mo felt superfluous, and he looked on as if he were in a theatre. Suddenly he felt as if he was invisible again, or not even in the same room. Miri Li was so busy with Leif that he felt left out. Yet she was even more beautiful in her see-through nightgown than he remembered. She was wearing a white towelling bathrobe over her nightgown, and the belt which was supposed to tie it had come undone: the thin fabric underneath traced every limb of her flawless slender body, as if she were standing naked before him.

Ever since Andy Mo had been living among the humans, a body of flesh and blood had held a strange attraction for him. He felt that the beauty of spirit and soul could only be fully expressed with such a body of pulsating life.

He wanted to touch Miri Li, hold her hand, feel her breath, and despite her closeness he was further away from her than before. He followed her every movement, and with all clarity he became aware that he was not like her. He lacked Earthly life; he was made only of shadow and light. As if Miri Li had sensed his feelings, she suddenly turned to him.

"I'm sorry, Andy Mo", she said, her gentle voice still sounding somewhat sleepy. "I didn't properly greet you. I assume you've already treated the wound – a cut like that usually bleeds a lot more."

Andy Mo nodded, wondering how she knew that so well. But before he could ask her, she gave him the answer herself.

"My father was a boxer for a while, you know – in the featherweight division", she added as she closed the first aid kit. "What do you want to drink? Shall I fix you something to eat? The fridge is full."

Leif asked for some cola, but Andy Mo shook his head.

"First I need to learn to eat and drink", he explained, "but I'd love to watch you."

All the same, Miri Li brought three glasses and placed them on the table along with the opened bottle. Then she snuggled into an armchair and wrapped her bathrobe more tightly around her shoulders.

"Now please tell me what happened", she said. "You don't show up at my house in the middle of the night for no reason."

Leif looked at Andy Mo and nodded, whereupon he recounted his dream. Miri Li listened attentively. To the surprise of her friends, however, she showed no fear. She remained calm and collected despite the danger she was in.

"If I understand the matter correctly", she said, "there isn't much we can do at the moment. Install fire alarms, increase the insurance, and stay alert. Or pay the mafia", she added after a brief pause. But Leif cautioned her.

"I'm not sure if the arsonists from Andy Mo's vision are really the same people extorting protection money from you. They'd be more likely to set fire to the restaurant than the house, wouldn't they? Something's not right here."

Andy Mo agreed with him. "Baphomet has many minions. However, it's likely that there's one who's running everything from here – if we can expose them, we'll have solved our other problems too."

"That's if you're right about your conspiracy theory", Miri Li mused. "But maybe it's all just coincidence, and we're really just dealing with small-time crooks. Who beat up Leif, for example? And why? Was that also related to your spirit mafia?" Andy Mo couldn't help smiling, despite the seriousness of the situation.

"I'm afraid so, though Leif should tell you about that himself."

But Leif avoided the issue.

"That's got nothing to do with the whole affair", he stated firmly as he stood up. "I must go now. Miri Li is safe for the time being – I'm sure nothing else will be happening here tonight."

Andy Mo nodded and rose from his chair as well. "You really can sleep soundly", he said to Miri Li, stroking her hair tentatively. "I'd sense it if you were in immediate danger." She looked at Andy Mo gratefully and hugged him warmly; he could feel her scent and her warmth. Content, he noticed that she was a little more distant from Leif. But maybe he was just imagining things.

*

As they stood in the street, Leif called a number on his mobile phone. "Where have you been? Yes, I had to leave for a while. Okay. In half an hour." Then he put the phone away and looked Andy Mo openly in the eye. "I'd rather do this on my own. Are you offended?"

Andy Mo shook his head. He was hurt, not offended. He felt he had been sidelined by Leif. He had gotten the goons off his back, and now he was withdrawing his trust. Leif realised he had made a mistake and looked down in embarrassment. When he looked up again, Andy Mo had disappeared.

"Andy Mo, where are you? You don't need to get in a huff about it and run away. I just don't want to get you involved in this, understand? Please come back!"

Leif looked around, searching, and Andy Mo realised that he couldn't see him anymore. His friend didn't want him around, and so he had automatically become invisible to him.

Andy Mo decided to take advantage of this situation. He sensed that Leif genuinely regretted hurting him, and he wanted to follow him unseen. Perhaps Leif would need his help again, he reasoned. Leif continued turning in circles, even looking up into the trees; then he shrugged in resignation and walked to the bus station. Andy Mo stayed by his side.

Just as he had suspected, they went back to the nightclub. He was surprised to see there was still a lot of life outside the club – visitors were still arriving, despite the late hour. Some teenagers were standing in front of the entrance in an excited mood, and a girl shrieked before letting one of the boys kiss her.

Andy Mo looked around. It wasn't loud or merry, but the coerced frenzy of the noisy dance hall lingered on within the young people, and it continued outside the hall in a similarly unnatural way.

Suddenly he could clearly sense that they were being watched. Since he himself was invisible, the object of interest could only be Leif Andersson. Andy Mo immediately managed to locate the direction from which the glances were coming. While Leif stood about indecisively and seemed to be waiting for someone, Andy Mo followed the signal. It was coming from a blue Jaguar parked about fifty metres away. The driver's long, dark hair was tied back; he had ice-cold, unflinching features, and his slanted black almond eyes were fixed steadfastly on Leif. He was in the process of concealing a handgun in the inside pocket of his leather jacket. Then he retrieved a small metal case from the back seat and took an envelope from it.

"It's only a thousand euros", he said, grinning. "We'll let him squirm around a little longer." Then he hissed at the other man in the car: "Get out of here now – we mustn't be seen together."

As Andy Mo looked more closely at the guy sitting in the passenger seat, he was startled. It was one of the goons from earlier. He had to warn Leif.

With a lightning-fast mental leap, he transported himself back in the hope he could make himself visible to his friend again. Leif, who had been waiting around indecisively until now, was about to enter the nightclub when Andy Mo blocked his way. He wasn't at all surprised to see him.

"I should have guessed", he said, smiling.

"Are you snooping on me, or trying to save me again? The people I'm meeting are okay – they're going to help me. They're on my side."

"I wouldn't be so sure", Andy Mo disagreed, and he described what he had just heard and seen. "They're damn tough guys, and they're working together. You can't trust them."

Leif turned pale. But before he could reply the goon was already there, pulling him to one side.

"I'm obviously too late", he remarked dryly, looking coolly at Leif's puffy eye. "Here's the money."

Leif quickly regained his composure. Without taking the envelope, he said:

"That's only a thousand – where's the rest? And since when have you been carrying a gun around? Did I come to the wrong address?"

Now it was the goon who was taken aback. Startled, he fumbled for his gun, then looked at the envelope in amazement.

"Man, you're good. Are you psychic? You're almost a Clear – you're better than the boss."

"That's who I'd like to talk to", Leif replied, and with a quick grab he took the money after all. "Where can I find him?"

But the goon's mobile phone rang before he could reply. He held it briefly to his ear, then exclaimed "Damn!" as he turned to Leif: "The police. It's a raid, get out of here!" and he was gone. It all happened very quickly.

Andy Mo had originally intended to follow the goon, but now he had to take care of Leif. It would be a disaster if the police found so much money on him. While the Jaguar disappeared like a shadow up a side alley, the two friends ran to the bus stop. But it was too late. Tyres screeched, car doors slammed, and then a policeman was standing in front of them, politely but firmly asking Leif to follow him to the van. He had aroused suspicion by running away. Before he was pushed into the police vehicle, Andy Mo just managed to take the envelope full of money which Leif had been hiding behind his back. They strip-searched Leif, but fortunately they couldn't find anything else on him. Then they took a note of his name, asked how he got his injury, and let him go again.

Relieved, Leif stood in the street and puffed the fresh night air through his lips as if he were blowing out a candle.

"That was close", he said to Andy Mo. "You saved my skin again. Thanks. I hope I can repay you for everything one day."

Leif hadn't had any real friends in his class until now. That was due not only to the age difference, but also to his challenging, cynical nature. He had experienced more than the others as well. He had lived in Sweden, Israel, and Thailand, and felt just as much at home in New York as in Vienna. His father had been in the diplomatic service of the Foreign Ministry for many years and had been posted as ambassador to various countries. For the sake of appearances, he had always taken his family with him. So Leif had mastered four languages and discovered half of the world, but the frequent change of schools had also brought disadvantages. When they moved to Vienna after his parents' divorce two years earlier, he had missed out on the transition to senior high and had to repeat a grade.

His mother had never cared much about him, and had always left the upbringing to the current housekeeper. She was an actress, and her career meant more to her than her family. She had lived in

New York since separating from her husband, and Leif hadn't seen her since. But he wasn't very devoted to her.

His relationship with his father wasn't particularly cordial either. In fact he was only his stepfather: he didn't know his real father. Dr Andersson had adopted him so he could present a whole family to the world, but he'd never shown any particular interest in his life. He treated him fairly, but otherwise he was as distant to him as he was to his employees and servants. All the same, Leif had never found this difficult. On the contrary: he appreciated the freedom it gave him, and he made use of it. He frequently came home early in the morning, and he skipped school during the day as well, but nobody asked him where he'd been. Dr Andersson didn't even look at his school reports. After the divorce he had moved from the civil service to the private sector, and he travelled a lot as chairman of the supervisory board of a large chemical company. For the most part it was only short trips abroad, but if he was in Vienna – which was rare – he usually stayed with his girlfriend, who was another young actress. As a rule, Leif was alone in the large villa with the new housekeeper, who came in the morning, cooked, and disappeared again in the evening. He could do whatever he wanted. With his adventurous character it was no wonder he fell into bad company.

Andy Mo sensed his friend's suppressed loneliness and felt sorry for him. Leif also gratefully acknowledged the sincere feelings of friendship. Neither of them suspected the tragic fate that would bind them together beyond death. Without a word, Andy Mo held out the money to him.

"I'm tired", was all he said. "Infinitely tired." Leif nodded.

"I'm totally exhausted too", he replied, reaching hesitantly for the envelope. "You can spend the night at my place. I don't live far from here." Andy Mo thanked him but declined.

"I need to get into my element. That's the only place I can really relax. Thank you for taking me to Miri Li's – I'll see you at school tomorrow."

Andy Mo decided to walk on the Earth's undersurface, where

he could move more easily. He scanned for the boulder on Michael's property and was actually able to pinpoint it. Leif confirmed that the direction was correct.

"Six kilometres straight ahead", he said, and could just see his friend begin to flicker as he sank into the ground and disappeared.

Almost instantaneously, Andy Mo arrived in Michael's garden. It was much easier than the day before – he was learning. Exhausted, he lay down on his bed and fell asleep immediately. This time he dreamt of nothing.

*

It was already light outside when he woke up again. Feeling well rested, he climbed out of his boulder and consciously breathed in the fresh morning air, full of the power of the sunlight. As he did so, he could feel the previously unknown energies of the human realm supplying him with new life force.

Earth spirits purify themselves by cleansing their thoughts and feelings and distancing themselves from everything unnecessary and unpleasant they've absorbed into their consciousness during the day. They purge negative thoughts, anxiety-provoking ideas, and depressing feelings by realising that they don't wish to have them, and therefore that they aren't a part of their being. On the other hand, they retain positive moods, hopeful thoughts, and good intentions by consciously repeating them in their minds and thus firmly anchoring them within themselves. Normally this is done in the evening, but since Andy Mo had been too tired the evening before, he did it in the morning. He was so focused that he didn't even notice Michael stepping out of the old villa and rubbing his eyes sleepily.

After the friends had said goodbye, Michael had returned to search for a book his grandfather had treasured, and he had fallen asleep while reading it. It was about the beyond and life after death. Now he felt as if a seed was sprouting within him that had been planted the evening before. Only now did he realise the full implications of his encounter with Andy Mo. He now knew what he had previously only considered to be vaguely possible: spirits and a spiritual world existed. And if there were spirits, there also had to be a spirit within humans which – like the spirits – could live without a body. That meant there were also angels, a God, and an afterlife in which his mother now lived. It had taken an encounter with another spirit for him to become aware of his own spirituality. He felt as if he had been reborn.

"Good morning, Andy Mo – are you an early riser too?"

"Sure", Andy Mo replied, climbing down from his boulder. "This is the best time of the day in your world. At night you're noisy and hectic like demons." Michael looked at him in surprise.

"I really needed you yesterday", Andy Mo explained, following his friend into the house. "But your bed was empty and I couldn't find you. I didn't know you were sleeping over there." While Michael made some tea, Andy Mo told him about his terrible dream vision, his adventure at the nightclub, and their visit to Miri Li to warn her. He didn't mention anything about the police for the time being. Michael listened to him attentively, and he was simultaneously impressed and concerned.

"We should meet again today and discuss everything together. If we wait until Sunday, it might be too late." Andy Mo agreed with him.

"Our opponents are operating on two planes. Baphomet and his princes operate in the Shadow Realm, which we cannot penetrate. But their Earthly minions are pursuing us here. We can get to them – and once we expose one of them, we'll have them all, because their thoughts will lead us to their centre. Then we'll know exactly what they're planning. I suspect we'll find a lead to my father there, too."

"Do you think there's a magical Lodge behind it?" asked Michael. "The Book of the Master mentions one."

"I hadn't even thought of that", replied Andy Mo. "But maybe you're right – the princes influence priests, wizards, and scientists just as much as drug dealers and thieves. Please make a copy of the book for me. Maybe I'll find a clue there as to where to look."

"Take the original", said Michael, retrieving the manuscript for him. "Christian left it here yesterday. He prefers to use a copy so he can make notes and underline things."

As Andy Mo held the book in his hand, a strange feeling gripped him. Although he hadn't even read it yet, he had the sudden impression that he had taken a big step closer to his father. All at once he was confident again and full of energy. And as if he had read his thoughts, Michael said: "This book is a guide. It opens up a world to everyone which would otherwise remain closed to them. We'll surely track down the missing volumes. Then we'll have everything we need to solve your problems – and ours, and everyone's."

"Before that, I need a guide to the human realm", Andy Mo stated dryly. "Is there such a thing as a drawing of the surface of the Earth? I need an overview so I can orient myself better." Michael briefly disappeared and returned with a detailed map of the city.

"Over in the library there's a globe – that's a replica of the whole planet. But I think this map of Vienna will do for now. This is where we are," he explained, circling a spot, "and this is where Miri Li lives."

Glancing at it for only a second, Andy Mo immediately knew where he was. Like all earth spirits, he had a fantastic sense of location and space, and he knew he'd soon find his way around as well as a bus driver. He excitedly traced his finger across the map.

"There's the nightclub, and this is where I walked. Now please show me where the school is and where Kathi, Christian, and Leif Andersson live."

Michael marked these places for him as well. Then he made another mark. "This is the other restaurant owned by Miri Li's parents. There could be a fire there too."

Andy Mo flinched; it was barely perceptible, but Michael noticed. "You've fallen in love with her", he stated matter-of-factly. And when Andy Mo nodded, he added: "I can see why – she really is like an angel or a fairy. She's like a dream."

Andy Mo nodded again.

"For me she must remain a dream. I'm well aware that I have

no chance whatsoever. For starters, I'm a spirit and don't possess a real body; and secondly, she loves Leif. You should have seen how lovingly she treated his wounds."

But Michael shook his head.

"She'd never take him on. That was pure pity. She's devoted to the weak, the sick, and the poor. She doesn't like the super-strong guys – wait until he gets well again. Then she won't look at him twice. Besides, you two are somehow alike. You both have the same big dark eyes and the same unfathomable gaze. You could be mistaken for siblings."

Andy Mo glanced at him gratefully. Even though he felt Michael was wrong, his friend's comforting did him good. He felt that he wasn't alone. Then he turned his attention back to the city map. "We can't watch the house and both restaurants around the clock", he noted, and suddenly he paused. "The shop that belongs to Christian's parents: it's right next to the Li family's restaurant, isn't it? Who owns the shops to the right and left of those two? They were empty, if I remember correctly."

Michael didn't understand what Andy Mo was getting at and bent over the map as well. "They both closed last week. They were given notice and the buildings were sold. A filthy rich developer by the name of Goldstein bought both properties at a crazy price – there was even a TV report about it."

"I thought as much", said Andy Mo, slapping the table with his palm. And then Michael also understood what he meant.

"You mean that high-class mobster is behind this? Could be. He was planning a large, modern shopping centre in the district, but the Greens have managed to stop it so far. He actually wanted to buy Christian's parents' house, too."

"That would at least be a lead we can follow up", said Andy Mo. "But don't you have to go to school?"

"You're right, it's time. Are you coming too, or would you rather study the books in the library?"

"I'll have time for that later – let's go." Andy Mo stood up and folded the map. "I'll need this in case we get separated."

While they were waiting for the bus, Andy Mo pointed out to his friend that he was invisible to other people and didn't need a ticket. Then he mentioned the confused bus driver, and Michael burst out laughing – which of course promptly caused the other waiting passengers to stare at him. All they could see of Andy Mo was the city map, which was no less embarrassing. Held by an invisible hand, the map was floating in mid-air as the bystanders gazed on in astonishment. It's not often that you see someone talking to a flying city map. When Michael recognised the phenomenon, he snatched the map like a fly in mid-flight and put it in his pocket. Then the bus arrived.

"That was a great magic trick", said a little boy, sitting in the seat next to him. "Can you tell me how to do it?" At first Michael was irritated, but then he grinned.

"It's very simple", he explained. "You just need an assistant spirit. Mine's called Andy Mo. Watch closely: Andy Mo, please open the bag and take out the map of Vienna."

Andy Mo played along. He did as he was told, unzipping Michael's backpack and pulling out the city map. Then he made a few circular motions with it, unfolded it and folded it up again, and finally slapped Michael on the head with it.

"Know, dare, will, stay silent", he lectured. "These are the four pillars of magic. Those who cannot remain silent will lose their magical power. We'll talk about it later."

"My apologies", Michael muttered. "But it was just too tempting." Then he jumped up and pushed his way towards the exit – he hadn't noticed they had already arrived at school. Andy Mo simply hopped through the closed window. All the bewildered boy next to him saw was the city map flying through the window. Fortunately he went to a different school.

EINSTEIN AND THE QUESTION OF SPIRITS

It was only a little way to the high school. Students of all ages were heading towards the building. Cars stopped briefly to discharge their cargo; some students arrived by moped or bicycle, and even a teacher was among them, parking his mountain bike in one of the bike racks out front.

"That's Einstein", Michael explained, waving to the professor. "Everybody knows him, and everybody loves him – he's always there for you. There's no problem he can't solve. He fixes mopeds, computers, and broken hearts. All the while he teaches philosophy, chemistry, and physics." Einstein also raised his hand in greeting, but then suddenly stopped and turned slowly around. For a brief moment, Andy Mo felt as if the teacher had noticed him. He looked the earth spirit straight in the face. But then his gaze was lost in the distance, and he shook his head imperceptibly.

"Hello, Michael! What's your father writing?"

"I haven't heard from him for two months."

"Are you getting along okay? Do you need money?"

Michael smiled gratefully at him. "I'm fine, thanks. But I have a question: what is the human spirit? Is it the same spirit that spirits are made of?"

Einstein (who actually looked like Einstein) stopped abruptly and grabbed Michael by both shoulders. His small, clever eyes sparkled like fireworks. "What a question!" he exclaimed. "Did you hear that? Listen up everyone. Eureka! We have another golden question:

"Is the human spirit the same spirit that spirits are made of?"

The school building was bustling like a railway station at this time of day, yet silence fell almost instantly. Everyone knew Einstein, and everyone knew: not only did whoever asked the golden question receive a gold coin as a reward, but so did whoever gave the best answer. And Einstein did in fact carry a gold ducat with him

97

at all times for this very reason. Solemnly pulling a red-checked handkerchief out of his trouser pocket, he laboriously unknotted it and handed Michael his prize. The bystanders applauded; some of the teachers had also stopped, but unlike the students, most of them disagreed with the teaching methods of their popular colleague. Mr Kleindienst made no secret of this and shook his head in anger.

"There are no spirits. What a load of nonsense. And the fact there is no such thing as a spirit or the ether has already been proven by another Einstein, hasn't it, my dear colleague?"

"Michael is asking about the human spirit", explained Einstein, emphasising the word 'human' without responding to Kleindienst's provocation. "And this spirit is not in fact omnipresent." Now he earnt more applause, and the teachers laughed as well. Mr Kleindienst retreated in a huff. Then the bells rang and the circle that had formed broke up.

Einstein put his arm around Michael's shoulder and followed him to his class. His first lesson was there, and he seamlessly continued where he had just left off:

"Answering Michael's question requires two things. Firstly, that we assume we humans not only have a body of flesh and blood, but also a body made of spirit. And secondly, that other beings exist who are formed only of spirit. So for the time being, we are forced to assume something which cannot be scientifically proven: namely, this spirit. Even though we use the term in philosophy, we don't know what to concretely imagine." A student raised his hand and Einstein nodded at him.

"Socrates taught that Nous, the spirit, is the absolute being which...", he began to say. "Poppycock", Einstein interrupted him, making a hand gesture as if to chase away a fly. "I'm not teaching you philosophy so you can tell me what someone thought 2500 years ago. I want you to learn to think for yourselves. You must even think beyond the ancients. I'm sure that if the philosophers of antiquity had possessed our present scientific knowledge, they would have drawn conclusions from it about the spirit and taught something quite different. It's not just the natural sciences and technology which have evolved, but also philosophy, the science of the spirit. Today we understand the laws of nature better, and consequently we know more about the invisible connections of our being. We're conquering outer space and penetrating hidden microworlds – we must try to penetrate the spiritual worlds as well. So, how do we find the spirit? Where could we look for it?"

"Within ourselves", replied Kathi. "I think the spirit is what I am."

"Very good. You say you think the spirit is what you are. So you're seeking yourself, and you do so by thinking. You ask yourself: 'Who am I?' and you expect that what you find will be something spiritual. So you search and find yourself in thinking. I think, therefore I am. Someone else has already said that. Who?"

"Descartes", said the clever boy from earlier.

"Correct. And what does it mean? It means that thoughts must be something. If you only begin to exist in thoughts, then you need thoughts to exist. Then you experience yourself in your thoughts, then you support yourself with thoughts, then thoughts are something very concrete rather than nebulous figments of your brain. A logical conclusion would be: thoughts are made of spirit, or spirit is made of thoughts. Thoughts are the true molecules of the 'I'. I think, therefore I am. I live because I think."

"I live because I feel", said Miri Li, and everyone laughed, knowing Miri Li's romantic, sentimental streak. "I live because I love. I love music, I love the smell of flowers, I love beautiful things, reading, travelling, swimming, and lying in the sun. I feel, therefore I am. I am more than my thoughts. I not only know something, but I also feel something as soon as I think. There are feelings within me as well. I get scared when I think about my appointment at the dentist. I get angry when I think about the mafia. I get sad when I think about Elisabeth, who's been in a wheelchair since her accident, and I'm looking forward to the holidays because then we'll be flying to Thailand to visit my grandmother. I haven't seen her for five years and I love her more than anything. I feel, therefore I am. I experience feelings very closely – they touch me. I just look at the things that I think. For me, thoughts are like pictures of a landscape – they pass by. So, I am because I feel."

"And why do you feel?" asked Einstein. "You feel because you think. You just said it yourself: you get sad when you think of Elisabeth sitting in a wheelchair. Strictly speaking, therefore, you don't exist because you feel, but because you know that you feel. And you only become conscious of it through your thoughts. But Miri Li is right. As soon as you search for yourself by thinking and seem to find something of yourself, you discover that you also feel. So there is something else which is intangible yet moves us and touches us inside – something worse than a dentist's drill. Feelings. Emotions. Hopes and fears. Love and hate. Joy and suffering. But if you observe your feelings more closely, you realise that they always arise together with a thought. Sometimes it's a thought which awakens a feeling, and other times it's a feeling which gives rise to a thought. Feelings are mysterious powers which animate thoughts, connect them with one another, and touch and move us. Not only inwardly, but also very concretely. Because as soon as you feel something, you usually wish for something as well. You want things to stay the same, or you want something to change, and you act. And so we have found something else spiritual, namely the Will."

"I think things are getting complicated now", said the young philosopher who had already spoken up several times, and who was obviously reaching the limits of his wisdom. Miri Li also made an exasperated face and asked:

"Do I exist now because I think, or do I exist because I feel, or do I exist because I want something? Or am I whatever just experiences and observes the thoughts and feelings and desires like an inner landscape? Or interacts with them", she added after a short pause, "putting them on and taking them off like clothing?"

Einstein praised her and nodded. "That's a good comparison. After all, people also speak of a soul garment. But it gets really complicated when we try to distinguish between spirit and soul. We'll save that for later. I suggest that we consider all terms denoting the invisible inner life as ethereal for the time being, and instead of spirit and soul we simply assume the existence of an ethereal body. In doing so, however, we shouldn't make the same mistake as the bishops at the Church Council of Constantinople in 869 and simply abolish the spirit. Rather than humans consisting of spirit and soul, they said that the soul has spiritual qualities.

"On the other hand, we believe that the spirit can command its soul, just as it can command its body. Because there is indeed something else which perceives thoughts and feelings. It observes. It thinks and feels and wants something. The 'I'. The consciousness which says of itself: 'I AM'. This 'I' is as intertwined with its thoughts, feelings, and desires as it is with the body. Everything is somehow connected, and – as we experience and perceive it – it's just as real to us as the tangible, gross material world. But none of it is really there materially or spatially. That is why we refer to this reality as 'ethereal', and the landscape in which everything takes place as the ethereal plane. Religions call it the beyond. Strictly speaking, a substantial part of us already exists within this ethereal world."

"So, I'm still sitting here", one student observed while others laughed. "How do you enter the spirit world? And where's the portal?"

"With your spirit", Einstein replied. "And you'll find the portal leading into that world within yourself. What we are discussing today is spirit physics and soul chemistry, not philosophy. The laboratory is not in school, it is within you. If you wish to know spirit and the spirits, you must research and search within yourself. You can experiment with your thoughts and feelings just as you can with molecules and electricity. Try to grasp a thought or a feeling – that is, to master it. You'll get the shock of your life. There's more energy and explosive power in the spirit than in dynamite. Thoughts control our lives, not the other way around. Just think how often you do something you don't really want to do – it almost always starts with a thought." Einstein looked at Beate, who was grossly overweight. "Imagine you're sitting in front of the television, and someone in the movie is eating a cake. Immediately you think of snacking too.

It's just an idea of a taste, a thought of a feeling of pleasure. But that thought triggers a desire, and you move your body towards the fridge. You could almost say thoughts are like little spirits which come and go. They can be intrusive like mosquitoes and you can't swat them away easily. They can create images and desires, and if you don't master them, they'll become powerful demons which move you against your will. You don't need to summon the spirits: you already have plenty of them inside you."

Andy Mo was following the lesson with great enthusiasm, and again he felt as if the professor was looking in his direction. But his gaze didn't fix on him, and Andy Mo remained unnoticed. Einstein paused his discourse briefly, as if he were suddenly far away, and then he continued:

"I spent some wild years in India during my youth. I was searching for the meaning of existence, for God, for truth, for self-realisation. I hoped to find an initiate there, a guru, who could impart higher knowledge to me. So I set out on my journey, and it was no pilgrimage, I can tell you. It became a crazy trip into my own underworld. The path inwards is more exciting than any other adventure. At first I found only lunatics, scoundrels, and charlatans: the same kind of gurus who advertise in the newspapers here. There were some pious sectarians as well – sure, it was all Indian, but everything they taught was trash, superstition, and 'Hallelujah!' So there was nothing to be found in the ashrams – that's what the enlightenment centres are called there – other than a few western recreational yogis and occult tourists exchanging their dollars for the ultimate enlightenment. I meditated, I fasted, I held my breath and twisted my limbs for hours on end, but I didn't get any wiser. Quite the contrary. Then I smoked the hashish someone had recommended to me, and instead of Nirvana, which is the Buddhist heaven, I ended up in prison. Only for three days, but it was enough."

The class had long since gone quiet. For the first time, they had learnt something about their favourite teacher. There were enough rumours, but no one really knew him. They knew that he owned a

Porsche but rode a bicycle, and that he lived in a luxury penthouse but spent most nights in his laboratory at school, sleeping on a mattress. They also knew he was very wealthy, but they didn't know where the wealth came from. He had published a few books, appeared as an expert on television, and was committed to environmental protection, animal transport, and street children in underdeveloped countries. He was versatile, very successful, but nobody knew how old he was. He could have been thirty or fifty. He lived like a twenty-year-old freak, yet he had the kindness and serenity of an old gentleman. You wouldn't guess that he knew five foreign languages besides Latin and ancient Greek and had two doctorates.

Einstein continued his story: "Then I went to the mountains of Tibet. The higher I got, the dirtier both the pilgrims and the monks became. I learnt how cold, hunger, and tired legs can paralyse both the body and the spirit – that is, consciousness. I became ill. Fortunately, a shepherd found me and carried me to a nearby monastery where I could finally find rest. It was a different world. I don't know if it was due to my illness, the lack of oxygen in the air, or the old Lama who took care of me, but I became a different person. I lived detached from myself and saw myself as a stranger. Life passed by like a movie. I had sought the truth and found peace. I stayed there until spring, then I was bid farewell. 'Go back to your country', said the monk, 'and follow your own path. Don't seek it in others or in books, because what you're looking for lies within you. Know yourself! Ask yourself, who am I? Ask yourself, what is that which can say of itself: 'I AM'? You will never truly find yourself, and if you do, then it will only be for a moment; but you will recognise what you are not. And you will learn not to lose yourself anymore. Whatever you seek, you will find it within you.'

"Which brings us back to our topic. Kathi mentioned it earlier: I think the spirit is what I am, the spirit is within me. So I could have saved myself the trip to India. And I can assure you, the journey within has become even more exciting than the journey to distant lands."

Einstein went to the blackboard.

"So, let's summarise: spirit is not materially detectable, but it exists in the form of our thoughts, our feelings, and our will." He wrote down the words so that they formed a triangle. Then he drew an eye in the middle. "This is consciousness, which perceives and recognises itself and the environment. This gives us a vivid symbol for our further reflections on the spirit which can say of itself: 'I am'. Next time I'll show you how to meditate properly – the Tibetan monk taught me some valuable tricks back then."

"Now you've gone too far, my dear colleague." No one had noticed that Kleindienst, who had the next double lesson, was already standing in the class. None of them had noticed the bell. Einstein glanced down at his watch and apologised, but Kleindienst was upset and indignant. "Your background is very interesting, and so are your theses. I see we have a cult leader at our school. I will be reporting it."

A commotion arose in the class. The students began to murmur, and Michael looked at Andy Mo. "Can't you do some magic and show him that spirits exist? Do something, please!" The other friends who could see him were also looking expectantly in his direction. But Andy Mo had a vague feeling that he should stay out of it. Something was holding him back. Besides, he suspected that it was impossible to convince sceptics. But then he changed his mind: after all, his task was to convince people that the world of the spirit and of spirits existed. And that was obviously what Einstein was also trying to do. Should he allow the path which the mysterious teacher had just shown to be blocked again? No. Resolutely, he went to the blackboard, took a piece of chalk, and wrote:

"And there really is a spirit, and spirits as well!"

As if the volume was slowly being turned down, it gradually became silent. It was like a conductor entering the orchestra pit; all the noise died away, and everyone who saw the writing that had appeared as if written by a spirit's hand fell silent. The silence was filled with the tense anticipation of what would happen next. Einstein was sitting at the desk of a missing student at the back of the classroom; even he seemed surprised and slid off the desk.

Too late, Andy Mo realised that he had made a mistake. He distinctly sensed the thought: "Erase! Erase it immediately!" and he realised that Einstein was the transmitter of this thought. Then Einstein's gaze swept over him. Could the teacher really see him, or was he just imagining it? Andy Mo rapidly shifted gears. In a flash, he wiped the writing off the blackboard with the sponge and guiltily disappeared into the wall.

But the catastrophe failed to materialise. Mr Kleindienst, who had been following the magical writing closely, began to laugh grudgingly. Then he soberly stated: "Chemistry – a good magic trick, my dear colleague. You probably learnt it in the laboratory rather than India. But now please stop the show. We're not in the circus. Take out your notebooks."

Life slowly returned to the classroom. Einstein took his bag from the desk where Mr Kleindienst was already sitting and walked thoughtfully to the door. There he turned once more and looked inquiringly at Michael, and then at the spot where Andy Mo had just disappeared. Then he raised his hand in salutation and left the room, shaking his head.

*

Andy Mo was relieved that his magic hadn't had any unpleasant consequences. He strolled leisurely across the schoolyard, heading towards the old elder tree. He wanted to surprise Krux with his visit. But he was already standing at the window and waving to him from afar. Next to Krux he could recognise the two tree spirits Plit and Plomp, whom he had met on his way to Michael. They all greeted him warmly and were happy to see him back safe and sound.

"We watched your performance in the classroom – it was great fun. But where have you been for so long? We were worried about you. Why didn't you check in?" Andy Mo also felt as if he'd been gone for an infinite amount of time. Yet it had been just twenty-four hours. Time seemed to pass differently around humans; at least it didn't feel the same as in the spirit world, where a day and a night are like a moment.

"I've experienced so much – much more than in my entire life", he enthused, not knowing where to begin. Then he related everything in chronological order while the others listened attentively.

Once he had finished, Plit, who was long and thin like a reed but could think as fast as lightning, summed it all up: "Andy Mo has come a long way in the search for his father. He has found humans who can help him, but these friends are already under pressure from the Prince of Shadows. Now they have problems of their own, and Andy Mo must help solve them. This has made the whole affair even more complicated than it already was. Besides, Baphomet also has helpers among the humans. We must find them. We already have some clues – there's this millionaire Goldstein with the properties, for instance. Then there are the humans who are stalking Leif Andersson – highly suspicious. They want to win him over and soften him up. We're following up on these leads, but we also leave traces which remain visible to Baphomet, for a few hours at least. For example, following the path Andy Mo took didn't pose any difficulties, and that's how we ended up here with Krux." Plomp, the other tree spirit, who unlike Plit was spherical and silent, nodded.

"We too leave tracks wherever we go. And the more often we take the same path, the clearer they become. Even humans perceive our spirit paths. They call them telluric currents. It can't be a coincidence that Andimo, the king, also passed by here. And there must be a reason why there's still a passage to the upper world right here in the schoolyard."

"Perhaps because of the children", replied Krux. "The human realm is corrupted by the influence of Baphomet. Every selfish thought obscures the path to the spiritual world, and the confused ideas of the 'believers' consist only of fanaticism or superstition – they are will-o'-the-wisps which lead nowhere. All ill-gotten money and gold casts a dull shadow in the spirit world and hardens into a lump with which Baphomet can wall up the portals. Due to selfishness and lack of pity, the cement which holds these lumps together solidifies instead of connecting people in the form of compassion. Ignorance and immorality allow Baphomet to close the portals up, and they can only be averted by the innocent spirit which still exists in young people. There must be someone in this school who is countering Baphomet and who specifically nurtures the childlike power of faith – a magician, or somebody who doesn't yet know that they have within them the power and the force which regulates events in both worlds."

"Well, it's definitely not Mr Kleindienst", Plit added, and they all laughed, then looked at each other in concern.

"It could be Einstein", said Plomp, voicing what everyone else was thinking.

"I think he noticed me", confirmed Andy Mo. "Not immediately, but he may have seen me when I made the writing spell on the blackboard. I'll check out his lab – maybe he's doing alchemical experiments. Then I could teach him something. My father has taught me many things. In any case, it's likely that he's on our side."

"Be careful", Krux warned. "You can't trust anyone. What if we're wrong and Baphomet has a minion at the school? Perhaps one of his secret centres is located here." The others nodded and became serious.

"It's a pity we can't go with you to the human realm", Plit lamented. "We could support you better then. I also know lots of magic tricks, and it would be great fun. I'd teach Kleindienst another lesson straight away, for example."

"You can help me better from here", Andy Mo comforted him. "I need allies in both worlds, just like Baphomet. But maybe we really should give Kleindienst another lesson. A teeny tiny one. Let's see what we can do." While the others were still enthusiastically agreeing, Andy Mo transported himself back into the classroom with a mental leap. This method of transportation no longer posed any difficulties for him. Without hesitation, he went to the blackboard and wrote:

"Of course there are spirits!"

At first no one noticed, but gradually more and more students saw it, and whispering and giggling broke out. Mr Kleindienst looked up in irritation, and when he still didn't understand, Michael pointed to the blackboard: "The spirits, Professor. The spirits are back." Kleindienst turned around and went red.

"Who was that?" he yelled, but then he realised that no one could have passed by him unnoticed. It must have been written by Einstein. Angrily fetching the sponge, he set about erasing the writing. But that wasn't so easy. Andy Mo had deliberately written at the top of the blackboard, and he had spaced the words so far apart that the sentence spanned the entire three metres of the green surface. Then he had jammed the mechanism so that the blackboard couldn't be lowered. Mr Kleindienst climbed onto his chair and had to move it a metre after erasing each word. And that's when the mishap happened. The chair tipped over, and the teacher just managed to grab onto the top edge of the board before he completely lost his footing, leaving him hanging onto the blackboard like a monkey in a zoo.

Andy Mo immediately seized the opportunity, swiftly writing:

"August Kleindienst's circus act."

The amusement of the onlookers knew no bounds. So Kleindienst, who always signed the exams only as 'A. Kleindienst', was called August. Somebody started clapping their hands, and the laughter swelled into a raging hurricane. The students could no longer be contained.

But then something happened which Andy Mo wouldn't soon forget. He felt someone grab him from behind, and for a moment he couldn't move. But when he finally managed to turn around, there was nobody near him except Mr Kleindienst, who was still hanging helplessly from the blackboard. So he was still invisible – he could tell because everyone was looking at the teacher rather than him. Only the tall, greying man at the door – who nobody had noticed entering the classroom – was looking in his direction with dark, deep-set eyes. His distinguished features were serene, disciplined, but icy cold and hard. Or was he imagining things again? Was it the hunchback standing behind him who had thrown him a glance? Andy Mo scrutinised the two of them, but as before with Einstein, the visitors were looking past him now. Still, he sensed danger looming from that direction.

"The headmaster!" someone whispered, and the classroom fell silent. Obviously he was either feared or highly respected by everyone there. Suddenly there was a deathly silence. A movement of his head was enough, and two students freed Mr Kleindienst from his embarrassing position. Andy Mo had erased the writing himself in a flash.

"This must have consequences, Mr Headmaster. I won't stand for it! Einstein prepared the blackboard to embarrass me."

"Prepared the blackboard?" The headmaster feigned surprise. "How did he get you up there?" A few students got the joke and grinned, but none dared laugh out loud.

Kleindienst was confused and gestured behind him. Then he turned around and turned pale; it was only now that he noticed the writing had disappeared again. Before he could comment, his boss ended the discussion.

"I regret the mishap, dear colleague. Fortunately nothing more has happened. I'll arrange to have the pulley on the blackboard repaired, and I'm sure nothing like this will happen again." It might have been a coincidence, but at that moment he glanced briefly towards the corner where Andy Mo had retreated. Kathi noticed, and she was startled. Could her father see the earth spirit? As if he had also registered her invisible thoughts, he now looked at his daughter. It seemed as if he wanted to say something else, but then he nodded briefly at her and left the room abruptly without a greeting. The hunchback followed him silently like a shadow. Life returned to the classroom.

*

Andy Mo was confused by the unpleasant situation he found himself in. For the second time that day, he had made a mistake. But he took comfort in the fact that the others had also revealed themselves, for he now knew that the headmaster could probably see spirits as well. This didn't necessarily mean that Einstein and he were working together, but it was likely that at least one of them was on Baphomet's side. The Prince of Shadows tries to win over anyone who finds a path into the world of spirits. He had to keep an eye on these two: this was a promising clue which might lead him to his father.

Now Kathi had a problem as well, he reflected further, and he felt sorry for the girl. She surely loved her father and admired him; he was a powerful personality. But the promise to her friends to keep quiet about her contact with the spirit world put her in a serious inner conflict. Conversely, how could she still trust her father when he might be in the service of dark forces?

Thoughtful, Andy Mo returned to his friends in the elder tree. He chose the path across the schoolyard again, and he was surprised that he had adapted to humans so quickly. He felt just as connected to them as he did to his spiritual friends in his spirit world.

They were waiting for him with serious faces, as they too were aware of the danger of the new situation. Their suspicion that there was a magical centre at the school seemed to be confirmed. And if it were true, their Earthly opponents had now been informed and warned about Andy Mo.

"I need to learn more about the magical power structures and secret connections among the wizards", said Andy Mo. "I'll study the Book of the Master today. Michael has left me a copy – we'll surely get the missing volumes in the next few days, and we'll probably find more clues there."

Andy Mo said goodbye to Krux, who promised to keep an eye on the school and the teachers. Afraid they would get lost on the way back, Plit and Plomp joined Andy Mo. He would have preferred to walk on the surface of the Earth, but they couldn't follow him there, so he chose the path he had taken before.

They were surprised at how easy and fast it was this time. They reached their destination in a few moments, despite the fact that Andy Mo made sure they didn't pass under inhabited houses – they didn't want to disturb sensitive humans who can detect spirit paths. Now Plit and Plomp also said goodbye. Their trees stood close together behind a cemetery chapel on a hill above the city.

Andy Mo walked the last stretch of his journey above the ground, in the manner of humans. He loved the light-filled landscape, which was full of life, and now he understood why his father would have preferred to have been born human. He also envied his human friends for the opportunities their world of earth, sun, air, and water offered them, and he was about to conquer this world. He felt more and more familiar with the special circumstances here. Thanks to his photographic memory he had the city map in his head, and by now his fabulous sense of direction was working again, so he was home in three mental leaps.

He immediately fetched the Book of the Master from Michael's house and made himself comfortable on his boulder. The stone was pleasantly warmed by the sun; nothing stirred, and only the tops of the tall firs moved quietly in the summer breeze. He was alone with his thoughts; there was nothing to hear other than the chirping of the birds. Curious, he began to read.

Printed books were something completely new to him. Writing didn't exist in the spirit world – thoughts and information were stored and transmitted differently there. While some insights could be easily conveyed using their method, general education was much more difficult for spirits. There were huge libraries containing all the works ever dreamt up and written by gods, spirits, or humans, but they couldn't be read. They were more like film cassettes. Moreover, these books only opened to those spirits who, due to their nature, already had access to the subjects they described. Other spirits only saw light and shadow. It wasn't that you read words and sentences; rather, the content unfolded before you like a landscape you had entered. You were practically immersed in the knowledge. You gained insights into a world which broadened your horizons, and you experienced first-hand what you wanted to know. However, you didn't enter foreign, unknown realms by 'reading'. Although the experience made you smarter, it didn't open up new planes to you. That's why the spirits, and even the angels and gods of the highest hierarchy, didn't fully comprehend Creation. Their knowledge always remained limited to the particular sphere of life for which they were responsible. So although many spirits became much wiser than human beings in their field of expertise, they didn't have the same overarching perspective as humans.

Andy Mo was excited to discover how different it was in the human world. Here you not only recognised what you were looking at, but you also had the opportunity to read about something you previously couldn't even imagine because you knew nothing about it. Reading gave you insight into areas you had never seen in your mind's eye before.

Andy Mo was fascinated by this new method of reading. He skimmed through the pages and immediately grasped what he was reading, just like a scanner. It was incredibly fast. The book was exciting, and although it was written in the form of a novel, hidden between the lines he could find a lot of information about the connection between humans and spirits. Gods and angels were described there, as well as intermediate beings living among humans which he hadn't known about before.

One of those beings was a raven. His name was Yks, but because he was so clever, they called him 'Professor'. Yks could speak, read minds, and see a few seconds into the future. He was funny, drank a lot of beer, and it was said he always showed up when someone needed help. The sly bird had been overlooked by the circle of friends, and Andy Mo immediately realised they needed to contact this funny chap. He sensed that the raven could help them find his father and expose Baphomet's criminal minions. The thought gave him confidence: it couldn't have been a coincidence that the king had led them to this book. Perhaps the raven was the key.

Andy Mo finished reading the story in half an hour. He was so enthralled by human books that he walked over to the library to look for more reading material. But he didn't know where to start. There were thousands of volumes, and every work seemed interesting. However, on the sofa he spied the book Michael had been reading the night before: *The Mischief of Living and Dying, and the End of Mischief* by Prentice Mulford. As Michael had mentioned, it was his grandfather's favourite book. Even before the friends arrived, Andy Mo finished this book as well. It dealt with the very subject Einstein had talked about in class: the power of thoughts and wishes as an active spiritual force.

"Every thought and every desire is an energy which wishes to manifest itself and alter life in its own interests", writes the author.

Andy Mo was surprised by the unimagined possibilities which were open to humans due to their special nature, and how few initiates there were who used the power and force of their spirits to shape their destiny. Rather than consciously and autonomously shaping their lives with their thoughts, they all allowed themselves to be moved by their urges, impulses, and unthinking desires. These spiritual 'mechanisms' had nothing to do with magic. Anyone could 'do magic' by following these simple rules, if only they tried.

Now he also understood his father, who had once said that humans had to learn magic from spirits, even though they could perform magic without them. They imagine that the beyond is like a more ethereal version of the here-and-now, and that the substance of the spirit is merely more subtle matter. But that isn't so. The spirit is not a fleeting mist of light and shadow or a blind energy like electricity: it is a living being. In everything visible in the spirit world, there is a spirit. Behind every movement in the spirit world stands an active being.

"Humans no longer need us spirits", his father had once said. "As soon as they learn to master the spirits of which they themselves are composed, they master the whole spiritual realm. Each of their thoughts is a small living spirit and could be a helpful spirit for them. Every thought summons a similar spirit from the spirit world to its vicinity; in this way, people are constantly in contact with angels and demons without knowing it."

This is what humans must learn: to master themselves. After all, human beings are themselves made of spirit, and therefore they have many spiritual beings within them. Every thought and every desire they perceive within themselves is the manifestation of a spirit. And whoever masters their own thoughts and impulses has already mastered the lowest hierarchy of spirits.

Andy Mo now knew how to begin his lesson in 'magic', which is actually the true science of the spirit, and he could hardly wait for his friends to arrive.

But when Michael finally showed up, he arrived alone. Christian's father had suffered a heart attack and had been admitted to hospital.

"He's still unconscious and in intensive care", Michael said. "It's not clear if he will regain consciousness. Christian and his mother are with him."

Kathi couldn't come either. She had to help her father at the law firm – the secretary was sick and there was an important dispatch due to the upcoming school trip. Then Miri Li called: she was needed in the kitchen because a cook was absent. Lastly, Leif had sent his apologies because he had an urgent matter to attend to. So the meeting had been rescheduled for the next day.

"I'm afraid I have to leave right away as well", Michael stated after going through the mail. "The bank has permanently blocked the loan. I want to talk to the bank manager – maybe he can still give us an extension."

Andy Mo was disappointed and worried. He had brought bad luck to his friends. The weather as well as the mood had turned gloomy; clouds from a low-pressure zone were spreading and it had become colder. The whole atmosphere had changed. The world suddenly showed its dark side. Obstacles and delays were accumulating, and their magic circle began to dissolve before they had even started to work properly.

Andy Mo thought over ways to help his friends with a spell. At some point he had to start intervening and fighting back; it couldn't go on like this.

"I'll come with you", he said to Michael. "I'll use a thought packet to make your banker think in the right direction. But first I must bring Christian's father back to life. After all, we have the elixir; that will save him. Show me which hospital he's in on the map of Vienna."

Michael marked the spot.

"They flew him to the Vienna General Hospital. You can't miss the huge, dark bed towers. You don't have to worry about me – I'll take care of this myself. I want to convince the bank manager of our seriousness with entirely normal arguments. I feel it's a matter of honour, somehow. There will always be time for magic later."

Andy Mo was sympathetic to his friend's wish and found his view reasonable. The most obvious thing should always be done first. He too had gotten into the habit of using Earthly options – in some respects, they were even easier and more purposeful than magic. For instance, no mind could transmit thoughts as clearly and quickly as a mobile phone. Moreover, he suspected that the bank wasn't at all interested in securing the loan. The bank director was probably in cahoots with the others, or he had an interest in this property himself. The quiet location was truly unique, and perhaps the old château held a secret they weren't aware of yet. He had sensed a strange impulse when he followed Michael's thoughts while he was talking about the bank director.

He had to help Mr Freiwald in a different manner. Following ancient gnome tradition, he planned to lead him directly to a gemstone. This stone had to be absolutely superb, so large and valuable that he could cover all his debts with the proceeds. But first he had to learn more about the surface of the Earth. He wasn't yet capable of transporting himself all the way to Colombia, as he didn't even know where it was. He still had a lot to learn.

"Okay", he said to Michael, who was hurrying and already standing at the door. "I'll get the elixir and check on poor Mr Baumann. After that you'll find me in the library – I'll be doing some research, and then I'll look for an emerald for your father." Michael didn't hear the last sentence. The bus was leaving in a few minutes, and he was already outside.

The huge buildings of the Vienna General Hospital were easy to locate, as they were mentally impossible to miss as well. Andy Mo could also sense his friend, and he transported himself to his vicinity. He landed directly in front of Mr Baumann's bed.

The intensive care unit looked like a modern torture chamber: wires, tubes, technical devices, monitors with flickering curves and spikes, and in between – lifeless and small, as if it had shrunk – lay the body of Christian's father. Christian and his mother were sitting outside the glass wall, crying. So it didn't look good. Andy Mo was able to commence treatment unnoticed. First he made some magnetic strokes with his hands over the unconscious patient. Then he moistened the pale forehead with the elixir. When that didn't work, he added a few drops to the transparent infusion container to which Mr Baumann was connected. The effect was almost immediate. The patient moaned, and the insistent beeping of one of the devices changed its signal. The waveforms on the electroencephalogram began to show strong activity again, and a siren went off. A doctor immediately rushed into the room with Mrs Baumann, who was also wearing a doctor's coat; the doctor attended to the patient, who was moving and slowly opening his eyes.

"He's coming to!" cheered Frau Baumann. "He's made it! My God, he's made it." The attending doctor quickly administered an injection to Mr Baumann, who finally awoke, his eyes filled with life. While the hospital staff and doctors rushed over to test his reflexes and reactions, Andy Mo also confirmed that Mr Baumann was indeed responsive again. He nodded reassuringly to Christian, who had noticed him in the meantime and was watching everything through the glass wall, and who immediately understood who was responsible for the miracle.

There was nothing left for Andy Mo to do. Waving to his friend, he transported himself back to the library – now he wanted to take care of the next father. He had to guide Mr Freiwald to a gemstone, but he didn't yet know how difficult that was going to be.

*

Andy Mo soon found what he was looking for. A large old atlas and the modern illuminated globe on the mantelpiece provided him with sufficient information about the dimensions and conditions of the Earth's surface. He was surprised at how much water there was between the continents, and he hoped it wouldn't hinder him. After an hour he had studied many maps and all the relevant books on geology, memorising the essentials. He realised that while humans possessed extensive knowledge of the chemical and physical structures of matter, they had no conception of the living spiritual beings involved in the formation and growth of ores and crystals. Most of their scientists considered nature to be a lifeless, three-dimensional computer game.

Conversely, Andy Mo reasoned, the spirits had no real conception of the human realm either. In the spirit world, cause and effect were always visible together. In the human realm it was different: most of what happened there followed rules and impulses which remained hidden from the observer. Everything took much longer as well, and once something existed there in gross material form it had more permanence. Changing something cost time and energy. So events took on more significance, and possessions gained value. And not only rare gems – every brick had to be laboriously transported before a house could be built with it. While the thought-buildings which an architect devised in the spirit world were already visible, nothing of them could yet be seen in the human realm.

Andy Mo admired the patience and perseverance with which humans attempted to fathom the laws of creation and destruction in nature, and he was amazed at the great number of insights they had already gathered. In the library he found books on all kinds of sciences, and the knowledge opened up a completely new perspective on the world for him as well. Realities and facts stretched out before him, as well as fantastic theories which he had never encountered before. He was particularly astonished by the infinity of the universe and the mystery of consciousness. Until now he had never thought about space, time, and his ego. The world of the gnomes is limited to what lies beneath the earth, and he knew more about that world than any other being. He also knew quite a bit about the worlds of the water spirits, the air spirits, and the fire spirits, as well as the realms of the demons, angels, and gods. But until now access to these spheres had largely been denied to him as a spirit.

On a theoretical level, at least, the human realm suddenly offered him insights into all the planes, be they of visible or invisible existence. He didn't know what to read first. Dozens of volumes which he wanted to study were already piled up in front of him. He found the scientific works describing tangible things just as interesting and exciting as the different explanations and theories of the humanities about esotericism, religion, and philosophy. Humans weren't as ignorant as he had originally thought. There were books on magic and mysticism from the time when the spirit world was not yet closed off to them. They had obviously just lost interest in the other world.

He read and studied, and although he only skimmed over some works, by the evening he had gained a sufficient overview of the state of human knowledge. But the unaccustomed study had tired him. With the new insights came new questions, and he would have liked to discuss them with Einstein. If they pooled their experiences, they would add up to more than the sum of their knowledge. Andy Mo felt they should confide in the funny professor – he had intended to discuss this with Michael, but by the time he got home Andy Mo had fallen asleep from sheer exhaustion.

*

Michael didn't wake him up. He had achieved nothing at the bank and didn't know what to do next. He tried calling his father several times, but the line to Colombia was constantly disrupted. Now only a miracle could help. The situation had also worsened for his other friends: Mr Baumann had finally been charged with embezzlement, and Miri Li's parents continued to live in fear, as a new threat had turned up. Nevertheless, all the friends had agreed to stop by the next day, and he was wondering what to cook. It was a holiday and he had planned to grill a chicken in the garden, but the weather forecast didn't look good, so he decided to use the chicken for a pan dish. Normally he bought chicken breasts and legs so he didn't have to carve them, but now the whole chicken was already in the fridge. He could prepare and season it in the evening, and the following day he would just put it in the oven on a baking tray with the vegetables and soup greens. He made sure he had everything he needed in the house, and then he began to carve up the chicken with a sharp knife.

RECIPE

CHICKEN SKILLET
For about 4 people

Ingredients:
1 chicken, carved, or 3 chicken breasts and 3 chicken drumsticks
1 onion
1 courgette
Tomatoes
A bundle of 'soup greens' (= 1 piece of celery, 1 carrot, 1 yellow turnip)
4 potatoes

Preparation:
Halve the potatoes. Season chicken pieces with salt and pepper. Place on a baking tray with the vegetables and potatoes. Pour on some water and roast in the oven for about an hour. Serve with white bread or a baguette.

For dessert, peel a fresh pineapple, slice it, and then cut it into small pieces and serve.

Cooking was like meditation for Michael. When he cooked, he forgot about the world and lost himself in his dreams. He always listened to music while cooking, and this time he put on 'Carmina Burana', an opera by Carl Orff. Kathi had given him the CD, and his thoughts gravitated towards his girlfriend. Naturally he had also noticed her father's strange behaviour, and there was obviously a suspicion that he knew more than all of them put together. But whose side was the headmaster on? Michael was so lost in his thoughts that he didn't even hear Andy Mo knocking on the door. It was only when he called him telepathically that he turned and called him in. "I was just with you, but you were asleep."

"And now you're asleep", Andy Mo observed. "And while you're working as well – it's lucky the chicken's already dead. A surgeon couldn't afford to do that."

Michael set down the knife he had been using to cut the chicken into smaller pieces and nodded thoughtfully. "You're right. We sleep even when we think we're awake. Life isn't so very different from a dream either. Everyday life, the daily grind – it all becomes routine until you don't even realise that it's you who's living it. And when you actually plan something consciously, it usually turns out differently than you thought it would. In fact I was planning a barbecue in the garden for us tomorrow – everyone likes that, but it's going to rain, so we can't be outside."

"What's a barbecue?" Andy Mo asked, and when Michael explained how it worked, he was glad it wasn't going to happen. He was afraid of fire. "I'm more afraid of heat, embers, and flames than I am of Baphomet", he confessed to his friend. "For me, any fire is hell. But tell me, what did you achieve at the bank?"

"Nothing", Michael sighed. "The bank manager was stubborn and wouldn't listen to reason. But he pretended to be very nice, and said he wanted to help us with the sale – if we sold it privately, we would get more than if the bank auctioned the house. He already had a potential buyer: a wealthy antiquarian by the name of Büchli from the antiquarian bookshop Büchli and Wolfe. The manager already knows the house. I don't think he cared about the outstanding payments or any collateral; he didn't even ask about them. He just kept talking about selling. He wants the property or the villa for this antiquarian."

"You might be right", Andy Mo agreed with him. "Even if Baphomet is behind this, he must first awaken a personal need in whoever is going to carry out an action for him. He can't force anyone to do anything evil, and everyone takes a different bait. But perhaps Goldstein is also involved in this. It's likely that they know each other, and that would be another lead to him. I'll look into it. Do you have any idea where he lives?"

"He has a chateau somewhere in the first district and a villa on the city outskirts – I'll look in the phone book right away." But Andy Mo waved him off.

"Not today. That can wait until tomorrow. I'm tired. I think I'll read some more and then go to sleep."

"I'll watch the evening news", said Michael, turning on the television. "Then I'm going to bed too."

THE RAVEN YKS

Exhausted, Michael fell into a fitful sleep an hour later, just like Andy Mo. They both dreamt of barbecuing.

But in Andy Mo's dream there was a raven on the spit rather than a chicken. The black bird swore and cursed, demanding that he be set free without delay – then he would lead Andy Mo to his father as a reward. The vision was incredibly vivid, and even after waking up, Andy Mo still had the bird's rasping voice in his ears. He immediately thought of the raven from the Book of the Master. Obviously the intelligent bird which could talk really existed, and someone was holding him captive like a parrot. He clearly sensed this was a lead he had to follow, and he tried to follow the impulse he had picked up straightaway. But he could no longer make out anything in his waking state, apart from a direction pointing out of the city. And when he put himself to sleep again, he ended up back

121

in Michael's dream world, who was asleep in the annex, still dreaming of barbecuing and cooking.

Andy Mo recognised his situation and didn't allow himself to be distracted. He knew that the planes of consciousness of spirits and humans who are close to each other can mix during sleep, and he continued to concentrate his full thought power on the raven.

For a brief moment he thought he saw a luxurious villa with a spacious terrace and a huge heart-shaped swimming pool, tiled in red and terribly kitschy. The whole thing was pompous and repulsive, and simultaneously filled with such lifeless emptiness that he was flung back to where he had started by disgust. He had seen nothing of a raven. Irritated, he decided to stop trying.

Andy Mo had the feeling that he could no longer control his abilities as he had prior to living among humans. It was as if his spiritual muscles were atrophying in the human realm.

It was probably because you didn't use them all the time, he reflected, and this realisation prompted him to try again for the third time. Once again he concentrated on the bird. At the same time, he set his sights on the villa where he suspected the raven was, and this time he had more success. The landscape changed and he found himself back on the terrace with the pool. However, it wasn't a dream: he was there with all his senses.

He looked around attentively. The fantastic view over the twinkling lights of the city was impressive. The owner of the property must be immensely wealthy. In front of the double garage were a silver-grey Rolls-Royce, a black Porsche, and a huge pink Mercedes. The gravel paths and the swimming pool were brightly lit, and the lights were also on in the house. But there were no residents to be seen.

Andy Mo listened into the silent night and tried to make contact with the raven. But no matter where he reached out with his spiritual feelers, not a single bird was to be found in the whole area. Neither in the house nor on the terrace, not even in the trees of the park. That was suspicious. Something was wrong. There was dead silence.

It was just like back in the Borderlands, Andy Mo thought to himself, and he remembered the dangerous situation at the beginning of his journey with a shudder. Now, too, he was suddenly paralysed by the eerie silence, and it was difficult for him to form a rational thought or decision. He felt as if he had shrunk into one of the many garden gnomes standing around, without a life of his own – as if, like the tables and chairs on the terrace, he was already one of the owner's possessions, lacking any will. But strangely enough, this didn't bother him. He was tired and would have preferred to stay where he was. Time had taken on a different quality.

Even his natural surroundings seemed lifeless and empty. The illuminated flowers along the paths looked as if they were made of coloured paper, while the splashing of the fountain in the middle of the pool – which he hadn't previously noticed – sounded glassy and hollow. Even the tall old fir trees shone stiffly and unnaturally, as if they were synthetic Christmas trees. The modern glass façade of the villa also looked hackneyed and hollowed out like a stage set.

But all at once the situation changed. Someone slid the wide glass door open, and two men stepped onto the terrace. Andy Mo recognised one of them immediately: it was the guy from the Jaguar. The second man was elegant and tall, and he pushed the first man out through the half-open door, hissing:

"You're lucky nobody saw you. Leave the property through the back exit – if you show up here again, you're out of business. And take the pictures back with you. I told you I don't want them, they're too hot for me."

The second man wanted to reply, but he was forced to be silent by the demanding look of the first guy, who was obviously the owner of the house. With a swift movement he threw the large bound package he was holding at the house owner's feet and disappeared wordlessly into the darkness. The other man watched him angrily.

Now Andy Mo was convinced that he had come to the right place. All at once his spirit came back to life. Curious, he examined the man standing on the terrace, whose gaze was gliding over the lights of the city and the shadows of the night as if he owned everything. He wore a cashmere jacket by Knize, trousers by Armani, and the leather of his tailored shoes seemed softer than glove leather. A thick golden Rolex was flashing on his wrist. He was about forty years old, tanned, and the contrast between his alert bright blue eyes and his naturally wavy black hair lent him something extraordinarily exotic. His profile looked like it had been carved out of stone. The dynamic, slightly bent nose and the disciplined but sensual mouth made his features appear sensitive yet cold at the same time. He had an impressive, almost unearthly beauty. You could sense that he knew it, too, as he wore his vanity so openly that even this weakness lent him dignity.

The man looked angrily at the parcel, seemed to think something over, then took out a mobile phone and dialled a number. His instructions were brief: "Take care of him. No. Not here, of course. Yes, that's fine." Suddenly his entire demeanour changed. Focused and alert like a tiger, as if he had heard or seen something, he stared out into the darkness of the bushes and trees.

For a moment Andy Mo thought he had spotted him. But then he could hear it too. It was a cry for help, and it was coming from the house. It wasn't a voice, nor was it a sound – it was a telepathic shriek, at the same frequency as in his dream. It was Yks. He had found the raven. "I'm coming", he called back silently; then he stopped abruptly, startled.

But the man couldn't hear the cry. He relaxed again, took the package, and made his way down the gravel path to the garage. He opened the gate with a button on his mobile phone, went inside, and returned empty-handed after a short while. Then – again using his mobile phone – he turned off all the lights and spotlights and disappeared into the villa.

Andy Mo followed him into the house. He would have liked to see the pictures the guy from the Jaguar had brought, but the raven was more important now. He was relieved to see that the elegant homeowner had gone upstairs; he didn't think he could see him, but since he had perceived the telepathic cry, he probably had other psychic abilities. He had to be careful.

Curious, he looked around. The furnishings of the spacious rooms were just as lavish and impressive as the architecture of the façade and terrace at the front of the house. Avant-garde chrome tables and chairs stood alongside magnificent antique furniture: Empire, Biedermeier, and Art Nouveau. Surrealist paintings and collages hung on the walls next to the venerable paintings of old masters. Although it wasn't as tacky as the pool area, the ostentatious display of wealth was still tasteless.

Andy Mo moved cautiously through the rooms. He had memorised the direction he had to take and followed the mental trail to the cellar. The wide staircase leading down was carpeted with precious rugs; the crystal chandeliers on the wall and the gilded Venetian mirrors gave you the impression you were in the foyer of a luxury hotel rather than a cellar. The stairs led down two floors. Then he was standing before a locked, video-monitored door.

Andy Mo felt his way through the wall and discovered that the entire floor was built like a fortress. A single, huge vault was hidden behind the elegant fabric wallpaper. Bunker-thick concrete walls and electronically secured steel doors made unauthorised entry impossible. "No ordinary burglar could get in here", he thought, and he slipped through the wall. To his astonishment, however, there was nothing behind it but a spacious, luxuriously equipped sauna, a jacuzzi, and a fantastically furnished fitness studio. At the very least he had expected a secret casino or a brothel, but there was nothing illegal or precious to be seen. There had to be more rooms. He slowly rotated and immersed his spiritual feelers in the silence. Then he found it: hidden behind the shower was a corridor, and at the end of it was life. He followed it and suddenly found himself in a spacious, eerie crypt.

What he experienced next left him breathless. He couldn't believe what he saw – it was like being in another world. Instead of lights, there was a bright, diffuse mist condensed from invisible sources, creating a surreal atmosphere. Mysterious music filled the room. The sound of individual tones crystallised into visible formations of light and shadow which flitted through the air like living spectres. Curiously shaped plants grew on the wall next to him – their black and red leaves were shaped like tongues, and they smacked their lips and murmured something suggestively to him. A waterfall splashed down silently from above him, sputtering onto a golden rock as if in slow motion, and each drop was an eye staring back at him.

Andy Mo was convinced he had fallen asleep again and was back in the spirit world. He was about to reach curiously for an eye when an excited voice stopped him:

"Stop, don't touch anything! Everything is electronically secured. Like in a museum. I'm his most valuable piece."

Only now did Andy Mo spot the raven. The bird was sitting on a perch in a massive, spacious steel cage which was hanging from the ceiling on a long chain.

Despite the grotesque situation, Andy Mo was relieved to have found him.

"At last. I thought I'd never find you. Come on, let's get out of here quickly. I don't like it here."

He wanted to free Yks immediately, but the raven tried to restrain him again. "Stay where you are. There's a mental barrier around my prison: thought molecules based on magnetic fields. It doesn't react to humans, but it does to spirits."

But the warning came too late. Andy Mo had transported himself into the cage with a mental leap, and he had crashed into an invisible obstacle. He was held firmly by it, and he felt like a fly in a spider's web. He was helplessly stuck to strange mental threads which threatened to constrict not only his limbs but also his consciousness, and in a wild panic he tried to free himself. Summoning all his concentration, he began to amplify the structure's pulsating vibration, which had begun with the violent impact of his collision. And he succeeded. He slowly swung back and forth as if he was on a swing, and when he reached the bars of the cage he clung to them. But the metal was electrified. Andy Mo was thrown back with tremendous force. Sparks flew, bolts of electricity frizzled, and the touch burned his fingers badly. But he was free again. Dazed, he crouched on the floor and looked up at the raven. "Your cage is electrified", he stammered in confusion, slowly regaining his senses.

"That was your lucky break", said Yks, flapping his wings excitedly. "The shock of the pain catapulted you out of the danger zone. Are you hurt?"

"I don't think so. I just feel sick and exhausted, and I'm infinitely tired. I'm afraid I'll lose consciousness again."

"That's because of the spirit trap", Yks explained, clacking his beak like a stork. "It would have killed you in no time. But there's nothing bad that doesn't also have some good in it. What's keeping me here saved you. He knows how much I hate that liquid fire – that's why he designed it that way. I would never touch those bars."

"Neither would I", Andy Mo confessed, "I won't be touching that a second time. Electricity and fire are hell for me. But how do I get you out of there now?" Disappointed, he looked around. "There must be a switch for the electricity and this devilish system somewhere."

"There is", Yks confirmed. "But not here. He controls everything with his mobile phone. We can't get to that. Besides, he uses a code that he changes every week. It always takes me several days to filter it out of his thoughts. Around his neck he also wears a small golden key for the cage door. But the spirit trap is sturdy – once the magnetic field is charged, it stays active for months. There's no way to turn it off. You can't get me out of here alone." "The main thing is that I've found you. My friends will help us – we'll get you out, trust me. But how did you end up in there? Who locked you up and why?"

"That's a long story", Yks replied, pointing to a screen just outside his cage. "I'll tell you everything later. Take a look at this first."

Andy Mo was surprised to see that a modern office had been set up at the back of the crypt. There were three monitors, several phones, a laptop, and other high-tech equipment on a large glass desk. Two of the screens were displaying stock market trends and charts; the rows of numbers were constantly changing. The computer had to be directly connected to a stock exchange. On the third screen there was a film playing: a raven was impaled on a spit and was slowly rotating over glowing coals. It was still alive and screaming horribly.

"Disgusting!" Andy Mo exclaimed indignantly. "How perverse. I'm guessing you don't watch this voluntarily. What's the point of all this?"

"To make me afraid. I'm supposed to keep seeing what will happen if I don't do what he wants. I have to speculate on the stock market for him – he knows I can see a few minutes into the future, and he takes advantage of the fact. We buy currencies, shares, and options which I can see are about to rise, and we sell them again as soon as they've reached their peak. That's what all banks do, incidentally – it's just that they're not clairvoyant and they often lose their money. He earns millions, on the other hand. Before I escape I'm going to give him a false tip. I'll trick him and make him bankrupt."

"Who is this guy?" Andy Mo wanted to know. "And why's he hoarding all that money? He already has more than he can spend, doesn't he?"

"He can never get enough", Yks explained. "And besides, he also has debts. He needs the money for research. There's a lab somewhere in the city, and others spread all over the world. There are other humans like him who fund certain projects, and who sponsor schools, universities, and private scholars. But they're also involved in corporations themselves, and they have influential managers and high-ranking scientists working for them, most of them without even knowing it. There are physicists, chemists, and computer specialists among them, as well as neurologists, astronomers, and philosophers. They all have a common goal: to copy nature. They conduct research on genetics and molecular biology; they build technical devices and are as interested in modern data processing as they are in alchemy. Initially they constructed small robots which actually behaved like simple living beings – he had a toy of that kind here. When several of these little vehicles encountered one another, they grouped themselves together like molecules and formed themselves into patterns without being programmed to do so. Then they built ever smaller and more complex structures. Their latest creation is Adele, the artificial plant behind you, as well as the loudspeaker Max, which produces those visible sounds buzzing around like swarms of colourful insects." Yks spoke rapidly in short sentences and didn't allow Andy Mo to interrupt him, even though he twice wanted to ask something. "They think they're like gods, but in truth they themselves are directed by the gods and guided along like puppets."

"Are you also one of those lab creations, or just a normal bird which can talk?" asked Andy Mo, deeply offending Yks.

"Since when do normal birds speculate on the stock market? I'm a normal spirit just like you, except my spirit has been stuck in a bird for six hundred and fifty-two years. And unfortunately, that bird has been stuck in this prison for a year. I was too curious. That's when he caught me and locked me up. I fit perfectly into his collection. But let's figure out what we're going to do. I can't move through the walls like you, and you can't get to this damn cage. How do we solve this problem? Andy Mo?! Hey! What's wrong with you?"

Andy Mo couldn't help it. He had begun to flicker and felt himself slowly losing consciousness. But it was more than a fainting spell. The effect of the mental spirit trap threatened to dissolve his entire being. Then he remembered the elixir – it had saved his life once before. He had to go back. With the last of his strength, he managed to focus on his boulder in Michael's garden. He just managed to wave, then he disappeared before the baffled raven's eyes.

He had hidden the vial in a hollow of the boulder he inhabited. He opened it and moistened his forehead with the liquid, then fell into a deep sleep.

*

It wasn't until the next morning that Andy Mo regained consciousness. He still felt weak and dizzy; the spirit trap had taken its toll on him. He wondered if he should take more of the elixir, but he didn't want to waste the precious medicine. Instead, he did his vitality meditation: he breathed in consciously seven times and imagined light and life force flowing into his consciousness with every breath. Then he consciously exhaled seven times, and as he did so, he imagined the last shadows of his leaden tiredness flowing out of him with the exhaled air. Finally he tensed all his muscles, and rather than heaviness he could feel the accumulated radiant vitality tingling in his limbs. After that he felt better again.

It was pouring rain above him, with dense clouds drifting across the sky. Despite the gloomy weather, Andy Mo was in good spirits. He had the first concrete lead which might lead to his father. He was convinced that at least one of Baphomet's minions was living in the strange, luxurious villa. This would also help solve his friends' problems. Yks certainly knew more about the network and the machinations of those involved. They were getting a lot closer to their goal.

He reconstructed the experiences of the previous night in his mind. Suddenly he realised with horror that he had made a huge mistake; he hadn't oriented himself. He didn't know where he had been. He couldn't even determine the direction in which the villa lay. Journeys of consciousness which begin in dreams are very difficult to reconstruct later – and mentally locating the raven was impossible from a greater distance. The grid of the spirit trap acted like a jammer on any form of mental communication. This was something he had already noticed.

Resignation and panic began to well up inside him again. The raven was waiting to be released; he was depending on it, and he might already be in the process of economically ruining his tormentor with a false stock tip. Andy Mo had a new problem on his hands.

He felt an urgent need to talk to someone, and he realised how much he already felt connected to his new friends, and how many of their habits he had already adopted. Since he had been in the human realm, he talked much more than he had in the land of the spirits. Something was constantly being discussed here among the humans. They chatted and talked about everything, even things which were completely meaningless. In the spirit realm it was different. The spirits are closer to each other, but because they are mediated by their ideas, each of them lives more independently in their own spiritual world. The verbal exchange of thoughts between spirits works differently than between humans. It's similar to reading: thoughts are transmitted from one consciousness to another as easily comprehensible packages of spiritual experience, just like text messages, and they're received just like your own ideas and perceptions. This requires more concentration and leads to only the essentials being communicated. Spiritual beings don't gossip.

But what Andy Mo felt compelled to tell the others seemed really important and earth-shattering to him. The raven's life and their own future depended on it.

"Michael is surely awake already", he reasoned, and he went straight to the library, sensing that he was there. But to his surprise, all his friends had already gathered together. It was much later than he had thought. The dense rain and cloudy sky had given him a false impression of the time; they were already waiting for him, and Christian was just suggesting that they summon him using their crystals.

"You can save yourselves the effort", Andy Mo interrupted, apologising for his tardiness. "How is your father doing?"

"You saved his life", Christian said, hugging his friend. "I don't know how you did it, but the doctors are talking about a miracle. He's not in intensive care anymore."

"I almost died for that last night", Andy Mo declared. "But the excitement was worth it. I have some good news and some bad news. First, the good news: I've found the clever raven from the Book of the Master. He'll be of some help to us."

"Yks?" exclaimed Kathi, clapping her hands enthusiastically. "Professor Yks, the funny bird who drinks beer, who can see the future, and who steals thoughts like a magpie? He really exists, he's alive – can he actually speak? Why didn't you bring him with you?"

"That's the bad news", Andy Mo explained. "He's been locked in a cage, and I can't free him alone. I need your help. But I can't remember where the villa is where they're keeping him captive. I lost track of him and I can't locate him anymore."

The friends fell silent in disappointment. The mood sank and spread like the damp cold which crept through the old walls. Michael stood up and made a fire in the fireplace.

"Are there no specific clues?" Leif asked. "Anything out of the ordinary? Who's holding this strange bird captive? Did you see anyone?"

"Yes, there was a man. Vain, wealthy, and as cold as ice. In fact the whole villa was cold and impersonal. Nothing inside the building was normal either. Everything seemed pompous, even the cellar. It was secured like a bank, and there was a cabinet of curiosities in a secret vault." Andy Mo didn't mention the guy from the underworld – he didn't want to compromise Leif again. But he related everything else he had seen and experienced on the previous night. When he had finished, the friends looked at him in disbelief. No one said anything. Only Leif voiced what the others were thinking.

"It sounds like fantasies from your spirit world. Maybe you were just dreaming?"

"No", Andy Mo replied firmly. "The villa is in this city." And then he remembered the swimming pool. "The pool!" he exclaimed. "There's a swimming pool in front of the terrace, heart-shaped with red tiles. Tasteless. We could look for that."

"We need an aircraft", Christian remarked. "We could hire a helicopter."

GOLDSTEIN

"That won't be necessary", Kathi said. "I think I know where Andy Mo has been. I know that pool and villa – they're not far from here at all." She rummaged around awkwardly in her school bag, then found what she was looking for and placed a crumpled newspaper clipping on the table. "Is this the criminal who's holding Yks captive?"

"That's him", Andy Mo confirmed. "But that's your school, and your father's standing next to him! What's he got to do with that crook? How did you get this photo? Who is that man?"

"That's Goldstein, the architect who speculates in real estate. We suspected him right away. He renovated our school two years ago – on that occasion his Prosperity and Knowledge foundation donated an elaborate new physics classroom. The whole basement was converted for the purpose. The lab is sensational, and the electronic equipment reportedly cost a fortune. He threw a party when everything was ready – it started at the school and ended up at his villa. The newspapers covered it, and even the television cameras were there. Now scientists from all over the world visit us here to carry out experiments. Goldstein keeps bringing in new people."

Andy Mo became serious, and the others also understood what this might mean. Kathi, too, fell silent and looked distressed. The suspicion that her father was also working with these people could no longer be dismissed. Michael was the first to compose himself.

"Let's think over what we actually know. Either we've been afflicted by a random cluster of problems, or Andy Mo is right and the demon prince Baphomet is behind it all. He wants to prevent us from helping Andy Mo find his father in this unfamiliar world. He wants to break us up or distract us, and to that end he's got our parents into trouble. But that doesn't necessarily mean there's only one culprit behind everything. The Prince of Shadows probably has many minions. Goldstein isn't the only suspect. The head of the insurance company and the bank director have also been behaving suspiciously. And, of course, there's the Chinese mafia who have been threatening Miri Li's parents."

"Goldstein is definitely involved", Kathi agreed. "We can start with him." The terrible suspicion her father had suddenly fallen under almost made her feel complicit herself, and she wanted to do something about it immediately. Michael sensed her conflicting emotions and put his arm around her shoulder comfortingly.

"She's right. We should grill Goldstein first", Michael said. "We must free the bird anyway – maybe he'll know more then."

Kathi looked gratefully at her friend and snuggled closer to him. Andy Mo nodded.

"There's nothing bad that doesn't also have some good in it. Look, Goldstein knows Kathi's father, and he can probably remember her too. That gives us access to his house", Andy Mo said, turning to Kathi. "Call him. Tell him you want to conduct an interview with him for the school newspaper. Topic: the secret of success."

The others were immediately enthused by the suggestion – except for Michael, who had reservations.

"We must be careful. If Goldstein really is the mastermind, he knows every one of us and may be luring us into a trap."

"Do you think he wants to cage us like that poor bird?" asked Leif, and everyone laughed. But Michael shook his head impatiently.

"Kathi can't go to his house alone. At least one of us must accompany her." But Kathi reassured him.

"Please don't worry about me. He was really charming to me back then. I'll have him wrapped around my little finger, three times. Goldstein may be terribly vain, and he's probably a criminal, but he still behaved like a gentleman towards me."

"Of course someone's going with you", Andy Mo interjected. "I need someone to help me free the bird – I can't do it alone. Only someone made of flesh and blood can get through the spirit trap unharmed and unlock the cage. However, we need to think carefully about who is going to accompany Kathi. Goldstein must not become suspicious. And Michael's right: if he's the head of the gang, he knows every one of you."

"We still have to risk it", Miri Li agreed. "When he wanted to buy our restaurant, it was a lawyer who came to see my parents, not him. So he certainly didn't see me."

"Nor me", Leif said. "We don't own any property that would be of interest to him."

"It's still possible that he knows you", said Andy Mo. "The guy from the nightclub was with him. He threw him out, but the two of them are probably in cahoots." The others looked at him uncomprehendingly, but Andy Mo continued. "As Miri Li said, we have to take some risks. I think it's best if Kathi and Miri Li do the interview alone. Then, without Goldstein noticing, I'll let Leif onto the property via a back entrance in the wall. While the girls distract Goldstein with their questions, I'll guide him into the house through the cellar."

Naturally Michael and Christian wanted to come too, but Andy Mo insisted that only he and Leif would enter the villa.

"Leif is the oldest of you. This situation is dangerous – it's not child's play. Goldstein has underworld characters with him. No one can see me, but if they catch any of you spying, you'll be killed or end up in a cage. These people are not to be trifled with. We must be extremely careful."

Alas, Andy Mo had no idea how justified his fears were. Since he had been living in the human realm, he no longer had the same psychic abilities as he had in the spiritual spheres. But the others trusted him and agreed.

"Okay!" said Andy Mo. "First, we need the current code for the mobile phone so we can turn off the alarm system and the power in the cage. I'll pay the raven a visit and take care of that. I hope he's already uncovered the numbers."

"And I need an appointment for the interview", Kathi said, reaching for the Nokia lying on the table. Directory enquiries gave her three numbers; on the very first attempt, she gave her name to a secretary, explained that it was a private call, and was put through to the real estate mogul. He remembered her immediately and even seemed pleased that she'd called. He also didn't mind that she would be accompanied by a friend equipped with a tape recorder and camera. They arranged to meet the next day, straight after school. "We're supposed to take our bathing suits", she announced after the conversation was over. "The pool is heated."

"That was too easy", Christian observed suspiciously. "I fear he's trying to probe us. Maybe he just wants to learn how much we know about his shady dealings."

"I think it's more likely that Andy Mo cast a spell on the crook",

135

Kathi said. "After all, he dissolved at the same moment Goldstein answered the call." Only now did the others notice he had disappeared.

Indeed, Andy Mo had transported himself to the villa while the two were talking on the phone; using the thought link that had been created, he attempted to influence Goldstein with his imagination. But when he reappeared flickering before them, he shook his head pensively.

"That man is impossible to figure out. His brain is like an open book, but I still couldn't follow his thoughts properly. His mind is a kaleidoscope of dark shadows, with no illuminating light, and there are no feelings in between. We can't take any chances with him."

"If we had enough money all our problems would be solved", Leif said. "Christian's father could replace the paintings and wouldn't lose his business; Miri Li's parents could buy their way out of trouble with the mafia; and Michael could pay off his overdue instalments. Why don't you just go through the wall of a bank and get what we need?"

But Miri Li protested.

"Would you do that if you could walk through walls?"

Leif Andersson nodded.

"Well, sure. Why not? I'd even take a lot more than we need and distribute the money to the poor."

"But that would be just as much theft as if you walked through the door."

Leif shrugged in reply.

"Andy Mo could just put it back later, when we are in a position to do so. It would be a loan. After all, that's what credit institutions are for, right? The bank directors are all crooks themselves. They take the money from the small investors and speculate with it, or distribute it to the big corporations, which then go broke."

"Miri Li's right", said Andy Mo. "Even if a spirit steals money from a bank, it's still theft. Magic isn't for getting rich or playing Robin Hood. Every spell is a loan from fate and must be repaid with interest. We'll talk about that later. I must help you in some other way – besides, it would be highly suspicious if Christian's father suddenly had half a million euros. They would immediately claim he'd sold the paintings elsewhere and was trying to commit insurance fraud. We must find the paintings. And I think I know where they are."

The others looked at him expectantly, and now Andy Mo told them about the shady character at Goldstein's house, and the package Goldstein had involuntarily taken from him before ordering him off his property.

"They were valuable paintings. He said he didn't want them – they were too hot. The fact that he hid them in the garage afterwards rather than keeping them in the house also suggests that there was something wrong with them. I'll transport myself right back into the villa and take a closer look. I assume you'll be eating soon?"

"Yes, I think we're all hungry", Michael confirmed. "Let's go and have some food. There's chicken skillet and fresh pineapple for dessert."

"Bon appétit", Andy Mo said and waved. Then he transported himself back to the mysterious villa. The path was familiar to him now.

*

In the meantime, Goldstein had received a visitor. The guest was about sixty years old, elegantly dressed and appeared distinguished, aloof, and self-possessed. His smooth, intelligent features were unremarkable – it was only his gaze which was fixed, fanatical, almost insane. The man seemed to consist only of eyes. In those dark, black holes – they were expressionless like empty caverns or murky mirrors – hid a cold, pitiless gaze which dominated his entire personality.

Although Andy Mo was convinced that the pair couldn't see him, for safety's sake he stayed in the background of the salon. They were seated on modern chairs upholstered in white leather; each had a glass in his hand, and a bottle of champagne in an ice bucket stood on the table. The visitor was in the middle of explaining something.

The conversation revolved around brain research and relevant experiments. Apparently the visitor was a neurologist or a psychiatrist, as well as being the director of a psychiatric clinic. Goldstein listened to him attentively and kept asking questions.

"What happens when the subject dies? Do the brain waves change slowly, as if the subject were falling asleep, or do they stop immediately, no matter what frequency was measurable at the time?"

"That depends on whether we're deactivating a conscious patient or one who's already unconscious. The problem is that we still haven't managed to rebuild the electromagnetic field of a brain once it has collapsed. A lifeless heart can be restarted with an electric shock – even after some hours, it will begin to beat again. We can't do that with the brain. We've tried all kinds of frequencies, but a dead brain – even if it's still warm – can't be brought back to life. We have a huge turnover of test subjects. True, we can artificially generate part of the spectrum of alpha, beta, and theta waves in a magnetic field, which then vacuums up elementals and elementaries and becomes an artificial spiritual field. But it terminates immediately. The transfer of the electromagnetic field to a brain has not yet been successful."

"The so-called spirit trap you developed works perfectly, though", praised Goldstein, refilling the glasses. "My refuge is as secure as a bunker, so even my own unpleasant thoughts don't bother me."

"That was a by-product", the visitor replied, pulling out a videotape from a briefcase on the floor beside him. "However, we're continuing to make good progress. Everything so far indicates that what we call consciousness consists of two complementary fields: one that's formed within the body, and one that interacts with it from the outside. It's the same phenomenon as lightning, which also only strikes where a field of negative ions has built up. We're now working with a new theory of two fields of consciousness. I've brought documentation of the last series of experiments: the EEG clearly shows a flicker on the waveform before everything goes out. It's a most unusual frequency."

Meanwhile Goldstein had slid the videotape into the recorder. What Andy Mo saw now sent cold shivers down his spine. The guinea pigs weren't rabbits: they were humans, mainly children and teenagers, not animals.

"This is the special section of our secure ward", the doctor explained, looking impassively at the gruesome scenes. "Thanks to the generous support of your foundation, we were able to convert the attic for this purpose and purchase the necessary equipment. Now we have a physical and a biochemical laboratory – completely inconspicuous, of course, with access only for proven, selected personnel." For the first time, something like a wry grin appeared around the man's mouth.

"And the patients?", Goldstein wanted to know. "How do you explain the high mortality rate to the authorities?"

"Officially, the inmates of this ward have already been released. Everyone who ends up here no longer exists: they have already disappeared or died. We receive a constant supply via a police physician. Arrested illegal immigrants, junkies, dopeheads, homeless people, asylum seekers. The ailing flotsam of the streets. But private patients from wealthy families who want to get rid of their heirs also end up here. The patients in this ward are already dead to the world. Now they are dying again for science."

The walls of the hospital room now visible were a poisonous green. There were two beds in the room, and the camera panned to a dark-haired boy of about fifteen, his face distorted with fear. His arms were fixed to the edge of the bed with leather cuffs. Electrodes were attached to his clean-shaven head, leading to a monitor on which the waveforms of his brain frequencies were recorded. He was unable to resist as an orderly with an expressionless face inserted a needle into his vein. His tense body immediately relaxed. At the same time, the peaks of one of the waveforms on the screen flattened out noticeably.

"Valium", the doctor explained. "Watch this – now he'll get an overdose of insulin." The orderly inserted a cannula and hooked the patient up to the drip.

The film played silently, without sound. But it was precisely the eerie silence which accentuated the overwhelming horror for the viewer. Even Goldstein, who stared open-mouthed in fascination at the screen, stroked his sweaty hand over his trousers and reached for his glass.

*

Andy Mo couldn't bear to watch the horror any longer. Disgusted, he turned away and left the room. He tried to locate the raven but couldn't get through the mental shield. To avoid ending up in the spirit trap again, he chose the normal path via the stairs to the basement, feeling his way along the walls of the gym and the sauna until he was standing in the corridor in front of the vault again. He carefully slipped through the last wall as well, but for safety's sake he stopped again immediately. The strange silence numbed him more than the most terrible noise. Slowly he adjusted to the glimmer of the living light which darkened rather than illuminated, and he gradually recognised the contours emerging from the fleeting shadows.

"Hello, Professor, wake up – you've got a visitor!"

The raven had dozed off on his perch and was jolted awake.

"Goodness, you scared me. You've come to get me at last. I was afraid something had happened. The code for the alarm system is currently AH2041897."

"I'm alone", Andy Mo dampened his joyful anticipation. "The operation isn't happening until tomorrow – can you hold out that long?"

"What choice do I have? Fortunately Goldstein doesn't suspect anything yet. I practically ruined him yesterday with a few stock options, but he still doesn't know how lucky he is. The shares I bought won't plummet until the day after tomorrow. We'll be continuing with the same strategy today – he's thrilled about the new idea. He trusts me completely and has promised to release me if I get him fifty million."

Yks wanted to explain what options were, but Andy Mo waved him off. Instead he got Yks to describe the hidden mechanism which unlocked the doors in the sauna and the room beyond. It wasn't complicated, but the clever bird wasn't sure whether turning off the alarm system would also turn off the surveillance cameras. Even if the girls were distracting Goldstein, there was a chance that the butler or someone else in the house would spot them on one of the monitors. Just to be safe, Andy Mo – who was invisible – would go on ahead and hold something up in front of the lens.

Suddenly the raven became agitated.

"He's coming. You've got to get out of here. He's with somebody." Andy Mo also felt something coming towards them.

"I'll see you tomorrow at four", he called out, and with a mental leap he transported himself upstairs, as he still wanted to search for the pictures. He walked around the house and slipped through the wide, locked aluminium door into the garage.

But the stolen paintings were nowhere to be seen. There were no cupboards, only shelves, and everything was neatly tidied away. Unless Goldstein had already taken it away, the package could only be in one of the two luxury cars. Oblivious, he opened the boot of the Rolls-Royce first – and sure enough, there it was. But a siren began to wail at the same time. A motion sensor had detected the change to the car and triggered the alarm. Andy Mo hadn't expected this, and he stood there paralysed, not knowing what to do. He spontaneously grabbed the package, but it was too heavy for him. He couldn't even lift it out of the car. Hastily, he began to untie it. He wanted to take at least one of the pictures with him. But underneath the paper, the box was sealed with special tape – Christian's father had expertly packed the artworks for transport. While he was searching for a sharp knife, he wondered why no one had checked on him yet. Then he remembered that Goldstein was in the soundproof cellar with his guest. That gave him some time. What he didn't realise was that the alarm system was linked to the nearest police station – a patrol car would be arriving within a few minutes.

Hurrying feverishly, he untied the package and took one of the pictures out of the boot. And as he pushed aside the soft, foam-lined special foil, he could have cheered. It was indeed a winter landscape by Dombrowsky. Rejoicing at his first success in the human realm, he immediately wanted to teleport himself with the painting to Michael's garden. But he couldn't get the painting through the wall. The frame was too massive to penetrate the matter.

Andy Mo looked around. The window was barred, and he didn't want to take the back exit through the house for fear of bumping into Goldstein. Nervously, he looked for the garage door switch. But just as he found it, the metal rattled upwards by itself.

Two policemen were standing with their guns drawn in front of the door, and above them a strobe light was still frantically flashing. Seeing no one, they called out to each other and crept towards the cars, first the Rolls-Royce and then the Mercedes.

"There's no one here", one of them stated, lowering his gun. "Another false alarm. That's the third one this year." He turned on the lights and switched off the alarm system.

"The homeowner must be here, though", the other policeman said. "There's his Porsche and someone else's Citroen parked in the driveway – he's obviously got visitors. They're probably sitting in the sauna and didn't hear anything."

Then he spotted the painting lying on the floor.

"That certainly doesn't belong there. I think something has been going on, and the alarm scared them off."

The policeman's colleague approached curiously, bent down, and deciphered the signature: "Dombrowsky, 1942. That's a winter landscape by Dombrowsky – I heard something about that. Can you remember?"

Andy Mo telepathically helped their thoughts along.

"Oh, yes. Now that you mention it, something comes to mind. There was a news story recently. Three works by this painter were reported stolen. Someone's stocking up on Dombrowskys – I think we need forensics after all."

But then they noticed the boot was open, and they found the other two paintings, still packed.

"Well, that's odd. Who packs stolen goods before stealing them?

Now I think we need the homeowner as well. If these really are the paintings they're looking for, we must clarify matters. I wouldn't want to be in his shoes right now."

"I wouldn't mess with him", the policeman's colleague warned. "He has influential friends."

While one of the policemen went to the car and informed the officer on duty at the police station, the other disappeared into the house to look for Goldstein.

*

"He was shocked", Andy Mo told his friends half an hour later; they had finished eating in the meantime. "You should have seen him. At first he was completely surprised and didn't know what to say. But then he quickly regained his composure. 'These pictures don't belong to me', he asserted firmly. 'I have no idea how they got into my car.' He was cool again right away."

"Did the inspector believe him?" asked Christian. "And are they really father's paintings?"

"There's no doubt about it. I assume they're already in the process of notifying your parents. This news is surely the best medicine for your father. We've solved one problem, but I'm on the trail of a new outrage."

Then Andy Mo told them about the psychiatrist and the secret research he was doing.

"We need to find out who this guy is and where he's carrying on this abominable affair. This special ward could be in any major hospital. People are being killed there like mice for research purposes."

"We can sound out Goldstein tomorrow", Miri Li said, but the others shook their heads sympathetically. Christian voiced what they were thinking.

"Do you really think he would betray his accomplices to us? If he even suspects we're about to unravel his network, we'll end up in that perverted hospice ourselves."

Andy Mo winced and began to tremble. He had a dark, terrible premonition, but he betrayed nothing.

"I need to get some fresh air", he said, and walked quickly to the front of the house. Despite their success with the paintings, a serious mood came upon them again. Unconsciously they could sense that the evil of this world was not to be trifled with.

Christian followed Andy Mo and sat down with him on the boulder. The storm hadn't passed by yet, and the dark clouds still hung low, obscuring the sky. Only the wind had died down.

"Thank you for your help", Christian said. "We could never have done it without you. Now we're off the hook."

Andy Mo brushed it off.

"If it wasn't for me, I dare say your parents would never have gotten into this dreadful situation. It was only your friendship with me which brought you and your family to Baphomet's attention. But I'm still convinced that my father had a reason for letting you find the book. Somehow everything fits together, even if we don't know how the story continues."

Christian nodded.

"I also think things had to happen the way they did. We're a good team and we'll overcome the other problems too." Then Miri Li also came out of the house and sat down with them.

"Do you think everything will go well tomorrow?" she asked anxiously. "I'm a little afraid of the interview, to be perfectly honest with you."

THE LIBERATION OF THE RAVEN YKS

The next day the weather was glorious, contrary to expectations. Right after class they drove to Goldstein's place. They took the bus and reached their destination twenty minutes later. They had to walk the last stretch; it was a private road which led up the hill through a wooded area. Before they got to the high wall surrounding the entire estate, they separated. Andy Mo led Leif to the hidden back entrance and – as spirits are wont to do – transported himself to the other side of the enclosure. Then he slid the iron bolt aside from the inside and opened the rotting gate for Leif.

Kathi and Miri Li went to the main entrance. The two girls rang the bell at the ornate wrought-iron gateway, which opened as if by magic. A friendly voice from a hidden loudspeaker invited them to enter. Along the wide gravel path they reached the villa, which was more reminiscent of a castle. Miri Li felt like she was in a movie. They were welcomed by a distinguished butler, who escorted them through the house and out onto the large terrace. He asked them to take a seat, and they took their places at a rustic teak table. Then the host arrived: tanned, radiant like an Olympic champion, wearing a white polo shirt with a crocodile and tennis shorts. He had a thick folder in his hand and apologised for being late.

"Make yourselves at home. What would you like to drink? Are you hungry? What can I get you?"

They just ordered two colas, but the host instructed the butler to serve a snack as well.

"I'm sure you'll be in the mood for a sandwich in a minute. Swimming works up an appetite."

"But first we have to work", Kathi said, setting up the microphone she had brought for the interview. "We're very grateful to you for granting us an appointment so quickly."

"The pleasure is all mine", the host declared gallantly. "I really like the idea of sharing some secrets of success with young people. That's not something you usually learn at school. Besides, I'm very much indebted to your father."

The two girls let their gaze wander over the park, up the hill, and down to the city. The sea of houses spread out before them like a panoramic postcard and disappeared like an endless stony sea into the bluish haze in the distance. The slanting light of the afternoon sun lazily flooded the air and the rooftops, creating a surreal atmosphere: it was as if everything was a light-saturated Turner painting rather than reality. The view that presented itself to them was truly magnificent.

Miri Lee was impressed. "Fantastic!" she exclaimed as she took the first photos. "All this wasn't cheap. Do you really think you can learn to earn so much money and afford such luxuries?"

Goldstein nodded.

"I'm firmly convinced of the fact. Success follows very specific laws. Fact one: everyone gets lucky at least once in their life and has an opportunity. If they seize that opportunity, they can achieve a certain level of prosperity at the very least. Fact two: if they want more, they must follow certain rules. Then there are no limits at all for them."

"What are the rules?" asked Kathi, taking notes.

"First there are the four E's: expertise, entourage, effort, and envisioning. Then the four R's: recognition, risk-taking, ruthlessness, and remarkable luck. And finally there are the four B's: bribe, bestow, beguile, and bully."

"Bribing and bullying? That doesn't sound good", Kathi observed, looking up from her writing pad in confusion. "I wonder if that's appropriate for a school newspaper?"

"The world is not good. There is no law and order, only power and money. Believe me, there are different rules out there in life than those taught in school. It's a war. There are hyenas fighting over the scraps. If you can't impress someone or give them a gift, you must bribe or blackmail them. Everyone has their price."

"Are you saying that all rich and powerful people are criminal rogues?"

"Most of them, yes. At the very least, they're ruthless and will trample over corpses to get ahead. But naturally it's better if everything is handled via good friends. You need a network of people who are befriended or obligated towards each other. Even as a student, I attended every ball where architects and real estate magnates met. I hung around their construction sites, tennis courts, and golf clubs and showed them I was willing to help. Always free of charge, of course – that obligates them. Wherever someone was needed, I was there. I got to know everyone who had something to say in the construction industry. I even studied astrology and called them on their birthdays; sometimes I would tell them things that totally baffled them. This gave me insights into their private lives as well. Soon they were also inviting me to their parties. I knew them all, and today, they know me. When I finished my studies and started my first company, I immediately had a lot of orders. They remembered me and trusted me." Goldstein paused and seemed to ponder. "You need friends, confidants, and slaves, you can't achieve anything alone. That's the whole secret of success."

"You believe in astrology? A moment ago I thought you were a sober businessman."

"Believe? You don't need to believe in astrology like you believe in God – you can test it out anytime. Astrological forecasts are like economic forecasts. They're not made to come true, but rather to set your course in a timely manner. It's information which indicates a prospective development, like a weather report or a road condition report – if you act on them, you'll simply drive better." He smiled. "Today isn't a good day for me, astrologically speaking. To avoid losses, I cancelled all my business appointments and decided to use the time privately. I'm enjoying the company of two lovely young ladies, and rather than encountering any problems I'm having a great time, despite the bad constellations."

As he was speaking, the butler brought the drinks and snacks on a serving trolley. They were delicacies like those found in a luxury restaurant. Lobster, salmon, and shrimps; various kinds of ham and cheese; exotic fruits and deliciously crunchy red, green, and yellow capsicums; radishes, carrots, and tomatoes. There was even a can of Beluga caviar on a mound of ice. Next to it, under a huge glass dome, was the dessert. Candied fruits, fine sweets. Cakes, cream slices. The girls' eyes opened wide.

"Dig in and enjoy", Goldstein urged them, and then he turned to the butler. "Send me Leo, he has to take this file to the ministry."

"It's his day off today, Director. There's no one else in the house either. But if you no longer need me here, I can take care of it. I assume it's the documents the Minister of the Interior left here yesterday?"

"Yes. He's still in his office waiting for them; they're confidential papers. Go to him and give him my best regards."

Andy Mo had been lurking in the background the whole time, and he breathed a sigh of relief. No one was in the house: that would make their plan much easier.

Miri Li was completely taken aback by the friendly demeanour of this alleged evildoer. She had imagined Goldstein quite differently. He smiled kindly at her, spread some butter on a piece of toast, and heaped caviar on it with a small golden spoon. Then he slid the morsel into her mouth.

"You have to try this; it was delivered yesterday." He also served Kathi. They all ate with relish, and he poured them more cola. "You see, we can manage on our own." Then a phone rang somewhere and he excused himself.

When he came back, he was wearing a bright red bathrobe. Under his arm he carried two huge fluffy towels and handed them to the girls. He placed his mobile phone on the table.

"You can change inside. No one will disturb you." The girls laughed and disappeared. Goldstein also slipped out of his bathrobe and went to the pool. His swimming trunks were as red as the bathrobe and the tiles of the pool.

Andy Mo was startled.

The key. No one had thought of the key. Around his neck Goldstein wore a gold chain with the key to the cage hanging from it. How was he going to get to it now? He couldn't follow him into the water.

"Take off the chain", he suggested. "Take off the chain!" He bombarded Goldstein's brain with these thoughts, but he didn't react. He never seemed to part with that extravagant piece of jewellery. Instead, he jumped off the diving board into the pool and waved happily to the girls who had reappeared, dressed in lovely bikinis, and were sitting down at the edge of the pool.

"It's not cold at all", Kathi rejoiced, splashing her feet playfully, then she too slid into the water with a little yelp.

Miri Li was still hesitating, and that gave Andy Mo the opportunity to explain the problem to her. She grasped the situation immediately.

"I'll tell Kathi", she murmured, speaking behind her hand and without turning her head so Goldstein couldn't see that she was talking to someone. "She can distract him, and I'll open the clasp on the chain. I'll put the key in this flowerpot." Then she too jumped into the pool.

While Goldstein was climbing back onto the diving board, she informed her friend. Kathi nodded and gestured, but Andy Mo didn't understand what she meant.

Despite that, everything went as planned. Following Goldstein, Miri Li also climbed onto the diving board, wobbled a few times on her toes, and then slid into the water in an elegant arc without splashing. She dived through until she collided heavily with Goldstein, who had turned his back on her and was now talking to Kathi. Startled, he whirled around, probably more out of concern for her, because he grabbed her by the hips and pulled her up to the surface. As he did so, he too disappeared briefly beneath the waves. Taking advantage of the intense turbulence, Kathi opened the karabiner and Miri Li was just able to grab the key as the heavy gold chain sank to the bottom of the pool. It all happened in a flash. Gasping and panting, Miri Li swam to the edge of the pool, where she put the key between the flowers, as arranged. Goldstein hadn't noticed a thing.

"Are you okay?" he called out, following her, but before he could reach her she had jumped over his head back into the pool.

Kathi tossed her the big ball which was bobbing in the waves, and a casual ballgame began, with Goldstein joining in.

*

A car pulled out of the garage – it was the butler with the files. Now Andy Mo knew the coast was clear. He quickly retrieved the key from its hiding place, then searched for Goldstein's mobile phone and entered the code: AH2041897. It worked. A red message on the display blinked, signalling that the alarm system had been disabled. He hadn't expected that, and he had no idea how to delete the incriminating text. He didn't dare turn off the mobile phone either – he was afraid that he would break contact with the alarm system and activate it again. He couldn't take it with him either. It would immediately arouse suspicion if it suddenly began to ring in the house, or even in the cellar. Goldstein had programmed an unusual, penetrating signal; they would surely hear it. He spontaneously slid the mobile phone under the large-format daily newspaper lying on one of the deck chairs, hoping they would return before Goldstein used his mobile phone again. Then he waved to Leif, who had been waiting behind the bushes for his signal, and they both disappeared into the villa through the back entrance.

Yks had explained to him exactly how to get to his prison the 'normal' way, as Leif couldn't go through the walls. They got past the wide entranceway without any problems: the surveillance cameras were switched off, along with the alarm system. The concealed jib-door to the fitness room was also unlocked, as expected. Andy Mo immediately led Leif into the sauna. A mechanism disguised as a tap was supposed to open the hidden door to the secret passage leading to the ghastly chamber. After two attempts they found the right tap. First Andy Mo pressed the gold-plated handle; then, like a safe, he turned it three notches to the left, two to the right, and one to the left again. Sure enough, the shower wall slid silently to the side, revealing a short, discreetly lit, wood-panelled corridor; a comfortable couch and a huge mirror gave the impression of a relaxation room. The exit wasn't visible, but Andy Mo knew where the vault was, and Yks had also told him how to lift the mirror so the passageway would open. Andy Mo quickly found the right spot, and the mirror eerily turned into a sliding door, uncovering the way.

Although he had prepared himself, Leif still couldn't believe what he saw. The suggestive, vivid sounds and the strange tangible light immediately captivated him and stifled his consciousness, just as bad air in an unventilated room takes your breath away.

"This is horrible. Worse than the worst trip", he groaned. "I think I'm going crazy."

"Get me out of this prison first", Yks interjected, fluttering his wings excitedly. "We've got to hurry. Something's wrong, I can feel it in my feathers." Understandably, the bird was hopping impatiently around behind the bars, visibly nervous. As Leif unlocked the cage with the key Andy Mo had quickly thrust into his hand, Yks zoomed past him like a rocket, flew through the corridor, and waited in the sauna for the others to follow. Leif, still dazed and unable to think clearly, instinctively locked the cage door and then followed Andy Mo, who was also extremely nervous and waving impatiently at him. The mirror slowly sealed the chamber behind them, and a few seconds later the shower wall in the sauna clicked back into place as well.

The whole operation had taken five minutes at most, but it felt like an eternity to them. It was as if they had come from a distant, foreign land. Yks had tears of joy in his eyes and sat trembling on the toilet cistern. The excitement had made him sick to his stomach, and he took the opportunity to relieve himself. Ravens are known to defecate vertically, and he hit the toilet bowl with precision. Afterwards he artfully pressed the flush and tried to say something, but Andy Mo urged them to hurry. He too suddenly sensed that something was going to go wrong, and he felt afraid. After all, they had broken into the villa, and it would have disastrous consequences for Leif if he was discovered – not to mention the poor raven's barbecue party. They hurriedly crossed the gym and slipped through the jib-door into the hallway. Leif bounded up two stairs at a time. He wanted to get out of there as quickly as possible; he wouldn't soon forget the horror in the cellar. But then it happened. After the second flight of stairs, he lost his orientation. Indecisive, he stopped.

"Hurry! There, to the left", Andy Mo pointed. "Run through the kitchen. There's a side exit that leads behind the house into the garden. From there go straight down the hill and you'll be back at the wooden door in the wall."

Leif hurried around the corner, stumbled, and ran straight into Goldstein, who had just come out of the kitchen with a bottle of mineral water.

"Who the hell are you? How did you get in here? What are you doing in my house?"

The homeowner seemed more horrified than outraged at the intrusion of a trespasser, and he stared at him with eyes wide in disbelief, almost fear.

Leif quickly regained his composure. Goldstein's uncertainty immediately restored his own confidence.

"The gate was open", he claimed cheekily. "I called out, but no one heard me. I'm looking for Kathi and Miri Li – we had an appointment here. Unfortunately I got delayed." He looked Goldstein in the eye with an innocent look. "I take it you are the great builder. Please excuse my tardiness."

Goldstein's features relaxed.

"Oh, I see. Yes, of course – it's alright. It's just that somebody tried to break in here yesterday, so you're suspicious when someone's suddenly standing in the middle of the room again. Come on. The interview is finished, but your colleagues are still here. We're sitting outside. Please follow me."

In the entrance hall, Goldstein checked the alarm system. He pressed the buttons of an intercom on the wall, but the monitor of the surveillance camera remained dark.

"This damned shoddiness. It's broken again. Either the butler forgot to close the gate, or the electronics are going haywire. I dare say the system got messed up yesterday. But let's go," he said, holding up the bottle, "the girls are thirsty. Get a glass from the kitchen too."

Leif followed him, relieved. Through the kitchen window he could see the raven disappearing among the treetops of the old firs. He was lurching in the air like a drunken bat; you could tell he hadn't flown for a long time. So the bird was saved.

When they stepped through the large glass door and onto the terrace, the light blinded him. The two girls showed no surprise at seeing him and waved. Andy Mo had rushed ahead to throw the key for the chain into the pool, and he had already informed them of the problem. He had also reactivated the code on Goldstein's mobile phone, and now he was following the freed prisoner into the bushes. He had to show him the way to Michael's house, where they were to meet afterwards.

Goldstein went straight to the table, quickly filled the glasses, and then looked for his Nokia to check for a faulty connection. But everything was OK. He shook his head in irritation, then clutched his chest and turned pale.

"The key's gone. I've lost the key." His voice sounded broken and hoarse.

The others played dumb.

"Can we help you, Director?" asked Kathi innocently, looking at him with wide eyes. "What kind of key was it – what did it look like? Where did you keep it?"

"It's a safe key. I wear it on a gold chain around my neck. In fact it's an amulet I never part with. It was still there when I changed my clothes."

"Then it must be here somewhere", Miri Li said "– or in the pool, you haven't been anywhere else."

The girls looked around the terrace while Goldstein and Leif went to the edge of the pool and stared intently into the glittering ripples.

"There's light reflecting here", Leif said. "You can't see anything; it will be easier from the other side."

But Goldstein jumped into the water and dived down to the bottom of the pool. He almost made it the whole length of the pool before coming up for a moment to breathe, and then immediately resumed his underwater search. He went about it systematically, and when he surfaced the second time he had already found the necklace. He swung it happily back and forth, dived under once more and then came up gasping with the key. His relief was evident.

"Thank God", he beamed, "this piece of jewellery has a very special meaning for me." He checked the clasp and immediately put the chain back on.

The Nokia rang out, and at the same time a phone could be heard in the house as well.

"I think we should go now", Kathi said. "We've already taken up too much of your precious time."

While their host took care of the calls, the girls changed their clothes. Goldstein insisted on ordering them a taxi.

"At my expense, of course", he said, discreetly placing a hundred euros into Leif's hand. "But please send me a copy of your newspaper."

Then he escorted his guests out and walked with them to the gate. The car arrived at the same moment.

ONLY CHILDREN CAN DEFEAT BAPHOMET

The sun hadn't yet set when the taxi stopped in front of Michael's property. Andy Mo had already brought the exhausted bird to their destination with a mental leap, and so everyone was happily reunited.

Leif was the hero of the day, but Yks stole the show. He had recovered surprisingly quickly and was strutting back and forth like a peacock on the large table in the library.

"We showed him! He'll be surprised when he gets back to his refuge! And tomorrow, when he's broke. Do you know what he used to call me?" Yks sobbed theatrically and covered his face coyly with his right wing.

The others looked at him expectantly.

"He called me lucky piggy. He called me his lucky piggy because he made a lot of money with me every day."

"That is indeed impertinent, dear Professor", Kathi sympathised with him. "May we bring you a beer to fortify yourself? It says in the Book of the Master that you love this noble beverage of hops."

"No thanks, I've been abstinent since I was captured. If I hadn't been drunk back then, that criminal would never have caught me. Mineral water please, and a cheese toast. I haven't had anything to eat since yesterday evening."

"I think I'll get us all something to eat", Michael announced and disappeared into the kitchen. "I've made a Liptauer sandwich spread." He returned straight away with a laden tray. Kathi had followed him and brought the drinks and cutlery. She had prepared a double decker for Yks on the electric grill.

RECIPE

LIPTAUER SANDWICH SPREAD
For about 4 people

Ingredients:
120 grams of butter
250 grams of quark
1/2 onion
1 clove of garlic, crushed
2 gherkins, cut into small cubes
10 capers, finely chopped
Salt, pepper, and caraway
1 tablespoon of mustard
1 teaspoon of paprika powder
1 teaspoon of sour cream

Preparation:
Beat the butter with the salt, mustard, and pepper. Add the caraway seeds, paprika powder, garlic, onion, gherkins, and capers and mix well. Mix in the quark. Stir in the sour cream. Serve with wholemeal bread and toasted white bread. Garnish with tomato slices, bell pepper strips, radishes, and chopped chives.

DOUBLE DECKER

Ingredients:
White bread (a proper loaf tastes better than pre-sliced toast)
Ham (or sausage)
Cheese (Emmental is best, but sheep's cheese also goes well with

a spicy sausage)
Mustard
Butter

Preparation:
2 slices of bread per person. Spread one slice of bread with mustard. Layer with cheese and ham. Place the second slice of bread on top. Spread butter on the outside of both slices of bread. Toast on an electric grill until the bread is golden brown and the cheese is melting. Garnish with ketchup and pickles.

APPLE COMPOTE

Ingredients:
5 apples
5 tablespoons of sugar
2 cloves
zest of an unsprayed lemon, about the size of a thumbnail

Preparation:
Peel and core the apples, cut into small pieces. Place in a saucepan, add sugar, cover with water, and cook slowly until they begin to disintegrate. Chill. Serve with whipped cream.

*

The two girls were still full from Goldstein's buffet, but the boys ate their fill. Andy Mo, who also wasn't eating, asked Yks what he knew about his father.

"Do you at least have a suspicion as to where we might look for him? How did you meet him? What was he up to?"

"We've known each other for a long time. Whenever he came to the human realm, he'd call me and I would come, no matter where I was. He showed up again unexpectedly about two years ago. However, he didn't tell me what he was up to this time. When I pressed him to confide in me, he said he didn't want to put me in any danger. So I don't know who's holding your father captive, nor where they're hiding him. But I think I know why they deprived him of his freedom."

Everyone looked eagerly at the raven. He swallowed a mouthful, thought for a while, and then continued.

"It must be related to the mysterious lost scroll he was looking for. He told me about a document which describes how humans are really nothing more than the milking cows of the gods and demons, and..."

"But that's already in the Book of the Master", Kathi interrupted him. "It explains exactly how these super-spirits feed on the impulses, feelings, and emotions of humans. Since they can't be born in a body of flesh and blood themselves, they miss out on many experiences which can only be had in the human realm. They only have access to those perceptions and emotions which they can imagine because they correspond to their nature. They can't grow beyond themselves like humans and gain new experiences. They rely on the humans whose impressions they adopt, and who they exploit for their own advantage, just like we milk cows."

"That's right", Yks confirmed. "But Andy Mo's father has discovered that an important part of the document is missing. It's the pages which seem to describe how humans can free themselves from the power of the gods. It's the secret Formula of Nothingness which opens the gate to eternity. The Library of Alexandria went up in flames because of this scroll. But a copy of it still exists, and he knows part of it. I don't know if he's found the missing pages yet – the last time I saw him, he mentioned that he was still looking for the formula. Naturally the gods are afraid that this secret will be discovered. How many bosses would happily swap positions with their underlings? Baphomet is the one who has the most to fear. Without humans as his underlings, he would be a nothing within nothing."

Christian wanted to ask something, but Yks could read his mind and waved him off.

"I'll explain later. So I don't know if the king found this scroll, but he knows at least part of its explosive content. He was still looking for something specific, though, and that's when he ended up at your school."

"Do you think our school is one of those mysterious places where black magic is practised?" asked Kathi in dismay; she was thinking of her father, of course.

"I can't say. But I think he was there mainly because of the students. He had his eye on a few of you, and now I think I understand why. He said he had a plan. But before he could tell me what it was, he disappeared. At first I thought he had briefly returned to his kingdom, because he mentioned several times that he had to discuss something with Andy Mo Junior. He said it was a mistake that the Book of the Master was written for adults – it should have been a book for children."

"For children? Why?"

Yks paced pensively back and forth on the table, wondering how to begin. After all, it was the last Hermetic secret he was meant to reveal. The Gnome King had entrusted it to him. It concerned the victory of good over evil.

"Pay attention", Yks said. "Your father only recently discovered it himself and spoke to me about it. It lies within that document, and he is still looking for the last page with the secret formula. But he already knows this much: only children can free the world from the negative powers. Baphomet cannot be defeated by the religions or the priests; nor by the ideal institutions, the Masonic Lodges, or the political parties; nor by the 'good' people. Nor even by the magicians, or the heroes, or the saints. Neither magical power nor morality can defeat evil. Only children are capable of conquering it. He told me repeatedly: only young people do not cast shadows. Children still possess an openness to new things, have faith in the seemingly impossible, and possess the genuine, carefree enthusiasm necessary to delve into previously unimagined worlds. The Gnome King said that the truly powerful are the children." Yks paused and looked at each of them intensely. "The future lies within you. You shape the destiny of the world. You can make the world a better place. Your fathers and mothers have not been able to do so, nor can they do so in the future. That was the last thing Andy Mo's father confided in me. If we can find the missing page he was searching for, it would be a useful lead that could guide us to him. I suspect he was only taken out of action by the powers-that-be because he figured all this out. For these are truly new perspectives. If this becomes widely known, and if in the future children begin to occupy themselves with the science of the spirit, the human spirit will develop undreamt-of abilities. Humans will surpass the gods. They cannot remain indifferent to that fact. Unfortunately, I don't know the Gnome King's plan. But perhaps we are already in the middle of it without knowing it."

"That's entirely possible", Miri Li remarked. "After all, it all started with Christian's dream in which the Gnome King appeared to him and led him to the book in the cellar. The book then enabled us to bring Andy Mo to the human realm. Then we encountered Yks and were able to free him. And now he tells us that Andy Mo's father has found the secret documents. Maybe they were both taken out of action because they know their sensational contents. But now we also know: the future of the world depends on us children. It all fits together – it can't be a coincidence. But how should we proceed?"

"Isn't it strange that my father never mentioned these books to me?" Andy Mo asked the raven. "What did he tell you about them?"

"In fact he spoke to me about it several times. He said that the key to new thinking and true magic lay in the Book of the Master. He was also the one who kept the work from being destroyed by the forces of the Shadow down through the centuries, and who always made sure that it came to light again. It was never intended to be a secret document; rather, it should have been printed long ago. The time was ripe and as many people as possible should have read it. That's what was intended by the ONE which humans call God. But Baphomet and his princes have been able to prevent this so far. The esoteric publishers who intended to publish the book suddenly all went bankrupt, and so it has remained as a small edition for personal friends." Yks paused and snatched a slice of bread with Liptauer spread from Michael's plate. Then he continued. "Perhaps you will succeed in doing what Andy Mo's father last intended – namely, to write a Book of the Master about the spirit realm for children. They are ready for it now."

"What do you mean?" asked Michael, who had been mostly silent until now.

"If something is going to move the world, it must first be thought of by many people. That's the way it has always been. Just think of the conquest of space. Previously there were only utopian fantasies, such as the books of Perry Rhodan, the Star Trek and Star Wars movies, and so on. Millions of people have spiritually reproduced these images with their thoughts. In the meantime humans really are flying to the moon, and some of the technical devices which were described can be found in every office today. This development would not have been possible without the fantasy-fertilising images. It all begins as a fairy tale first: that's the real Harry Potter mystery."

It was Kathi who immediately understood what the raven meant.

"Just as Perry Rhodan prepared the minds of readers – and thus all of humanity – for outer space and computer technology, so Harry Potter and the Pokémon characters have filled the minds of children with images of the unseen worlds and prepared them for real magical practice. They now have a concept of magic and spirits, at least in their imagination. They're just waiting for real instructions to follow the fairy tales."

Yks nodded and looked at Andy Mo.

"Millions of people know Harry Potter, but no one knows you. Yet you actually exist, and you really can perform magic. If you write a magic book for children, you'll be even more famous than that fellow from the world of fairy tales."

Andy Mo laughed, then became thoughtful.

"Why not? If you start practising and we write about it, other young people will follow us. If we succeed in spreading these insights with an exciting book for young people, then other humans will also experiment and realise their true spiritual potential. As soon as the youth make full use of their power over the gods and spirits, a new age will dawn for humanity. They will become like the gods."

"This is already possible on your computer screen", Christian said. "Think of the games by the game designer Will Wright and his crazy life simulations, from tiny single-celled organisms to space travellers. Each player can invent their own characters and let them grow, with different characteristics resulting from the corresponding composition of a character's cells. You can even create a new planet for them to live on. His games create their own content, and people really do act like the gods. Only theoretically for now – but with our book, instructions for practice will follow."

"That means we are the Chosen Ones in the game of the powers", Christian stated soberly. "Andy Mo will show us how to perform magic, and then we will write a book together on true magic: a Master Book for young people."

"Don't forget Dr Stein", Miri Li warned, frowning. "He didn't have a moment's peace after he started rewriting the old manuscript of the Book of the Master in a contemporary form. It will be the same for us." "I fear she's right", said Andy Mo. "But we're already on Baphomet's hit list anyway. He'll keep coming after us no matter what. We should keep an eye on the book project, which was obviously a concern of my father's. I suggest we begin by each keeping some kind of diary, and then together we can compile an exciting book from the notes."

"But first we have to find the missing volumes", said Kathi. "As long as we don't have them..."

She was interrupted. Someone was knocking loudly on the large window from outside and pressing their face against the dirty pane of glass. "Mail. Urgent delivery, is anyone there?"

"Coming", Michael called out, disappearing down the hall to let the postman in. Apparently the bell at the gate was rusty and was no longer working. When he returned, he was lugging a heavy package – he heaved it onto the table with a flourish. "It arrived much more quickly than I imagined. Actually, it was supposed to be a surprise. But it came at just the right moment: we have the Book of the Master."

The friends stared at him incredulously.

"Who just cast a spell?" asked Leif, and the others couldn't believe that such a coincidence would happen either. "We shouldn't mention that in our book. No one would believe this story."

"On the contrary", said Kathi. "The very fact that the books were just delivered proves we're in contact with extraordinary powers, doesn't it? Where did you find them? Why didn't you tell us that you'd found them?"

"First I wanted to make sure that it was the Book of the Master that we were actually looking for, as there's a paperback with the same title published by Knaur. But our publisher is called the Archive of Hermetic Texts; they specialise in reprinting rare esoteric works. I found it by chance on Google under antiquarian booksellers. It's a small publisher, a family business. I phoned them and someone called Gloria Ogris took my order – a nice girl with an interest in magic, and the same age as us, incidentally. She'd be perfect for you, Christian."

Christian blushed and became embarrassed. Everyone knew that Gabi, his girl, had gotten involved with the gym teacher. Michael realised his mistake too late.

"Sorry", he said. "I was just thinking, 'Well, well, so this Gloria is interested in magic too', and she's the one who confirmed to me that these are precisely the Master Books we're looking for. Her father supposedly knew someone who appears in the story." Michael unwrapped the books as he spoke. Then he solemnly handed each of them five volumes. "The third, fourth, fifth, sixth, and seventh books – that's all there is, apparently."

Andy Mo also received his own copies and immediately began to leaf through them. Yks flew onto his shoulder and read along.

"These Master Books were your father's main concern", he said to Andy Mo. "He was worried whether it would ever be possible to disseminate them. But when he found part of the secret scroll, all he had in mind was a Master Book for children."

"I think that has become our concern now as well", said Christian. "We owe it to the old man. Andy Mo will show us how to perform magic, and then we'll write a book about our experiences with spirits."

THE FIRST LESSON IN MAGIC

Andy Mo closed his book and looked earnestly around. Then he nodded and asked Michael to light the two candles again, which were still standing on the chest.

"I've been intending to teach you magic for a long time. But since I've been in the human realm, I've begun to think differently about magic. You can change the world in accordance with your will even without magic. You already have a much better command of matter than most spirits – what you achieve by means of technology seems like a miracle even to me. Telepathy will never work as reliably as your mobile phones, for example. Today, I believe magic is only for spirits, and not for people who are stuck in a body. I'm convinced that once you master this art, you'll no longer use it."

"Why?" asked Leif, and the others were also very puzzled.

"Because you'll no longer need it. When you've mastered your spirit so well that you can use it to cast spells, you will also have mastered your destiny, and you'll be able to realise the few remaining wishes through your mind by quite normal means. I believe my father had something else in mind when he wanted to use magic to show children the power of the spirit.

"So what is magic? Magic is when you change something in the physical world without any discernible cause.

Any effect which is not achieved by mechanical, physical, chemical, or physical means in the physical, psychic, or spiritual fields should be considered magical.

I just happened to read this definition in the fourth volume of the Book of the Master. True magic is therefore nothing other than work with the spirit. Thus proper magical training always leads to spiritual perfection. And that is what matters, not the magic. I will teach you magic. But not so that you learn how to control spirits or change the world according to your wishes; rather, so that you change yourselves in such a way that the spirits and the world with its temptations can no longer change you against your will. Personal perfection, not magical power, is our goal. Do you understand?"

"Yes, yes", Leif said. "Don't make it so exciting. What's the first thing we have to do?"

"Magic always means working with the spirit. Either you work with your own spirit, which is primarily your ideas and thoughts, or you summon spirits like me. You can also make your own helpful spirits. I'll explain how to do that later; so in magic you're always dealing with the spirit and spirits.

"Now, I ask you: how do you think you can move or shape the spirit? Certainly not with your hands. How can you talk to spirits? No matter how loudly you shout, no spirit will hear you. If you want something from a spirit, you must somehow teach it what you want from it. Apart from the fact that you must summon it first, it can only help you if it understands what you expect from it. Even if you work with your own spirit, it must express exactly what you mean in the form of an idea. For example, if you want to influence someone with a thought packet, the idea of what you want must be clear and distinct rather than being expressed in blurry images or confused fantasies. But that is precisely what is not so easy.

"So, magic means working with the spirit. Therefore you must first train and develop your spirit. Einstein explained it yesterday: spirit manifests itself in thoughts and ideas. So the ability to master your thoughts and to imagine things is the basic requirement for magical experimentation.

- Lesson number one: you must train your imagination and learn to handle your thoughts properly, as well as those of others."

"That sounds complicated", Leif said. "Can't you just tell us a few magic spells – that would make everything much easier."

"Alas, spellcasting is not that easy. Spells are already little spirits, strictly speaking, and you must deal with them properly. But we'll talk about that later; we have to start from the beginning.

"So, what language is spoken on the spiritual plane?" "The language of images, I think", Kathi suggested. "Before I say something, I think about what I want to say. In the process, a picture – an idea of what I'm thinking – emerges."

"Exactly", Andy Mo rejoiced. "Under certain circumstances, these ideas can also be perceived by other spirits. Now let's do a little experiment. Take a closer look at the thought-images you're creating. Look inside yourself. Turn your gaze inwards so that you get to know the substance and the energies you'll be working with. It's not just the stuff which dreams are made of; the whole spiritual world is built with it. Even you yourselves consist of this spirit. Look at them – your ideas, thoughts, and fantasies."

Kathi looked at Andy Mo with incomprehension. Then she understood what he meant and closed her eyes. The others followed her example. Silence fell in the library. After about five minutes, Yks looked at the clock standing on the marble mantelpiece; Andy Mo nodded, and the raven crowed as if he were a rooster. Life returned to the group.

"You really are going to end up on the backyard barbecue", Michael said, looking a little dazed. "Why did you wake us up?" Miri Li was rubbing her eyes as well.

"Is this what they call meditating? I almost fell asleep too."

"So that's exactly what you're not supposed to do", Andy Mo replied. "On the contrary: you're supposed to awaken. The most important goal of all magical training is to be wakeful. I don't mean not sleeping, but rather having a clear distinct awareness: I AM. The conscious recognition that you are, and that you are here. That you are a spiritual being. But we'll talk about that later – it's still too early to work with consciousness yet. You've just looked purposefully into your inner world for the first time in your life. What did you experience, Miri Li?"

"Well, not much really. A lot of things went through my mind. I wasn't thinking of anything at first, but then I realised that I actually was thinking about a lot of things. About Goldstein, about the delicious tropical fruits and sweets, about the beautiful view, about the water in the pool. Then Bangkok came to mind; the sea; my grandmother; I suddenly thought what it must be like to die, and about the mafia, and..." She thought for a while, but nothing else came to mind, and she fell silent.

"You've remembered a lot", Andy Mo praised her. "You were very wakeful. That's good. But then you started dreaming. Kathi, what did you experience in your inner world?"

"Again, the exciting events with the key. Then I thought about my father, and about whether he really is working with Goldstein. That's when I remembered our class trip – Kleindienst will be accompanying us rather than Einstein, and I wanted to ask you if we could influence that with magic, because yesterday I didn't manage to convince my father to assign Einstein to our class..."

"What, we're getting Kleindienst?!" Leif was horrified. "If he's going, I'm calling in sick."

"Me too!" Michael declared, and the others were also visibly upset by the bad news.

"What's a class trip?" Andy Mo wanted to know.

"The whole class is going to Neusiedl am See next week. We'll be staying at the Segelhafen West Hotel for a week – it's really great, we stayed there last year too. But with Kleindienst we won't be learning to sail or surf; he's planned an excursion to Hungary, where we'll be visiting some dusty museums."

Andy Mo got the picture. "I think something needs to be done about that – what do you think, Professor?"

Yks, who sensed he was being addressed, nodded thoughtfully. A sly twinkle flashed in his small eyes.

"I know that midget. He's already caused trouble for your father; it will be my pleasure. Just let me handle it. Please continue with the instruction: we stopped at thought control. That's the first thing we had to learn in school, too, but I still haven't mastered it completely."

"I'm having trouble with it again here in the human realm too", Andy Mo admitted. "It's as if thoughts are extra rebellious around humans." Then he continued.

"You've just realised that there's a whole lot going on in your head which you don't normally notice. Yet you only realised a fraction of what actually crossed your mind, and only a part of it remained in your memory. Now we're going to repeat the experiment. But this time you're not simply going to look inside yourself – you're also going to try to consciously grasp all your thoughts and ideas. You'll be surprised at what's going on and how much you've been overlooking until now." Silence fell again.

After five minutes, Andy Mo signalled to the professor again. This time he rang like an old alarm clock rather than crowing. The meditators were startled.

"Man, oh man!" groaned Leif. "How did Goldstein put up with you? You belong in a circus as a ventriloquist. But I'm glad you brought me back to reality. There really was a lot going on; it's like a dream in there. What a mess! I feel like a lunatic."

"I felt the same way", Christian remarked. "Leif's right: it was pure chaos. If my room looked like my head, it would drive me crazy. I would never have believed that you could think of so many things in such a short time. If Andy Mo hadn't told us to pay attention, I wouldn't have noticed any of this. Within a split second I was thinking about Gabi, about the police, about the paintings that had surfaced, about my father, about Yks, about having to go to the toilet, and I probably missed a lot as well – all while I was convinced that we were sitting here meditating and I wasn't thinking about anything. It was only when I paid closer attention that I noticed what was going on. I'm beginning to doubt my mental state."

"You're perfectly normal", Andy Mo reassured him. "I'm sure the others didn't fare any better. Normally, the sequence of thoughts is as disjointed as a video clip. But how is a spirit supposed to recognise what you really think and want? And another thing: you believe you've thought of many different things and situations. But that's only half the truth. It's not you who have been thinking, but rather the thoughts have made you do what they wanted to do. They came and went as they pleased. I'll prove this to you right now. Look once more into your inner world, and now try to control your thoughts. Think exclusively of the upcoming holiday week, and don't think of that perverse pink swimming pool at all."

After five minutes, the raven squawked "toot-toot!", sounding just like the old-fashioned horn of a vintage car. He had learnt it from a parrot in New York. Life returned to the group.

"That was mean, Andy Mo. You set us up", Kathi said indignantly. "Of course I kept thinking about that stupid pool and a hundred thousand other things, and least of all what I should have been thinking about."

The friends nodded; they had had the same experience. The raven chirped like a nightingale, and tapped his wing against his head as if to say they were cuckoo. Andy Mo laughed.

"Be glad your laptop works better than your brain. Imagine if the data in your computer scrolled across the screen as quickly and incoherently as your thoughts. No one would be able to make sense of it. The same is true of your projections into the spiritual world. First you must learn to order and control your thoughts and ideas. If you want to achieve something on the spiritual plane or work together with other spirits, you must first learn to form thoughts clearly and maintain them longer. You must be able to concentrate on a single idea; only then can another spirit perceive it and grasp what you mean. All other disruptive images must disappear."

"I'll never be able to do that", Miri Li said despairingly. "I'd rather stick to my prayers."

"Spiritual training isn't meant to replace praying – it's meant to make your call to the heavenly beings more intelligible. You'll learn it, it's not so difficult.

"There are various techniques for getting rid of or controlling stubborn ideas. You can't think or push thoughts away, but you can try to ignore them. You can treat them with indifference by realising that they don't interest you because they're completely meaningless.

You can also replace unpleasant thoughts by focusing your attention purposefully on other ideas – on the idea of silence and calmness, for instance. You'll notice that the better you can concentrate on a single thought, the fewer disruptive ideas will arise. So it's all about the ability to concentrate. Attention works like a beam of light which you direct towards an object. You can even visualise this when you practise. And you have to practise, otherwise you won't get anywhere.

"I'll share a trick with you, a so-called magical gesture: imagine that your two index fingers are like the headlights of a car. If you close your eyes and stretch out your fingers side by side and point them at the thought you want to keep in your consciousness, you won't lose sight of it so quickly. If you perform this magical gesture often enough, it will soon work automatically. Then you can concentrate more easily as soon as you point this spiritual laser beam towards the spiritual object.

"I'll reveal another secret to you – and a magical formula which you can use to sweep the realm of your consciousness clean of unpleasant, unwanted thoughts.

- **Every thought is a small spirit.** A living being. We'll talk about this in more detail later. When a thought appears in your consciousness, it enjoys it because it comes to life and can romp around in the realm of your consciousness, your soul garden. But your thought spirits also know that you are the boss.

Therefore the formula is: "I see you!" As soon as you think this, the uninvited thoughts sense they are being watched and withdraw. The path of consciousness in front of you becomes free.

So in the next few days, try to repeat the three steps we just took. However, don't think of this as homework – think of it as a mind game.

- **Firstly,** whenever you have the opportunity, look at what's going through your mind in a relaxed and calm way. You don't have to become a recluse; you can do this on the bus or train. After a while you'll notice that fewer and fewer thoughts will arise all by themselves.

- **Secondly,** focus your attention on a single train of thought and think about it without drifting off to another topic. For example, imagine going home after school. Or think about a particular person you like, or an activity you enjoy doing.

- **Thirdly,** liberate yourself from thoughts. Concentrate only on your breath. Just as you observed your thoughts before, now observe your breath. And if you succeed in doing this, concentrate only on yourself. Only allow the idea 'I AM' to fill your consciousness as the sole thought. Breathe in and think: "I AM." Breathe out and think: "I AM." Under no circumstances should you fall asleep or fall into a trance – this will plunge you into the shadowy realm of dreams and demons. On the contrary, you should be completely wakeful and be entirely conscious of yourself as a spiritual being.

You can only communicate with another spirit from this clear state of consciousness. All the other exercises that I'm going to show you will only succeed from this inner wakeful stillness.

But you must practise for a long time to reach this magical state of consciousness. So don't be discouraged if you don't immediately succeed in achieving inner silence.

- And if things become too turbulent and your ideas slip away, then realise: you are the observer of your thoughts and feelings. You yourself are unmoved, no matter what is happening in front of you. You're just watching, calmly and serenely. Think of the immobility in which you find yourself, and the stillness will transfer to your thoughts."

Andy Mo paused his teaching and seemed to be thinking. Then he said: "I think that's enough for today", and silently extinguished the two burning candles.

*

Outside it had become dark. The wind had picked up again and a brief shower of rain pattered against the windows. Michael had gone over to the house to make apple-peel tea; he had dried the apples himself the previous autumn. Kathi was taking notes from Andy Mo's first instruction, and Miri Li was engrossed in the Master Books. She shivered briefly and it was clear she was freezing.

"The thick old walls are still cold from winter", Leif said, trying to start a fire in the fireplace. Yks and Andy Mo, both of whom had a healthy respect for the spraying sparks, retreated from the danger zone.

"What are these experiments this devil in a lab coat is doing?" Andy Mo asked the bird. "Do you know him? Do you know where his clinic is?"

"No", Yks replied. "I only saw him once when they installed the spirit trap around my cage. But this much is certain: he's trying to bring the dead back to life. In the lab they're artificially creating the electromagnetic field which surrounds the brain cells of every human being while they're alive, and then they're transferring it to a deceased human. They haven't succeeded so far – none of the patients have woken up again. But if they succeed, demons could incarnate in human bodies in this way. The special magnetic field already acts on mental images and spirits like a hoover. That's what you experienced when you fell into the spirit trap."

"Please don't remind me of that. We have to put a stop to this guy as soon as possible, if only for the sake of the unfortunate victims. The police will take care of Goldstein now, so we can pass on a tip to them. Maybe he'll come clean then."

"But we can't tell them to interrogate him about your father's disappearance as well. Imagine the announcement: "Earth spirit missing, distinctive feature: taller than other gnomes." The raven let out a shrill, sarcastic laugh. "I doubt the police will help us find the king."

Michael returned with the tea and helped Leif with the fire, which wouldn't catch light properly. But he couldn't get the flames going either.

"Let's call it a day", he suggested. "We can go over to my cabin – it's warmer in the kitchen than here."

No one objected. They were all tired. First there had been the stress of the interview, then the rescue of Yks, and even the first lesson in magic had been exhausting. They had imagined learning magic would be easier.

Michael extinguished the embers and the remaining candles. Just as he was about to lock the gate, Leif returned; he had forgotten his Master Books.

"Put the key under the pot", Michael asked, "and turn off the light again." Then he followed the others, who were already waiting. Once they were all gathered around the big round kitchen table,

Andy Mo began: "Let's summarise what we know. The new member of our group, Yks, needs to be filled in as well."

"I am most honoured", said the raven, taking an elegant bow. "Fire away!"

"So, my father was searching in this city for a lost scroll. It describes how people can free themselves from the power of the gods and demons. He found part of this document, and he's been missing ever since; we assume that Baphomet had him captured so he couldn't pass on his knowledge. Fortunately, the king entrusted the secret to Yks before he disappeared, and that's why we also know: only children can defeat the dark forces. We've also found the Master Books in the meantime. Even if we fail to free my father, we have been initiated into the mystery and will reveal it in a book for children, just as he wished. Baphomet must suspect this fact and is also trying to destroy our circle by any means necessary. He's using his minions among the humans to do so. They probably have no idea that they're mere puppets of Evil."

Leif interjected: "Do you think the humans don't know what they're doing? Do you think each of them is simply following their own interests, and we're just random side characters to them?"

"In fact I'm convinced of it. Baphomet can't force anyone to do anything for him. He can only use a bait to lure his servants into acting in his interests. He must have discovered that Yks also knows the secret, and so he sent Goldstein after him. Goldstein is unscrupulous and money-hungry, and he captured the clever bird so that he could speculate for him on the stock exchange. Goldstein is also after Christian's parents' house – not because he wants to harm them or us, but because he needs the property. That's why he arranged for the paintings to be stolen. Of course, the fact that the thief subsequently refused to play along was not part of Baphomet's plan."

"Obviously there are also good forces which are on our side", Miri Li stated with satisfaction, and Andy Mo nodded.

"There are, without doubt. The fact that we're sitting here together and have already achieved a great deal is surely due in large part to these positive attendant spirits. I believe you call these spirits 'angels'. But even they are only allowed to guide people in the right direction through inspiration; no spiritual power is allowed to directly interfere in the life of a human being. Even Baphomet must abide by this rule. So we're not dealing with a black magical Lodge whose members are acting together against us: I believe we are dealing with individual perpetrators." "When it comes to the Chinese mafia, I have no problem understanding that", Christian remarked. "They want money and nothing else. But what about this physician from Doctor Frankenstein's horror clinic?"

"Even he has no idea who is inspiring him to do his work. He is surely unaware that he may be preparing an invasion of demons with his inventions. I heard him tell Goldstein that the spirit trap was just a by-product of his research; he's convinced that spirits are nothing more than bundled electromagnetic fields. But even if our opponents are lone wolves, that doesn't make them any less dangerous. On the contrary: it makes it more difficult for us to find out which of them is holding my father captive. If there were a common centre, then we would know where to look for him."

"Who else is under suspicion besides Goldstein?" asked Christian. "Who else could be in the service of the Shadow?"

"The Chinese mafia, of course", Miri Li agreed. "Whether these bandits were hired by Goldstein or are acting in their own interests is irrelevant. These people are real. I saw them when they were at my parents' house."

"That's right", Andy Mo confirmed. "But I doubt they're capable of holding my father captive. Only a powerful mage – or possibly this Dr Frankenstein – can do that. You see, my father has been completely shut off. I can't locate him at all. Either he's unconscious or he's stuck in one of those spirit traps. So the first thing we must do is find this diabolical clinic."

"Apparently there's a magic centre at our school as well", Kathi remarked, swallowing. "Just because my father is the headmaster doesn't mean we should ignore that fact."

"Perhaps the school is a centre of light", Andy Mo mused. "But you're right. We should investigate the lab in the basement more closely. This has nothing to do with your father: anyone who has access there is suspicious. Not just your father or Einstein. For example, I noticed a strange guy with a hunchback. Who is this man who creeps along the corridors like a ghost? I've met him twice, and I had a strange feeling each time he looked in my direction. He possesses mediumistic abilities as well."

"You mean Quasi, our mute school caretaker. We call him that because he looks like Quasimodo, the Hunchback of Notre Dame. He's harmless. He lives at the school and keeps everything in order – a good-natured oddball. He was hired three years ago when we had dirt in the basement from the big construction site. When the renovation was completed, the old school caretaker died, and he took over his job. A friend of my father's vouched for him."

"I'm still going to keep an eye on him", said Andy Mo. "There's something about him I don't like. That makes six people we should watch out for."

"Seven", Michael corrected him. "We mustn't forget the bank

manager. It's pure caprice if he doesn't extend the loan. After all, he's admitted that he wants to buy our villa for this antiquarian." Leif looked at his watch and switched on the television.

"Maybe they'll have something on Goldstein and the paintings on the local news. I still think he's the head of the gang: he knows the guy who stole the paintings, he's working with Dr Frankenstein, and he's after our parents' properties."

Although he disagreed, Andy Mo said nothing. He didn't mention that Goldstein hadn't recognised Leif, even though he should have known him if he'd also set the painting thief on him. "The network of evil is woven by spirits, not by secret superiors conspiring against the rest of the world", he thought to himself. The powerful among humans all work for their own benefit; that much Andy Mo had already learnt. They're easily seduced into acting in the demons' interests. If they see an advantage for themselves, they are willing to do anything. As if to confirm his thoughts, a government minister appeared on the television screen spreading a new lie about his aspirations to protect the environment. Andy Mo wondered why people fell for the sick, lousy characters involved in politics and helped them gain power. It was very different in the spirit realm: no prince or king would abuse their position. But there they weren't elected either; rather, they attained their position of leadership all by themselves due to their special qualities and abilities.

Suddenly Andy Mo flinched. Leif also turned pale when he saw a close-up of the face of a dead man they had just pulled out of the water. It was the guy with the money and the gun, the man who had been at Goldstein's with the paintings. The report was brief. The body of the unknown man had only been in the water for a few hours, and a request was made for any pertinent information that would enable identification.

Andy Mo immediately grasped the situation. Goldstein had obviously concluded that the guy had broken into his garage in order to set the police onto him. He made short work of his opponents. Now Leif's life was also in danger, for as soon as Goldstein discovered the raven's disappearance, he would consider him to be an accomplice of the dead man. He had been wandering around the house without authorisation, and it couldn't be ruled out that Goldstein would also suspect the girls.

"Leif, how close did you get to the edge of the pool before Goldstein found the key?"

"We were both standing right in front of it as we were searching the ground. Why?" And then Leif understood too. Not only had he gotten into the villa, but he was the only one who could have thrown the key into the pool without being noticed. Leif wanted to say something, but then he thought twice. He knew who the dead man was, but he had to handle his own business – he didn't want to get his friends involved. Besides, he was still convinced that it was a coincidence, and that his connection with these people had nothing to do with his friends' problems.

Andy Mo deliberately avoided probing Leif's thoughts. It wasn't customary for spirits to pry into people's private concerns. But he decided he would talk to Leif privately about the matter.

"That was the visitor who brought Goldstein the paintings that night", he explained to the others, who were still unaware of Leif's story. "He didn't survive the deal." Then he voiced the fear he was harbouring: "We must be doubly careful now. Goldstein is more than just dangerous – he's ruthless. Under no circumstances must he link any of us to the break-in."

Meanwhile they were showing the weather report on the television. There hadn't been a word about the break-in and the seizure of the stolen paintings at the Goldstein villa. That could only mean Goldstein hadn't been arrested.

"I'm tired and exhausted", said Miri Li. "This has been an arduous day. Who's taking the next bus with me? It leaves in six minutes." Leif and Kathi joined her. They had to hurry and said their goodbyes quickly.

Christian had been allowed to stay with Michael while his father was in hospital, and he helped his friend with the dishes and tidying up. Andy Mo and Yks made themselves comfortable in front of the television. Andy Mo watched every free minute of TV, and so he had learnt more about humans in a few days than in his whole life previously. The raven also had an enormous appetite for information after his long period of captivity. They didn't notice the drama that was unfolding nearby.

THE PASSAGE THROUGH THE DARKNESS

Just as the bus was arriving, Kathi discovered that she had left her notes with the interview and the minutes in the library. "Go without me", she called after Miri Li and Leif, who had already boarded.

"I'll take the next bus. I forgot my notepad."

She turned around and ran straight across the meadow to the villa. She knew where the key was, but she struggled to unlock the large old gate, and as the lock clicked an oppressive feeling came over her. Her footsteps on the tiled floor echoed eerily off the walls. The sculptures in the alcoves stared at her with hostility, as if she had entered their world of dead forms against their will. They looked as pale as propped-up corpses in the pale glow of the moon which fell through the high windows. Kathi began to shiver inside.

"This isn't the first time I've been in this house", she thought, irritated with herself, but something was suddenly different. She hurried and felt very childish.

She searched nervously for the switch in the library, but the cold light of the crystal chandeliers only emphasised the shadows of the heavy black furniture. A creaking came from the beams of the old, wooden ceiling above her; a figure seemed to be moving behind the curtains, and her pulse throbbed in her ears.

Kathi was close to running away, but she pulled herself together. Looking around anxiously, she spotted her papers lying on the marble mantelpiece above the fireplace. Relieved, she took them and was about to quickly leave the room when she caught the cuff of her jacket sleeve on a decoration on the fireguard. She tried to free herself, but something got stuck and was holding her back. With an impatient movement she tried to break free, bending the iron scrollwork on which she was hooked, and then the thin linen fabric tore with a horrible sound. Startled, Kathi stopped moving: she didn't want to ruin her jacket completely. She carefully untangled her tattered sleeve from the bulky obstruction. It was a small, cast-iron goat's head, staring viciously at her on an unnaturally long, shaggy neck. Despite her fear, she bravely pushed the silent head back into its former position. And then it happened. The neck of the strange figure was actually the lever of a hidden mechanism. A section of the bookshelves rotated with a creak, revealing a narrow passage. The smell of must and cellar wafted towards her. Kathi had found the hidden chamber which Michael's grandfather had told her about. So the secret passageway really existed.

Now her curiosity was greater than her fear. Kathi squeezed through the opening and peered into the small chamber. That's when it befell her. Before she could prevent it, the wall behind her slid shut again, trapping her in the gloomy silence of the grave. As if a demon had swallowed her up, she had disappeared. She had the impression of being in a strange, distant universe, and she felt completely cut off and isolated from her surroundings. A wild panic gripped her in the pitch-black, impenetrable darkness. She wanted to scream, but her throat was tight. Only a hoarse rattle came out. Exhausted, she huddled in a corner and began to cry.

The absolute night all around her penetrated her like a damp chill, making the narrow space she was in seem like a vast, infinitely large cave. Fearfully, she pressed herself against the wall. She knocked and called out, but no one could hear her. The shock she was feeling only slowly dissipated. She had to do something. At the earliest, her friends wouldn't notice she was missing until the following morning at school. She groped blindly around her, frantically searching for her backpack and the mobile phone inside it. That was when the next misfortune occurred. As she carefully stood up, she was overcome by a slight dizziness, and she unintentionally staggered sideways, stepping into the void. Instead of a wall for her to lean against, there was a narrow staircase leading down into the depths. Kathi fell down some steps and lost consciousness.

*

"There's still a light on in the library", Christian said as he happened to look out of the window. "Is anyone still over there?"

Michael replied in the negative. "That must have been Leif. He was the last to leave and probably didn't turn off the lights. The gate will still be open too – it's best if I go over there now and sort it out."

Just as he had suspected, the key was still in the lock. Shivering, he walked down the hallway, and as he entered the library an oppressive feeling came over him as well. Michael could still feel some of the fear which Kathi had felt as a premonition of what she was going to experience. And he felt her closeness. But he couldn't interpret the strange mood. He rapidly left the room and locked the gate.

The cosy atmosphere in the kitchen soon made him forget what he had experienced. He sat down at the table with his friends and followed the conversation attentively. Andy Mo was currently engaged in a heated discussion with the raven – both had discovered that they couldn't see as well in the human realm as they could in the spirit world, and that their magical abilities didn't work as well as they used to. Andy Mo thought it was their own fault.

"I don't think we're practising enough", he opined. "Our spiritual muscles are atrophying because we don't have to use them as much here as in our own world."

But Yks disagreed. He believed that external circumstances were to blame.

"Your father had the same problem. He too felt weakened, and eventually he even had difficulty returning to the spirit world. I believe that the longer a spirit stays in the human realm, the denser it becomes, until it can no longer move at all. If I hadn't slipped into a bird when I got lost, I'm sure I wouldn't be alive today."

"Maybe the king isn't imprisoned at all", Michael said. "Maybe he's lying helplessly somewhere, and you can't locate him because he's unconscious."

"Right now I can't even locate living humans", Andy Mo complained. "This Dr Frankenstein has vanished right off the face of the Earth. Although I can imagine that my father is being held in his torture clinic, whether he's conscious or not. The first thing we must try to do is find this doctor."

"Goldstein would know where he is", Christian said. "You could trick him into thinking about it and then read his mind."

"A fine suggestion", praised Andy Mo. "That's one possibility. Kathi calls him again tomorrow, using a question for the interview as a pretext, and I get close to him and monitor his thoughts. That could work – if he hasn't been arrested after all", he added. "But right now I can't even see that much. A lot has changed within me since I've been living in the human realm. Perhaps I really have become more material."

"It's the opposite for me", Michael remarked. "Since I've known you and learnt about the world of spirits, I've somehow become more mediumistic, alert, and sensitive. I sometimes sense what someone is saying even before they open their mouth. And just now when I was in the library to turn off the lights, I felt as if the spirits were calling out to me – as if someone was holding me back and wouldn't let me go."

"You clairvoyantly perceived the atmosphere of the library", Andy Mo surmised. "This room is indeed a magical place. There's a spirit in every book, you see – the thoughts of the author and the thoughts of all the readers who have engaged with them. And thoughts are like little spirits, as I've already explained to you. We've probably awakened some of these spirits with our presence and our conversations about magic. After all, every conversation leaves invisible traces, creating a special mental environment in which spirits corresponding to the topic can frolic like fish in water. However, those aren't real spirits like me – they're fleeting elementals which only gain importance when you engage with them and thus animate them, or when you consciously and purposefully keep them alive in order to use them as helpful spirits. Let me explain how that works in more detail. It's..."

A strange noise interrupted him. It came from the curtain rod and sounded like someone sawing a tree trunk. It was Yks: the raven had fallen asleep and was snoring like a drunken tramp.

"To be honest, I'm tired too", Christian said. "If you don't mind, I'll retire as well."

Michael nodded.

"I think we're all exhausted. This has been a draining day; we should call it a night and go to sleep."

Andy Mo also got up.

"I would love to spend the night with you guys," he said, "but I have to go back to my spirit world. It's the only way I can preserve my abilities." He waved, began to flicker, and disappeared.

*

While the friends drifted off to sleep, Kathi regained consciousness. At first she didn't understand where she was. She thought she was dreaming. But slowly her memory returned, and she realised what a terrible situation she was in.

She was surrounded by complete darkness. Her head felt like it was about to burst, all her limbs were aching, she was cold and thirsty, and her body was shivering all over. With difficulty she managed to hold back her tears. Despite her fear, she was attempting to keep a cool head. First she felt all the painful spots and was relieved to find that nothing was broken. Then she stretched out her arms, but she reached out into the void in all directions. The steps she had fallen down had to be somewhere. Afraid of falling again, she cautiously crawled on the floor until a wall blocked her way. She struggled to stand up and felt her way along the wall like a blind woman; her clammy fingers brushed over cold, damp stones, and she reached an alcove, but realised it wasn't the chamber she had been in before. She had crawled in the wrong direction. Now she had absolutely no idea which way to turn; she had completely lost her bearings, and she began to cry uncontrollably. She called out and screamed for help, but no one heard her. Her voice was completely swallowed up by the thick walls which surrounded her. The underground passageway had become an underworld of demons from which there was no escape. She was terrified.

For the first time in her life, she became aware of the importance of light. Even the slightest glimmer would have given her hope and courage and helped her to choose a direction. But the impenetrable darkness enclosed her more tightly than the stonemasonry above her. She felt absorbed by the lack of light, and her spirit was also about to lose itself in the darkness. The light of life within her was slowly flickering out. Only the dull silence that thundered in her ears was keeping her awake. Kathi knew she had to get back, as they would never find her here. But she was too weak and completely exhausted. Weary, she huddled on the cold floor. She wanted to rest for a few minutes, but she couldn't find any peace. Something moved next to her feet, and when she flinched in alarm it squeaked away. Horrified, she realised that there were rats there. And worse was to come. When she had huddled on the floor, she thought she had felt a wooden stick, but as she fumbled to defend herself with it she realised it was a thighbone, and the large smooth stone next to her was a skull. She was sitting next to a human skeleton.

Disgusted, she pulled her light jacket tighter around her shoulders and searched her pockets for a handkerchief. As she rummaged around, she came across a hard object. When she realised what it was, she could have cheered. It was Andy Mo's rock crystal. Kathi knew immediately that the magic stone was her salvation. She had no doubt that Andy Mo would get her out of this underground labyrinth. As if a light had been lit inside her, the thought of her invisible friend and the faith in her rescue gave her hope and confidence again. All she had to do was summon him. His seal would lead him to her.

Kathi remembered what they had learnt before. You can only talk to spirits from the inner silence, Andy Mo had explained. She had to bear that in mind. Despite the terrible situation she was in, she tried to relax. She focused her attention on her breathing and felt herself slowly becoming calmer. A peaceful silence descended over her.

Cool and smooth, like a magic wand, the elongated crystal lay in her hand. Using the inner light of her imagination, she spiritually drew Andy Mo's seal in the darkness. With all her might, she concentrated on Andy Mo while carving his seal into the ground: the curved line which ran from top to bottom like a mountain and then ended in a figure-of-eight loop, forming two caves, and the three horizontally layered lines next to it. The spell worked immediately.

*

With a violent jolt, Andy Mo woke from the dreamless sleep into which he had just sunk. He knew immediately that he had been summoned. Although he was still dazed, there was no doubt that someone was using the power of the crystal and the secret seal to bring him closer. It had to be one of his friends who needed his help. He couldn't tell which one of them was in trouble; all he could sense was that the call came from the human realm, and that it was insistent like a cry in dire need. Andy Mo rapidly scanned for the direction and was astonished to discover that the person was underground. For safety's sake he took his lantern and followed the pull of his thoughts, which took hold of him like a tractor beam and led him to Kathi.

It all happened very quickly. From one moment to the next he landed in the underground passage and materialised right before her eyes. Kathi could also recognise him in the darkness thanks to his magic lamp. She threw her arms around his neck in relief and began to cry uncontrollably with joy. Andy Mo held her protectively in his arms and waited patiently for her to calm down.

"How did you get here?" he asked in surprise. "Where are we anyway? What is this strange vault?"

"We must be somewhere near Michael's villa", Kathi explained, briefly recounting what had happened. "I don't know how long I was unconscious. I can't have gone far."

Andy Mo quickly confirmed that she was right. He spiritually scanned the area and then he knew her exact position. Indeed, Kathi hadn't ventured far from her starting point in the darkness; a transverse passageway led into the alcove where she had sat up, and she had followed this path by mistake. They were in an underground labyrinth which probably dated back to the time of Maria Theresa. Andy Mo knew that the princes and counts had built escape routes and connecting passages between their small castles and fortifications. In that bygone era, the gnomes still had contact with individual humans. He resolved to examine the tunnel more closely later – perhaps he would find a clue that would lead him to his father. But first he wanted to free Kathi from the darkness.

Resolute, he took the exhausted girl by the hand and carefully walked with her back along the corridor until they reached the secret chamber behind the library. The small room was empty except for a large old chest standing in the corner. Wiping the dust from its surface, he realised it was an archaic artefact with ornate metal fittings. The contents had to be valuable. He would inspect the box later; first they had to find the exit.

He lit up the walls with the light of his magic lantern, and immediately he spotted the narrow door along with the small brass knob set into the wall which opened it. When he pushed the knob, it budged and released them to their freedom. Andy Mo immediately wedged a thick book in the opening so it wouldn't latch shut again, and Kathi turned on the light. They both breathed a sigh of relief and dropped exhausted onto the old leather sofa. There was still a bottle of mineral water on the table. Kathi emptied it in one go.

"I think that it was Baphomet himself who lured you into that underworld and made you disappear", Andy Mo said. "Whether he deprives his victims of spiritual or earthly light, he banishes them with darkness. We must be more careful in the future." Andy Mo sensed that another calamity was about to happen, and he was seriously worried because he couldn't see where the new danger was coming from. But he kept his thoughts to himself.

Kathi had found her backpack in the chamber and rummaged around for her watch and mobile phone. Surprised, she realised that it wasn't as late as she had thought. She had the impression she had been in the dark basement room for an eternity.

"If I take a taxi, I'll be home before my parents. They've been invited to a friend's house and won't be home until midnight."

"That's good", Andy Mo replied. "We mustn't make your father suspicious. He doesn't know about our magical alliance yet; until we know whose side he's on, he mustn't even suspect that you're connected to me."

"You've just saved my life. I don't know how to thank you for that."

Andy Mo shrugged it off.

"You brought me into your world, and I brought you out of the basement. We just make a good team. Together we'll succeed in freeing my father as well, no matter which world he's trapped in."

They decided not to wake Michael and Christian. They could tell their friends what had happened at school the next day. While Kathi ordered a taxi, Andy Mo went outside to get the key. Then he opened the front gate for Kathi and accompanied her to the street. The car she had ordered came faster than they thought.

Andy Mo waved goodbye and then went back into the villa; he wanted to see what was in the box. But to his disappointment, the lid wouldn't open. The chest was fitted with a complicated lock which he didn't want to destroy by force. He needed more light to study the ingenious mechanism: the glow of his lantern and the dim light of the candlestick he had fetched from the library weren't sufficient. Since he couldn't lug the heavy object out of the chamber alone, he had to postpone his project until the next day. He carefully extinguished the candles and went to his refuge, where he fell asleep almost instantly.

SHADOW WORLDS

This night wasn't over for Leif either. He had accompanied Miri Li home and tried to kiss her at the front gate. But she didn't want to. Gently but firmly, she withdrew from his embrace.

"I like you", she said, "but not like that. We're just good friends. Give me some time." Then she disappeared before he could hold her back.

Leif was disappointed, and his pride was hurt. They had become closer since their adventure together at Goldstein's. In fact it had all begun that night when she had tended his wound – her touch had been very different, much more loving than that of a nurse. Since then, he couldn't help thinking about her increasingly often. He had fallen in love with her, and he believed that she also had feelings for him.

But he had other problems. He looked at his watch and then called a number.

"Did you happen to watch the local news?... Well, the dead guy in the water... What?... But that was the guy who brought me the money. You must know him... Okay. I'll be at your place in ten minutes."

Leif walked quickly through the narrow suburban streets, passed the entrance to the Westbahn train station, and a short time later he was standing in front of one of the typical municipal buildings from the fifties. A figure emerged from the darkness of the front gate and stepped towards him.

"You have to believe me, I really don't know who this guy is. When you hit me up for money, I reported it to the group leader. He said he would talk to the old man. That's all. I don't know anything else."

"Who is this old guy?" asked Leif. "Why hasn't anyone seen him? Why is he hiding?"

The other person shrugged his shoulders and shook his head.

"I have no idea. All I know is that he's filthy rich. But I can give you the phone number of the group leader. He said that you're an important asset to our organisation and that we should look after you. You don't think one of us killed him, do you?"

"No", said Leif, saving the number on his mobile phone. "It wasn't anyone from the group – I know who did it. But there's still a problem. I need to speak to the old man personally." The other person got curious, but Leif brushed him off and quickly said goodbye. He walked back to Hietzing and was about to go down to the underground when his mobile vibrated.

"You want to meet me", someone said. "And I'd like to know who killed poor Ricardo. If it's not too late for you, we can meet today."

Leif was pleasantly surprised. It had worked – the old man was granting him an audience. He looked at his watch. It was half past ten.

"Okay. I'm on the Kennedy Bridge. Where can I find you?"

"Stay where you are, I'll come to you. I'm close by."

Leif looked around. For a moment he actually felt as if someone was watching him, but he couldn't see anyone suspicious. Nor did he know what the man he was about to meet looked like. Nobody from the group had seen him yet. However, there were many contradictory rumours about him. Some said he was the spiritual leader of a secret occult Lodge; others believed he controlled the drug scene and dealt in weapons, and that he recruited new blood for his dark business through the youth groups he sponsored. Both might have been true. Some of the group members used hashish, and the books they propagated within the group covered a wide range of occult topics: they discussed everything from Aleister Crowley to the dubious Aryan ideals of the neo-Nazi scene and the pseudo-occultist works of the Scientologists. However, punctuality and cleanliness were strictly observed, and the only criminal was the guy who had handed him the money.

Leif expected he would have to wait at least half an hour, and he wondered if he should buy a cola at the hot dog stand across the street. But something held him back. Indecisive, he stopped and looked absentmindedly down at the black water reflecting the lighting of the bridge arches. The white foam of sewage drifted lazily past beneath him; it had the smell of a canal and of seaweed. Suddenly, the noise of the traffic seemed to recede into the distance. A strange mood took hold: the darkness cast its spell on him. Then he felt again that he was being watched, and this time he was not mistaken. A beam of light lit him up and a huge white luxury car resembling something from a Hollywood movie floated slowly and majestically like a ghost ship towards him. The rear door opened, and without realising it, he walked to the car like a remote-controlled puppet and got in.

There was a strange atmosphere inside the vehicle. As he sank into the soft upholstery, something within him also sank. He felt as if he had dropped out of time and was removed from everyday life. Outside was another world. But inside him, too, something had suddenly changed. He felt light and untouched by his environment or his problems. The car glided silently through the streets like a balloon ride; it was as if the sound of the television had been turned off. Nothing had changed; life went on, but differently than before. Reality played itself out behind a thick wall of glass: inconsequential, meaningless, and uninteresting like a film you've already seen, as if the future had already happened.

"You're doing well in the group", someone said. "You're appreciated and people listen to you. You've read an amazing amount." The words were strangely powerful to Leif, and yet they seemed to come from far away. Something was swallowing the sound as if they were underwater, and only the meaning was being transmitted. Later he wouldn't be able to describe the voice.

He hadn't immediately noticed the old man. Even now he couldn't really see him, although he was sitting next to him on one of the snow-white, glove-soft leather seats. The interior of the Maybach limousine was designed like a luxury salon. In the dim light, Leif could make out a minibar and a television made of fine burl wood behind glass; on a small round table, an opened bottle of champagne and a cola had been placed in a silver ice bucket. The driver could only be seen in black and white via a video system, and even the houses and people outside were filtered out through the strange atmosphere inside the car, making them seem eerily dead and distant. What was outside stayed outside, like a billboard passing by. You couldn't tell whether the car was moving or stopped at a junction. It was a timeless, spaceless sense of floating, like a dream.

"And you seem to know a lot", the man continued, and although the words he spoke were inaudible, again they touched Leif and penetrated his innermost being as if he were hollow. A sweet and strangely numbing smell filled the room.

"The voice; that soundless voice is within me", Leif realised. "It's as if I myself am speaking rather than the old man." Somewhat dazed, he waited for the man to continue speaking and tried to focus on him, but he evaded his gaze. Whenever he thought he saw a face, a flash of light or a flitting shadow altered the features and he looked different to how he had moments earlier. Even when the old man leaned forward and refilled his glass, the face remained a moving mask.

"All that vagrant Goldstein wants is money. Not even power and influence can seduce him. Sure, nobody can live without money: gold is the blood of this world. But there are other worlds, young friend. We aspire to higher spheres. The gold of the spiritual planes is our goal."

Had he already told him about Goldstein? Leif couldn't remember. Was it the toneless voice, the strange smell, or the peculiar violet light which seeped out of the cracks of the limousine like a luminous mist and kept forcing him to close his eyes? Several times he got the feeling that he'd fallen asleep and was dreaming it all. The old man spoke of angels, spirits, and demons. And he answered him, but he couldn't hear his own voice either. Thoughts burst like soap bubbles and appeared as the subtitles of a wordless dialogue in his consciousness. He didn't even know if it was him or the old man who was speaking.

"Good and evil do not exist", he heard within himself. "Where there is light, there is also a shadow. Light only stands out from the darkness. If everything was just light, there would be no contrast and you wouldn't be able to see anything. Imagine if your screen only had bright pixels." There was a pause in Leif's thoughts. Then the voice continued: "Light alone is not visible. Only when a ray of light hits matter is it illuminated. In the same way, the very thing that some people demonise as earthly and evil leads to spiritual enlightenment. Do you know what Lucifer means? It's Latin and means light-bearer. The so-called fallen attendant spirits mediate the visible universe in which we live. What could be evil about that?"

"But in this world there is limitation, destruction, and death. Humans inflict suffering and pain upon each other. That's clearly evil. Isn't that why we strive for a different, spiritual, unlimited existence? Perhaps we're only trapped here and there are spheres where light, not matter, forms the basis of existence."

"Now you're living on the Earth, and here the foundations of life are limited. In order for the new to emerge, the old must be destroyed. The humus for new growth is created from dead plants. You can learn from blows of fate. There is nothing bad which doesn't also contain good. The negative, destructive principle is also part of Creation and must become part of your being if you wish to rule in both worlds. Only if you have experienced everything within yourself will you become complete."

"But surely you don't need to support or do evil for that." Who said that? Was it him or the old man? Or was it another voice? Was he hearing the voice of conscience?

"How else can you master it?" it resounded back.

"By refusing to do it or alleviating its consequences in others. There's enough suffering in the world, it doesn't have to be increased by me. You can also do good and so compete with the negative powers."

The dialogue was taking place inside him. Not a single word seemed to be spoken. One thought followed another; voices spoke.

"You're on the right path. But you must also learn the left path. The lord of this world is Baphomet. They fear him because they do not know him, and because they do not know him, they do not control him. Those who have not experienced the dark cannot reach the light. I will show you the path. We have the formula, and you will provide the wand."

Leif wiped his eyes in irritation. The wisps of violet mist were still hanging in front of his face and could not be driven away. As before on the bridge, he was now absent-mindedly standing outside his front gate, trying to remember what had happened. The bridge, the car, the old man; they had discussed good and evil. What else had he said? He robotically unlocked the door and went to his room, as if in a trance. Without undressing, he lay down on his bed in a daze. Something crackled in his pocket. The old man had slipped him an envelope: the rest of the money for the dealer. He was rid of that worry. But it was blood money. Slowly the memory came back to him – he had divulged everything. He had betrayed Andy Mo and his friends, and he was going to steal from them. He had agreed to it. He was going to provide the wand for an incantation of Baphomet. The old man had managed to convince him after all. He had to face the power of evil. He wanted to rule both worlds: the earthly world and the world of spirits. In both worlds there was light and darkness. He would not hide from Baphomet.

Only the chosen ones, the best from each group, were going to participate in the ceremony. "You will be alone", the old man had said. "I only show the direction. The strength to follow the path is granted by another. And everyone must walk it themselves."

Leif had made up his mind. He wanted to take this path. But he was afraid.

AUGUST KLEINDIENST'S CIRCUS ACT

"I'm afraid for you", said Andy Mo the next morning after telling Michael and Christian about the nocturnal adventure in the underground passageways. "You're all in more danger than I thought. If Baphomet and his princes intervene themselves, we have little chance. We're no match for those forces."

"Don't panic", Yks reassured them, gleefully consuming the special toast Michael had just prepared for him. "Everything has turned out fine. You eventually saved Kathi – what more do you want? And besides, there's nothing bad which doesn't also have something good in it. Think of the chest – who knows what's inside there?"

"My grandfather searched for that hidden chamber for years", Michael said. "I think he even bought the house because of that rumour. I suggest we forget about school today and go straight to seeing what's behind the mystery."

"That old chest isn't going anywhere", Yks protested. "But you'll miss out on my big performance in front of Kleindienst. I was supposed to take him out for a week so Einstein could take over the school trip."

"I almost forgot", Michael apologised. "What are you going to do? How are you going to manage it? Are you going to peck his eyes out?"

"No, I'm not Goldstein. Just let me handle it – I already have a plan. By the way, what happened to that criminal? Did they eventually arrest him? Have you heard anything about him? I'm afraid I fell asleep last night. Theoretically, he should be broke by now. Go on, turn on the radio, maybe they'll report something on the news. I think…"

But Christian interrupted the raven's torrent of words and urged them all to leave.

"Kleindienst is teaching the first two hours. If we want to catch the bus at half past seven, we have to go. Unless you'd rather fly, there's room in my backpack for you." But Yks declined with a shudder.

"No thanks, I know where the school is. See you around. I guarantee it's going to be fun."

Andy Mo raised his eyebrows and shook his head as he watched the bird swoop out of the kitchen window with an Indian war cry. He was about to shout something else to him, but he was already gone.

"I hope he doesn't do anything foolish. Who knows what he learnt from that pervert Goldstein."

Michael nodded.

"After all, for months he had to watch that violent video of his own brain roasting on a grill. If every thought is a little spirit, then the poor guy invited a whole lot of evil spirits into his inner world. If they emerge today, Kleindienst is not to be envied."

On the bus, Michael sent Kathi a text message. Immediately afterwards his mobile rang. The conversation lasted a long time. While she was describing to him everything that had happened, Christian chatted with Andy Mo.

"How come we can actually see you while you remain invisible to everyone else?"

"If someone doesn't believe in us spirits, we take it as an insult", Andy Mo explained. "It's like someone telling you that you're lying. So anyone who doesn't believe in spirits can't see us; they turn and move away from us. No spirit could appear to them, even if they wanted to. Only a few of us are able to condense ourselves so powerfully that even unbelievers can perceive us."

"But what about well-known ghost phenomena? Surely there are…"

"Who are you talking to?" the boy next to him interrupted. It was the same student who had sat next to Michael last time; he was sitting near him again in the hope of witnessing a new magic trick. "Do you see ghosts, too, perhaps?"

"Sometimes", Christian said. "But sometimes we just sense them. That's when they grab us by the ears and pinch our noses."

Andy Mo took the hint and sprang into action. The boy turned pale; startled, he grabbed his nose and felt his ears, which had just been pulled. At the same time he looked around in all directions, but he couldn't see any suspects. Smiling uncertainly, he muttered something about suggestion and rotten magic and then sat down somewhere else, just to be safe.

Kleindienst would say the same words a short time later, before he lost his mind. The tragedy began innocently enough, but it didn't end as happily as the fun on the bus.

As usual, Kleindienst had entered the class with a stalwart "Good morning, everyone!" and had immediately begun his lesson. However, he was soon interrupted. First a theatrical voice in the schoolyard called out, "Ev-ery-bo-dy!" It sounded really great. The call of death came from all corners of the large square, just as it did in the performance of the well-known drama Everyman at the Salzburg Festival. It was eerily haunting, and even those who didn't know the play had chills running down their spines. The strange echoing sound made them aware of the transience of life. The class fell silent, and even Kleindienst, who was usually not easily disturbed, interrupted his work at the blackboard and stepped to the open window with interest.

"Who's rehearsing? Which class is performing the play? You mustn't disturb the lessons. What's going on out there?" He leaned far out and closed the window indignantly when he could see nothing. Visibly annoyed, he went back to the blackboard and continued writing. However, a loud knocking immediately came from the windows. Kleindienst, still trying to keep his composure, said quietly in a clenched voice: "I ask for silence. I urgently request silence!" But when the knocking continued, he lost his nerve and turned around. "Who is responsible for this? I forbid it! I will not have my lessons disturbed."

"A raven", someone said, and a girl began to giggle hysterically. "It's a raven knocking on the window, Professor." Then Kleindienst also saw the bird, which was pounding violently against the window with its beak. He took a step towards it, bent down, and stared at it in amazement with wide-open eyes. Then he jerked upright and nodded.

"A raven, indeed. A raven knocking on the window." "Open up", Yks shouted impatiently, again banging vigorously on the panes. "Open up!"

"He's talking", Kleindienst observed, opening the window curiously. "It's a mynah, not a raven. Ravens can't talk." "I can", said Yks. "But I'm still not a raven – I'm a spirit stuck in this raven's body. I'm one of the spirits which supposedly don't exist, okay?"

Kleindienst froze. For several seconds he was unable to respond; then he slowly backed away without taking his eyes off the bird. As he wasn't looking where he was going, he tripped over a backpack and fell. Yks flew after him and politely inquired if he was injured. Two students helped the teacher back to his feet; he already looked slightly confused.

"I can think too", Yks said. "For example, you just made a mistake. Up there on the third line – the square root of 169. That result is wrong!"

Kleindienst looked at the blackboard and became jittery. He had indeed made a mistake. Initially it seemed he was going to start crying, but then his features contorted into a sly grin.

"Einstein. A conspiracy. You're doing it with your mobile phones. But I'm not stupid. All mobiles on the table! Class president, please get the headmaster. You can't do this to me!" Apparently aimlessly, Kleindienst rushed through the classroom with great strides, moving hither and thither like a startled bat, first hurrying to the blackboard and correcting the mistake, then wiping it all away and writing instead in large letters: "There are no spirits!", then laughing maniacally and turning triumphantly around.

"I won't let you drive me crazy. It's just technology and suggestion. This is an ordinary bird. Who brought it? Where is the animal?"

Meanwhile, Yks had perched on the edge of the blackboard and was looking down at the bemused teacher with his head tilted. Everything was going according to plan. One more comment, he thought, and he'll be ripe for the clinic. Quietly, so that only Kleindienst could hear him, he whispered to him:

"Here I am. But I'm no ordinary bird. There's something extraordinary within me. We could perform together in a circus, August – you'd become famous with this act. World famous. 'Professor teaches ravens to count.' I did that on stage years ago, you know. You want to be on TV like Einstein, don't you?"

Kleindienst stared up at the raven with his mouth open. He felt trapped. In fact, he *had* been dreaming of becoming famous. No one knew about those secret fantasies – and no one was allowed to know, either. Furious, he grabbed the nearest object within his reach and hurled it at the bird. It was his drinking glass, which shattered against the wall and splashed water in all directions. Kleindienst got wet and was already looked pathetically haggard.

Meanwhile Yks had taken refuge on one of the six globe lamps hanging from the ceiling and was cursing loudly.

"Murderer! Help! He's going to kill me!"

But the enraged professor was out of his mind. He followed his victim, throwing the mobile phones the students had placed on the tables in front of them at his request. Two of the lamps were shattered in the process. This was too much for Yks. He had achieved what he wanted. Just before the headmaster and the school caretaker entered the class, he flew out through the window into the courtyard, where he disappeared between the branches of the elder tree.

Kleindienst threw a few more mobile phones at him. Now he was talking complete nonsense and couldn't be calmed down. The headmaster and the hunchbacked caretaker had great difficulty holding him down until the alarmed school doctor arrived to give him medical attention. Then the ambulance arrived and took him to the clinic.

"A mynah", the class president explained. "It seems a tame bird strayed into the schoolyard. He knocked on the window and said: 'Open up.' That upset him."

The headmaster nodded, then shook his head and surveyed the devastated classroom. "Please note down how many mobile phones Professor Kleindienst threw and the names of their owners. We need the data for the insurance. And you," he said, turning to the school caretaker, "please clear away the broken glass and put everything back in order. The two lessons that Kleindienst was supposed to teach are cancelled." He was already at the door when he turned around again: "Our colleague Einstein will replace him during the school trip." The students were thrilled.

Andy Mo observed with surprise that Kathi's father didn't notice him this time. Nor had the hunchback taken any notice of him, even though he was in his line of sight. Had he imagined everything? Had the stern look last time just been a coincidence?

*

The five friends met in the schoolyard under the elder tree. Yks was sitting on the lowest branch and was about to recount his latest adventures to the tree spirit, whom he knew from before. He was showing off, of course.

But Kathi waved at him and applauded. "You were really fantastic. Your idea with the loudspeaker was great – luckily no one was in the office at the time. You did it! Unfortunately, something unpleasant has also happened. Goldstein called this morning and asked about Leif. He wanted to know who he was, where he lived, and how long I had known him. I told him I had to go to class and would call him back later."

"Thank you", Leif said, and you could see that the news worried him. "But I'm afraid his people will find me anyway. You can go ahead and tell him who I am; I'll have to handle this another way."

"What are you going to do?" asked Miri Li anxiously. "Maybe we should tell the police what we know after all? If Goldstein finds out what really happened, he'll have us all killed."

"In fact we don't know if he really has knocked anybody off", Christian pointed out. "Maybe the man just fell into the water and drowned."

Michael agreed with him. "The TV only mentioned an unidentified corpse. Not murder."

Andy Mo nodded.

"We'll call him in the evening. We were planning on doing that anyway so I could spy on his thoughts. Now Kathi has a plausible reason to do it. When I search his mind for the horror clinic I may also come across scenes involving the dead man, as well as his thoughts about Leif and our interview. Once we know what he knows, we can decide what to do."

"Why don't we call him now?" suggested Leif, handing Kathi

his mobile phone. He hadn't left it on the table, perhaps wisely. "Then we'll immediately know where we stand."

But Andy Mo objected.

"I can't concentrate so well here", he said. "And besides, there's something interesting to report. Kathi, please tell us what you experienced tonight."

Now Kathi described her nocturnal adventure in great detail. She made it exciting, and everyone was deeply impressed. Christian and Michael had already been filled in by Andy Mo, but they also listened attentively, and even Leif became serious and thought of his own experience the night before. He too had been confronted with evil.

"That could have ended badly", he remarked, nodding appreciatively at Kathi and her rescuer. "I'm beginning to wonder what else is in store for us in the next few weeks. However, we now have the Book of the Master, so we can learn how to confront these powers," he added confidently. "We will face the Shadow."

Michael nodded, but Miri Li shuddered and said she'd rather not confront the Shadow. She was certain she wouldn't have coped.

"From now on, I'll never leave home without the crystal", she said, not suspecting how badly she would need it the very next night.

Then the free period was over. They decided to go to Michael's house together right after class. They were all excited and wanted to know what was in the chest.

*

Andy Mo didn't follow them to class; instead, he slipped into the tree to give Krux an update. As he did so, he noticed that he was having difficulty entering the spirit world. Something was hindering him. It wasn't anything tangible, but he felt as if he had to wade through deep water. Just a few days ago he had effortlessly returned to his spirit world, but now he had to overcome resistance. Even in the cosy living room of the tree spirit he felt cramped, and it took a few minutes before he could orient himself properly and move normally again. It seemed that his stay in the human realm had already altered the constitution of his being.

Krux noticed his temporary uncertainty.

"You spend too much time with the humans", he said worriedly. "You shouldn't stay out there so long. It hasn't been a week and already you're losing control over your element. I didn't imagine it would happen so quickly. You were only supposed to leave the spirit world for a few hours at a time."

"The days pass much faster for humans than for spirits", explained Andy Mo. "When I think about all the things I've experienced this week, it makes me dizzy. Still, everything you undertake requires more time than it does for us. I can't explain it to you, it's all completely different. It's much better: I feel just as comfortable on the surface of the Earth as I do in my element."

"It's not our world", Krux warned. "The danger of getting stuck over there and not being able to return doesn't get any less just because you feel comfortable there. Then you won't be at home in either world, and the consequences are unforeseeable. First you become tired, then you get denser. Soon afterwards you can't move properly, apparently. And eventually you lose consciousness. At some point in the human realm, everyone loses consciousness and dies. You should stay here for a few days now to regenerate."

"I can't do that", Andy Mo said firmly. "Think of my father. With each passing week things are getting more critical for him as well. Either he's stuck in a spirit trap or he's already unconscious, so I can't locate him. We have some leads, but still no concrete clue leading to him." Andy Mo told Krux what they had learnt so far. "We assume that the king is being held captive by an Earthly minion of Baphomet, so anyone who obstructs our search is a suspect and must be investigated. My father isn't being held by Goldstein, we know that much. But Goldstein knows this perverted doctor who probes people's minds, and he'd be capable of holding an earth spirit captive as well. I'm hoping Goldstein's thoughts will lead us to the horror clinic. We want to grill him about it today."

"Don't forget the school", Krux said, glancing over at the building. "I'm sure the king had his reasons for beginning his search for the lost document right there. Who knows what's going on over there?"

"That's true", Andy Mo agreed. "The headmaster, the caretaker, and Einstein: all three of them are suspects. Nevertheless, I'm reluctant to poke around in Kathi's father's thoughts. I couldn't find anything in Einstein's mind, but I must admit that I'm not as good at clairvoyance since I've been living among the humans. I feel like a thief breaking into someone else's home, and that's obviously blocking me. Naturally I'm still going to deal with the school caretaker, and we'll investigate the labs in the basement down to the last nook and cranny. We also have to find the Chinese mafia bosses. The people who approached Leif are no ordinary dealers either. They've got something planned for him. So there's still a lot of work to be done, you see."

Yks knocked on the window, urging them to leave.

"We want to study the Master Books too. Stop gossiping and come on."

"Investigate the bank manager too", the tree spirit called after them. "He's trying to purchase Michael's house for a man who may also be engaged in magic. Since there's a spiritual power spot on the property, anyone interested in it is suspect. It seems that the old villa belongs to a magical network, just like the school and Goldstein's estate. You would have to know the key connecting the places or the people involved. Somewhere is the centre or the place where they're holding your father. Maybe you'll find a clue in the chest that will reveal the secret."

THE GARDENER, CHRIST, AND BAPHOMET

A few hours later, the friends pushed the huge chest out of the chamber and into the library. In fact they had wanted to examine the secret passage first, but then Kathi had discovered the key in the dust on the floor, and the prospect of finding a treasure changed their plans. Michael inserted the large, elaborately crafted skeleton key into the lock. At first nothing budged, but after a few futile attempts the complicated mechanism moved, and they lifted the heavy, ornate lid.

"Books", said Leif, sounding disappointed. Like the others, he had been hoping for a treasure trove of gold. "Books – nothing but books."

But Michael seemed satisfied.

"I think my grandfather would have been ecstatic if he had lived to see this. The mystery of this villa has been solved: a secret passage and a chest of ancient books. I suspect they are extremely rare works."

Andy Mo stepped closer and examined the leatherbound copies Michael was stacking on the table.

"*Aureliae occultae philosophorum*", he read. "*Symbola aureae mensae duodecim nationum*. These are alchemical works", he explained. "To a practitioner, these instructions are more valuable than gold. If you understand them correctly and work in accordance with them, you can make gold yourself."

However, the books weren't just about alchemy – most of them dealt with the subject of magic and astrology.

"The books here are all much older than the ones in the library", Andy Mo noted. "A priceless treasure for a researcher and collector. If you sell these, you'll be rid of much of your debt."

"My God, what luck!" rejoiced Michael, who could hardly believe it. "The previous owner obviously hid them from the Nazis during the war. They clearly didn't bring him any luck, as he still perished in a concentration camp. Under Hitler, anyone who dealt with such subjects was imprisoned and had their property confiscated."

Then Michael took another thick leather folder from the chest. It contained old manuscripts on parchment. Curious, Andy Mo approached and explained that they were documents and protocols concerning the Order of the Templars. There were also notes of a more recent date in between them, presumably from the builder of the house. Finally, they discovered a strange, ornate brass object at the bottom of the chest.

"That's an astrolabe", Christian noted. "We used to have one in our shop. In the old days it was used by astrologers to calculate horoscopes, when there were no tables of houses and celestial positions. Today you can find the daily position of the planets in the so-called 'ephemerides'. They're even calculated by NASA."

"Since when have you been interested in astrology?" asked Leif in surprise. "Do you know anything about it?"

"No, but I was in the shop when we sold this thing. The buyer explained to me how it worked – he was an antiquarian who regularly stops by for books, a certain Büchli."

"Büchli?" exclaimed Michael. "Is that Büchli from the Büchli and Wolfe bookshop – a gaunt old guy with a long white chin beard like old Chinese men wear in pictures?"

"Exactly", Christian confirmed. "He told me that he's a bookworm himself. 'Never mess with books,' he warned me once. 'You'll become a slave to the spirits hidden within them.'"

"That's what my grandfather used to say too. He said if you have more than a thousand volumes, you don't own them – they own you. The two knew each other, incidentally. When my grandfather bought this house, Büchli also wanted to buy it. However, he couldn't raise the necessary amount. The bank director who refused us the loan told me that yesterday. He's still after the villa."

"Or after this chest here", Andy Mo agreed. "That leaves us with another suspect. Maybe he knew something about the secret passageway and the hidden treasure; Krux had a suspicion in that direction. I think we're slowly getting to the bottom of the mystery."

"I can pay the bookworm a visit right now", volunteered Yks, who was busy with one of the old works. "Or we can call him and tell him about the chest. He'll be thrilled about it and come right away. Maybe he'll buy one of these musty old tomes off you, then you can pay the next instalment and you'll be off the hook for a quarter."

But Andy Mo dismissed him with a wave.

"First Goldstein. That's where we're most likely to find a concrete clue. But we'll wait another hour before we call him. My second sight is better in the dark." Only Leif understood the joke and grinned.

Meanwhile Kathi was curiously examining the leather folder with the loose leaves of parchment. On the very top she found an oversized horoscope drawing which not only depicted the planets and astrological fields, but also a park landscape. As she looked more closely at the picture, which was painted in the early medieval style and had no perspective, she realised that it was Michael's property. Andy Mo's boulder was depicted, as well as the old villa. Only the walls, though – the house was still under construction. Various tools were lying around: a trowel, a spirit level, and a plumb line, as well as a floorplan which was spread out and weighted down with a compass and square. The picture seemed older than the other drawings and documents in the chest. It must have been made earlier.

Kathi looked in fascination at the parchment leaf. The only person in the garden was a gardener who was planting a rose bush. Next to him was a watering can, and scattered in the grass were his tools: a planting stick, a rake to loosen the soil, and an artfully shaped pair of scissors to prune the roses. The colours of the flowers shone so vividly that you thought nature was alive: you could literally smell the fragrance of the flowers. A large fountain and an old-fashioned balance scale were drawn in the middle of the strange horoscope; the two scale pans were hanging to the right and left of the fountain down to the very bottom of the strange drawing. Above one of the pans, Jesus Christ was floating in an aura of radiant light, raising his hand in blessing. On the other, dark side, enthroned on an unhewn stone, was a strange figure whose arms and legs seemed to have grown together with the boulder below them. He wore a crown on his bearded head, and his sad eyes were fixed in the distance, lost in thought. On the old man's forehead was a blood-red heart, which suddenly began to pulsate. Then he looked at her. Kathi was startled and froze. Time had stopped. Nothing moved; only the faint splashing coming from the fountain punctuated the eerie silence. The fountain was uncovered, and in its dark water the stars of a constellation were reflected. A hypnotic power seemed to emanate from the murky depths. It was as if the stars were glittering and moving, slowly but surely turning in circles like the Milky Way in space. The two scale pans also rose and fell as if time was breathing through them, and a strange vibration filled the room. It came from the taut strings of the balance scale, and it gave the impression that the whole world was hanging from them. At first it was only a faint sound, as soft as cobwebs; then it became louder, more insistent, as if the overstrained nerve fibres of a tortured person were screaming and struggling. Was there no one there to hear it? The balance scale was a harp of horror – who was playing it? The room began to spin around Kathi; she was overcome by dizziness, and she felt as if a suction was pulling her into the dark fountain. She cried out and the parchment leaf slipped from her hands before she fainted. Michael just managed to catch her, so she didn't hurt herself.

Andy Mo rushed over and stroked her forehead several times with his hand.

"That was too much for her", he murmured. "First last night, and now being confronted again with the passageway and the chest. Bring her something to drink. Quickly."

Miri Li handed her a glass of water and Kathi slowly regained consciousness.

"The fountain," she groaned, "and that sorrowful look. That was Baphomet. Where is the drawing?" Kathi searched around for it. Yks spotted the parchment leaf, which had glided under the cupboard; he placed it on the table.

"She's right. That's Baphomet. And that's how the Freemasons and Templars portray him as well. The same depiction of him is also in the Book of the Master. How did the Bearded One end up on a plan of this house? Who built it?"

The others approached, but no one said a word. Everyone recognised the image of Baphomet. How had it come to be there? Were they in a former Templar hideout? As usual, Leif broke the spell.

"I'm hungry", he declared. "Let's call it a night and go over to the cosy kitchen. In any case, the annex is not on this mysterious plan."

Michael nodded.

"I've prepared a delicious vegetable soup. There's buttered bread, cheese, and peppers to go with it. And for dessert, fruit salad.

RECIPE

VEGETABLE SOUP
For about 4 people

Ingredients:
2 onions, 2 leeks, 2 carrots, 1 piece of celery, parsley, 2 potatoes, 1 clove of garlic, 1 stock cube, salt, nutmeg, olive oil.

Preparation:
Chop onions and vegetables and fry in olive oil. Crumble the stock cube and add. Pour in about 1.5 litres of water, add salt, and simmer gently for about half an hour. Remove the vegetables and puree them very finely with some of the soup and the crushed garlic clove using a hand blender. Mix again with the rest of the soup and serve. Serve with buttered bread topped with cheese and green and yellow pepper strips.

FRUIT SALAD

Ingredients:
1 can of sweetened fruit cocktail from the supermarket, 1 apple, 1 banana, 1 kiwi, 2 oranges

Preparation:
Put the contents of the can into a large bowl. Cut the fruit into small pieces and add it to the bowl, then add some orange or mango juice. Serve with whipped cream.

GOOD AND EVIL

"Who were these Templars?" asked Christian after they had eaten. "And who is Baphomet? What do we know about him? Does he really exist, or is he just a legendary figure like the devil?"

Andy Mo thought for a long time before answering.

"Well, the Templars lived in the twelfth century. They were Crusaders. They formed a Christian order which looked after pilgrims in the Holy Land, and their members were into magic and mysticism. The order soon had an enormous amount of money at its disposal. This made it too powerful for the Pope, who had them all executed. The reason given was that the Templars worshipped the devil."

"Was that true?" asked Leif. "Or was it just a pretext to get hold of their wealth?"

"Nobody knows exactly. For the Templars, Baphomet was the ancient, eternally young spirit of nature. Baphometus means nothing other than 'the man with the beard'. The All-Father in nature, who animates, destroys, and reshapes it. But because he is so closely fused with it, he can never leave it, and he only attains his consciousness within it. Thus he remains forever a Shadow, because – like a shadow – he is dependent on matter. However, since humans also seem to attain their consciousness only in a material body and survive only thanks to nature, the Templars did indeed worship Baphomet like a god."

Leif interrupted him. "But surely that means that not everyone sees Baphomet as the spirit of evil? If you see it as the Templars did, then Baphomet is closer to us than any other distant god."

"I wouldn't see it that way", said Andy Mo. "Baphomet probably isn't a spirit at all. And that's what makes him so dangerous. We spirits don't know him. None of us have ever seen him. He exists only as a Shadow, and he would be nothing if humans didn't cast shadows whose outlines are also the outlines of Baphomet and his princes. Nevertheless, he possesses more power than all other spirits. For he is everywhere where a shadow falls. But he needs humans and lives on what arises from their nature."

"Then how is it possible that he can oppress us?" asked Christian, astonished. "How does he defeat humans? What ensures his power?"

"His invisibility", Andy Mo answered immediately. "He seduces you without you realising it. He tempts you, inflames your passions, or saps your energy. He reinforces your weaknesses, such as selfishness, laziness, or fearfulness. He simply traces your thoughts, desires, and cravings and makes you feel everything more strongly: fear or confidence, love or hate, lust or displeasure, impatience and anger. This leads to excess, because anything which is too much or too little escapes your control and degenerates, and therefore it is bad. Personal emotions follow the spirit like shadows, and the great Shadow lives on them.

"In this way he succeeds in turning even harmless idealists into foolish, blind fanatics who unwittingly disturb the peace and sow hatred and discord in the name of some god. He even turns well-intentioned people into his minions. Instead of acting consciously of their own accord, many people become their own shadows and are motivated by their unconscious impulses, ideals, habits, and drives. If people controlled their thoughts, feelings, and emotions, Baphomet would have no power over them.

"And that is precisely the goal of all magical training. As I said:

we don't engage in magic to change the world or to summon spirits. Spiritual training is solely for the purpose of changing yourself so that the world and its shadows can no longer change you in accordance with their will. The spirit of evil is just as real as you and I and all other spirits. Evil is even closer to you than you think. For it is within you. It is inside each and every one of you. And it is constantly striving to seduce you. Whenever you stray from a good intention, act against your conscience, allow yourself to be driven by negative moods, act impatiently, selfishly, or recklessly, in short: act as you did not actually wish to act, a spirit of evil has seduced you."

"Does evil really have more power in the world than God?" asked Leif, and the others were also wondering the same thing. Andy Mo explained:

"It's not about God or the Lord of Darkness, it's about people's freedom to choose between good and evil.

Baphomet is probably no worse than the other gods and attendant spirits of the spiritual world. They all live from the energies of human beings in one way or another. Conversely, we also need the beings of the Hierarchy. The dark powers seduce people, and that moves us, while the powers of light illuminate (that's reason). Only by inspiration do the gods and demons move the world. They never intervene directly. They can awaken impulses which produce lust, for example, or which encourage you to control lust. They can supply thoughts which lead you astray, or they can impart knowledge which prevents that from happening. They can awaken ideas which evoke feelings, be they positive or negative, selfless or egoistic, but it's always the human being who must act. Humans are the only free beings in creation. All spirits envy you for that reason. You have freedom in your thinking, in your decisions, preferences, and goals, and you can change them independently at any time if you so desire."

"But most of us would much rather just let ourselves go", Michael said. "It's much easier. And besides, we can never get enough – we probably have Baphomet to thank for that as well. I just wonder what he gains by seducing people into these excesses."

"He thrives on it", explained Andy Mo. "Anything which is too much or too little finds no restraint and ends up in his realm. It falls to the Shadow. It becomes evil, as people say."

"I see", pondered Michael. "Too much courage becomes over-confidence and leads to excess. Too much caution paralyses you, but without fear there would be no brake on your actions. Even fear is good if it isn't felt excessively strongly, and courage becomes bad as soon as it leads to carelessness. Without the instinct of self-preservation, it is unlikely any living creature would survive. In animals we speak of instinct, but in human beings many things degenerate into pure egoism." "That's not the whole problem", said Andy Mo. "Anyone who produces for the Shadow Realm is automatically connected to the twelve Shadow Princes. The Shadow power has many names and guises. This connection intensifies over time, and if someone is associated with one of the princes long enough, it becomes ever easier for that prince to seduce them into further excesses."

"That explains why leaders of people become dictators", Michael reflected. And Kathi added: "And why you can develop a habit so quickly. Especially the pleasant things in life. I had given up on snacking, but for a few days now I've been eating a piece of chocolate every evening again. And every day it gets a little bit bigger." She shook her head. "When I think there's an invisible being snacking along with me, I immediately lose my appetite."

"So with every thought and every impulse you should ask yourself which of the spirit parasites you're attracting", Miri Li noted with a shudder. "But I still can't believe that we're the milking cows of invisible beings. I have problems with this new theory."

"It's not such a new idea", Yks said. "Even in ancient times, the gods were seen as the shepherds and guardians of humankind. Socrates mentions this in a conversation with his students about suicide, which was already forbidden at that time." The clever bird had flown onto the table from the curtain rod on which he usually sat, and he lectured: "As Socrates said to his pupil Cebes, 'So if one of your herd should kill itself when you had not indicated that you wished it to die, you too would certainly be angry with it and punish it if you could' – end of quote."

"Thank you, Professor", Kathi said. "But how are we supposed to do it then? On the one hand we feed Baphomet and the gods if we dance to their tune, and so we lose power to them. But on the other hand we need them to inspire us to act, and to motivate us to do things."

"This is indeed an art", said Andy Mo. "As always, the good lies in the middle: using your skills without becoming one-sided; following your ideals without being fanatical; being critical of your impulses without stopping them altogether; not being seduced by the world and its temptations against your will, yet not withdrawing completely from the world. Always keep a distance from your thoughts and feelings and thus from the influence of demons and gods. Ensure balance and don't think or want the same thing for too long. Also tolerate opposing opinions and consciously develop qualities and abilities within yourself which are foreign to you. Evil exists in the world, but you don't have to choose to do it."

Kathi nodded.

"Even if things really are this way and we're grazing in the shadow of Baphomet, there is still the GOOD SHEPHERD. I believe in Christ too. And I sense him: he's much closer to me than this Prince of Shadows. I feel him within me – not always, but often. Temptations seem to come from the outside and seduce you, but this inner voice of conscience is inside me."

"Kathi's right", Michael agreed. "There must also be a balancing, restoring force. Attraction and repulsion, light and darkness: it's a law of nature. And everyone has the opportunity to choose between good and evil. Isn't that what makes life interesting? No power in the world can take away your free will."

"I believe that, deep down, even the evil spirits long for Christ", Miri Li speculated. "Perhaps Baphomet also just wants to be loved and redeemed."

Leif mocked her:

"Love, light, and scrambled eggs, are the good gods' humble dregs." For some time, Leif had been like a changed person. Andy Mo glanced at him briefly. Christian shook his head, while the others remained silent. Leif pretended to be remorseful. "Sorry, Miri Li – I didn't mean to offend you. I don't mean the Christ who was probably a great magician. What disgusts me so much is this hallelujah nonsense of the New Age movement. With their simplistic beliefs, their followers are no different from all the other stupid sectarians. They believe the world is good and God will fix everything, but just look at the world. It's ruled by criminals, and there is no justice. It can't be that simple. If I interpret light as knowledge and love as compassion, it's precisely these two qualities which are most lacking in the world at the moment. And I doubt if it has ever been any different – the other day I was reading a book by Barbara Tuchmann about the Middle Ages called *The Distant Mirror*. You shouldn't close your eyes to evil. If there really are these divine spheres of love and light, then they're certainly not on this planet. Just look at this world. It's all just crime, corruption, and oppression. All of it perfectly legal, whether it's politics, economics, or religion. In the past they called it the mafia, today it's lobbying by interest groups. If you were the good Lord, would you be satisfied with your work? I wouldn't be, in any case."

Everyone fell silent. They felt Leif was right. "Maybe he's not even finished with his work yet", Kathi pondered. "Or maybe he expects people to help him with it."

"All the more reason to work for good", Miri Li replied. "But I didn't mean the hallelujahs of the New Age sectarians. I'm thinking of the deep faith which comes from the heart. Given the fact that this faith exists, and that there is genuine compassion which makes people act selflessly, surely there must also be a spirit and good spirits which correspond to this light." And then she added quietly: "Every person has the opportunity to choose which spirit to serve in every second." "That was a beautiful closing statement", said Andy Mo. "I think we'll leave it at that. The mystery of evil cannot be solved by theory. We won't find any definitive answers to these questions. But the very fact that we're able to think about them is a step towards liberation; and the fact that we can believe in goodness is something of a miracle." Andy Mo rubbed his forehead and closed his eyes. "Actually, we should call Goldstein now as we planned, but I'm too tired to do so. I'm afraid I can't concentrate. If you don't mind, let's postpone the whole thing until tomorrow."

Miri Li asked anxiously how they could help him. But Andy Mo waved her off. "I'm just tired. Living between two worlds is exhausting." Then he dissolved and disappeared into his refuge.

THE BAPTISM OF FIRE

Andy Mo wasn't going to get any rest that night either. First he fell into a fitful sleep and had a terrible dream: Yks was trapped in his cage again, surrounded by raging flames and shouting something at him which he didn't understand. The desperate cawing grew louder and louder, and when he woke up drenched in sweat, he still had the cries of the raven in his ears. And it wasn't a dream, it was reality. Yks was reflected in the window of his boulder, fluttering his wings excitedly.

"It's burning! Miri Li! The house is on fire!"

In an instant, Andy Mo was wide awake and had glided up to the human realm in a flash. The bird was all ruffled up. He smelled of smoke and some of his feathers were singed.

"I couldn't wake her up", he cawed desperately, coughing as if he were choking. "You must get to her. Hurry, or it will be too late. I've already called the fire brigade."

The agitated bird was still stammering something unintelligible, but Andy Mo understood the situation. What they had feared had come to pass. He had expected it and was prepared; without thinking twice, he aimed in Miri Li's direction, focused on her, and transported himself into her vicinity. But he landed in front of the house on the street, not next to her. The flames had thrown him back. The smoke and heat were like an impenetrable wall for him – as an earth spirit, he was no match for the element of fire.

Powerless, he stood in front of the burning building and didn't know what to do. When he saved the nixie in the water, he had simply surrendered himself up. He had passively followed the undertow that had swept him and Amue away, as he was willing to dissolve himself in order to save her. Back then, his feelings had carried him forwards. But now in the fire it was different. Here too he had to sacrifice himself, but it wasn't selflessness and devotion which were called for – it was courage and strength. Now nothing was pushing him; he himself had to mobilise his energy and plunge into the flames like a warrior. He had to decide: "Me or you?", and consciously, of his own free will, risk his life. Did he want to save Miri Li or preserve his own life? No earth spirit can break the power of fire. He had learnt that at school. All he had to do was to retreat to his spirit world and he would be out of danger.

But was he still an ordinary earth spirit like the others? He had escaped Baphomet's Shadow Realm. He had survived the elements of water and air unscathed. And he had learnt to move in the human realm. Didn't he also feel the fire within him? Wasn't the unbridled power to defeat Baphomet ignited within him, and hadn't the passion of love long since blazed in every fibre of his being? Nothing would prevent him from saving Miri Li.

The lower floor of the house was already burning in several places. The curtains and other easily flammable objects were already on fire. The heat increased suddenly, and a windowpane shattered, but there wasn't any sign of Miri Li. It was dark in her room on the top floor. She was asleep. If she didn't wake up immediately, she would suffocate helplessly in the poisonous smoke. He had to get her out of this hell before the fire brigade arrived.

It was deliberation rather than fear which was holding him back. He searched for an escape route which was open to him. In his mind he assessed the possibilities and then made the decision: they could use the rear exit which led into the courtyard and garden. The conflagration hadn't reached this area yet.

The decision to save Miri Li was made, and it catapulted him directly into the inferno. A bright, dazzling light flashed and blinded all his senses. A hellish heat burnt every one of his cells. He knew he had to die, but as long as he was alive he fought his way courageously through the flames. The alien element pierced him like jagged arrows. Pitiless, the heat took his breath away. Dying in water or in the air would have been merciful, he thought – there he would have dissolved or evaporated. But in the fire, he burned. The searing pain cut him like a thousand sharp knives. He felt every single cell detaching from him and he burst in every conceivable direction. There was no escape from this flaming hell. Yet his love for Miri Li was greater than his fear of pain and death. He could not die, not yet. And strangely, he did not die. The power of his will was transformed into an indestructible spirit and lent him a sure footing for his 'I'. His will lent him the substance which did not burn, protecting his consciousness from the destruction of the blaze.

The flashover blew out and ignited the last objects that were not yet burning. But despite the inferno, he was surrounded by an impenetrable, sooty darkness. Not even the flames could be seen through the dense smoke. No human being could find their way around here anymore. Andy Mo crawled on the ground, where there was a little less smoke. He bravely struggled forward, and it felt as if eternities were passing. But he made it to the top floor sooner than he had expected. There he found Miri Li motionless in her smoke-filled room. With his concentrated thought power he roused her from her sleep, but the girl was completely dazed. If he had been a human being, he would have simply grabbed her and carried her downstairs. But he reached into the void as he took her in his arms. She was too heavy. He couldn't condense himself that much, and he reached through her without grasping her. Desperate, he tried to draw her attention to him, and eventually she felt his presence. Now she reached out her hands to him herself, and he felt her touch. It was a completely new sensation for him. For the first time somebody touched him in this way in the earthly world, and he felt love and life. She had given him something of her living substance; he knew they would survive the fire. Joyous, he took her by the hand and she followed him. A minute later they were out in the open, sinking exhausted into the dewy grass.

They sucked the cool night air into their tortured lungs as if they were thirsty. An explosion shook the house, windowpanes rattled, and the fire brigade's sirens could be heard in the distance.

Miri Li was completely out of breath. She was still holding his hand, and she looked gratefully into his eyes. Then she rested her head on his shoulder. She said nothing, and he was glad of that, because now any words would have been wrong and would have destroyed what her wordless gesture had accomplished. "I love you", he thought, and she felt what he could not say. "I love you, Miri Li, but I know..." – but she closed her eyes and shook her head. Then she kissed him very gently on his lips.

Tyres screeched outside the house; it was Miri Li's parents. Embracing their daughter happily, they did not see her rescuer. Then the first fire engines arrived.

Andy Mo waved goodbye to his girlfriend and withdrew. He was exhausted. Nevertheless, he felt as if he had been reborn. He sensed he was no longer the same as before. First, in the intermediate realm, he had defeated the paralysing power of darkness and conquered the densest layer of the earth, the place where life no longer existed. Then he had plunged through the waters of the nixies without dissolving and had entered the human realm. He had also flown through the air without losing himself in lightness, and now he had survived the burning heat of the fire element, dying and rising again as a spirit in the dazzling light. Consecration through the four elements was usually reserved for human beings. He had experienced it.

In fact he wanted to be alone now. But first he had to tell Michael and Christian about Miri Li's rescue. Yks had surely informed his friends about the arson attack.

*

When he arrived, they were just calling a taxi to take them to the burning house.

"She's been saved", Andy Mo said, dropping exhausted into an armchair. "We can't help her any further for now. There were no deaths or injuries. Her parents are with her." Then he looked around nervously. "Do you have anything to drink? I think I'm dying of thirst."

They all stared at him. Yks flew over and sat on his shoulder. "Since when do spirits get thirsty? Are you alright? Have you been hurt?" The bird couldn't believe it and was completely beside himself. "Just don't start with beer", he warned urgently. "That almost cost me my life."

Michael put a glass of water on the table. But when Andy Mo tried to drink, it flowed right through him and all ended up on the floor. Andy Mo shook his head in amazement at his human desires, which he obviously couldn't satisfy. But then, to his surprise, the need was satisfied anyway.

"The heat", he tried to explain. "Probably an earthly reflex to the flames. I just experienced hell. Or perhaps not. I think I was in heaven."

Yks tapped his head.

"I hope you didn't blow a fuse."

Andy Mo looked at him reproachfully. "What do you know about love?" he thought, but of course he didn't say it.

"I think you'll have to excuse me now. I'm tired. I'm going to retire to my retreat." He raised his hand in parting and waved to them as casually as the Austrian Emperor.

"Sleep well", Michael said, and the other two also wished him a good night. But Andy Mo didn't move from the spot. He just flickered briefly and became invisible, but he couldn't pass through the wall. It was only on the third attempt that he managed to jump into his spirit world.

THE FORMULA OF NOTHINGNESS

Andy Mo was troubled. He wasn't the same as before since he'd been living in the human realm. He attributed the weakness to his exhaustion and the unfamiliar stirrings he was suddenly feeling first-hand, but how was it going to end? It seemed earth spirits were more hindered than inspired by love. He wasn't human. And he wasn't here for his pleasure. He had a mission to accomplish.

Despite his tiredness, sleep was out of the question. Everything within him was unsettled. What further consequences would the consecration through the elements have for him? He was already aware that he would never be the same as before, but the idea of struggling with feelings upset him. He had enough problems as it was. At the same time, however, he wanted nothing more than to be human. And that was what worried him the most. But the situation had also become worse for the others. The attacks from the Shadow Realm were becoming more and more brazen, and now even the lives of his friends were threatened.

Unable to relax, he decided to sift through the old documents and drawings from the chest. He had brought them to his refuge the day before to take a closer look at them. He leafed through the folder attentively; it mainly contained the descriptions and sigils of spirits, as well as a ritual of the old Templar Order whose members had tried to summon these spirits. That wasn't so interesting to him. But then he paused: an ancient parchment lay before him, inscribed with Egyptian hieroglyphics. It was probably a copy of a scroll from the Old Kingdom which had long since decayed away. And what he read made him tremble. It said something about children: *"The children will be the ones who will free the world from the power of evil"*, and as he read he could have rejoiced. After deciphering all of it, he knew: in front of him was the missing page his father had been looking for. It must have been written centuries ago. The characters were hard to discern, and the parchment threatened to crumble away if you touched it.

Andy Mo felt confident again. He decided to transcribe the text into contemporary human writing and immediately set to work; he wanted to surprise his friends with it. They were on the right track. So this house and the secret passageway had been in his father's sights, and at some point he would have tracked down the chest and come here. They could try to follow the trail in the reverse direction. By morning he had finished his work and translated the message from the realm of the past. Satisfied, he read what he had written:

EXCERPT FROM THE DOCUMENT

"It will be the children who free humanity from the dark forces which rule the world. Only children's souls cast no shadows. They have no prejudices. They are open to new thoughts. They are unprejudiced, flexible, and adaptable. They are innocent because they lack the experience which imposes responsibility.

If they grow up without fear of a 'hell' or death and instead train their spiritual abilities, then through their thinking they will not only change themselves and their soul gardens, but they will also change the entire world, including the otherworldly spheres of the gods and demons. Only children can defeat the evil which rules the world.

If children already learn to consciously control their bodies and their urges of their own free will, to refine their souls and train their spirits, this world and the hereafter will no longer be the same.

THE "FORMULA OF NOTHINGNESS"
CONSCIOUS BEING AND IMAGINATIVE POWER
MULTIPLIED BY FAITH
DIVIDED BY RECEPTIVITY
EQUALS SPIRITUAL REALITY.

But then he hesitated. Something wasn't right! Andy Mo looked at the second page more closely and now he discovered a place he had overlooked before. A word had been changed in the Formula of Nothingness. Instead of 'receptivity', it had originally said 'affection', then 'love', and later 'feeling'. And instead of 'faith', it had previously said 'light'. Someone had been scribbling on this page like you do on a blackboard and then they had erased it again. The whole thing had previously had a different meaning. The production of secret inks had long been known to humans; they knew how to make writing visible and invisible again. Who had written this document and who had changed the text afterwards? The paper wasn't as old as the parchment on which the prophecy about the children had been written. The statement that only children can save the world had been written in the script of the initiates and was undoubtedly genuine. Andy Mo could determine that exactly. But the Formula of Nothingness was written on different paper using Phoenician characters. The letters were written from right to left – a technique still used by magicians as a secret script today, as Andy Mo knew.

"That twists the meaning like a mathematical formula", Andy Mo thought. The whole thing reminded him of another formula, but he couldn't figure it out straightaway. Then he had it! Einstein. There was a formula that was supposed to explain how an effect can act on other distant processes. It concerned mass and speed and the energy which was contained within them.

"Energy equals mass times the speed of light squared, and vice versa", he thought he remembered. The Formula of Nothingness also contained 'plus' and 'times' and 'divided by', but there was no 'squared'. Back then only gnomes knew the complicated systems of calculation which Einstein only used much later. Someone had obviously been philosophising, and rather than using numbers, they had experimented with the concepts which determine human consciousness. Mathematics and philosophy were Andy Mo's forte, and so he managed to solve the riddle surprisingly quickly.

Suddenly illumination came to him. He had solved the mystery concerning the Formula of Nothingness. His father hadn't been searching for a written page on which this formula was written;

rather, he was looking for the solution to the problem! It may well have been the king himself who had deposited this text in the human realm centuries ago. The correct formula was not yet known at that time; this mystery had not yet been solved. The king was looking for the answer to the question of being, and he wanted to represent the fundamentals of consciousness in a formula. The fact that he was seeking it in the human realm rather than thinking it over and researching it in his gnome laboratory meant that the solution could only be found in the human realm. "But why?" Andy Mo wondered. Everything that came into being on this Earth had been prepared on the ethereal planes by the attendant spirits and elemental spirits. Their knowledge surpassed that of human beings. He could have figured it out much more easily in the spiritual world.

A hot shudder abruptly overcame him. He had the solution and was deeply moved: of course the key to this secret lay in the human realm. But it wasn't hidden in a secret hiding place – it was within human beings themselves. People had to search for it within themselves. You had to be human to understand the secret; only in a human body was it possible to experience and understand the mystery of being and non-being.

"Alas, humans don't know what they're looking for", Andy Mo thought sadly to himself. "They're searching for the formula of matter, space, and time rather than the data of the spiritual world and eternity. And he himself was an earth spirit, not a human being, so he would never discover the secret Formula of Nothingness. This mystery and its solution were reserved for human beings; this was another task he could not solve. What had he achieved so far? His father was still missing; he had got his friends into trouble; and he himself was entangled and trapped in foolish, hopeless feelings of love.

Deep sadness overcame him once again. Nothing seemed more desirable to him than to be human, yet nothing was further from him than that.

EVERY BOOK HAS A SOUL

Before the sun had risen, Andy Mo had already squeezed his way up through his boulder into the human realm to do his exercises in the red glow of dawn. In the last few days he had neglected them, and he was feeling the consequences. Now it was easier for him to transport himself to the surface than to return to his Gnome Kingdom from there. It used to be the other way around. His stay among the humans had changed him more rapidly than he had feared. Not only had he become denser, but he was also taller. He wondered how much longer he would be able to wander back and forth between worlds. He had to hurry to complete his mission: the time left for him to find his father was running out.

But they had also made a little progress. The discovery of the chest had almost cost Kathi her life, but it pointed to a new lead they could follow. Andy Mo even entertained the possibility that his father had also found the chest, and that he may have been interrupted at the last moment and prevented from bringing its contents to light. The ancient texts probably came from the highest hierarchy of the spirit world and must have been transmitted to a human being many centuries earlier. They were surely the records the Gnome King had been seeking.

So now Andy Mo was pleased with what he had achieved after all. He knew that even if the formula was wrong, he had solved the puzzle of what it was all about. It made him sad, because he also knew that he would never find out the true wording of the formula, but thanks to his help, perhaps his friends would figure it out. Now that he could explain to them what they needed to look for, it should eventually be possible for them because of their magical training. And the foreclosure could be avoided for the time being if Michael sold the books from the chest.

Andy Mo felt that they should contact the antiquarian bookseller Büchli that day, not only to sell the books for the best possible price, but also because there was a suspicion that he was working with their adversaries. In any case, he was after the villa. He seemed to be involved in the case in some way, and they had to risk it. Maybe a lead from him would lead to his father.

Initially Andy Mo wanted to go straight to the bookshop to spy on the antiquarian's thoughts. But then he dismissed that plan: perhaps Büchli had been seeking the chest for many years, and if he saw it he would be more likely to reveal what he knew. Emotions release thoughts which you would otherwise keep to yourself.

Michael interrupted his thoughts: "Good morning, Andy Mo!" He had just returned from his jog. Andy Mo hadn't even noticed that he had left the house. "Are you feeling better today? Did you get some sleep, or were you up rescuing pretty girls from the fire or the underworld again?"

"Enough joking around. Listen, I have some news", said Andy Mo, reporting in detail what he had discovered. "It's no coincidence that the documents concerning the secret of the children and the Formula of Nothingness were hidden right here in this house. The plaque with the well and the old picture of the house your grandfather bought must be part of it. It makes sense, it's a secret code we have to crack."

Michael was impressed and agreed with him.

"It really looks like the Gnome King followed specific signs. You ended up here, after all. We need to take a closer look at that underground passageway – maybe it will lead us to our goal. But first I'm going to call the antiquarian bookseller. I hope you're right and he'll buy the books from me so that I can pay off part of the debt. I don't expect anything from my father in the near future. Last night I was informed that he's seriously ill with malaria. He won't be able to return to the mountains for a long time."

Even though it was so early in the morning, Büchli answered immediately. And when he heard what the call was about, he wanted to come right away. They arranged to meet at 4 p.m., when the other friends would also be present. Then Michael had to go to school, and Andy Mo went over to the library to read.

*

Mr Büchli arrived on time, and they were already eagerly awaiting him. He was short and gaunt, and he walked bent over with a cane. He wore a silky black work coat and an old-fashioned beret, despite the early summer temperature. The long and sparse white beard on his chin was reminiscent of a Chinese man. He moved slowly and stiffly, as if in pain, and spoke in a chalky voice. Nevertheless, it was difficult to estimate his age because his vivid, flashing grey-blue eyes lent him a highly vigorous air. He got straight to the point.

"So where is the chest with the books, young man? I knew your grandfather – we were friends, you might say. We both searched for it for decades; he sought it in this house, and I looked all over the world. So he was right, the poor man. If he hadn't smoked so much, he'd still be alive. But I warned him. Where was the chest hidden? And where is it now?"

Büchli, who spoke Swiss German, clumsily slid a pair of large round glasses onto his nose and looked around searchingly. As he did so, he spotted the other friends and nodded to them.

"Aha, visitors! I hope I'm not disturbing the young people." Then he saw the chest and strode towards it. His hands fluttered like bats as he rummaged frantically through its contents. He took out the books which were still in the chest and placed them on the table with the others. Then he straightened up with difficulty and looked quizzically around.

"Documents – were there no documents?" The old man was visibly disappointed.

An inner voice held Michael back from saying anything. He exchanged a brief glance with Christian, and in silent agreement they decided not to reveal anything about their find.

"Documents? What kind of documents? Don't you like the books?"

Only now did the bookseller realise that he had been behaving tactlessly. He was visibly embarrassed. Irked, he searched for words to explain himself.

"Forgive my improper behaviour. The books are good. They are all scarce works. Rarities. Very valuable – but I already know them.

I was hoping to find private notes. Loose leaves, yellowed old manuscripts; it concerns a very specific manuscript."

The friends looked at him questioningly, pretending not to understand, and the bookseller understood: his hope had not been fulfilled. He slumped as if the strings of a puppet had been cut.

"May I sit down? I'm 92 years old. I get tired easily."

Leif quickly pushed one of the heavy leather chairs towards him and Kathi poured him a glass of apple tea.

"Is it something specific which you and Michael's grandfather were searching for in vain for decades?"

The old man shook his head slowly.

"The truth, young lady. We were looking for the truth. Whether that is anything in particular, I highly doubt it today; you can't find it in books, anyway." He took a sip and looked absent-mindedly at the leather-bound folios.

"Never start collecting books. Throw them away. Throw them all away, preferably in the trash so no one will ever find them. You think you own them, but in reality it's the other way around. I know many book lovers; they are my customers. They study, compare, collect, and hoard, and they don't realise that it's the books which are driving them, as if the sheep were tending their shepherd. They wander between their books and their dubious contents like they're in prison, chasing after them and still not getting enough. What they collect they can no longer read, let alone think about. I did the same. I'm still not cured.

"Books are receptacles of spiritual power. Every word is an active being, every sentence a world of its own. There are spirits in every book. The spirit of the author, the spirit awakened by the content and manifested in the readers' consciousness, and the spirit of all readers who engaged further with the ideas presented. Spirits can help, but they can also make you obsessed. It's no different with the spirits in books. When I realised this, I opened my bookstore, and then I was forced to part with books again. In the process I came to another important realisation. You also have to part with the opinions you've absorbed from the books. That's the only way to remain free for new ideas. These days I try to read my own thoughts."

He struck the ground energetically with his stick and looked around with his bright, flashing eyes.

"You're still young. Don't let an old man talk you into anything. You still have many books to read. Absorb the spirit in these thick tomes into your heads, but don't let it seduce you." Then he rose and was about to leave, but Michael begged him to stay.

"I was hoping you would buy the books from me. I need money urgently. If I don't pay the next instalment, everything here will be auctioned off soon. The books, the property, and the house."

The old man sank back into his chair.

"I know", he replied seriously and nodded. "I was offered the villa. If I still had the means, I would purchase everything – the books, the property, and the house – for the sake of the chest. Somewhere there must be a chest like this one, and that's the one I wanted. Within it lies the document I sought. It describes a formula: the formula of life and death. That's all I know, and your grandfather didn't know any more either. He was convinced the document was in this house. I came for those papers, but I can't buy the books. I have no money."

When Mr. Büchli saw their disappointed faces, he raised his arms helplessly.

"I'm really sorry, but I'm broke. I only found out yesterday. I speculated everything away on the stock market – or rather, Goldstein did. You might have heard about him on the evening news. He's wanted for theft, embezzlement, and murder."

They hadn't heard.

"Goldstein!" Michael exclaimed. "What about him? What do you have to do with that crook?"

"Goldstein is one of my best customers. Magic and alchemy – he's a friend of Hermetic science. I entrusted him with all my money. Until yesterday he was advised by an immensely successful investor. Now they've both disappeared: Goldstein and Rabe, that was the name of the man who provided him with stock market tips."

A mournful sound was heard from the curtain rod. Then there was a long silence.

Michael was close to telling the old man about the documents, but again something held him back.

"Maybe I'll find a good buyer for the books", the antiquarian promised, pulling his cap down over his almost bald head. Then he stood up and looked into the chest again. "This one work alone is worth a small fortune: *Statuta gallica summi magistri murariorum et rosaecrucianorum*, 17th January 1795 etc. The same work is located under number 15159 in the manuscript and incunabula collection of the National Library. I've studied it. It's a Lodge manuscript and describes how to make the Philosophers' Stone." The old man shook his head absent-mindedly. "Now if you will please call me a taxi. I am tired, I must go."

RECIPE

APPLE TEA

Four unsprayed apples. Remove the core. Cut apples into large pieces. Simmer apple pieces gently in a litre of water for five minutes (along with a thumbnail-sized piece of lemon peel or a slice of lemon, if desired). Remove from the stovetop and leave to infuse for twenty minutes. Strain and sweeten to taste.

*

"So Goldstein got away", Leif stated soberly after Büchli had left. "Baphomet's minions can't be taken out like normal criminals. The Shadow which protects them is simply more powerful than we are."

Andy Mo was also mulling over the situation, and he was in despair. The antiquarian bookseller who was supposed to buy the books was broke. They hadn't made any progress. He wondered if he should 'persuade' the bank manager to extend the loan to Michael's father; even though Michael had rejected the use of any magical influence, he saw no other way to help him. In the poor condition he was in, he probably couldn't lead Mr Freiwald to an emerald. He couldn't even transport himself to his refuge if he wanted to. Resigned, he summed things up:

"First Christian's father is robbed and driven to having a heart attack, then Miri Li's house burns down and she almost dies in the flames. And yesterday Kathi almost lost her life in the underground labyrinth. We're all so busy with our own worries that we can hardly concentrate on the goal we've set ourselves. I doubt whether I'll be able to complete my mission."

"I wish it was all just a bad dream", Miri Li sighed. "But the power of Baphomet is very real. We can't fight against this spirit. I'm already afraid of what he's planning to do to us next. Who will he target?"

"At least you managed to save me", Yks tried to interject with something positive. "So he's not all-powerful. All the same, I fear your worries are justified. I can feel an uneasy tugging in my left tail feather, you see. It only happens when danger is looming, but I can't locate it or see where it's coming from. We must remain vigilant."

None of those present could imagine how right he was; none saw the disaster which was to come, and which would tear apart their oathbound coterie. They were all still together.

"You've experienced a lot, Professor, and have more experience than we do. Is there no way to defeat this Shadow power?"
"Baphomet and his princes cannot be defeated", Yks grumbled. "He must be starved out. Evil will not disappear so long as it can hide within human nature. It is fed by humans, and only in humans can it be conquered and overcome."

"Then Baphomet's minions, who spread evil in the world through politics and economics, should be systematically eliminated", Leif said. "You obviously can't get at them by legal means."

"That would be wrong. For that is precisely how you would

supply the Princes of Darkness with new sustenance. You would then be acting entirely in their interests. As soon as you physically or emotionally hurt, humiliate, offend, anger, frighten or otherwise harm someone, the negative emotions which are released nourish the negative Shadow beings. But conversely, the positive feelings of joy, comfort, and compassion strengthen the constructive powers which ensure a balance of the existing order in the cosmos. Whenever someone makes life easier for someone else and brings them hope, Baphomet suffers a defeat in the world."

"That brings us back to morality", Miri Li rejoiced. "It suffices to behave virtuously and do good, as the religions teach. Where one spreads light, darkness fades."

But Yks added a note of caution.

"Unfortunately, that alone is not enough. The balance of power has shifted. Baphomet currently rules the entire world. Today you must fight to regain the power you've lost. But you shouldn't fight against the demons' minions like clueless fanatics; rather, you should fight against the evil within you. The first adversary you will have to deal with directly is yourself. Hatred, anger, fear and rage, ruthlessness, lies, avarice and greed, ruthlessness, laziness, slovenliness – there are many qualities which keep Baphomet and his princes alive if you nurture them. Above all, beware of hatred, for it instantly connects you to the power of destruction. Naturally it doesn't happen so quickly with laziness, addiction, or other bad habits, but then the contact with the spiritual underworld is all the more lasting. You must master yourselves and eradicate everything negative within you. The battle takes place within you, and you must be strict with yourself as you proceed. Outwardly, on the other hand, you follow the impulses of your compassion."

"Nothing is good unless you put it into practice", Leif pragmatically quoted Erich Kästner. "But before we think of making the world a better place, we should solve our own problems. We mustn't lose sight of our goals. We want to find and save the Gnome King, and we want to write a book for children which illuminates the secrets of the spirit world and magic. And we will do it, too –

we have sworn to do it, and no one shall stop us."

"Alright, so let's get to work!" exclaimed Yks, making a hand-clapping noise like Kleindienst (he was doing it with his voice, of course, but it sounded remarkably genuine). "Where do we start? What do we know? What can we do? Andy Mo thinks the king was here, or on his way here. What was he doing in this house? The documents in the chest must hold another secret. It can't be the formula because that's wrong or incomplete, as Andy Mo discovered. The secret of the children was already known to the king. And as an expert, he probably knew the alchemical instructions by heart. So why did he target this house? Where did he come from and where was he going?"

"Maybe we should take a closer look at the underground passageway", Michael suggested. "I imagine we might come across a clue down there which would lead us forwards." Everyone was immediately enthusiastic about the idea except for Kathi, who had reservations. She was afraid of descending into the underworld again after having just escaped unscathed.

"I'll study the documents again while you're down there. So many people have been looking for these papers, including Andy Mo's father, and I believe there's something in them that we've all overlooked."

"The records are still in my refuge", Andy Mo said. "I'll bring them up." He closed his eyes and began to flicker, as he always did when he was about to transport himself underground, but he didn't move. You could tell he tried several times, but he remained where he was.

"Bloody hell!" said the raven, imitating Leif's voice so that everyone was looking at Leif rather than him.

Eventually Andy Mo succeeded. He disappeared and reappeared shortly afterwards with the documents.

But meanwhile Kathi had changed her mind.

"I'm coming with you", she announced bravely, tucking the folder Andy Mo handed her into her backpack. "I'll look through the whole thing at home – I won't be able to concentrate on it now.

It's cold down there, so let's dress warmly."

Michael was already making sure they had adequate clothing and lighting. He brought torches and lanterns from the last summer festival. Soon the little expedition was ready to go, and Andy Mo operated the secret door's opening mechanism disguised as a goat's head. Cool, clammy cellar air and darkness wafted forbiddingly towards them.

In the light of the lanterns, the small chamber behind the library looked no less spooky than the day before. Deep shadows concealed the end of the stairs which led down into the tunnel. Michael patted Kathi approvingly on the shoulder: "Brave girl, I would have peed my pants in here."

Leif took care of Miri Li. She had fallen behind in the darkness, the candle in her lantern had gone out, and she dared not go any further. She was trembling with fear. He took her by the hand.

"We're just in a cellar. A normal old cellar tunnel." Suddenly the piercing whistle of an approaching train sounded. The raven had played another of his pranks. He had strapped on a small torch and now he was flying around while he made the sound of a plane. The spell was broken.

They followed the passageway until the first bend. Andy Mo felt through the walls in gnome fashion, but he couldn't locate anything out of the ordinary. Just earth, sand, and rock. Christian had taken the old ship's compass which stood as an ornament on the library mantelpiece, and he laid out a map showing the course of the tunnel. Beyond the bend the passage led slightly downwards, which they hadn't noticed without light on the previous day. Then they reached the spot where the tunnel divided.

"This is where it was", Kathi whispered, pointing to the alcove. "There it is." The others approached cautiously and stopped respectfully at some distance from the skeleton. The bones were scattered among scraps of fabric and remnants of clothing; the skull Kathi had felt the day before lay completely un-anatomically two metres away from the other bones. The raven hopped around excitedly and carefully inspected every corner.

"He hasn't been dead long", he expertly noted. "Thirty, forty years at the most. He didn't decompose; the rats disposed of him. Hence the bare bones, which should still have tissue attached if you compare them with the condition of the clothes." Something flashed in the light of his torch. It was a solid gold medallion hanging from a long, refined chain. On one side an elaborately stylised balance scale was engraved, and on the other the artist had depicted the constellation Libra with four small diamonds and two rubies. Yks recognised this immediately; not only was he an astrologer, but he was also well versed in astronomy.

Kathi approached and looked at the jewel with interest.

"Goldstein wore the same medallion together with the key he lost in the pool", she said with certainty. "He had a second chain with this pendant hanging from it. But it couldn't be Goldstein – you don't decompose that quickly."

Miri Li also came closer and looked at the find with interest. The reddish gold shimmered warmly in the glow of the lanterns. Something began to make sense in her mind, and then she had it.

"I've got it!" she exclaimed. "The same symbol is also hovering above the well and reflected in the mysterious water on that enigmatic drawing of Michael's house and property. Surely that can't be a coincidence."

"It's certainly strange", Yks confirmed. "The constellation isn't visible everywhere in the northern night sky. And it's usually depicted with only four stars. The two rubies are stars which appear to belong to the constellation visually, but which are actually far behind it at a great distance from the others. They're not normally assigned to the constellation."

"We keep coming across new puzzles rather than finding solutions", noted Christian, who had been very silent lately. "I feel like I'm in a film where I'm both a viewer and an actor at the same time."

"I feel the same way", Miri Li said. "Let's go back; I don't like this whole affair. In fact we should report the discovery of the body to the police."

"That's completely impossible", Michael said firmly. "Then they'll immediately want to come into the house and ask a lot of questions we can't answer. Now that we're here, I think we might as well explore where this secret passageway leads. That's what we've set out to do, and we should see it through to the end."

Initially they followed the tunnel which turned to the right, and they made good progress. The ground was dry, and the passageway was high enough for them to walk upright. But after about two kilometres it abruptly came to an end. The ceiling had collapsed and there was no way forward behind the rubble. The passage had been bricked up and a small but massive iron door blocked the way.

"End of the line!" called out the raven, who had flown ahead. "Now it's up to spirits like you, Andy Mo. Make yourself thin and go through the wall."

But Andy Mo failed to penetrate the solid matter. He was able to transport himself, so he disappeared, but then he flickered and bounced off the wall like a rubber ball. He tried repeatedly, but he couldn't get through. The friends watched his futile efforts with concern until Michael put an end to it.

"Don't strain yourself: you're overtired. Let it be. We'll try it another time. Then we'll tackle the rusty lock on the door. We've achieved enough for today."

"Yes, please", said Kathi. "Let's turn around already. I'm terribly cold and tired."

When they were gathered in the library again, they all had the impression that they'd been away for an eternity. Yet the whole adventure had taken no more than two hours. Kathi immediately compared the constellation on the jewel with the symbol on the drawing. Both glyphs matched each other exactly.

"I can't help thinking this is a hot lead. I don't know what it's pointing to, but we need to keep an eye on the constellation Libra."

"There's something behind that wall too", said Andy Mo. "I wasn't tired. I couldn't get through because something was obstructing me, almost like the spirit trap in Goldstein's villa. I'll have another look at that on my own." He didn't know now that it would be too late.

232

Michael wanted to prepare something for dinner, but they were all tired and exhausted. No one felt like staying any longer. Everyone was preoccupied with their own problems and thoughts. As twilight fell, the friends said their goodbyes and arranged to meet again the next day.

THE EMERALD

A strange silence hung in the air – or rather in the boulder, for Andy Mo had awoken in his refuge without realising it. He thought he was still dreaming when he realised in a daze that he was back in his spirit world. The night before he had tried several times to transport himself to his element, and when he failed he had lain down on the leather bench in the library to sleep.

Somewhere he was stuck fast to his thoughts, and feelings were stuck to those thoughts, forming a threatening world from which he could not break free. They were feelings of fear. He tried in vain to liberate himself from the swamp of shadowy moods and memories which he could neither grasp nor dispel. He thought he was in a hospital, lying in a bed, motionless and tied up, guarded by demons. Only slowly did he manage to separate himself from the images of the night which clung so persistently to his consciousness, and he finally realised where he really was: in his refuge, in his boulder, in the spirit world.

But his relief was short-lived. For suddenly he knew again that this clinic wasn't a figment of his imagination: it really existed. With a shudder he remembered the video recording of the experiments from the horror clinic, and he knew they had to keep looking for his father in that direction. At the same time, he also sensed a hidden warning of impending danger. He struggled to dispel the feelings of fear which still lingered within him as macabre remnants of the night.

He was glad that he'd woken up on his own plane. He hadn't told his friends about the problem yet, but at some point he had to confide his condition to them. They'd already noticed that it was difficult for him to transport himself into his world, but they didn't realise how much it was weakening him, and how he was finding it even more difficult after each unsuccessful attempt. They had only noticed that he had become denser, that sometimes they could touch him, and that he had grown almost as tall as they were.

Andy Mo stayed in his refuge. It seemed there wasn't much happening at the school. There was hardly any teaching so soon before the school trip, and Kleindienst was absent, so there was no fun to be had. Since he was currently in his element, he preferred to take the opportunity to finally lead Mr Freiwald to an emerald druse which would put an end to his financial problems. Time was running out. He had to find a suitable stone while he could still search for it. If he couldn't transport himself into his gnome world anymore, it would be too late. He could only do it while he was still within his element. He wouldn't find a gemstone so easily from the human realm.

But he had no idea if he could get that far. He had to travel halfway around the world to get to Muzo, a small town 160 kilometres from Bogota. He had examined it all very carefully on a globe. That's where he would find Mr Freiwald.

The fact he was currently ill wasn't necessarily detrimental for his plan. On the contrary: rather than condensing himself in the human realm, he could meet Mr Freiwald in the spiritual Borderlands – that is, in his dreamworld. Entangled in delirious fantasies, the human spirit exists on a plane of consciousness in which both the earthly and the spiritual worlds are mirrored and mixed together. This was going to make his work much easier and simpler. He could lead Mr Freiwald to the discovery site via a vision, which would be easier than working on him with thought packets and guiding him through the real world.

Andy Mo couldn't simply break a gemstone out of the mountainside and lay it at Mr Freiwald's feet. Even back in the time when elemental spirits and humans were in close contact and could see each other, spirit beings weren't allowed to change a person's fate with such a precious gift. And if they were urged to do so by a magician using a spell – or even forced to do so with a diabolical threat – the people concerned usually had to pay dearly for it later. Making your life easier with a spell has always been a costly affair. In the human realm, magic serves exclusively to train and research the spirit, not to change your circumstances. Using spiritual power to move nature is reserved exclusively for spirits. Andy Mo had already learnt that much. Under no circumstances are you allowed to interfere with the intended course of destiny or the existing laws of nature.

Andy Mo had made extensive preparations for this expedition, but he didn't know whether he would be successful. Too many unknown dangers lurked along the way. He also wasn't allowed to delve too deeply into his Gnome Kingdom, as he might not be able to find his way back. So he had to move along the undersurface of the Earth. But an ocean lay between the continents. For an earth spirit, this was an almost insurmountable obstacle. While it would be much easier for him to move through the human realm with mental leaps, if he couldn't transport himself into his element at his destination (which was likely in his current state) he wouldn't be able to search for a suitable gemstone there, and all his efforts would have been in vain. He also suspected it would be exhausting, *really* exhausting.

Andy Mo would have liked to say goodbye to his friends, but the risk of getting stuck in the human realm and not being able to return to his spirit world was too great. He hadn't yet figured out why the transition was easier for him at some times and harder at others. He suspected that it was related to astrological influences, and he planned to investigate this possibility. If it was then he could take advantage of favourable constellations in the future. He had no idea how much time he had left in which to switch between worlds, or when he would finally find his father.

So instead, he tried to inform Krux of his plans. But he couldn't reach his friend, even though he lived on his own spirit plane. The tree spirit wasn't responding to his thoughts. That, too, worried him. He couldn't ignore the fact that his mental abilities had been enormously impaired since he had been in the human realm. That wasn't a good omen. But despite this, Andy Mo still didn't lose heart. Determined, he packed up his things: his lamp, which illuminated the densest mineral kingdom for him, a map to orient himself and show what lay above him in the human realm, and the elixir. But then he placed the small glass bottle with the red liquid back into the stone from which he had taken it. After all, he would only be meeting Mr Freiwald in his dream world, not in the real world. He couldn't risk leaving his plane, nor could he risk materialising in a foreign land without the protection of his friends, and thus being at the mercy of Baphomet's minions.

Although Andy Mo didn't have much hope that it would succeed, he initially wanted to try to mentally leap his way along the undersurface of the Earth to his destination. Michael had shown him a lot of photos of the area and he knew exactly where to focus. A river divided the rugged mountain range where the emeralds were mined into two halves. On one side was a productive mine where exhausted, half-naked workers toiled all day like slaves for a monthly wage of $600; on the other side was the town.

Michael's father wasn't employed at the mine. Nor did he have his own staked claim; rather, he searched for the valuable green stones in the mountain wilderness without a concession. This was not without danger. It wasn't just corrupt policemen who were after illegal adventurers; there were also bandits, who were even more dangerous. In Muzo, no one left their house without a gun. Successful gem seekers and traders were murdered every month. So far, however, everything had gone well for Mr Freiwald. He lived in a simply furnished hut below a mighty rock face on the outskirts of the town. Andy Mo took aim at this wall of smooth blasted rock, and to his great surprise it caught him. He hadn't imagined it would be that easy.

He immediately began scanning the area for gems. It had to be a particularly beautiful emerald – the effort needed to be worth it.

Mr Freiwald had to be able to pay off the mortgage on his house with the proceeds, and it also needed to be enough to live on for a few years so that he could take better care of Michael. Finding a piece like that wasn't going to be easy, Andy Mo thought to himself. He focused on the lighter veins criss-crossing through the mountain. The white structure of the calcite vein in which emeralds are found felt very different from the empty grey rock. It enveloped the crystals growing within it like a protective womb. Andy Mo felt their living tingle and probed every crevice. He came across many beautiful specimens, but he had to find an emerald which was close to the surface. Mr Freiwald couldn't work with explosives and had to painstakingly break each chunk of rock out of the rockface with a pickaxe and an iron bar. Then he discovered what he was looking for: a vein divided upwards and downwards, forming an open cleft and ending in a narrow cave which a human could only just enter from the outside. The emerald was growing from the upper spur of the vein straight down from the ceiling. It was of indescribable beauty and enormous size.

The green colour of emeralds comes from chromium. The coloration began at the surface of the stone and spread a hypnotic shine, filling the entire crystal with an infinitely deep green as if it were a piece of solidified ocean. A fist-sized emerald was embedded in the druse along with an equally large sky-blue aquamarine; the emerald and the aquamarine were fused together and of flawless purity. Lacking any inclusions, they were as transparently clear as the most expensive diamond. You had the feeling of drowning in this rare interplay of colours; like looking at the sea and the sky, your gaze was lost within it. Andy Mo had never seen such a perfect jewel. No maharajah, no sheikh, no king had ever possessed such a gem. An earth spirit would never release such a miracle of mysteriously flourishing magical beauty from his realm.

But Andy Mo saw things differently, of course. He knew that any oil sheik would pay a fortune for this gem, and then Mr Freiwald could pay off his indebted villa a hundred times over. Michael's problems and those of his friends would be solved. Now he just had to make sure that Michael's father found the stone.

Andy Mo had memorised Mr Freiwald's photo well and tuned in to him. He immediately sensed that he was asleep. He still had a high fever, and his spirit was still roaming on the outskirts of his soul garden, as expected. There, as with every person when they are asleep, the images of the real world were reflected and mingled with the ideas and feelings which had been occupying him lately. His thoughts and his hopes for a valuable discovery also drove him to the mountains in his dreams, making him search for gems in the rockfaces and gorges as he usually did. Andy Mo watched him from some distance, but even when he approached he remained unnoticed. Mr Freiwald was too engrossed in his own fantasies. Andy Mo didn't speak to him: he feared he would wake him up and drive him out of the dreamscape. He thought of how his father had silently led Christian to the book in the cellar, and he wanted to do the same thing as the Gnome King had.

He positioned himself in the path of the sleepwalker, but some distance away; that way he would surely be noticed. He waved in a friendly manner, and it worked. Mr Freiwald smiled and waved back in just as friendly a manner. So contact had been made, and Andy Mo was pleased.

Now came the most difficult part of his plan. He had to use his imagination to change his fellow traveller's dreamscape so that it corresponded to reality, and so that later in his waking state Mr Freiwald would be able to find the site to which he was about to lead him. But this was far more difficult than sending normal thought packets. The images Andy Mo formed were constantly being overlaid by the dreamer's fantasies. Only with the utmost concentration was he able to direct Mr Freiwald's attention away from his dreams and towards the landscape he was creating for him. Eventually he realised that Andy Mo wanted to show him something and followed him.

Now it was becoming easier, and soon they were standing in front of the bizarre rockface in which the cave with the gemstone was located. Andy Mo found a path through the difficult terrain which was also passable in the human realm, and he beckoned Mr Freiwald to follow him up the mountain.

They were only a few kilometres from the sleeping man's body, but it seemed like an infinite distance. After waking up and recovering, would Mr Freiwald actually find his way back here?

The concentrated effort had exhausted Andy Mo immensely. Suddenly Mr Freiwald also seemed tired and disoriented. He stopped and looked around enquiringly. Apparently he could no longer see Andy Mo. The entire landscape began to flicker like a mirage in the hot desert sand, threatening to dissolve. With the last of his strength, Andy Mo managed to consolidate the vision and re-establish contact with him. Together they continued the ascent. They were both exhausted, and neither of them had noticed that they had been watched for some time. Andy Mo mistook the Shadow following them for a dream figure, and so the disaster took its course.

After twenty metres they arrived at the narrow opening in the rock. It was more of a wide slit than a cave, just high enough for an adult to squeeze through on their stomach. Andy Mo pointed to the hidden entrance and Mr Freiwald understood. He crouched down to enter the cave. That's when it happened. An eerie rumble of thunder made the whole mountain tremble, and the violent shaking shredded the thought images he had painstakingly constructed; it was as if the landscape was being blown up. Andy Mo lost control of himself and his world and fell into deep unconsciousness.

THE SECRET OF A PACT AND A GOOD SALAD

When he regained consciousness he was in the library in Michael Freiwald's house. He had been thrown out of his plane. He was in the human realm. It was night-time. He registered these facts in a daze and then fell into a deep, dreamless sleep, awakening again only when his friends gathered for their discussion and woke him up.

"Andy Mo!" Miri Li exclaimed. "What are you doing here? We haven't seen you for three days." She understood that something was wrong with him and held his hands affectionately. The others also looked at him anxiously.

"I messed up", Andy Mo said, sitting up. "I didn't make it. It was all in vain. I found the biggest, most beautiful, most valuable emerald and I lost it again." And then he told them in detail what he had experienced. He couldn't believe that he'd been away for three days.

Michael was the first to grasp the full implications of the situation. He was worried about his father. Now he was at risk as well.

"Now my father is in danger too", he said out loud. "None of us are safe anymore. Whoever is after us and wants to harm us, they can obviously find us anywhere in the world."

"No matter if it's in this world or the next", Christian added sombrely. "Don't forget that the whole thing played out in a dreamscape, after all. Or have I misunderstood something?"

Andy Mo nodded.

"It was somewhere in the intermediate realm. A plane where the realities of both worlds mirror one another. So I don't know what the consequences will be – everything is connected, after all. Thoughts and ideas are manifested, and vice versa; what we do and what happens to us changes our inner spiritual world. But it's difficult to follow the chronological sequence of cause and effect. I have no idea what happened last outside the cave, but I fear there will be consequences."

"Before you were flung out of Mr Freiwald's dreamworld, did you see if he managed to climb into the cave or at least get a glimpse inside? Do you think he saw the emerald before everything collapsed?"

Andy Mo's features brightened.

"In that case there would be a real chance of him getting the stone after all, because he's bound to find his way back to the rockface with the cave if he looks for it."

"Unless Baphomet or one of his minions stops him", Leif pointed out. "That was a mental entity which was following you, a Shadow being. I thought Andy Mo hadn't noticed it. That spirit can inspire someone else to get the gem in exactly the same way as you did. Or if Michael's father has already found it, it can get one of the many bandits running around Muzo to take the emerald back from him."

"You're right", said Andy Mo. "Mr Freiwald is in danger. We must warn him. But I can't go back to him myself – I can't move on the surface or the undersurface of the Earth at the moment. I couldn't even manage a mental leap across this room. Watch what happens." He tried, but he didn't budge. He didn't even reach the flickering state; he just remained where he was. Watching his futile efforts in alarm, the friends realised that Andy Mo was no longer quite the same. The world had changed him. The laws of nature also applied to spirits, and it was becoming increasingly difficult for him to resist the Earthly forces which rule time and space and maintain order in the world.

"You're too exhausted. Let it be", Miri Li comforted him, putting her hand around his shoulder. "I'm sure Michael can reach his father in some other way and inform him."

"Unfortunately not", said Michael. "Not at the moment – he doesn't have a phone or an internet connection. And his mobile phone doesn't work in that region. You have to imagine this settlement as an old-fashioned gold-mining town. It wasn't my father who called me from the post office last week, it was his neighbour."

"But you can write to him. Write to him that the dream of hiking to the cave in the rockface was a reflection of reality, not a dream. You must tell him that there's an emerald hanging from the cave ceiling up there. But maybe he already knows that – perhaps he had a quick peek or crawled inside before the mental rockslide occurred."

"Maybe a real rockslide occurred at the same time and the entrance to the cave is buried", Leif mused. "Then he wouldn't be able to retrieve the stone."

"I fear he'll be in even greater danger if he finds the emerald," said Andy Mo. "We should try to prevent that. The bandits are more dangerous than the bank executor."

But Michael disagreed, and the friends all agreed with him.

"We need the money. The foreclosure can no longer be averted. Surely the fact that a Shadow followed you through the dreamworld proves Baphomet already has him in his sights; stone or no stone, it doesn't change anything. But if my father finds the stone, he'll have enough money to go into hiding, and then at least the Earthly minions won't find him."

"You could sell the books from the chest, couldn't you?" suggested Andy Mo. "Even if the antiquarian is broke, I'm sure you can find another buyer. Take them to a pawnshop and have them pawned or auctioned off."

Everyone looked at him.

"He doesn't know yet", Michael said, looking first at the group and then at Andy Mo. "You couldn't know because you weren't here. The chest has been stolen. It's gone, in any case. The precious works are no longer here, alas. The antiquarian must have told someone about them, and we'll never see the books again. Luckily Kathi took the documents home with her, otherwise they would have been lost as well."

Only now did Andy Mo understand the full extent of the disaster and the seriousness of the situation. They hadn't made a single step forward; there still wasn't any money. Baphomet was always one move ahead of them on the chessboard of destiny. Mr Freiwald had to take the risk.

"I'll write and tell him everything", Michael said. "Then he'll have to decide for himself what to do. But I'm convinced he will get the stone. And he'll be careful: he doesn't just believe in good spirits, but evil ones as well."

Andy Mo nodded.

"If he didn't believe in spirits, he wouldn't have been able to sense my presence. I hope he gets well soon and finds his way back, because I'm not in a position to help him a second time."

"But you can make a map with everything marked on it."

"The location of the discovery has been erased from my consciousness. I tried several times to recall the whereabouts of the cave, but I couldn't. I always see things from the undersurface of the Earth, not from their own perspective."

"Is Baphomet also responsible for this memory loss, or is it because you're weakened and tired?" asked Kathi, who had remained silent until now.

"Neither. It's the law of the gnomes and it conforms to our regulations. I was allowed to guide him because he believes in the existence of spirits, and so he was able to follow me. Not every dreamer could have done that. It was all a spiritual process. But it would be grossly material and a betrayal if I were to put the location in writing, like stealing in the spiritual world. It would be the same as laying the stone right at his feet. That violates the laws of destiny, and he would have to pay for it in some other way. It would be equivalent to making a pact. All values, both spiritual and material, must be obtained through your own labour and striving, otherwise they have no value."

"I thought you only ever made a pact with the forces of evil", Leif commented. "That's when you sell your soul to the devil. Does that really happen, or are those just fairy tales from books?"

Just as he said the word 'devil', there was a distant rumble of thunder which turned into a gloating laugh. The raven had once again showcased his aptitude for mimicry. With an elegant curve he glided off the curtain rod and landed in a hop on the large table.

"A pact is a deal, an agreement between humans and spirits. But believe me, it's not worth it. Everything has its price, and when you're asked to pay you always regret it. There are two kinds of pacts: intentional ones and unintentional ones. Intentional pacts are hardly ever made nowadays. They're far too difficult. People can't even see spirits anymore. But they were still common 970 years ago in my youth."

"What do people have to offer the spirits?" asked Kathi. "And how do you sell your soul? What happens to you then when you die?"

The raven closed his eyes and contemplated for a long time. You could see he was thinking hard and didn't know where to begin.

"That's a very difficult topic", he eventually said, raising his head theatrically and pretending to be an actor on a stage. "Let's begin with your last question. Just as a helpful spirit, when it's functioning..." – he glanced very briefly at Andy Mo, who luckily didn't notice – "just as such a spirit can move unhindered through space and time due to its ethereal nature, and can therefore be of service to humans, who can't move unhindered here, so the human spirit can travel through the four elements over in the spirit realm because it consists of those four elements. That's something spirits can't do. Andy Mo wouldn't have made it across the Sea of Souls or the River of Oblivion without the help of the nixie Amue. And he only made it to this material world with your support. A human who has trained their spirit (and spirits only make pacts with such people) is not only able to move through all planes, but can also oversee them all simultaneously. So, you see, humans can also be very useful to spirits. I would even argue that spirits need humans more than vice versa, because if..." But Leif interrupted the lecturing raven.

"Didn't you just say that pacts are no longer made these days? What's the deal? If I promise Lucifer that I'll take him for a spin after I die, will he get me a fancy Porsche in the here-and-now?"

Yks started laughing and was barely able to stop.

"Did you hear that? He wants to trouble Lucifer! The chief of the densest spirits. You might as well pray to the dear Lord that he takes you evildoers to heaven. Lucifer would simply laugh at you! You'd be better off trying to get Volkswagen to send you a Porsche as a gift. As I told you, the spirits only serve a magician who has mastered their own spirit. What have you mastered about yourself? Have you mastered your thoughts? Have you mastered your emotions? Have you mastered your impulses and urges? Snacking, smoking, drinking, sex? Have you mastered yourself? Besides, Lucifer has never served any human being. Those who claim so are mistaken: they've been duped by a trickster spirit pretending to be the Prince. I'm hungry. Isn't there anything to eat today?"

Now it was the others who were laughing. Michael stood up.

"I'll get you something right away – I've prepared some meatballs, and there's salad to go with them. But after we eat, explain the second kind of pact you mentioned."

But the raven interjected.

"Wait, I haven't finished yet. I won't starve. So, what do you need for a pact? What do you have to do to get a spirit you want to win over to serve you? Leif will tell us." He suddenly took on Kleindienst's voice, and he was also imitating his jerky chin movements. Leif went along with it and stood up.

"If you want to make a pact, Professor, you must draw a spirit's attention to yourself. You must invoke them. You must summon them. You perform an invocation ritual, and to do this, you need a magic formula, a magic wand, and a magic circle in which you stand as you perform the invocation. You place a triangle with the seal of the manifesting spirit in front of the circle."

"Nonsense. Superstition. Middle Ages. A magical evocation like that is far too difficult. It's also no longer necessary today: no graveyard, no sword, no magic circle. You haven't been paying attention, sit down. In the third millennium, the whole thing happens without any hocus-pocus."

"Namely by simply grabbing the bird and putting it in a cage", Leif said, grinning from ear to ear. Andy Mo was visibly amused too; overhearing the insult, the raven was offended and didn't respond.

"The only thing that's still necessary today for collaboration with a spirit is the invocation. And as I mentioned before, it mostly happens unconsciously these days. You have no idea how many pacts are being made every day without the people involved even realising it. Humans and spirits work much more closely together than they used to, despite the fact they know less about one another today than they did a thousand years ago – or perhaps precisely because of this fact. Thanks to the Enlightenment, humans have pushed the spirits out of their consciousness, but they haven't gotten rid of them. They're no longer able to invoke spirits and summon them up in a circle, and the spirits can no longer make themselves visible; but despite this, many more invisible beings influence the world today than they did in the past. And it's more powerful beings who are asserting their influence now – not some curious adolescent gnomes who swoon at the slightest opportunity."

"Or imaginary ravens who swan around drunk and end up in exile", countered Andy Mo. "But what our bird is claiming is true. I read it in this guardian angel book by Emil Stejnar. Humans have evolved and become smarter. Today, they're inspired by intelligences which are far cleverer and have a greater overview than us simple nature spirits."

"Stejnar only mentions some of the attendant spirits", Kathi chimed in. "Franz Bardon has described all of the intelligences in his book *The Practice of Magical Evocation*. Behind every idea there is a spirit who fully identifies with that idea and lives for it, and who therefore has an interest in bringing what they live for to fruition. To this end they inspire suitable individuals who then think like them and manifest their ideas. Behind every invention, behind every work of genius, behind every ideal or grand project, there is a spiritual being. Anyone who achieves above-average results is inspired and strengthened by a spirit. There are attendant spirits responsible for the development of technology, intelligences for science, art, politics, religion…" "And good cooking", Michael interrupted her. "Come on Kathi, people are hungry – let's get the food."

RECIPE

SWEDISH MEATBALLS

Ingredients:
500 grams of mixed minced beef and pork
1 onion
2 boiled potatoes
1 egg
1 tablespoon of salt
1 tablespoon of sugar
1 teaspoon of ground white pepper
10 tablespoons of breadcrumbs
10 tablespoons of water

Preparation:
Stir the breadcrumbs and sugar into the water and leave to soak for ten minutes. Grate the potatoes very finely. Finely chop the onion and fry lightly in fat, then mix all the ingredients loosely in a bowl. With wet hands, form balls of about 3 to 4 cm in diameter. Heat the margarine and fry the meatballs on all sides. Do not overcrowd the pan so that they can fry well on all sides. Reduce the heat and fry for five minutes.

POTATO SALAD

Ingredients:
About half a kilo of waxy potatoes
1 onion

Preparation:
Boil the potatoes in their skins in salted water until soft, let them steam off a little and peel them while they're still hot, then cut them into thin slices. Add the sliced onion. Pour dressing over them. Cover and leave to infuse for at least half an hour.

DRESSING

Ingredients:
1/8 litre hot water or stock, if available
3 tablespoons sugar
1/2 teaspoon salt
3 tablespoons of Hesperides vinegar or white wine vinegar (5%)
3 tablespoons sunflower oil
1 pinch ground white pepper

SAUERKRAUT SALAD

Ingredients:
Approximately 250 grams of fresh sauerkraut from the market, or
1 pack of organic sauerkraut from the shop
1 small onion
2 apples

Preparation:
Cut the sauerkraut into smaller pieces to make it easier to eat. Chop the onion and apples and mix them in. It's ready. No dressing is needed, it tastes perfect just as it is.

CUCUMBER SALAD

Preparation:
Finely slice a cucumber and its skin with a vegetable slicer. Sprinkle with a teaspoon of salt, mix well and leave to stand for half an hour. Pour away any liquid that has settled.

For the dressing:
1 tablespoon of vinegar, 2 teaspoons of sugar.

To nibble on afterwards:

RAD ROLLS

Preparation:
Crush or grind 200 grams of butter cookies in a mortar, grind 200 grams of ground nuts, mix 200 grams of icing sugar with 1 tablespoon of cocoa, add 2 tablespoons of melted butter and 2 raw absolutely fresh eggs, mix everything together, knead it and form into a roll.

*

As always, everyone thoroughly enjoyed the meal. Yks happily took the last meatball. "Tastes fantastic", he munched. "The philosophers are looking for the meaning of life, but they'd be better off worrying about good food – then they wouldn't ask stupid questions."

The girls were delighted with the salads and wanted Michael to tell them how he had made them so well.

"The secret of a good salad is sugar. That's what the famous Austrian chef Gerald Höhenberger told me: wherever there's vinegar, there has to be sugar. But now it's Yks' turn again. Please tell us the secret of the unintended pact."

The raven had been waiting impatiently for his turn, and he didn't need to be asked twice. Positioning himself as he had before, he closed his eyes, twitched, and then began:

"Actually, instead of unintentional, one should say unconscious. It can transpire that a human enters into a pact with a spiritual being without knowing it. There's nothing signed in blood – it's spiritual blood which establishes and fixes the relationship with a being."

"What is spiritual blood?" asked Kathi.

"Spiritual blood refers to thoughts and feelings, for these are the mediators of life in the spirit world. Everything which preoccupies and moves humans also preoccupies and moves the spirits. In fact it's the other way around. It's the spirits who inspire humans and motivate them to cherish certain thoughts, feelings, and desires.

They are the ones who benefit, because these fragments of human consciousness are their life element. Behind all the religions, politics, inventions, or ideals Kathi mentioned earlier, and behind every extraordinary ability, sporting achievement, or artistic talent, there is an invisible being striving in the same direction. And thoughts and feelings form the connecting element between these beings and humans."

Briefly pondering how to explain this, Yks glanced at a meatball, but he controlled himself and continued speaking slowly.

"For example, someone who's very enthusiastic about pop music and who uses their painstakingly saved pocket money to buy a keyboard, and who then plays and practices diligently on it – they will attract the attention of a spirit, namely the one responsible for pop music. This spirit is attracted to them and approaches them increasingly often. It experiences itself in the human being's consciousness, and an increasingly powerful connection develops between the two, despite the fact it can't appear to them and usually doesn't even notice that it has come into contact with a human being. It's a slow process. What the music spirit can do is transferred to the person through their proximity. It nurtures their talent and inspires them, so they become increasingly absorbed in their preoccupation with music until they have nothing else on their mind and no other desire than to make music and perform on stage. The spirit spurs them on, gives them melodies, and helps them achieve better and better performances, in most cases leading to the desired success. The human has no idea to whom they owe all this.

So it's an unconscious pact", the raven concluded. "And believe me, it's made faster than you would imagine is possible. But it's not always so spectacular. There are even spirits behind the fastidious housewife possessed by the cleaning devil who constantly wields her cleaning cloth, or behind the grandfather who cultivates his roses or tends to the orchids in his conservatory; the spirits take pleasure in these pastimes, and so they ensure that humans act in accordance with their will, rather than making themselves comfortable in front of the television or a good book.

"You need to understand this. If you're too committed to something and spend too long on a particular matter or idea, you attract the attention of the spirit lying behind it and summon them into your proximity."

"In that case every thought and every wish is the summoning of a spirit, and every ideal you follow is a pact", Kathi reflected. "That's terrible when you think about it. Then the affected individuals are already enslaved to the being which is helping them, not only after their death but also while they're still alive."

"No, it's not quite that bad. Only the gullible idealists, the deluded fanatics, and the zombified sectarians indulge themselves to such an extent that they lose themselves in the idea. Only people who have nothing else in their minds apart from a single goal and life purpose abandon their consciousness to the spirits which inspire them, and so gradually lose their own identity. If you maintain enough distance from your ideals and the goals you pursue, this can't happen."

"What about when someone sits in front of his computer for hours on end and does nothing but play games?", Christian wanted to know. "Is there also a spirit behind that, urging them on? The Book of the Master mentions spectres, which are spiritual entities created when you constantly wish or do or think the same thing. In essence, you create these parasites yourself. How do you tell them apart from a genuine spirit from the spirit world?"

"That's a good question", replied Yks, "but it's difficult to answer. All spiritual beings are essentially real. They only differ in their strength and quality – that is, in what they represent and want, and how they have come to be. After all, there are far more spirits than there are people and animals, and they all have a self-preservation instinct. The thought-spirits and grant-me-a-wish-spirits of human beings are intrusive but fleeting, and they dwindle away if you don't constantly supply them with your consciousness via your attention. These include the image of the moped you want to buy, the craving for a cigarette, or the melody you can't get out of your head, as well as the idea of a career goal which becomes so powerful that it determines your entire life. Even religious or political opinions which cause people to kill one another are these kinds of spiritual constructs which have taken root in the consciousness of affected individuals. Initially it's only an idea which impresses the person concerned, but then it robs them of their sanity.

"Besides the elementals and elementaries – which are actually your spiritual molecules – and the complexes and spectres which form like tumours from thoughts and feelings, there are also elemental spirits and nature spirits like Andy Mo and myself, as well as demons. And at the very top of the hierarchy there are the angels and intelligences of the planetary spheres, which are the beings from the so-called divine realm. They actually stand before you, and they were there even before this planet existed.

"There are more spirits than there are text messages and emails buzzing around. And they're constantly increasing. The jogging spirit which makes millions of people run, and the walking spirit which persuades even mummies armed with canes to go hiking – they didn't exist before."

"Are those also just spectres which move people?" Christian wanted to know. "Or is there a general sports spirit behind them?"

"It's hard to tell. The spiritual inner life is far more complex than the anatomy and physiology of material bodies. There are also organs, limbs, and cells of being there, but they lead a life of their own and are constantly in motion. In any case, regardless of how the spirits which influence you come about, whether they're your own thoughts, spectres, or inspirations, they can be significant. So it's important that you become aware of and control everything which you think, feel, and want. The moment you perceive something within you, it becomes a part of yourself, no matter whether it's your own imaginings or inspirations from other beings."

"Do the spiritual beings which influence us also consist of thoughts, feelings, and will like us? Are they also made of four elements and self-aware?"

"No", Andy Mo replied firmly. "Most spirits are made up of only one, or at most two or three elements. We earth spirits, for example, have certain qualities and abilities which are subject to the earth element of creation, and we see it as our duty to actually do what we are capable of doing. We feel compelled to do it; that's what fulfils our consciousness, nothing else. Work, diligence, and reliability. We think of nothing else and want nothing else; there were no feelings which would have moved me elsewhere. In the realm of the nixies it was different. These subtle beings seem to consist only of feelings. I only noticed the difference when I had to pass through their water element; there, I had only fear, hope, and the desire to help Amue. In fire, on the other hand, the will was stronger than feelings; there I wanted to take action. I didn't think over whether I would succeed in saving Miri Li, I simply wanted and had to do it. And then in the air, when the branch broke and I fell from my gnome world, for the first time in my life I asked myself who and what and where I was. In the air I seemed to consist only of thoughts, perceptions, and reflections. I experienced myself exclusively in my thoughts, and I thought that if I stopped thinking, I would be dead. I already possessed consciousness before, but it was only when I also came to know the air element that I became aware of my Self. For the first time, I thought 'I AM', and I knew without that thought I would lose myself."

"We humans are the same", Michael said. "We also constantly lose ourselves in our thoughts, or we get caught up in an idea or whatever is currently occupying our mind and driving us forward. Very little that we do is actually done consciously. Sometimes we're so engrossed in a book that we completely forget ourselves and the world around us. At other times we get angry and say something foolish without thinking, which then has unpleasant consequences. Or we lose our minds because of all the happy or unhappy feelings. The trick is probably to use all four members of the spirit at the same time. Then you would have everything under your control, i.e. yourself and what you need in order to be. But who is capable of doing that?"

Andy Mo nodded. "The ability to find your personal centre and focus your attention equally on thinking, feeling, willing, and consciousness is the highest art imaginable. Only human spirits are capable of it because they are the only spiritual beings consisting of five elements. Whoever masters this art surpasses all other humans and spirits. That's why it has remained the secret knowledge of magical-mystical orders, and only a handful of individuals know about it. The mystery was revealed for the first time in the Book of the Master.

"The mystery of the spiritual cells and members of being upon which consciousness is based is thus a very important matter which we still need to explore in great depth. We'll also discuss and describe this in detail in our book. Think it over and we'll talk more tomorrow. I'm dead tired, so I'm retiring for today."

But Andy Mo couldn't immediately transport himself into his gnome realm this time either. He flickered intensely but remained where he was. Only on the third attempt did he vanish from the sight of his friends.

"I'm really worried about the little one", said the raven with concern, staring at the spot where Andy Mo had just disappeared. "If he loses his magical abilities, we won't stand a chance against Baphomet. We can't get anywhere without him. After all, it's not just our own affairs; our book project is just as important. The future of all humanity is at stake. Humanity can only be saved if we succeed in enlightening the children about the true nature of their spirits, and if they learn how to properly deal with their thoughts and feelings before it's too late."

"You're right", Kathi agreed. "In our book we should illuminate and describe the mystery of these spiritual molecules which constitute us and the magical power of our imaginations from all angles. After all, some things have already been revealed in the Book of the Master; but I think Andy Mo can tell us more about this tomorrow."

THOUGHTS ARE SPIRITS

The next morning, a radiant blue sky lifted the sun above the horizon. Andy Mo crouched on his rock, pondering how he could explain the mystery of the ethereal components of being to his friends even more clearly. His father had mentioned this fact repeatedly, but it was only since he had been living among humans that he had truly grasped the mystery. It was described in detail in the Book of the Master: just as the human body consists of material cells and molecules, so the human spirit consists of spiritual cells and molecules. However, these components of being – i.e. the thoughts and feelings which mediate consciousness – are themselves little spirits.

Even in the spirit world this wasn't known by all beings. The insight is sensational. And it explains why positive thinking works.

Humans don't need to conjure up spirits – they can create their own helpful spirits. In fact they themselves are even comprised of these spirits. Every thought is such a spirit. People just need to mobilise them in accordance with their own intentions. However, most humans are moved in the opposite direction by their spirits. They feel that something is constantly stirring within them, urging them to say or do something they don't actually want to say or do, but they're not aware that their inner impulses are little spirits. Spirits which anyone who has mastered them can work magic with, but which can become independent and act against you if left unchecked.

This is why magical training is important even for those individuals who don't wish to engage with magic, Andy Mo reflected. Not to change the world or your own destiny with a spell, but to strengthen your own spirit so that it's you and not some inner impulse which determines what you want. This had become increasingly clear to him since he had begun to observe humans. He had to explain it to his friends.

"Actually, you don't need magic at all", Andy Mo stated in the afternoon. "You can also perform magic without incantations and rituals. You don't need spirits; you can use your own spirit. Every thought can be a helpful spirit, a messenger carrying your wishes to an angel. The light of unwavering faith, the attractive force of your own desires, and the concentrated images of vivid thinking become an irresistible command which shapes the future.

"The teaching of positive thinking has long proven this. For example, if for half an hour every day – even in summer – a skier imagines themselves speeding perfectly down the slope and crossing the finish line as the winner, this spiritual exercise is just as much a workout as physical exertion in the gym. The power of the spirit is just as real as the strength of muscles.

"However, this can also act as a curse, because it also works in a negative sense. You can precondition negative things with your thought images. And a thought can also be the messenger of a demon which harms you if you overlook it.

"Just fearing something is enough to attract it. That's why you still need magic, or rather magical training; for this is nothing other than training the spirit and soul muscles, and it enables you to learn how to deal with your thoughts and feelings correctly. You must master not only your drives but also your thoughts and feelings, because otherwise they'll take on a life of their own."

"Franz Bardon teaches that too", Christian said. "He calls these entities elementals and elementaries. He explains how thoughts don't just happen in our heads, but can detach themselves from us, and you can directly achieve things with them without summoning a spirit."

"Exactly", Andy Mo confirmed. "Thoughts, ideas, and feelings do indeed behave like autonomous little spirits. If you're unable to master them – that is, if you're unable to master yourself – you're certainly incapable of mastering other spirits which are not your own. Since you yourselves are made up of spirits, this is a dangerous matter. It's like a bus driver not being in control of their vehicle.

"Every thought is a living part of your being and must be felt as such. You don't let your limbs flap about; you decide where your legs should take you. It's the same with thoughts and desires. They're parts of you, essential components of your spirit. Just as the limbs of your body carry you, so your thoughts and feelings carry your spirit. And if you don't control your spiritual limbs, they'll carry you into those worlds which correspond to them, not where you actually want to go.

"Every thought, every wish is an independent little being which wants to realise itself, no matter whether it's good for you or not. These tiny spiritual entities have a self-preservation instinct and wish to survive – that is, to be thought and felt. For those who harness these spirits, they become helpful spirits; for those who fail to control them, they become demons."

"It makes me uneasy to imagine living beings stirring within me", Miri Li remarked. "I would rather think of them as growths of light and shadow, growing like plants. Plants proliferate just like fantasies if you don't prune them in time. We have a strawberry patch behind the house. If I didn't weed it every week, it would soon be overgrown. Weeds grow much faster than you think – at first you don't even notice them, then suddenly everything is full of them. A thought is rarely immediately decisive. At first it's a small, fleeting idea. Positive thoughts must be nurtured and cultivated like strawberry plants, while negative ones must be promptly removed from your consciousness so they don't overwhelm you."

"Which brings us back to our first exercise: thought control", Andy Mo remarked. "You see, the school of magic we want to describe in our book isn't about gaining magical power – it concerns an effective training of spirit and soul which grants you the qualities and abilities to shape your own life."

Michael had briefly disappeared, and now he returned with the iced tea he had prepared earlier in the morning. He looked around in search of something.

"Has anyone seen the plate with the rad roll? There was a big piece left over yesterday; I made twice as much on purpose. Where is the rad roll?"

"Here!" Yks called out. "It's here!" But Michael couldn't see anything. The raven was lying on the leather sofa, visibly exhausted, and had stretched out his legs and wings. "Yeah, here it is", he groaned and belched. "I ate it."

RECIPE

ICED TEA

Preparation:
Put 1.5 litres of water into a large pot. Add one tablespoon of tea, one slice of lemon, and two slices of orange, including the peel (this is important). Once the water begins to boil, remove the pot from the heat and let it steep for about ten minutes. Then strain everything through a sieve. Next, add four tablespoons of honey, one tablespoon of raspberry syrup, and three tablespoons of freshly squeezed orange juice. Then add sugar (brown sugar if you have it) until it's sweet enough and chill the tea. Pour some of it into an ice cube tray and place it in the freezer, then put it back into the jug when serving.

THE CONJURATION AT THE CEMETERY

"Tomorrow is the day", said the old man. "You've already got yourself the wand, haven't you?"

Leif nodded, unsurprised that the old man knew that. At the same time, he felt ashamed for stealing from his friends. After the last meeting, under the pretext of forgetting a book, he had returned to the library to take the wand from the chest. However, he fully intended to return it after the experiment. "No one will notice", he thought to himself. "I'll return it tomorrow."

"There will only be five of you", said the old man, interrupting his thoughts. "You will stand in the shape of a pentagram. You will lead the ceremony. Everything has been prepared. You will be expected at the first gate: arrive punctually at eleven, the others have already been informed. You will work with the ritual and formula from the manuscript I gave you last week. Handle the papers with care, they're originals – you don't make copies of something like that. By preserving the power contained in the papers, you can better harness it. Have you memorized everything?"

Leif nodded again; the old man had only given him three pages. The text on the yellowed leaves was written in both German and Latin. A note at the end of the manuscript confirmed that in 1789, seven monks who followed the instructions were able to establish a connection with otherworldly powers. The contacted entity was Lucifer. Leif was convinced that it would also work with Baphomet, who interested him more than Lucifer. He would just swap the names and hope the old man didn't notice.

The cemetery was located outside the city. It covered a vast area. As arranged, they met at the first gate. The huge carpark and the kilometre-long road next to the high wall were deserted. Leif was the last to arrive. The others were already there: Annika, Gregor, Peter, and someone he had never seen in the old man's group before.

"The Central Cemetery is the largest cemetery in Vienna and the second largest in Europe", the person Leif didn't know was explaining. "Only the one in Hamburg is larger. This gigantic burial ground covers 2,384,743 square metres. It's a huge nature reserve, home to 20 deer, countless hares, rare birds, and a host of other animals. There are almost 500,000 graves here, with over two million dead lying within them. And 25 more are added every day." When he noticed that the others were staring at him in amazement, he apologised: "I just saw a film about it on television." Leif shook his head too; they really had other things on their minds now rather than history.

Fierce gusts of wind drove dark wispy clouds before them, giving the full moon a chance to dim the already eerie scene even more with its pale light. Someone emerged from the darkness of the wall, waved, and led the small group through a hidden gate and into the burial ground. Then he walked ahead, showing them the path to their destination: a freshly dug grave selected for the invocation of Baphomet. They trudged behind him in silence, each individual busy with their own thoughts as if preparing for a challenging school assignment.

They crossed long avenues, walked through narrow streets, and followed hidden gravel paths past various sections and clusters of graves. There was a separate Jewish cemetery, a Buddhist one with a snow-white stupa, small churches and chapels of all denominations, and several crematoria and mortuary halls for the funeral ceremonies. Next to the lavish and pompous mausoleums and tombs of the rich were dilapidated graves overgrown with weeds and undergrowth which no one cared for anymore: toppled tombstones, weathered statues, hedges, bushes, and ancient trees. It was a place of transience and life.

The atmosphere was charged as if a thunderstorm was approaching. Oppressively heavy like mental jelly, the air bound them in a shared consciousness field of fear and tense anticipation. They walked through the night in silence. No one said a word. Somewhere a bird screeched.

The full moon was reflected on the polished marble slabs, and the statues on the tombs seemed to move. The soft light transformed the shapes into shadows, lending them sharp contours and giving the figures a new, grotesque appearance. Mists of light rose up, evoking the appearance of cotton wool, and where they disappeared they etched black holes into infinity.

From afar, a clocktower struck twelve. The church had to be somewhere out beyond the cemetery grounds. The drawn-out, off-key chimes faded away without finding their proper octave. Affected, the group stopped and listened. The tones created an uncomfortable echo within them. It was the witching hour. Gregor popped a bubble-gum bubble. As everyone stared at him in bewilderment, he spat it out. Nevertheless, the spell which held them captive remained unbroken. Silently they followed their guide and reached the grave after a few more steps. The old gravedigger who had brought them there disappeared silently in the darkness just as suddenly as he had appeared. Now they were alone.

A gust of wind – the harbinger of a storm – swept hissing through the tree branches. Immediately afterwards an eerie inferno erupted between the black clouds which, like the holes of an underworld, not even the brightest lightning could illuminate. Following each discharge there was a hellish noise, shrill and metallic like theatrical thunder, making the young people realise that this was no ordinary event of nature. Light and darkness, fire and water, order and chaos were raging there. Fortunately, just behind the grave was the half-ruined mausoleum of a forgotten poet, where they found shelter.

The storm disappeared just as quickly as it had erupted. There had been hardly any rain. But the steaming silence was even more ghostly than the roar of the forces before. Wisps of mist were reflected in the unreal shimmer of the distant metropolis, descending upon them and vanishing like living phantoms among the graves. There was just enough moonlight to fill the darkness with foreboding.

They had put on their black silk cloaks and pulled the hoods over their heads. The old man had given them these ritual garments, which supposedly came from a Masonic Lodge. Then they lit the candles in the lanterns they had brought with them and, as agreed, stood in a circle around the freshly dug earth under which the deceased had been buried a few hours earlier.

Leif began the invocation. However, he changed the text which the old man had provided and invoked Baphomet instead of Lucifer:

"Adonai, Lord of all worlds and beings, hear my call and bless my work.
In your name, I summon Baphomet."

He tried to give his voice a firm tone, but he couldn't entirely hide the fear which choked his throat and made him hoarse. The candles in the lanterns flickered, casting monstrous shadows reminiscent of the shadows of his own nightmares, and the shadows flew about like startled black birds, dissipating like the words of the nonsensical formula into nothingness.

"Baphomet, I summon thee.
I summon thee, Shadow of the world, born of light.
O thou whose heart bleeds.
Thou sufferest because thou are misjudged.
Thy realm, which is named darkness and which mercifully conceals the suffering of the afflicted, they call the underworld.
O Baphomet, whom they wrong.
Thou knowest the reason behind good and evil.
Thou art the Lord of this Earthly world, which divides light and darkness.
Thou black sun among the sleeping.
Thou bearer of light.
Thou liberator of the downtrodden.
The wretched will come to find solace in death and oblivion.
They will come to know the black secret of the graveyards.
Baphomet, we summon you."

However, since none of them could form a proper conception of Baphomet, and since they were unable to prepare the mental ground for a spiritual being, nothing much happened. The perverse words of the magic formula condensed the energy of their tense nerves, and fear created mental constructs out of their imaginations. But these were not stable enough for anything concrete to be discernible. What tried to form quickly dissolved and disappeared. Nevertheless, they mistook the haunting of their own spectres, which manifested themselves in the form of indefinable, eerie noises and violet veils of light, for a genuine spirit. They fell for the kaleidoscope of their own fantasies and shivered in awe at the extrasensory phenomena.

Then Leif, with a chill running down his spine, raised his wand imperiously and truly reached into the spiritual plane. With this wand, which had been consecrated by Andy Mo, a real being was touched. Sensing he was addressed, Andy Mo appeared, and everyone could indeed see him since they had all been expecting a spirit. Nevertheless, they froze in panic, as they believed it was Baphomet standing before them. Leif wasn't immediately able to recognise his friend in the flickering apparition, and he too was frightened. He suddenly didn't know what to say and lost control of the situation.

When Andy Mo realised who had summoned him to the cemetery and who they thought he was, he was outraged. How dare Leif dishonour this wand for such an evil purpose? How could he stoop so low as to steal from his friends? How could he betray their secret? Furious, he looked at the traitor and, astonished, felt something detach from him. The concentrated force of his agitation piled up like an avalanche and his anger, his rage, his disappointment, and his grief discharged in a violent detonation. The band of magicians rapidly dispersed, with everyone running off in a different direction. Only Annika and Leif remained standing. The latter stared at Andy Mo, whom he now recognised, in amazement and guilt.

Immediately Andy Mo regretted losing control. He knew that these were the truly dangerous demons: anger, rage, and hatred. Thoughts and feelings don't stay with the creator in the human realm; they become detached and escape the control of their originators. He quickly calmed down again and realised what he had done. Now the young people believed they had successfully summoned a spirit, and they would try again. They had seen him and believed that spirits existed, and now they would summon another one. Even though they were frightened to death today and abandoned their experiment, next time they would be better prepared. But they didn't know what really awaited them.

Just as the energy of his anger had detached from him and manifested in an explosion, so the energy of their tense feelings would detach and animate the idea they had of the spirit they were summoning. A phantom would emerge and perform a theatre piece for them: a new being created by humans which feeds on their emotions. Many 'gods' and demons have been created in this way in

Lodges, in witches' circles, and around shamanic fires. Once created, these unholy creatures never let go of their unsuspecting creators. They entice them to engage with them again and again. They pretend to be the being which the sorcerers imagine they've summoned, make them think they're nearby, make promises, talk them into doing or not doing things. They're vampires which feed off the affection and attention of those they have fooled. But the worst part is that if the phantom created in this manner actually corresponds to a real entity, because it has been given its name, quality, and seal, it automatically becomes an intermediary which connects the magician with that entity. Under certain circumstances, the phantom can serve as a body for that entity to manifest in. Andy Mo knew the young people were going down a dangerous path.

He felt guilty and regretted his emotional outburst. But then he recognised his opportunity. He could enlighten them. Precisely because he had appeared to them, they would believe him when he warned them against these nonsensical experiments. They would believe a spirit rather than a priest warning against the devil. "Call them back", he said to Leif, "I want to talk to you all."

Soon they were all gathered in the small ruin where they had taken shelter from the storm earlier. First Andy Mo made sure they could still see him, then he introduced himself.

"My name is Andy Mo. I am indeed a spirit, but not the one you have summoned. You called upon Baphomet, the Shadow, but with this formula you addressed Lucifer, the light-bearer. Fortunately, neither of them heard you. That I could appear to you was due to the wand, for my spirit is bound to it. The formula Leif recited had no effect. These invocations are as useless as the endless rosaries recited by pious women in churches, who do not meditate upon the compassionate Mary while praying, but think rather upon the next vexation they can inflict on their daughter-in-law or neighbour to make their lives difficult. They are as fruitless as the Jews' psalms from the Bible, the Muslims' recitations from the Koran, or the mantras rattled off by the Tibetans. They are just as ineffective as all the other mindlessly muttered prayers in this world, because while they are praying, the praying person's mind is somewhere else.

"But just as sincerely spoken prayers can sometimes have an effect, so invocations are not always ineffective either. And that is precisely what is dangerous about magic. For during conjurations, due to the power of faith and the excited anticipation of the participants, an energy is released which spirits who happen to be nearby use to temporarily manifest themselves. As a rule, these are not beings from the spirit world, but your own thought-forms which emerge and put on airs before fizzling out. However, this is a different spirit to the one in the formulas or the prayers. It is a trickster spirit, a mental soap bubble.

"A real spirit can only make itself visible or noticeable via the elementals, namely the ethereal building blocks you prepare for it. What the molecules and atoms constituting your body are for you humans, the ethereal elements are for the spirits: fire, water, air, and earth. Each spirit has a different task and quality and is made up of the corresponding element which most closely matches its temperament – that is, the temperament necessary for its task. Spirits, beings, and intelligences responsible for business matters, wealth, money, and economic success consist more of earthy components. Intelligences representing the intellectual principle and working for inventions, insights, science, and philosophy have more air in them. Socially and artistically oriented beings who represent imagination, empathy, and compassion consist more of cells of being from the water element. And the spirits responsible for sports, war, and ventures requiring drive, strength, and courage consist of cells of being corresponding to the fire element. Depending on the being in question, you must condense the element corresponding to it with your imagination and make that element available to it.

"When you think about an intention for a longer period of time, you attract the attention of the beings responsible for it. If your thoughts are combined with the power of desire and you're completely enthralled and inspired by your idea, you draw the beings closer to yourself. But only those who are simultaneously capable of condensing an element as a sensation and projecting it in front of them can bring it into the visible world under certain circumstances.

"When conjuring up a spirit, you must concentrate entirely on it without letting your thoughts stray. If a being is to appear visibly, you must not only have its image in mind, but you must also imagine its quality, its essence, its character, its spiritual reality, and the life element in which it spends its existence. If you were to summon a fish, it couldn't appear just anywhere – you would have to provide a bucket of water or an aquarium for it. It's the same with spirits. An earth spirit needs heaviness, an air spirit needs lightness, a fire spirit needs the fiery desire to move, and a water spirit needs cool, unmoving stillness. This elemental sensation must not only be felt within yourself; you must also spread it around yourself, as if the sensation is music which fills the entire space in which the spirit is to appear.

"Leif didn't do all that", continued Andy Mo, now addressing Leif directly. "During the invocation you must act as a spirit, not as a human being. You must forget your body and this world as well. You are a spirit and you speak as a spirit, namely on the spiritual plane. Only in this way will a spirit understand you. You must speak the formula silently, releasing it from within you with the exhalation of the thought. The essence of the formula is spirit, not audible words.

"And there's something else you need to know: the more you engage with a particular spirit, the more you fall under its spell. It doesn't matter if it's an angel, a demon, or a deity. It can be near you without you even seeing it."

"It's like drinking beer, apparently", one of those gathered said. "Once you get into the habit, you can't get rid of it. The beer spirit has you in its grip."

"And when you drink wine, it's the wine spirit", somebody else chuckled, and the others laughed along; but Andy Mo agreed with him.

"You'll find this hard to believe, but there actually is a different spirit behind every drug, partaking in the dubious pleasures of humans. It's not the addict who is addicted; it's the spirit which wants more of the illusory happiness of numbness or euphoria, for it knows nothing else. That sensation is all it consists of. It is the spirit which makes you addicted, not the drug or the brief enjoyment of a cigarette, crisps, chocolate, or alcohol. Those who are addicted to something or take drugs are slaves and milking cows for certain spirits, and they should try to free themselves from them."

"Well, if that's the case, you could make a sport of it", Gregor said, throwing the cigarette he had just been about to light on the ground and crushing it. "It's disgusting, when you think about it."

"Then what's the point of summoning spirits at all?" asked Annika. "You should be happy if they don't come too close. I'll just take care of my own spirit from now on. Of course, you're welcome to visit, Andy Mo", she added apologetically. "I learnt a lot from you today."

Andy Mo was glad that he had engaged the group, and he was pleased he had managed to instil some positive thoughts into their consciousness. They called themselves Light Bearers, and their foundation was darkness. They had to learn that although one complements the other, the human spirit represents the light and not the darkness. Only those who represent the light can maintain their consciousness in all realms of creation.

The night still hung like a misty veil among the trees as Andy Mo dissolved before the gaze of those present and left the cemetery in ghostly fashion.

MAGIC IS WORKING WITH THE SPIRIT

The time until the start of the school trip flew by. Another teacher had dropped out, so the headmaster gave their class the remaining days off. The friends met daily in the mornings for their magical discussions, and together with Andy Mo they went through the contents of the Master Books systematically. Very soon they understood that magical power cannot be acquired in a few days, and that there are no magic formulas to spare you the arduous training of your own abilities.

Andy Mo also learnt a lot, and he was surprised to find that magic is evaluated quite differently from the human perspective compared to the spirit plane. Magical training has a different meaning for humans than for spirits, whose task is to use their spiritual power to 'magically' shape and transform the world, and to influence humans and the world in accordance with Divine Providence. It became clear to him that there is a significant difference between the magic of human beings and the magic that spirits learn at school. While the art of the spirits lies in their ability as immaterial beings from the world of spirits to influence, move, and transform the world of gross material matter, human magic operates in the opposite direction. Humans must learn to control their spirits. Only then can they navigate the spiritual planes and communicate consciously with spirits. On the other hand, they can control solid, visible, gross matter much better with the techniques of physics and chemistry than with the spiritual practices of magic.

Andy Mo wondered how long humans who didn't train their spirit could survive without a body. After all, he had personally observed how quickly you lose consciousness in the human realm if you don't practice spiritual exercises every day. And he understood that humans were afraid of dying. They weren't at all prepared for life without a body – that is, for life with the spirit alone.

At each meeting Kathi summarised the insights gained in a document. Little by little, this was to become the Book of the Master for children. She read out what she had noted down on the previous evening:

"Magic is the science of the spirit. True magic does not strive to change the world or to summon spirits, but conversely to learn to change yourself in such a way that the world and the spirits can no longer change or dominate you.

"Engaging in magical practices therefore requires certain spiritual abilities. You can recognise serious magical training by the fact that it teaches techniques which help to develop these basic spiritual qualities. Accordingly, the four members of the invisible spiritual body are to be trained according to the four elements.

- Imaginative capacity: Those who wish to perceive and recognise spiritual worlds and beings must first be able to form their own spiritual worlds with their imagination and learn to see, hear, and feel inner images and ideas. Imagination exercises not only strengthen the power of concentration; they also develop the spirit's ability to perceive. Only when you're able to perceive your own ideas and images as reality can you also recognise other mental forms without error.
- Willpower: Those who wish to master spiritual worlds and beings must first master the spirits which form their own being and inner world – thoughts, feelings, and urges – and free themselves from unwanted impulses. Those who are unable to do so are controlled by these spirits and are inevitably plunged into life crises by their own weaknesses (everyone has different vulnerabilities). Self-mastery and self-refinement therefore count among the first exercises of every genuine magical tradition.
- Capacity for devotion: Those who keep their focus solely upon themselves and their own problems will never truly grasp their surroundings. Therefore sympathy, self-sacrifice, and compassion are prerequisites for expanding your personal horizons. Compassion is not only beneficial for others – it also prevents spiritual isolation and hardening.
- Consciousness: Those who wish to experience spiritual worlds and beings must be able to transfer their consciousness. Con-

sciousness is also spirit and can be released and fixed with the power of the imagination. If you concentrate your consciousness on the idea 'I AM' you become independent of other consciousness-bearers and can move yourself or the ideas of your surroundings in your spirit. You are conscious because you possess consciousness, sometimes more and sometimes less. Consciousness varies in strength and it must constantly be trained, like willpower. Whenever you become aware that you are a spirit stuck in a body, you make yourself conscious. When you are aware of yourself as an observer of your 'I', you have reached the state of magical wakefulness."

Kathi was interrupted as she read her transcript out. The old-fashioned landline telephone, which belonged to Michael's grandfather and still stood on the mantelpiece, rang out loudly. Michael said something in Spanish which no one understood. When he sat down again, his face was as pale as a sheet.

"They have either kidnapped or murdered my father. His neighbour wasn't sure, but father told him that he'd found a huge emerald. He felt as though he was being watched and was planning to hide it, and he disappeared shortly afterwards. They found traces of his blood in the house. That's all the neighbour could tell me. The police are already searching for my father – which is no less dangerous, because if he still has the emerald with him, they'll take it from him and kill him just like the other bandits. Even if he managed to hide the stone before it was taken, they'll beat the hiding place out of him. What Andy Mo was fearing has come to pass." "Baphomet is playing with us", Leif said gloomily. "We're helpless. How are we supposed to fight Shadows?!"

"I'll try to get close to him immediately", Andy Mo decided. "Please be quiet so I can tune in on him." But despite his utmost concentration, he failed to locate Mr Freiwald. Exhausted, he gave up after five minutes.

"Perhaps he's unconscious", Kathi suggested. "First the fever, then the attack – it wouldn't be surprising."

"You're right", said Andy Mo. "That would explain why I can't find him. But that might even be an advantage: as long as he can't reveal where he hid the stone, they'll let him live."

"If he's still alive", Leif thought, looking at Michael pityingly. "When is the auction of your villa scheduled?"

"It's in ten days. Then we'll be out on the street. But that's a minor matter now."

"Well I'll prevent that, at the very least", said Andy Mo, disappearing from their astonished gazes.

"So he hasn't forgotten after all", Kathi remarked. Despite the grave situation, a faint glimmer of hope was spreading. Little did they know that Andy Mo's calamity was only just beginning.

*

The rage which grows out of powerlessness had spurred Andy Mo on. He knew the bank where Mr Freiwald had the loan: it was opposite Baumann's antique shop, and he also knew the manager who was personally responsible for processing it. They had seen him in the coffeehouse belonging to the bank when they were last in Hietzing. The mental leap transported him directly into his office.

At that moment he was in a meeting. The brief glance he cast at his counterpart from his ice-grey eyes was cold. It was the typical vigilant gaze of managers of the upper echelons. His sensitive, controlled facial features made him appear serious and affable, but his movements were quick and impatient. He spoke softly in short sentences, in the manner of people accustomed to having their orders followed. You could sense he knew no one would contradict him. The power of the capital he managed was reflected in the modern yet refined office furnishings, and it surrounded him like a natural aura. Nevertheless, there was no trace of an independent personality. He had a grey, expensive, tailor-made suit, a parting on the left, greying temples, rimless glasses, and a small-patterned tie. This grey, global uniformity of his caste betrayed to the initiated that he too was only a pawn on the chessboard of the game of power: a puppet on invisible strings, interchangeable with anyone else with the same face.

"I will cut the strings which bind you to Baphomet", thought Andy Mo, spiritually severing the mental cords from which the man was unknowingly hanging.

With a "srrt! srrt!" his magical axe hissed through the air and the umbilical cords of evil fell to the ground like lifeless worms. The banker clutched his forehead, appearing confused, and reached for the carafe of water. Absentmindedly, he nodded to his counterpart and said goodbye. Then Andy Mo sent him the prepared thought packet.

"Remember Baumann's proposal. Rather than the commission on the sale, the villa will bring in more to the bank if it's burdened with an interest-generating loan. Goldstein is gone, the antiquarian is broke, and you're no longer under pressure."

The banker nodded as if Andy Mo was speaking to him directly; then he leaned forward and pressed a button on the intercom.

"Bring me the Baumann file. The application is approved. The auction won't be taking place." He searched briefly in the folder a secretary had brought, then found what he was looking for and signed the paper.

"That goes out today", he called after her. "Unfortunately our prospective buyer has dropped out."

Andy Mo breathed a sigh of relief. It was done! But when he tried to transport himself back to Michael's house, he found himself unable to move again. The work had depleted his last spiritual reserves, and he couldn't even leave the office with a mental leap. Fortunately he was still invisible and could at least pass through the wall. He decided to take the bus, but as soon as he was on the street he felt he was about to lose consciousness. Then everything happened very quickly. He tried to slip into a tree, but it was too late: he fainted in the middle of the street, amidst heavy traffic. The bus, the tram, the cars – all the vehicles ran over him, but Andy Mo no longer noticed.

This time he didn't get off as lightly as the time before, when the subway ran him over and tossed him around. His stay in the human realm had made him denser. This had made him more exposed to the gross material elements and more vulnerable. His whole being was fragmented, and he was barely able to grasp the thought 'I AM' before he lost consciousness.

THE SCHOOL TRIP

"Lake Neusiedl is a steppe lake; it's thirty kilometres long and up to ten kilometres wide", explained the sailing instructor assigned to the class. "It's not deep, but it's dangerous, so don't be deceived. You can stand anywhere, but all the same, close to twenty people drown every year. The weather is fickle and storms can come up quickly. So keep an eye out for the red flags which go up when there's a storm warning. For everybody, that means: return to the harbour immediately! If you're in distress or capsize, under no circumstances should you leave the boat. The lake is dreaded for its hard, short, high waves. They can knock down even the strongest of men. Nobody can stand up to them for long. As a rule, a thunderstorm clears up after three or four hours, then lifeboats swarm out to help those who have capsized. Even if you're driven into the reeds, you must stay with the boat. The reeds are razor-sharp, so you can't wade through the marsh to the shore."

They listened as if these were the instructions before take-off in a plane, when nobody pays attention regarding the oxygen masks and emergency exits. But here it would have consequences.

It was the first day of the school trip. They were staying directly on the north shore of the lake at the Hotel Segelhafen West, where they were accommodated in cosy double and triple rooms. The hotel was situated on a peninsula which jutted far out into the lake and offered a wonderful view. Dinghies, pedal boats, and an electric boat were moored at the jetty, while a huge barbecue area with tables and benches was set up in the middle of the meadow. A cosy wooden hut offered enough seats in case of sudden rain.

The sailing lessons on the first day had been filled with theory. But it had distracted them a little, as their mood had hit rock bottom. Andy Mo had been missing for days. They didn't know if he had managed to reach Colombia, Mr Freiwald's neighbour hadn't contacted them again, and they also didn't know if they could take Einstein into their confidence. He was one of the suspects who might have been in league with Baphomet. As a consequence they had decided not to let him in on their secret.

Most of the class had followed the young sports teacher to Neusiedl that evening. The programme mentioned culture, the old town, and heritage preservation, but everyone knew there was a disco there as well. Besides the five friends, five other interested students had gathered around Einstein and were listening eagerly to his words.

"I suppose the main reason I wanted to go to India was to find a guru", Einstein said, stoking the embers of the dwindling campfire with a stick until small flames flickered up again. They were sitting on the shore of the lake after a barbecue; the sun had set in a flaming red spectacle of colour, as if the fire had ignited the sky. A balmy breeze blew from across the water.

"When I began thinking seriously back in the forties, there wasn't the extensive literature on magic and mysticism or the trash which floods the book market today. A few treatises on yoga, a handful of banal writings on magic, and the dubious insights of the Theosophists and Anthroposophists. That was it. However, there were plenty of allusions to 'masters' who guard 'secrets' which they only pass on to worthy disciples. Without the personal guidance of a genuine guru, the books taught, it would be impossible to attain the great enlightenment."

"Isn't that what they're still claiming today?" asked Leif. "That whole thing about gurus is in almost every relevant book."

"Right. But in the meantime, some people with varying degrees of initiation into the occult sciences have released thought-provoking ideas and instructions for spiritual training which you can follow. If you inform yourself sufficiently, you'll find that most of these authors don't have much practical experience themselves, but you'll also come across some useful information and – if you make an effort – you'll find your own path. The best guidance I found was in the works of Franz Bardon [*Initiation into Hermetics*, Merkur Publishing], whom I consider to be a true initiate. With his books he prepared the way for the 'Magic and Mysticism of the Third Millennium' [Emil Stejnar, *Magic and Mysticism of the Third Millennium*, 13 volumes, Stejnar Verlag, Vienna]."

"So what about these initiates?" asked Kathi. "Are there really people who can perform magic? And do you need such an adept as a teacher, or can you follow your own path alone?"

Einstein fished about for a bottle of mineral water, took a hearty swig, and discreetly suppressed a belch.

"Maybe you shouldn't think of an initiate as a miracle worker who can do whatever they want. As long as somebody inhabits a body and has a digestive system, they must struggle with their bodily needs, urges, emotions, and their hostile environment, just like everybody else. An adept is more an adept because of what they do not do rather than what they do, as Albert Camus wrote. But if someone today claims to be an adept, I would be cautious.

"And as far as your second question is concerned, I'm convinced not only that you can, but indeed that you *must* go your own way. It may have been different in the past. Perhaps there were actual classes in temple schools; recent research on alleged initiations in ancient Egypt suggests the opposite. But regardless, that time is over. The priests of all religions and the masters of the Lodges, orders, and secret societies have magically and morally degenerated to such an extent that they can no longer achieve anything spiritually. They're incapable of initiating a neophyte and inducting them into magic and mysticism, as some Lodges promise. The same is true in India and Tibet, you can take my word for that. On the other hand, ordinary mortals today – and your generation in particular – are far freer and more independent, and thus wiser and stronger. You don't need a temple school; you just have to consciously go through the school of life. That will suffice.

"Stejnar has described all this clearly in his books. Everyday life is the best school to acquire magical power. You can use every resistance like an invisible fitness machine for your spiritual muscles.

"If you don't get out of bed in the morning and loll about for some minutes after the alarm clock rings, unable to muster the will to finally get up, you lose a lot of energy. On the other hand, if you consciously think before you get out of bed: 'I want to do it, and now I will', and then get out of bed with one swing of your legs, you instantly transfer all the energy you would otherwise have invested in effort into your spirit. Inertia is transformed into pure willpower, which is at your disposal at any time.

"A lot of energy is also wasted with gossiping; conversely, that energy can be gained for yourself if you master your need to communicate and don't immediately relay every piece of news. If you keep something you'd like to tell others to yourself, and if you don't constantly hang onto your mobile phone out of curiosity, you convert all the energy which compels you to talk into pure spiritual power. Strong personalities are always discreet people. Silence is the easiest way to learn to master the spirit.

"Self-discipline is the secret of all successful people. There are countless opportunities every day to keep yourself spiritually fit and to replenish your energy for successful action.

"For example, if you do your homework with frustration and reluctance, and you're already thinking about swimming or being on the computer, then all the energy you spend on the activity you dislike will be lost in the form of a bad mood. However, if you realise that you're a spirit inhabiting a body and you work on your brain so that it's available to you tomorrow as an even better tool for living in this world, then the whole process becomes meaningful and lends you a sense of achievement which strengthens your self-confidence. In this way you automatically become your own boss and gradually gain a better grip on your consciousness.

"There's nothing bad that doesn't also bring something good. You can transform every annoyance, every defeat, and every loss into a spiritual victory if you don't let it upset you, if you exercise self-control, and if you keep in check the negative emotions which wish to motivate you. You can even use laziness for your spiritual training. If you're sitting passively in front of the television, mindlessly staring at nonsense, you can also do it consciously and try to sit upright and motionless instead of slouching. In this exercise, too, you gain spiritual power instead of losing it." Einstein took another sip from the bottle and continued his lecture.

"Walk your own path. Walk the path of practice. Everyday life offers daily opportunities for conscious training of the spirit. Don't waste time searching for secret teachings. It suffices to gain an overview of the possibilities which exist so that you don't follow a single teaching unilaterally. That would be the only mistake you could make in the search for truth: to imagine you've found it.

"There are many paths, not only the path of mysticism and magic. Religion, philosophy, shamanism, alchemy, Kabbalah, tarot – they all try to explain the connection between the visible and invisible worlds. But so far only astrology has succeeded. The mystery schools and initiatory societies – the Freemasons, Rosicrucians, and the Christian orders which address these matters, depending on their tradition – are also groping in the dark. None of these paths leads to the destination. Nor do the pseudo-magical circles which conjure up spirits and demons behind graveyard walls; at best, fuelled by false expectations or real drugs, they unleash the pig of perverted ideas. The entirety of so-called esotericism is pure theft of time. It doesn't even offer vistas which broaden your horizon; rather, it blinds and obscures. That's why you must never stop and believe that you've found the truth; you must always go further.

"Of course, this also applies to the magic and mysticism which I'm portraying here. You shouldn't believe that the 'magic and mysticism of the third millennium' has all the answers to every question. But that is precisely why it surpasses the religions, philosophies, and Hermetics of the ancients: because it does not proclaim truths, but rather shows you paths which you can follow to gather your own insights."

"Is there such a truth?" the little know-it-all philosopher asked;

he had already attracted attention with his questions at school. "The religions make claims which we are obliged to believe. The esoterics tell fairy tales for adults about spirits, the afterlife, and magical power. Even philosophy, at best, can make statements about the limits of our knowledge and set rules about how to ask and answer questions so that logic isn't lost altogether."

Einstein nodded.

"That's a good question. But in magic and mysticism, practice matters as well, not just thinking. It's possible to have spiritual experiences which you don't only think about but actually live through: out-of-body experiences, for example, or the phenomenon of astrology and the miracle of succeeding in 'magically' changing reality with the power of your desire and imagination. But since belief and expectations also play a role when working with the spirit, you only ever deal with subjective experiences which cannot be scientifically confirmed or proven. In the science of the spirit, false expectations lead to distorted results or failures. That's what makes it so difficult to recognise an objective 'truth'. So you're right: what we believe is not a valid truth. But that doesn't mean it can't exist."

But the little one wouldn't let it rest.

"How about magic, Professor? You're not suggesting it exists, are you?"

"I believe in it, at least. I've experienced several things in my life which can be explained as being brought about by the power of the spirit. But you can never be sure whether a magical project – that is, work with the spirit – will succeed. Most of the time nothing happens; or only much later, when you no longer have any interest in it at all. A lot is coincidence or would probably have happened anyway. In any case, it's immensely difficult and requires a tremendously strong will, a crystal-clear imagination, and a colossal ability to concentrate. If you don't possess these spiritual abilities you'll achieve nothing magically. Without the power of the spirit, you cannot move the spiritual forces."

"Unless you possess a magic wand", interjected a Harry Potter fan, laughing. "Seriously, though – you obviously can't buy one in a supermarket for initiates, but maybe you can inherit one? And what about magical formulas? Are the reports about them all just tall tales?"

"No", Einstein replied, "they existed in the magical practice of all cultures, and people still work with them today. But they are merely aids for consciousness which help the shamans and magicians who use them to concentrate. By themselves, these objects do nothing. Franz Bardon describes this in great detail in his book *Initiation into Hermetics*. A magic wand must be charged, otherwise it is ineffective, and the same applies to swords, daggers, formulas, and rituals. You must constantly engage with your magical objects and make yourself aware of their contents over and over again, otherwise they lose their power very quickly. I'm not aware of any magic formulas which do anything on their own, except perhaps hallucinations or the short-term manifestations of spectres. Formulas must also be imbued with spiritual power and strength and pronounced correctly if you wish to achieve anything with them. There are no magic formulas which have supposedly been pre-charged by initiates or hocus-pocus which works by itself. The things that have been published on the book market and the internet in recent years have long since been squeezed dry like a lemon by thousands of curious would-be magicians. Even the formulas which were genuine are now completely ineffective. You won't succeed if you haven't mastered the spirit yourself, even if you use magic wands and formulas.

"Believe me, binding and moving the spirit is far more difficult than taking matters into your own hands. I assure you that anyone who is capable of doing so is also capable of achieving what they desire and wish to conjure by ordinary means."

"Then what's the purpose of magical power?" asked someone who was new to the group. "Once I finally have it, I won't need it anymore."

"That's precisely why you need it. Because you train your spirit via the exercises, and thereby develop yourself further. It's about the exercises, not the power. I would strongly advise anyone against taking up magic if they expect anything more from it than developing into a more confident, stronger, more sensible, and more understanding person."

"What about an abhisheka?" asked Leif. "I believe it's said that in India gurus can confer extraordinary abilities, i.e. magical power, on their disciples."

"Well, I personally haven't met a single guru who was able to do that. But I also don't know any disciple who would be sufficiently prepared for such an initiation. I've only read about it. There were initiations and consecrations in other cultures and traditions too. I believe, however, that they were more about imparting knowledge and insights than about the transmission of any dubious powers. Above all, it was about awakening the student's faith in themselves and their own abilities. Through an initiation, the person concerned is given the feeling that they have been chosen. It's a mental accolade. They receive confirmation of their dignity and authority. Such a ceremony can indeed have an impact.

"But even these disciples and priests often had to perform certain exercises for years before they were granted access to spiritual power through the initiation. Everyone has to earn magical power for themselves; it's a skill, a quality, and not a possession which can be acquired or given away like money. Those who receive money as a gift don't gain the ability to earn it themselves in the future. As a rule, it takes a long time to learn to influence other spirits with your own spirit, or even to influence the material environment by virtue of your will.

"Again, beware of anything which you can achieve by external means. By doing so you destroy the possibility of reaching your goal through your own power. All magical objects are at best aids for consciousness, crutches for the spirit, and it's best not to get used to them in the first place.

"You can use the power of the spirit to shape your life even without magic and grand enchantments. You don't have to be a great initiate and summon demons and spirits. Everybody has enough spirit within them which they can set to work for their own benefit. It even works automatically if you do it correctly. But we'll talk about that another time."

Einstein reached for a brown plastic shopping bag which he always carried around with him like a bum; he began to hand out the contents. They were paperbacks.

"*The Mischief of Living and Dying, The End of Mischief*", he declared aloud. "By Prentice Mulford – it's my favourite book.

"I obtained the German translation for you rather than the original English version because I think the lady who translated it – who called herself Sir Galahad – put it all far better than the author himself. This book has accompanied me throughout my life. I owe my success in life to this thought magic which Mulford teaches. This isn't magic with some dubious powers or forces which you must summon and which you do not understand. Everything you achieve in this way is created with your own power."

"This is a strange sailing course", murmured the little philosopher, thanking him for the gift. "Rather than sailing on the water, we're learning how to navigate through life."

HUMANS ARE THE NEXT SPIRITS

Afterwards the five friends met in the girls' room. Kathi had created an evocative atmosphere with the help of some candles from the dining room. They sat on the carpeted floor. Yks had gotten drunk out of concern for Andy Mo, and he was bellowing an old sea shanty in a raspy voice on the curtain rail when a knock came from the door. It was Einstein. At first they were startled, but the professor waved it off.

"No need to panic, I won't reveal our secret." He took out some apple juice, mineral water, fresh strawberries, and chocolate from a red and yellow plastic shopping bag from the nearby supermarket and placed them on the table. Then he sat down with the friends on the floor.

"I know you're a little more advanced than the others. But I don't want to learn your secret – I just want you to know that dealing with magic involves dangers."

"We've already noticed", Christian confirmed. "We're going ahead with it anyway, though."

"That's fine. I didn't expect anything different. Knowing, daring, willing, and keeping silent are four important qualities on the path of magic. By now, I'm sure you've also noticed that magic is not only dangerous, but also damn difficult. Magic is work with the spirit, and working with the spirit is the most challenging thing imaginable. Every profession is more easily learnt, every degree more quickly completed, every art is simpler than the science of magic and mysticism."

"We've come to realise that as well", Christian said. "But we don't want to conjure up happiness, success, and love, or summon spirits; we have something else in mind."

"It doesn't matter", Einstein agreed. "In magic, nothing works without the spirit. And spirit is neither a nebulous web of light nor an inanimate thing like matter or electric current. Spirit is alive. Spirit is always endowed with a life of its own. So you must master it. But you still don't need to conjure up spirits; you can also make the spiritual powers serve you in another way. It works according to the same rules as communication in the human realm. You just have to address the spirits correctly. Which spirits are closest to you here?" No one said anything.

"The earth spirits?" asked Michael, and he was right, but Einstein shook his head.

"The human spirits. You're surrounded by human spirits from morning till night. Everywhere you look there are humans. They're just like the spirits in the spirit world, only they inhabit a body. And if you want something, wish for something, need something, then you must always deal with people first. Without them, nothing works. You're always dependent on other people. They're the ones who help us or stand in our way and thus influence our lives. You need other people for your happiness, and you must be careful that they don't make you unhappy."

"That's obvious", said Leif. "What does that have to do with magic?"

"I'll explain that to you right now. Getting a human being to be favourably disposed towards you and serve you is no less difficult than enlisting a spirit's service. And it works according to the same laws. It's already hard enough protecting yourself from being exploited and harmed by others. But there are certain rules which govern the functioning of the human spirit. If you know them, you're already halfway there. Of course you might also call it psychology. Once you enter the professional world, you're dealing with people who are more likely to turn into hyenas than angels."

"You shoot hyenas", Leif remarked dryly. "Anyone who stands in my way gets taken out."

"That way you yourself become a hyena. You may be able to spread fear and achieve certain things, but you won't gain any friends who support you, and eventually someone else will shoot you. People will only serve you if they have to, or if they get something in return. They will only voluntarily help you if they like you. What does someone who doesn't like you expect from you?"

"Nothing", Leif replied. "Disadvantage at best – but now I understand. And you mean it's the same with spirits?"

Einstein nodded.

"In the case of magic, too, affection works according to the laws of sympathy. You don't need to invoke spirits. Instead of summoning them before you with a formula – which usually doesn't work anyway – you can contact them by bringing their abilities to life in your own consciousness. This captures their attention and makes you likable to them. An air spirit loves intelligent, curious, optimistic people. A water spirit is drawn to depth of feeling, so it loves romantics, artists, and empathetic people with compassion. Fire spirits are attracted to courageous, athletic, enthusiastic types. And earth spirits seek the company of serious, conscientious people who love order."

Einstein brought out the strawberries and chocolate and was pleased to see everyone enjoying them.

"Let's take a spell for financial success as an example. The earth spirits are responsible for prosperity. In the old days, people used to offer gifts to the gnomes they summoned – things they knew gnomes liked, such as a gold coin or a precious stone. They also offered fruits, grains, and bread, because gnomes oversee the growth of nature, which serves the prosperity of the people. Earth spirits provide, gather, and order things; they are industrious. They would never turn to a careless, superficial person who throws money away. In fact they would rather take care of a stingy egoist. If someone is thrifty and hard-working, the earth spirits find them likeable. They're attracted to them and will help them. So thrift is one of the secrets of success and wealth. That's not because thrift accumulates money, as a great fortune is not made through savings alone; rather, if you are thrifty, the earth spirits automatically take notice of you and help you to accumulate money and wealth. And if you're conscientious and diligent, they linger in your spiritual environment and inspire you to make the right decisions. They also inspire others to support you in your endeavours."

"Or they let someone die so you can receive an inheritance", Leif interjected. "There's a story about Aleister Crowley – he supposedly performed a spell for wealth, some kind of conjuration to raise a hidden treasure, and shortly afterwards he was granted a large inheritance."

"We don't know which spirit he summoned back then", Einstein said. "Supposedly it was a pact with a demon from the *Sixth Book of Moses*. There are different accounts concerning this matter; we might talk about these medieval practices some other time, as they don't have much to do with true magic and rarely have any effects. Crowley was a drug-addled eccentric rather than a magician. Although he had mediumistic abilities and wrote a lot about yoga and magic, today his writings are outdated, even if they were interesting at that time because there was nothing else. Nowadays, with Bardon's instructions, we have a systematic training of the spirit and soul which clearly reveals the mysteries of magic and mysticism. Moreover, we live in a different time. The boundaries between worlds have shifted.

"Today, spirits no longer have the same direct contact with humans as they did in the past. However, they perceive all the more clearly what emanates from us. And they still feed on our thoughts, feelings, and emotions, to which they react in a similar way as we do to our favourite music or food: we listen, we reach for it, and so do the spirits. Probably the spirits are as unaware of this as humans are – there's a constant exchange between the worlds without us noticing. All beings with the same qualities and interests are networked and interconnected with one another and are in spiritual contact."

"Does that also apply to negative qualities?" asked Miri Li. "That would be terrible. It would mean that with every bad thought and every unpleasant mood, you attract a negative being into your proximity without even realising it."

"Alas, this is also true for negative beings. That's why control of thoughts and emotions is the first thing a student of magic must learn."

Einstein looked up at the clock.

"We're way overtime. The sun has already risen in Tibet. I wish you all a good night." He turned around once more at the doorway: "I hope the young gentlemen will also be retiring to their rooms."

*

The next day was completely windless and calm again: it wasn't a good day for sailing. After the morning theory class, most of them spent their time with pedal boats and swimming. Some gathered around Einstein, discussing esotericism and magic.

"So how do I attain magical power?" asked Leif. "Transmission through a guru doesn't work. Initiations don't work anymore, and the real masters have died out. So I have to achieve it on my own. But where do I get the spiritual power so that I can perform magic?"

"Through yourself; specifically, from your body", Einstein stated. "It's a living fitness machine. The human spirit isn't born into the world; rather, it is born into a body. You owe it to your body that you are the way that you are. You can only realise all your abilities because you have a body. Everything you see of the world, you experience through the body. Through your body's sensory organs you perceive your surroundings; its impulses, urges, and needs awaken your feelings, and thanks to your brain you can process and coordinate everything. The body's senses convey impressions from this world to you. Its limbs enable you to act in this world. And its hormonal impulses are the energies which motivate and drive you. The body is the most valuable thing a human being possesses. Strictly speaking, we don't live in the world, but in our body. We aren't born into this world, but into our bodies."

"After all, we're incarnate – from Latin *in carne*, meaning to be born in the flesh", chimed in the little know-it-all philosopher.

"Well, sure", said one student. "Chilli con carne, we know that."

"Fiona con carne is even spicier", said another; he played the keyboard in Fiona's band.

"Shut up!" Leif said, grinning. "So what about training the will, professor? What is the will, anyway? If I understand the matter correctly, your will is ultimately directed against yourself."

"No", said Einstein, standing up to stretch his feet, which had fallen asleep. "The will is always a part of you. What is not part of you are your emotions, passions, and bad habits. These are outgrowths of you which you must straighten out. If these impulses are directed against your will, then you can fight against them, and if you are victorious, the energy of the conquered instincts, the mastered emotions, and the controlled impulses transfers directly into your spirit. Then the bodily drives and emotions become spiritual power and will power."

"But my urges are stronger than me, and they always seem to turn against me. I make a resolution not to smoke, but then I usually give in and light up another cigarette."

"You give up too quickly. Wait five minutes, and you'll notice that the compulsion becomes weaker, not stronger."

"That's true!" exclaimed Beate, who was constantly struggling with weight problems and was quite chubby. "I could devour kilos of chocolate, especially after dinner. That's when I stuff myself full of anything sweet. But if I manage to say no once, and steadfastly refrain from indulging myself, then the craving actually disappears, and after fifteen minutes I don't even think about it anymore. Then I note that I've just saved four hundred calories, and that satisfies me more than the chocolate. It strengthens me somehow. Sometimes a victory like that over my gluttony helps me for several days in a row, and I feel much better in general because I know I've succeeded. But I usually succumb again."

Einstein nodded.

"That's unfortunately the way it is. But don't let that irritate you or even discourage you. You've noticed it yourself: after every victory you feel a little better. You have more spiritual strength afterwards. That's why the urges which are bothering you are also good. However, you mustn't let them overwhelm you – only when you give your body too much freedom does it become your opponent. Otherwise it's your best sparring partner, a partner with whom you can consciously train your will and exercise your spiritual muscles. When something inside you stirs and wants something you think is wrong, you turn the tables and say no!"

"That creates a contradiction", Leif protested. "If I can fight my bad habits, then surely I already have the necessary willpower – and if I lack it, I can't fight them. Surely I can't pull myself out of a quagmire by my own tie?!"

"When you activate your will, you're not grabbing your tie, but rather the fixed point in the spiritual world which lends you support. It's like reaching for a branch on the riverbank. Start where it's easier for you: go jogging when you feel like having a cigarette. You'll probably find it easier to overcome yourself, and each triumph brings new willpower. As you're running, realise that you're stronger than the smoking spectre which lives through you and makes you want to smoke. And with every breath, think of the vital force flowing into you with the oxygen. Just as the energy from physical exertion is transformed into heat, so the energy which you expend in overcoming your inertia and which is released by your exertion while running is transformed into pure spiritual power. With that power, if you wish, you can even work magic.

"And take small steps. I don't just mean in running, but in training your will to gain spiritual power.

"You developed your habit gradually, and I'm sure you didn't enjoy that first cigarette. Now you reverse the process: you slowly get rid of the craving. Purposefully reduce your consumption. Make a resolution to smoke only a certain number of cigarettes per day – and when you do smoke, consciously delay the timing by fifteen minutes each time. Say to yourself: 'I smoke because I desire it, but I smoke when I decide and wish to. And I don't wish to smoke for another ten minutes.' Of course, this also works with chocolate, food, computers, the internet, and telephone calls.

"Anything which requires effort and which you do consciously and willingly strengthens your willpower. Not just sport: listening patiently, completing tasks instead of leaving them unfinished, suppressing anger, overcoming cravings for cola, chocolate, or crisps. Or conversely, doing something immediately which you really wanted to do later: homework, tidying up your room. These inner impulses and urges are not mindless energies. They are spectres – in other words, spirits which have a life of their own and which drain your spiritual energy if you follow their impulses. Equally, you gain spiritual energy when you defeat a spectre which seeks to make you do something."

"Now I understand why our virtuous grandfathers wagged their fingers", Leif remarked, grinning. "They practised magic without even knowing it."

THE MAGIC OF THE ATTRACTING POWER OF THOUGHTS AND WISHES

Word had spread that Einstein was holding a course on magic, and the next evening, instead of nine students, almost the entire class gathered around the beloved teacher. Due to a complete lack of wind, the sailing course had been cancelled once again. They had hired a bus instead and had visited Budapest. Now they were tired, and some of them had already retired to their rooms. Once again they sat around the large barbecue area, where the embers were still glowing. Yks was perched languidly on a tree; Andy Mo still hadn't shown up. They had considered calling him with the magic crystal, but then decided against it. "If he did make it to Colombia", Leif had said, "we'd only be disturbing him. We can't help him anyway." The others agreed with him, so they let it be.

"So what is magic, anyway?" Einstein began, looking questioningly around the table. At first no one said anything, because no one had thought about it that much. Then a girl spoke up.

"Well, when I want something and imagine it happening, and then it really happens, then –"

"Then it's a miracle", someone interrupted her, and everyone laughed. The girl's name was Michaela, and everything that could go wrong for her really did go wrong. But Einstein agreed with her.

"Michaela hit the nail right on the head. The foundation of true magic is the will and the imagination. There is no sorcery or miracles. Even behind these phenomena there's a system and an active spiritual power which can be traced back to will and imagination. If you achieve physical effects or other changes in the world or in consciousness by non-physical, non-chemical, non-electromagnetic means, that's magic. Or rather, it seems magical because you can't see the cause of the effect, which is on another plane. One plane is the gross material world in which we live, and the other plane is the ethereal world on which we think, feel, and will. All the non-material things – such as the thoughts, feelings, desires, and emotions which move us and make us think and act each and every day – are intangible, but nevertheless very real. Indeed, they constitute the most important part of our lives. That should be clear to you. You must control them, master them, and include them in your life as very real active forces.

"Magic involves grasping the hidden subtle relationships between cause and effect. The reverse is also true: if a physical impression alters your mind, i.e. your thinking, or the mood of your psyche, this is also a magical act. That includes ceremonies, rituals, and prayers, which are demonstrably capable of creating moods, arousing feelings, and elevating consciousness to a different plane. Any influence of one plane on another is magic."

"What is meant when we speak of a 'plane'?" asked the little philosopher.

"Good question. In simple terms, the Hermetics distinguish between three planes. Firstly, the gross material plane. That's the physical, tangible, visible world, which includes your body and all the galaxies.

"Secondly, the so-called astral plane, which encompasses all feelings, moods, hopes, and fears, in other words everything which moves you internally and subsequently prompts you to move your body because you want something, desire something, or feel like doing something. And thirdly, the spiritual plane on which thought-images and ideas emerge; you need these to plan things and orient yourself. We always speak of magic when the cause of an effect is nurtured on another plane."

"Wouldn't that make every musician and composer a magician?" asked Kathi. "Music is a vibration of the air, so it comes from the gross material plane, but it still completely changes the mood – that is, the astral plane – and can change and elevate a person's consciousness in a totally non-material way. Music can make you feel peaceful, awaken romantic feelings of love, make you sad, or totally disinhibit you and place you in a trance like a drug. In my opinion, sacred music such as the great masses can even replace a church, granting you that sublime feeling of eternity and closeness to God."

"I do indeed count the great composers as initiates", Einstein agreed. "But even comedians lift your spirits, and advertisers make you want something you probably don't need, thus interfering with your consciousness. We are constantly surrounded by magical phenomena without even realising it. However, we weren't intending to philosophise today, but rather to discuss magical practice.

"What is the aim of somebody who purposefully and consciously engages in magic? Unless they are driven by the search for knowledge, they wish to improve their own life or the fate of another person. It often revolves around everyday matters like money, health, love, and happiness.

"And now I'm going to reveal something to you. You can have all this much more easily. The whole secret lies in the power of thought and in the force of right wishing.

"How do the spirits and the powers of destiny influence people? They can neither touch us physically nor speak to us and tell us to do this or that. They can only inspire us by implanting thoughts within us to think something specific. These thoughts then give rise to desires, and these desires foment things. They make us think and wish to do, or not to do, one thing or another. The language of the spirits is thinking, and they move us through feelings. So if you want to be a free and independent individual, the first thing you must do is master your thoughts and feelings.

"If you wish to move the world, you must first move yourself. Who said that?"

"Socrates", replied the little philosopher dutifully, and Einstein nodded.

"And those who wish to master spirits should first master their own spirit. That's not from Socrates, that's from me. Magical training is nothing more than an ingenious practical system for learning to control your thoughts, feelings, and desires. Thoughts can be helpful spirits, just as they can sometimes degenerate into little demons which then connect you to the greater cosmic demons. With your thoughts, you can help shape your destiny; through thinking, you can free yourself from dependence on gods and demons.

"Magic, therefore, begins when you wake up in bed with positive thoughts, not just during a grand incantation in the temple or an invocation behind a cemetery wall. In fact that's where magic usually ends, because instead of working with your own spirit and the power of your thoughts, you enlist other spirits. And that always goes wrong. I know many shamans, sorcerers, and other personalities who practised magic in this way. Sooner or later they all failed.

"Before you can practice ceremonial magic successfully, a transformation of your being must take place. Those who still have weaknesses and are moved by any addictions or cravings against their will are never able to move other spirits. First and foremost, a magician must master their own spiritual components of being: that is, the thoughts, feelings, and bodily urges which move them and mediate their consciousness. Only then can they use them to call other spirits, impress them with their personality, and make it clear what they want from them.

"The stupidest thing you can do is believe that you have magical power. Even if you seem to have gained some successes – and everyone has them initially, and occasionally later as well – you are being fooled. It wasn't you who made something happen; it was fate or chance. But most often it was some little spirit who played with your thoughts like little cats with a ball of wool, thus making knots in the fabric of your destiny which must then be untangled.

"Incidentally, it's even more foolish to believe that someone else has magical power and would perform a spell for or against you. It's difficult enough to make something happen for yourself with spiritual power. For someone else, the effort is exorbitant. Only charlatans offer to do such things.

"That's something I didn't understand until much later", Einstein said, his gaze wandering into the distance as if he were seeking to recapture the past. "We don't need magic; we carry the power to change things within ourselves. An unassuming book led me to this realisation – the author was Prentice Mulford. As well as practice. Anyone who knows and practices the mechanisms of positive thinking recognised by Mulford is a magician who can mysteriously shape their future to their liking. At the moment you are still too young and impetuous. The desires you have now will not tolerate any delay; they want to be satisfied, like hunger and thirst. But as you grow older, your paths will diverge. Some will continue to chase after the short-lived pleasures and delights which seduce and tempt you, seeking to satisfy them immediately; others think further into the future and strive to shape it for themselves. They plan something and exercise their will to achieve it.

"Willing and planning: that is spiritual work. Spirit manifests itself in thoughts. And just as spirit expresses itself in thoughts, so thoughts sooner or later manifest themselves in the world. Thoughts are forces and energies with which you can alter and transform the whole world. Not just in your own head. Once you understand this, you don't need magic anymore: you know you carry within you the most powerful magic wand, as well as the spirits you can summon with it.

"Thoughts are not blind energies; thoughts are already little spirits, and they become helpful spirits if you use and control them correctly. Every thought of something creates an image and thereby calls forth a certain being of the thought, a spiritual manifestation of it. When you think of something, it exists as a spiritual image, and not only in your own mind. You're surely familiar with the phenomenon of wanting to call someone, and at that very moment the mobile rings and the person calls. Or you think something and someone else says it. Thoughts spread and can jump to others. Think of a mass demonstration where thousands of people, possessed by a thought, shout out the same thing.

"What's more, thoughts lead a life of their own. Especially if they're emotionally charged. Some thoughts and ideas you simply can't get rid of. There's more energy in a thought than in dynamite. It has the power of a hungry animal and resembles the human instinct for self-preservation. Thoughts wish to be thought further and manifested, and in doing so they behave like living beings; no one notices, however, because they are spiritual living beings."

The little philosopher spoke up again: "But Mulford said that thoughts are energies. I read your book all night long – he describes thoughts as ethereal powers which can be mobilised in a targeted manner."

"You're right", Einstein confirmed. "But a hundred years have passed since Mulford's death. Even the science of the spirit continues to develop and arrive at new insights. Bardon describes thoughts as little spirits and calls them elementals. I see in them the ethereal molecules, the spiritual cells of being, comprising our ethereal consciousness-mediating personality. I think we're both correct, because every thought connects with a feeling or arises from a sensation, and these are indeed forces which carry and move us – not just inwardly, but also very tangibly through the gross material world.

"The thought of the pizza in the fridge – perhaps it was just awakened by an advert – makes you want the pizza, and soon it makes you actually go to the fridge." Then Einstein looked at Fiona: "And the thought of that lovely bikini probably haunted you until you bought it." Fiona blushed and nodded.

"And in the same way, focused thoughts concerning a trait or skill you wish to acquire will actually lead you to develop that trait or skill within yourself. Similarly, the idea of a particular career goal will lead you to take certain steps, connecting you with people who'll help you to fulfil that desire. Experience shows that thoughts can also jump to other people.

"However, the attracting force is not craving, for that is connected with the feeling of lacking. You shouldn't dream about how it might be, but rather imagine that it already exists. It must be experienced and felt in thought as already manifested and present."

"But that's deceiving yourself", Kathi said. "I would have problems doing that."

"You needn't have problems with it, because what you imagine has actually already been realised and is present in your thoughts. And you must see it as something already manifested, not as a future dream. The mistake people make with so-called positive thinking is that they view what they desire as if they were watching a movie. But you must experience it as if you were standing on the stage yourself, right in the midst of the action. You should never sit in the audience while watching your life dreams.

"Let's conduct an experiment. Close your eyes and think of what you would wish for and conjure up if you had magical powers. Imagine it. Go through it in your thoughts in every detail. Experience it as vividly as if it were reality." After five minutes he clapped his hands.

"Who's ready to tell us what they experienced?" asked Einstein, and since no one came forward, he looked questioningly at Fiona, who everyone knew sang in a band and enjoyed being on stage.

"Yes, well of course I saw myself as a successful star standing on stage, cheered by my fans." Suddenly she realised what Einstein had meant earlier. "You're right. I wasn't on stage at all: I saw myself standing on stage, I was at a distance from myself. In reality I should have been watching the audience when I did that, not the other way round. The Fiona on stage was my idea of me; it wasn't me." Now Leif also spoke up.

"I had the same experience. The Porsche was in front of my house: I could envision it very well, and I saw myself getting in and driving away. I saw myself, but I wasn't actually driving away, because I was still standing in front of the house. And then there was another wish that was preoccupying me, and the whole thing became quite a chaos of thoughts. So it's not that easy; it's just as difficult as magic."

"Not once you figure out how it works. And it's more reliable than magic. You don't need to obsessively meditate on it for hours. Quite the contrary: that would be a bad thing, because then you would keep the thoughts which are supposed to work for you inside yourself, instead of sending them out so they can germinate like seeds in the soil of destiny. Brief reminders of what you desire are sufficient. I say reminders because you must imagine the wish as if it were already realised. It's like an order placed on the internet: the item is ordered, paid for, and the shipment is on its way. Granted, destiny's deliveries take a little longer, depending on the nature of the wish, but I guarantee you that when you correctly order something spiritually it will also arrive.

"The mood you feel when you think of what you want is particularly important, because it's your feelings which animate your thoughts and carry them in the direction of manifestation. There are numerous books on so-called positive thinking, but the fact you must also feel positive is rarely mentioned. Yet this is immensely important. Often the confident mood doesn't arise because you doubt your success. But it's precisely this cheerful, relaxed, even joyful disposition which is important, because as long as it prevails, no negative feeling can spread and hinder your belief in success.

"Now, let me tell you how I conducted my first experiment with Mulford's type of thought magic. I had already made up my mind to go to India before I completed school. I was obsessed with the idea of attaining great enlightenment there and was determined to find a guru. However, back then travelling wasn't as easy as it is today, and a ticket cost a lot of money. So I applied for a work permit in Sweden, where students could earn relatively large amounts of money in a short time. But the chances of obtaining the permit before the summer were slim, because the quota was limited, the demand was high, and I was a bit too young. In addition, you needed proof that you'd already found a job and a place to live.

"Every day on my way to school I had to cross the Ameis Bridge, under which the long-distance trains to Hamburg passed in the direction of Sweden. I never watched these trains wistfully as they passed. On the contrary: they were a promise to me. I knew that I would soon be on the seven forty-five morning train from Vienna, which I saw passing beneath me every day. I didn't have the slightest doubt. I always looked with joy at the long, modern carriages heading towards Sweden; spiritually, I already had the train ticket in my pocket. And I was indeed successful. Through a newspaper ad I found a job in a hotel in Jönköping – first as a dishwasher, but then the porter left, and I was allowed to replace him. It turned out to be a fantastic Nordic summer, and before winter had set in I was on my way to India."

Einstein was silent for a long time; he seemed to be reliving his youth in his mind. He got up and was about to walk to the lakeside, but he came straight back.

"Choose a life dream for yourself. When I said you shouldn't dream but rather envision specifically what you desire, that's not a contradiction. Many a success began with a dream. Numerous individuals who achieved extraordinary things were already convinced in childhood that they were capable of these remarkable feats and believed they would fulfil their life's dream. The biographies of geniuses are full of such statements."

"In that case I'll soon be a wealthy man!" exclaimed Hans Peter Bundschuh, one of the laziest students in the class. "I've long dreamt of living in the Seychelles and having the most beautiful girls swimming in the pool in front of my villa, all of them well-disposed towards me."

"Just wishing for a lot of money and dreaming about lying in the sun on a sandy beach doesn't help, of course. If dreams came true automatically, the world would be full of millionaires. You must start at the beginning of your dream and have as clear an idea as possible of how to earn the money. It goes without saying that it should be within the scope of your existing abilities – and if you don't possess them, you must acquire them."

"And what if that's not possible because I'm simply a failure?" asked Peter Stuppke, who really wasn't a lucky person. "After all, I embarrass myself constantly and I can't think of anything positive to say about myself."

"Even the biggest failure is perceived as a strong personality if they stand up for themselves – like you just did – rather than trying to appear more than they are to the outside world." The other students applauded and nodded encouragingly at Peter.

"You see", Einstein continued, "that's already precisely the first step towards success. You're no clumsier than the others, you just don't have enough self-confidence. And you lack a goal. Set one and you will achieve it. To be happy, it's not important to possess a lot, but rather to desire little. You don't have to be insanely clever to do that. Who do you think is richer: someone who wears only designer jeans because otherwise they feel inferior, or someone who prefers to wear cheap, casual, comfortable linen trousers and can't tell expensive Prada outfits from H&M clothes? A true personality doesn't need status symbols. On the contrary, they'd feel uncomfortable wearing the uniform of insecure snobs.

"And another thing is important", Einstein added. "Concentrate on only one wish at a time. It's like light. Focused light illuminates the spot where the beam is directed more effectively. What you imagine becomes clearer, so the powers of destiny also see what really matters to you and can help you more easily."

Einstein glanced at his watch.

"And now I'll reveal to you the most crucial aspect of so-called positive thinking. Silence. It's incredibly difficult not to talk about a goal you're striving for. The thoughts which move you wish to be spoken and thought about and aspired to by many people. But when you tell others of your plans and intentions, you tear something out of yourself and out of the spiritual soil where it should slowly ripen. You make your hopes accessible to everyone. You let the thoughts which should be working for you out into the world, scattering them before they're strong enough to manifest themselves for you. 'Only confide your ideas to true friends – perhaps one friend, or perhaps no-one at all', writes Mulford. Keeping secrets enhances their attractive power.

"So let's sum things up. Firstly, the dream of life must be preformed in your thoughts as a clear goal. Secondly, you must perceive the aspiration as if it were already realised rather than pushing it into the distance as a future event. Just as you know that the evening news starts at 8 p.m., so you also know that the powers of destiny are already in the process of preparing what you aspire to. Thirdly, it's important to keep silent about what you're spiritually preparing in this way. And fourthly, you can more easily manifest something which you desire with every fibre of your heart."

"If that's the case", said Christian, "then Gabi should have come back to me long ago. For weeks I've been carrying the longing for her within me. I think of nothing but being close to her."

"No. You're not thinking of being close to her, but of the opposite. You're thinking about her not being with you. You're thinking about how it used to be and how she's cuddling with Weiland now. You see her in his arms, not yours. You're feeling the pangs of love rather than that joyous feeling you experienced with her. You're revitalising the wrong spirits with your attention. You're yearning for her.

"Desiring something and yearning for something are not the same. The attracting force which is at stake here isn't unleashed by yearning for something. In truth, yearning always arises from the fact you don't have what you're longing for. Yearning is something painful and is usually associated with a feeling of hopelessness. Yearning often carries thoughts of doubt or of the unattainable, and it pushes what you desire even further away. When you long for something, you usually revive the spirit of loss, of the unattainable, and not the spirit of the manifestation of the desire. Thus the object of yearning, the thing you dream of, is spiritually moved into the distance and can't be realised. For the time being, leave Gabi to Weiland and find yourself another partner.

"Don't wish for a thousand different nonsensical things or something that's impossible right now. Strive only for what is truly important and significant. Every longing, every wish takes away some of the manifesting energy, no matter whether it's manifested or not. Happiness and success are like a prepaid mobile phone. You can't use it indefinitely. So use the credit on your happiness account sparingly; it doesn't recharge automatically. You always have to pay for it. Unsettled debts are usually paid later with a stroke of fate. So if in doubt, choose what will still be important to you in a few years' time, and not just whatever is urging you on today."

Einstein looked at his watch again. "It takes time to reach a goal, of course. The power of thought is not omnipotent. Thank God, I would say, because just as the positive thoughts help to manifest what you desire, so the thoughts of doubt will prevent it. The negative thoughts also attract what you fear and can manifest themselves. That's why it's so important to master your own thoughts. Learning to control your thoughts is part of the initial training in any magical practice. And one more thing. The powers of destiny don't perform magic; they must follow the earthly laws of nature. Support them by doing everything necessary and possible for success yourself, and do it at the astrologically correct times. Those who heed the cosmic tides, which even the gods and demons must obey, are already halfway to victory. Besides the magic of thoughts, there is magic with astrology. Astrology is the only truly reliable magical instrument at our disposal. And it proves that there are spiritual powers. But we'll talk about that tomorrow if you wish. I'm retiring for today; it's late."

*

Christian, Leif, and Michael disappeared into the girls' room as they had done the night before. They were all deeply worried. Yks had set out first thing in the morning to look for Andy Mo. As he was unable to locate him, he had flown to Vienna, but he still hadn't returned.

"Now we've been abandoned by all the good spirits", Miri Li stated gloomily. "He should have arrived back by now; he wanted to cover the sixty kilometres in two hours. It's almost midnight." No one said a word. Everyone was lost in their own thoughts.

"Maybe he's gone to lie down", Leif murmured. "I don't think ravens fly at night." Miri Li looked at him gratefully.

"If we lose him too, we don't stand a chance. We're not ready to take on Baphomet yet."

But Yks didn't show up the next morning either. The friends were taciturn and brooded over breakfast. They hardly touched their food, and later they followed the sailing lessons with little enthusiasm. The atmosphere didn't improve much during the day. The raven remained missing, and Andy Mo didn't make contact either.

ASTROLOGY: TIDES OF POWER AND LIFE

"Who among you believes in God?" With this question, Einstein opened his discussion circle that evening. Most of those present raised their arms. "Okay, and who believes in astrology?" About the same number of students raised their arms, and Einstein nodded. "But you don't need to believe in astrology. The cosmic tides can be verified. The phenomenon of a connection existing between certain astrological constellations and the nature, behaviour, and state of mind of human beings can't be explained, but it can be demonstrated. I therefore count astrology among the sciences which explain phenomena. Does anyone know what else falls into this category?"

"Meteorology", said the little know-it-all philosopher. "But that's considerably more reliable. I read my horoscope for next week in the paper this morning, and what it predicts for me doesn't meet scientific criteria at all. It's psychology, at best. It could apply to anyone.

It was something like 'don't get involved in conflicts or there will be trouble and strife.'"

The others laughed, but Einstein waved them off.

"Newspaper horoscopes have nothing at all to do with astrology. It's quite impossible to predict anything for an entire zodiac sign. A horoscope is a completely individual matter, and it must be calculated for each person individually according to the date and hour of their birth. Only then is it possible to make a statement about the person concerned and his or her life. However, even then it's impossible to make predictions about the future. A person's fate cannot be known even with a precisely calculated horoscope."

"My mother regularly goes to a card reader", Fiona revealed. "She always tells her fortune."

"It may be that there are psychic seers, but I would be cautious with that. I've only met three people with this ability in my life, and they didn't use their gift to make money. So don't ask a stranger what the future holds; ask yourself how and when you can best shape it. These are exactly the two questions which can be answered with astrology. Astrology doesn't present you with an inescapable fate; it helps you to shape your own life.

"After all, an astrological forecast is not a prediction of the future. Astrological forecasts are not made to come true; rather, they are meant to serve as information for the future by indicating a development. They become meaningful only when they bring about an intervention, a positive change. If I know I'll have an accident constellation during a certain period, then I'll be more careful with sport and traffic; that way I can prevent the accident."

"The stars do not compel; they create proclivities", the little philosopher interjected, quoting a well-known saying, and Einstein nodded patiently at him.

"Correct. Everyone can determine their own destiny if they vigilantly control their thoughts and desires and navigate consciously through life. No astrological current is obligatory. An astrological forecast is like a road condition report on the path of life you will be travelling. You must reckon with certain circumstances, but for the most part you yourself determine how you progress. Those who adapt their plans to the foreseeable circumstances make better progress. In critical periods when you can expect agitation, loss, and failure according to astrological experience, it's better not to make important decisions. Those who have the patience to wait for constellations which are suitable for their plans will surely be more successful. This applies to matters of career, health, love, and money. During a period in which your feelings of love are disrupted due to certain constellations, you shouldn't enter into relationships, and if a companionship breaks up at such a time, you can calculate when your chances will get better. Those who plan or forcefully pursue something at the wrong time will fail. Those who take advantage of favourable times will succeed.

"So a good astrologer doesn't predict the future; they prepare for it. Astrology helps you to shape the future yourself. But I'm not advising you to seek out an astrologer. Anyone can learn the basic rules of calculating and interpreting a horoscope.

"You know that I am neither a fantasist nor a dreamer. Logic and science are sacred to me. But if you asked me which insights impressed me the most and helped me the most in my life, I would answer that it was the results of astrology. It's a genuine aid in life which anyone can use. To those who master it, the science of astrology grants influence and power: over themselves, over others, and over their lives. Why do you think it was kept secret for millennia and only made accessible to a select few in the priestly schools? No ruler, no king, and no pope would dispense with the advice of astrologers. The question of when things are going to go well for you and when your enemy will be doing badly was of crucial significance for the state. But you don't have to be a statesman to benefit from it.

"We experience good times and bad times. One day you're in a good mood, and the next nothing brings you joy. Some days you succeed in everything you undertake, and other days everything goes wrong. With astrology you can see this in advance. Not only can you tell when you're going to be in good or bad form, but you can also tell this about the people you're dealing with. What's more, you can recognise the longer periods of life in which – apparently determined by fate – we only have worries and problems to master. Everyone has to go through these low points, but thanks to astrology you also know when things will start to look up again. That alone can be immensely helpful.

Naturally it's advantageous to adapt to these tides and know when you're capable of acting correctly and when you should be more cautious in making a decision. If I know there's going to be trouble, arguments, and resistance, then I won't challenge those around me with any demands or remarks at that time; instead, I'll hold back my opinion and act at a later, more opportune moment. In your professional life this can be of utmost importance for success and failure. A person who knows the astrological constellations can take the tides of the soul into account in their planning. Then they'll be well-prepared and particularly successful if they purposefully use their powers when their abilities are functioning optimally. And through caution and restraint they'll usually be able to avoid losses and bad decisions during critical periods."

"I'm curious about when I'm going to get more pocket money", said Denzl, whose father ran a construction company. "I urgently need a new moped. Is that in the stars?"

Einstein shook his head.

"The moped isn't, but the time when you can negotiate well for your pocket money can be calculated. With astrology you can not only calculate your own constellations but also gain insights into the nature and state of mind of other people you deal with. I assume your contact in this case is your father. When do you think he will be more understanding of your wishes? When he's having trouble in his business due to an unfavourable Mars aspect and he's fuming, or when Venus makes him peaceful and he feels balanced?"

"My dad won't give me any more money", said Denzl. "He can't have that much Venus. I have to go to my mother. But of course she has to be in the mood to give me something as well. She's just as stingy as my father."

"Okay", said Einstein, "so you have to argue and make it clear to her that the cost of living has gone up and her poor boy is under enormous pressure, but she can alleviate it. For this you need a favourable Mercury aspect. With this constellation you'll come up with exactly the right words to convince her. And then as soon as you have a favourable Jupiter aspect, there's a high probability you'll already be on the road with your new moped."

"How do you know which constellations are currently relevant to a project?" asked Kathi. "After all, there's hundreds of problems – not just pocket money."

"The lunar calendar", Fiona stated, bringing her mother back into the picture. "My mother has a lunar calendar. She checks it every day to see if she should do the laundry, cut her nails, or go to the hairdresser. It's all in the book. She swears by her fortune teller, and also by the moon. I'm pretty superstitious, but I think that's kind of silly."

"You're right", Einstein confirmed. "These lunar rules are indeed based on pure superstition and have nothing at all to do with astrology. All these claims, some of which date back to the Middle Ages, have now been clearly disproved. Neither the phases of the moon nor its position in the zodiac have any effect on the matters attributed to them in these nonsensical books. The moon doesn't influence hair growth or surgical procedures – not even the weather depends on it. That's a statistically proven fact.

In your birth horoscope, however, it is of enormous importance. It regulates moods and emotions. Only the Ascendant and the position of the Sun are of such importance for interpretation. For example, someone born with the moon in Leo attaches more importance to social recognition and appears much more self-confident than someone with the moon in Pisces. And the cheerful moon in Libra makes you more sociable than the serious moon in Capricorn. In each sign of the zodiac, the moon develops different needs and qualities of the psyche.

"The position of the moon in the birth chart also plays a very important role in forecasts. For example, if Mars is at this position, the person will be irritable and react strongly to resistance. If Saturn passes through this position, worries and depression are more likely to determine the emotions. If Jupiter passes into the moon's position, the soul becomes optimistic. Uranus' transit makes you hysterical, while that of Neptune causes confusion."

Einstein was interrupted by the philosopher:

"Do we know why this is the case? Can we explain this phenomenon? If astrology is actually true, that would be sensational, wouldn't it?"

"I'm afraid we don't know", Einstein admitted. "There are various explanatory models, but none of them meet scientific requirements. It's a matter of empirical knowledge which can be statistically proven but not explained. We only know that there's a causal connection between the movements of the planets in the solar system and the consciousness and life course of human beings. Anyone can verify the simple rules and follow them in practice. I don't know anyone who has personally studied astrology for a while and still doubted it afterwards.

For the calculations we use the celestial tables and sidereal time, which astronomers also employ in their work. After all, a horoscope is nothing more than a graphical representation of the planets of our solar system related to the time and place of your birth. In other words, it's a purely mathematical matter which can be calculated in five minutes. I advise you to study it yourself rather than running off to an astrologer. The right approach to astrology is a magical process. You look over the shoulders of the gods and gain insight into spiritual processes which remain hidden from others [Emil Stejnar, *Astrology: Navigation for the Journey of Life, Genetic Code of Spirit and Soul*, Stejnar Verlag, Vienna]. I believe in the old spirit model. There is plenty of evidence which points to the constant intervention of beings who are also making use of these tides, and that makes astrology all the more interesting. We come into direct contact with spiritual powers, and we know which ones they are. Astrology is the simplest form of magic. You don't have to be a priest or an initiate for this special form of communication with the gods. It's open to everyone.

"I can assure you, it's tremendously impressive to observe how the constellations actually have an impact and manifest themselves as the rules dictate, regardless of whether electromagnetic fields or spirits are behind it all."

"What about free will then?" asked Leif. "If everything is predetermined, or let's say predictable, then there's no room for free will. Apart from the fact that the starting point is largely predetermined by character and personal traits – that is, by genes."

"Nothing is predetermined by astrology. I'm convinced that there's enough room for personal freedom. The astrological tides merely ensure that life unfolds according to certain rules. They maintain order and regulate the spiritual traffic – that is, the flow of elementals circulating between the worlds. Even if this influences the course of destiny, the very fact that this is the case grants you the opportunity to consciously and purposefully shape your own life with the power of your spirit.

"It's true that many insights and behaviours are initiated unconsciously, and this is partly due to astrology; nevertheless, everything you plan can be consciously approved or rejected by considering reasons and counter-arguments. Character dispositions, convictions, and desires may serve as the foundation of the will, but they aren't the force of the will itself. You can also make decisions which are contrary to your desires and act differently to the way you're urged to. You can say yes or no to anything, and you can do it or not do it. You can even change your character and traits if you make an effort. You must take small steps to do so. Just as bad habits like smoking, drinking, and overeating only gradually become habits and then addictions, with a good intention you can slowly but surely overcome these habits as well as the negative traits, thus acquiring other, more desirable qualities and abilities. The spiritual laws which are recognisable in astrology also safeguard this freedom, which is open to everyone. Whoever creates enough elementals – that is, willed ideas of a quality or a goal – within their consciousness will be helped by these living images during the period of time when they can unfold."

"That brings us back to our topic from yesterday", Kathi remarked. "Positive thinking. Every action has consequences, and every spiritual impulse needs a certain time to mature and manifest itself. Even the self-fashioning of destiny is governed by cosmic tides."

"Exactly", Einstein said, looking at Leif. "Do you feel unfree when you have to wait at the intersection for the traffic lights to turn green? Is your freedom restricted if you adhere to the bus timetable? No. Because order ensures freedom. And if you know the cosmic order and align yourself with it, you are doubly free, because you can introduce and undertake something of your own accord at appropriate times. Gardeners orient themselves according to the seasons, knowing the time for sowing and harvesting, and thanks to astrology, sages recognise when the good and bad spiritual seeds within them will ripen. They also know when particular cosmic powers appear to act upon them from the outside, and they can be cautious."

A thunderstorm had been brewing unnoticed. Dark clouds were gathering, and strong gusts announced the approaching rain. Flashes of lightning danced over the lake, providing an impressive display of the forces of nature.

"I think we should retreat to the cabin", Einstein suggested, gathering his plastic bags. Then the first large drops of rain began to fall. That drove the students into the cosy refuge provided for such changes in the weather.

KARMA AND REBIRTH

"Now, how do we come by our destinies?" asked Fiona, probing her lip piercing with her tongue. "Why is one person born with a physical disability while another becomes a beauty queen? One is born in an African slum, another in a luxury Hollywood mansion?"

"That's karma", said one student. "If you killed somebody in your last life, you'll also be killed. An eye for an eye and a tooth for a tooth – that's also in the Bible. And if you were selfless and helpful in your previous life, others will help you today."

"That's totally illogical", Leif remarked. "It makes me wonder why it's the kindest people who suffer the most, and why billions of people are starving, sick, and unhappy. I think more innocent people are being tortured in prisons and dying an agonising death today than were living two thousand years ago. In the past were there really only evildoers who are now suddenly good people being punished for something they can't even remember?"

"That assumes that we actually are reborn", Einstein interjected. "We don't know that for sure. Karma merely describes the law of cause and effect. A hard fate need not be a punishment; it could always be a chance for probation. Conversely, a happy life would be a disaster for many people because they'd learn nothing in the process; instead, they'd become lazy and let themselves degenerate. Every experience of suffering is a test which allows you to really get to know yourself, and usually you emerge from the crisis a stronger person.

"If someone's sweating and slaving away in the gym, you don't think they're being punished – they're training their muscles. Similarly, when you experience difficult situations, you train your spirit and soul muscles, even if you don't master everything. Those muscles can weaken very rapidly when you're content. To perfect the spirit and soul, you must also get to know the underworld. Only what you've experienced becomes part of yourself. If you truly wish to conquer evil, you must experience it and overcome it within yourself. Only then can you be sure that you've risen above it. On the spiritual plane, it's not enough to philosophise – it is crucial to truly master these powers. But to do that, you must first become acquainted with them. When you're in a monastery or a cave in the Himalayas, life passes you by. Those who have been led through the underworld by fate or their own actions have likely learned more by the end than the virtuous, the fortunate, and the successful of this world."

"I'm not so interested in knowing why I'm Chinese rather than white or black", said Miri Li. "Rather, I want to know why I came into the world with these, my own personal characteristics, and not with others, for example with Leif's needs and views. Because even if astrological constellations do indeed influence our thinking, feeling, and willing, what ultimately happens – what I achieve, i.e. my so-called destiny – is still largely determined by my behaviour. The question is, how does a person acquire their character? How do you acquire your individual nature? How do you acquire the predispositions which determine your behaviour and thus the course of your destiny? Why does one person have particular talents, preferences, and abilities, and another person has different ones? It's undisputed that genes play a role, but what determines who is born in which body – a body in which these genes are currently unfolding, depending on the person's genetic make-up and the cosmic tides? The question is: why am I the way I am?"

"A golden question!" exclaimed Einstein, jumping to his feet. "Did you hear that? Why am I the way I am? You've summed up philosophy perfectly. Whoever finds the answer to this question will solve the mystery of existence." Einstein was visibly excited. "'Know thyself' is the first injunction to the student of magic. Who am I? What am I? Why am I? These questions have preoccupied the great thinkers for millennia, but to this day no one has been able to answer them. Starting today, we are going to ask ourselves: 'Why am I the way I am?' We'll take what we already know about ourselves and question it. In doing so, we take action and bring to life what we truly are."

"When you wonder why you are the way you are, you activate yourself. You then also ask yourself: 'Am I the way I am? Am I the way I could be? What moves me to be the way I am?' And in doing so, you recognise a great deal about yourself which you actually are not, and you begin to unravel the mystery of your essence. You explore your ethereal body and you realise: 'I am not just a body, some thoughts, and some feelings; those are only my members. I am more than that.'

"When you question deeply, you realise: you don't just consist of feelings, although feelings move and touch you. You don't just consist of thoughts, although thoughts awaken and carry you. You are not the character; you possess a character, and you are that instance of your personality which can determine your thoughts, feelings, and character traits. In addition to your gross material body with its organs and limbs, you possess an ethereal body whose members and organs are thoughts and feelings."

But Miri Li wasn't satisfied with the answer.

"That doesn't explain how we acquire our components of being, that is, our character. Is it possible that the spiritual cells we've acquired and mastered can be used again in our next life? Or do the ones we didn't master, and the ones we repressed because they wanted to express themselves forcefully, pull us back into a corresponding body?"

"Perhaps you come into the world with all the components of your being that you had", Leif suggested, "and the struggle begins anew in each life. Or you choose your components of being, regardless of the character you already have, in order to learn new things and to strengthen certain muscles of the soul which you need for self-realisation."

"But who says there has to be a purpose associated with you at all?" remarked Miri Li. "Maybe you enter a body because you want to help someone else or simply be close to them. Everyone talks about self-actualisation. But isn't selflessness the most important quality? Maybe the meaning of existence is to help someone else realise themselves. If I were really born again, I would want a gentle, patient mother to lovingly assist me in the early years of life, sensitive and understanding teachers to recognise and nurture my talents, helpful and reliable friends, and later a considerate husband. These are all selfless qualities which I hope for in others, whether they know themselves and have self-actualised or not."

"You deserve a second ducat for that statement", Einstein praised, solemnly presenting the golden trophy to Miri Li. It didn't surprise anyone that he happened to have a ducat in his pocket. "Perhaps astrology can help you in your search for an answer to this question. In any case, it's a tool which allows you to fathom what you are."

"But our question remains unanswered", Leif pointed out. "Why does one person become a thrill-killer while another enters a monastery? Do we incarnate into a body with genes which do indeed determine most of our characteristics and predispositions, like boarding a bus for a study trip to learn about different characteristics and how to deal with them, or are we in fact exactly who we are? How did we become the way we are? Sweeping it all under the carpet of a last life isn't an answer. If someone hides away in a monastery because they're afraid of the struggle of life, they won't be any braver in the next life. And someone who was a ruthless, murdering dictator won't automatically transform into a lovable person enduring one misfortune after another. How do we acquire our qualities? Can we choose them, are they assigned to us, or do we have to obtain a ticket for the journey of life?"

"No one can answer that for you", Einstein said. "Why we are born with certain dispositions cannot be explained, even if it can be traced astrologically and genetically.

"But not all dispositions are innate or fixed. As I mentioned before, you can change. Just as bad habits develop gradually, so desirable qualities and abilities can also be trained over time. You're constantly evolving in life. It usually starts unnoticed with a small impulse. You either let yourself go or you pull yourself together. You either succumb to a temptation or you resist it. A small carelessness can be the beginning of a decline, while a good resolution can lay the foundation for a new character and a new life. Impulses, thoughts, desires, actions, and habits – in this order, a significant portion of our innate dispositions are transformed into character traits. And we can intervene in this development at any time. We've already established that thoughts and desires can be helpful spirits, but they can also degenerate into demons. You just have to keep an eye on them and control them.

"But don't worry your head about philosophical questions which can't be answered. Life is just beginning for you. When you get older, you'll look back on yourself as if you were a stranger; you won't need to be reborn at all. Karma isn't just a consequence of the past, but also affects the future. Karma is an issue in every moment of this life, and it also affects the coming years of your life. Create good karma for yourself by living accordingly. At any time, you have the opportunity to purposefully change and shape your life according to your present ideas, regardless of what has been.

"Reincarnation theories are based on highly questionable notions. The Tibetan Book of the Dead states that you are reborn only a few hours after your death and you can also incarnate as animals. For me, this is a dreadful and illogical thought, as it would be a step backwards. Anthroposophists believe that you're only born every one to two thousand years. Franz Bardon assumes hundreds of incarnations. As you can see, the experts have entirely different perspectives. But the religions don't offer any reasonable concepts regarding life after death either. So set this question aside and concern yourselves with what you can get a handle on instead.

"Don't make the mistake of blaming your fate and character on any powers or past lives", said Einstein in conclusion. "You can change at any time and thereby reshape your future. Dante expressed this beautifully in his *Divine Comedy*:

THE HEAVENS SET YOUR APPETITES IN MOTION,
NOT ALL YOUR APPETITES, BUT EVEN IF
THAT WERE THE CASE,
YOU HAVE RECEIVED LIGHT
FOR BOTH GOOD AND EVIL,
AS WELL AS FREE WILL,
WHICH THOUGH IT STRUGGLE
IN ITS FIRST WARS WITH THE HEAVENS,
THEN CONQUERS ALL, IF IT HAS BEEN WELL
NURTURED.

THE SHADOW

"No one knows we are directing him", Baphomet thinks, and his thoughts fill infinite space. "No one suspects that he serves us. They all follow their own ideas, desires, and cravings, unaware that it is we who inspire them. Even the brave who are guided by their ideals are in truth following a phantom formed from their own imaginings and nourished by their thoughts and aspirations.

"We are powerful, but we are disturbed."

The princes nod silently. They know where it would lead if the Book of the Master which the children wish to write for other children were to be widely disseminated. It's not the potential danger of humans learning to harness the secret power of magic which concerns them; it's the hidden knowledge which poses a threat to their realm. They will draw conclusions. They will discover not only that their thinking can reshape science and technology and thus the world of matter, but also that they can alter the spiritual planes with it. The beyond, too, is constantly being rebuilt by the thoughts of humans. And once they know this, they will purposefully and consciously shape their own realms.

"Instead of merely believing or philosophising and changing the world and their lives with their insights as they did before, they will reshape themselves", thinks Baphomet, and his thoughts manifest as invisible echoes. The princes follow his words.

"The humans will also create their own spiritual realm. Not only will they overthrow us, the Shadow Princes; they will also dethrone the gods. Behind every religion there is a demon: a 'Lucifer' who pretends to be the ONE and allows himself to be worshipped, and never the ONE himself. They will see through this and rise above us. Then the creatures of the ONE will have triumphed. But as yet they know nothing of their power. We have managed to neutralise Andimo, the Gnome King, who could have enlightened them. And we have also hindered the progress of Andy Mo, his son, who was on the trail of the secret as well. He has an inkling of where the Formula of Nothingness is hidden, but he knows he will never find it. He is at the end of his tether. Even his friends can no longer pose a threat to us; they are distracted by their own worries. Only Leif still poses a danger to us." Baphomet glances at one of the princes, and he nods.

"I will take care of him."

AMUE

Leif couldn't get the nixie Amue out of his mind. Ever since they had been at the lake, he couldn't stop thinking about her. When Andy Mo had spoken about her a few days ago, he did it with such suggestive clarity that everyone thought they could see her in front of them. He described her seductive beauty, her charm, and the quiet benevolence which made her presence an oasis of peace and security. And he described her deep, selfless compassion, which lends true femininity its strength and lifts what appears to be soft above the power of the hard masculine. She and her subordinates have governed and nurtured life in all the seas and waters of the Earth since time immemorial. Even the life of humankind once originated there. Amue is the elemental force of love which eternally creates new life; she is the primordial mother of existence. Leif felt drawn to Amue and longed for her presence; he had never experienced the gentle patience and prudence of a mother, because his own mother had always prioritised herself and her career over him. He was surprised by his own feelings, which had become steadily more intense since he had been near the water. It was as if they had known each other for an eternity and were on the verge of a reunion. He felt he had to get out onto the lake.

It was afternoon, shortly after four. And rain was looming. Despite the calm, the lesson had been cancelled early because of a storm warning, and they had used long sticks to pole the boats back into the harbour. Manoeuvring in the doldrums was also something they had to learn. Now Leif, Michael, and Christian were sitting in the room listening to music.

Leif suggested using the time they still had at the lake to summon the nixie. He had already drawn her sigil – Andy Mo had revealed it to them – and he had impregnated it with his thoughts. But the other friends were sceptical.

"If it were that easy, Andy Mo would have summoned the nixie long ago and told her about his situation", Christian said. "You heard it yourself: nowadays it's not as easy as it used to be. The walls between the worlds have become denser. The time when every lake offered access to the realm of the water spirits is over."

Michael, too, was tired and wasn't in the mood for a magical experiment. He was worried about his father, about Andy Mo, and about Yks, who still hadn't returned.

"If the thunderstorm really does strike over the lake, it's going to be unpleasant out there. Why do you think we had to return early? I've seen something like this before in Colombia. No nixie could be so charming that I would want to go through that again."

Leif knew that his venture was not without danger. There were good reasons why they had been warned about the hazards of the lake on the very first day. It was all still fresh in Leif's memory, but he was determined to try. He had learnt to sail at the age of eight. Back then his father had given him a small Optimist dinghy for his birthday, and he wasn't afraid. He decided to sail out alone to invoke Amue in her element.

"I'm going out for some fresh air", he said, and he slipped away without letting the others in on his plan. Initially he thought of taking a pedalboat. But then he decided he could get out onto the lake faster and travel further with a sail, as a light breeze had come up in the meantime. The boats were all moored along the shore, and only a few sailors were still out on the water. He expertly unhooked a dinghy and turned it into the wind. And he ignored the red flag.

But the wind was stronger than he'd imagined. He had barely left the harbour entrance behind him when it suddenly blew from a different direction, forcing him to make a difficult manoeuvre. Then a gust caught him and pushed him off course. He found himself dangerously close to the reed zone and tried to get away from the shore. Although it had become noticeably cooler, he began to sweat. Then clouds began to gather, darkening the sky ominously. The weather service had been right. Leif had never experienced such a rapid change in the weather.

He struggled against the increasingly powerful gale and the short, choppy waves. Lightning flashed, and the first heavy drops of rain began to pelt down on him. A magical evocation was now out of the question. He would be lucky if he made it back to the harbour in one piece. By now it was raining so hard that nothing could be seen of the shore. The wind kept changing direction, eventually causing him to lose his orientation completely. The unleashed elements were raging all around him, and he felt as if he was held captive in the centre of the turmoil. Leif sensed that this was another realm, an evil, demonic world. The forces of nature had conspired against him. He felt so alone, as if millions of kilometres separated him from humanity, from the shore, and from his friends.

With the wet and the cold, fear crept into his bones. Mortal fear. That was when he felt Andy Mo's crystal in his jacket. But it was too late. He tried to jibe but made a mistake; the boom swung around and hit him hard on the head. Even as his consciousness faded away, he spiritually drew Amue's sigil into the watery air with the crystal. His call to her was a cry for help. Then he lost his footing and went overboard.

But Amue had heard him. She perceived him precisely because he had drawn the seal with his imagination alone rather than his physical hand. His affection and the power of the charged crystal compelled her into his spiritual proximity. She could sense not only him, but also Andy Mo. Two powers were drawing her and brought her into the human realm. At first she was confused, because she thought it was Andy Mo who had summoned her. But then she grasped the situation. With a few gentle strokes of her magnetic hand, she revived Leif's spirits. She kept him afloat for some time until he had regained his consciousness fully and had managed to climb back into the boat. When spirits embrace each other, it's as if they merge together. This was just such an embrace, and Leif felt it too when the nixie gently detached herself from him. She could feel it as well, and they both knew they would see each other again.

However, Amue had to return to her spiritual element. With a short formula she calmed the agitated natural forces. The mist lifted and the last rays of the setting sun broke through the clouds. Slowly, as if it was being moved by an invisible ghostly hand, the dinghy glided safely into the harbour.

"I got wet", was all he said as he entered his room. "What about Yks? Has Andy Mo been in touch? Any word from your father?"

Michael shook his head sadly.

"No Andy Mo, no word from my father. But Yks is back. He's totally exhausted and asleep."

Then the girls arrived.

"I'm scared", Miri Li said. "There's something wrong. I'd prefer to go home – I had a terrible dream. It was about Andy Mo. Ever since he disappeared, I've been feeling defenceless against evil."

"I have a strange feeling too", Kathi said. "I think there's something coming for us that we're not capable of handling."

THE ALCHEMIST

This time it took longer for Andy Mo to regain consciousness. After the car accident he literally felt like he'd been broken on the wheel. He had woken up near the scene of the accident under a tree in the Hietzing cemetery. Andy Mo knew the place because Michael's mother was buried there, so he was able to orientate himself quickly. With difficulty he set his sights on his refuge and transported himself into his boulder with a mental leap. But once again, he couldn't quite get through. He did penetrate the rock, but then he resurfaced like a cork in water.

Desperate, he looked over towards Michael's house, but he wasn't there. It was afternoon and he thought he must be out with the others or swimming. He didn't know that the friends were already learning to sail on Lake Neusiedl; somewhat disappointed, he transported himself back into the library. He hadn't yet lost the ability to pass through regular walls. What he couldn't manage was the leap into his spiritual realm.

Andy Mo couldn't believe that his weakness and the massive impairment of his magical abilities were caused solely by his time in the human realm. He hadn't been on the surface of the Earth long enough for this to have such severe consequences. In fact it had started in the underground passage, he reflected, and he became scared at the thought of going down there again. But it was the only viable lead he could follow. The chest, the documents, the gold medallion near the dead man which Goldstein also wore. And then there was the bricked-up area. Something there had reminded him of the spirit trap in Goldstein's cellar. He had to follow the tunnel to its end, no matter how dangerous it was for him. And he had to hurry, because there was no telling how much longer he could even pass through walls. The friends certainly wouldn't manage to get through the rubble and the wall.

On the mantelpiece lay the compass and the city map with the notes Michael had made about the tunnel's course. He took everything with him. As a precaution, he pushed open the secret door to the hidden chamber. Should the undertaking weaken him as it had last time, he could take the easy human route and wouldn't need to go through the wall.

His gnome lantern provided him with enough light even in the human realm, but he still pocketed a torch. He had learnt to appreciate the practical objects humans used since he had been living on the surface of the Earth. Human inventions were far better suited to life here than all the spiritual magic. Even though the human realm greatly hindered a spirit and severely limited spiritual abilities, on the other hand it offered fantastic opportunities, perspectives, and insights which remained hidden from those on the ethereal plane of the elements. Thus he hadn't had any idea of the immensity and infinity of the universe before, nor of the higher spiritual hierarchies of the angels, attendant spirits, and planetary beings which govern the destiny of humans. He had only been familiar with the spirits of the four elements. In his short time among the humans he had learnt more than in his whole previous life.

Andy Mo had no idea what was in store for him, but he sensed it would be crucial. With the same unease as jumping into cold water, he mentally leapt to the area of the collapse in front of the wall which had blocked their way last time. And again, he had the distinct feeling that he was on the right track. From now on he had to be careful. Instead of mentally leaping his way to the other side of the brick wall, he gingerly felt his way through the obstacle, gnome-style, and squeezed through.

As expected, the tunnel continued on the other side. Apart from a few interruptions, it continued almost straight northwards. However, its condition wasn't as good as before. Water was seeping in at some places, and twice there were piles of rubble which completely blocked his way. But Andy Mo had no trouble following it. He pushed his way through the boulders and made good progress. After about five kilometres the tunnel ended, but when he lit up the passageway more closely, he realised that it continued to the west at a right angle. Embedded in the wall in front of him he again discovered an iron door, but this time it had a modern and intact lock. And then he flinched. Next to the door, a bicycle was leaning against the wall.

And then Andy Mo got another surprise. When he compared the map of Vienna to the location where the notes indicated he must be, he found that he was standing directly under the school building. That couldn't possibly be a coincidence. So his suspicions had been confirmed.

Believing he had reached his destination, Andy Mo made a grave error. Instead of abandoning the venture and informing his friends first, he decided to get to the bottom of the matter immediately. The adventure had exhilarated his spirit, and success had lent him new energy. Finally, a concrete lead! His father had to be trapped somewhere in these catacombs. He felt strong and full of determination as he pushed his way through the iron gate.

An ancient stone spiral staircase led steeply upwards. After twelve steps there was a landing with a small door, just as old as the first, but locked. Without lingering, Andy Mo continued to climb. The steps ended in a square opening under the ceiling, sealed with a stone from the other side. He pushed through and found himself in a winding passage which branched off several times as he followed it, until a wall finally blocked his way. Here too he squeezed through without any problem; surprised, he found himself in the school's assembly hall. A cleaning lady was lethargically dragging her wet rag across the floor, not noticing him.

Andy Mo searched for the way back to the cellar, but he couldn't find his way anymore. On the first floor of the basement was the modern laboratory and scientific equipment donated by Goldstein. He didn't need to look for his father there. Then he discovered another exit, but this staircase was also old and winding, and the corridor he followed branched out through the structure, causing him to lose his orientation completely. This had never happened to him in his entire life. It must have been due to the unpleasant noise which had been haunting him all this time. He kept wandering until he finally arrived back at the place where he had started. The lower level had not been renovated. The cellar dated back to the seventeenth century, and the foundations were older still: that's what the newspaper article about the school renovation had stated. Although there was lighting, he used his magic lamp to avoid attracting attention. Its light illuminated his path. He passed by dusty chambers crammed with strange sculptures, curious objects, and old books; he peered into every room, but he found no trace of his father. Until the corridor ended in a windowless tower chamber. Andy Mo stood rooted to the spot: it was a fully equipped alchemist's laboratory. He recognised every item – the special furnace, the various retorts, ancient leather-bound works. But alongside them stood ultra-modern technical equipment, some of which seemed utopian. The Middle Ages juxtaposed with science fiction. The uneasy feeling that Andy Mo had felt all along, but which he couldn't explain, intensified. It was a faint but pervasive vibration that was making him tired.

Curious, he looked around him. On a huge wooden table lay an open manuscript. Andy Mo stepped closer and recognised his father's unmistakable handwriting. Shaken yet relieved to finally have a concrete clue, he sat down exhausted on the bench. "Where is my father?" he thought. "He must be around here."

"He's not here", came a deep, rumbling voice from behind him, and he turned around. It was the school caretaker; he had read his thoughts. Although the caretaker was much larger than him, he looked at him askance from below, lurking like a tiger and at the same time keenly interested, as if he wanted to explore every millimetre of him.

"You won't find him here at the school. I took him away because Goldstein was after him too. Your father didn't reveal the final secret to me. He refused and stalled me for a long time – he said he'd rather die. Yet all I need is one more operation and I will have the Stone." Then a sly grin flitted across his misshapen face. "But now you've come – his offspring, no doubt equally knowledgeable in the royal art. You will show it to me. You want to live; you even want to be human so you can love. You escaped me in class, but today you cannot escape me. Today I'm going to make a circus act out of you."

Their eyes met and clashed like the torsos of two sumo wrestlers. Andy Mo slowly stood up. He didn't take his eyes off the caretaker for a second; he could sense the secret power emanating from the alchemist.

"Where is my father?" Andy Mo focused all his energy into that thought: "Where have you taken him?" He pressed this question into his mind as if he were cracking a nut to get to the kernel, squeezing until he himself became dizzy. But he couldn't read his opponent's mind; the hunchback was inscrutable. He knew what Andy Mo wanted and whirled his thoughts around in circles, making them impossible to grasp.

Then Andy Mo grabbed his magical axe – the one he usually used to smash rocks – and struck. In a wild rage, he slashed at the caretaker with the broadside of his axe, hitting him several times in the head. But he wasn't allowed to kill him, and he held back. How else could he find out where his father was being held captive? Nevertheless, the attack had thrown his opponent off balance. He hadn't expected such a human, emotional assault. He was unfamiliar with this magical instrument and backed away in surprise. But before Andy Mo could prevent him, the caretaker himself had reached for a weapon. As quick as a flash, he flipped the lever on a device and stared expectantly at Andy Mo, triumphant. The effect was instantaneous. The exhausting vibration immediately intensified. It was as if a fan was spraying millions of tiny needles which penetrated his consciousness like tranquiliser darts. It was a hellish fiery stream of evil, infiltrating him from all sides and disrupting his spiritual structure.

"Now I've got you!" the alchemist shouted, raising himself up to his full height and standing in the alpha posture of an orangutan as he laughed. It was an eerie laughter which erupted from the deepest depths of his being. His relief was propelled upwards like boulders in an avalanche, and Andy Mo heard the chilling echoes of his triumphant feelings as they eerily faded away amid the basement stonework.

"Now I have you trapped. That is high frequency electricity. A deadly fire for earth spirits; you can't escape from here. Your father didn't make it out either."

Andy Mo could clearly sense that his opponent wasn't bluffing. He thought of the spirit trap in Goldstein's house, which had indeed almost killed him. And when he glimpsed a medallion hanging from the caretaker's open shirt, he felt utterly defeated. The diamonds of the balance scale flashed in the glow of the lantern. He, too, belonged to the secret society. Resigned and confused, he conceded defeat and stepped backwards.

"I only want to know one thing: is my father still alive?"

The caretaker flipped the lever again and pressed another switch. A light above the door began to blink.

"Who knows if a spirit is still alive? You're all just glimmers of light or shadow. No human can tell who lies behind it. But I know that you're alive. You will explain the final operation to me. If you refuse, both of you must die." Then his mobile rang. "Yes, director. I'll take care of it at once." As he spoke, he became crooked and much smaller again. He turned around at the doorway: "Don't get too close to the walls of this room; it will mean instant death. The electricity runs through a special grid in the wall."

Andy Mo was alone again. Everything within him revolted at the thought of defeat. He couldn't give up. If he could find his father, the elixir would bring him back to life. He would rather die than become a minion of evil. The gold would empower the wrong people, and he would be complicit. He didn't know who else was working under the sign of the balance scales.

He thought about his mission. This didn't just concern him or his father; the future of humanity was at stake. He was no ordinary earth spirit, and he had defeated fire once before. In an instant he became calm again. Now he knew what to do. "I'll just have to go through the fire again", he thought, and he prepared himself by identifying with the element that was otherwise so alien to him.

Andy Mo proceeded systematically. Initially he thought only of warmth, of the body heat which sustains all humans. When he felt it in his gnome body, he condensed the warmth at his centre into a small spark; igniting it with his imagination, he caused a fire to burst forth from him in blazing flames. Then he intensified the heat into an energy which surged outwards with the fervour of a volcano. He imagined the expansion, the pressure, the agitated vibration – the energy which lends strength to every action and power to every will. He felt the heat within him, sensing the hot, electric tingling on his skin and feeling the primal quality of the element detach itself from him as radiant light. Andy Mo experienced himself as the highest manifestation of fire, as light. He identified himself with that light, concentrated on his refuge, and leapt. Just as he had done back in the burning house, he transported himself to the other side of the wall with a courageous mental leap, breaking through the obstacle which denied him freedom at the speed of light.

However, he did not arrive at his intended destination. He had managed to pass through the wall of his prison, but even in the form of dazzling light he had failed to penetrate the barrier separating this world from the next. Instead of landing in his refuge, he was still in the human realm. The way back to his realm had been denied to him once again. To change planes, you need a different medium of consciousness. The Earthly light was not the light of knowledge which penetrates the barrier to the beyond.

Andy Mo only gradually managed to find his bearings. The electricity trap had affected him more than the accident on the road. He had ended up in the tunnel beneath the school, and he could hear the siren of a fire engine from above. His escape had evidently caused a short circuit or an electrical fire. He hastened to get away, but he was too exhausted. Having just managed to drag himself past the first bend in the tunnel, he squatted down to rest. When he tried to continue, he realised that he had lost his magic lamp and his axe. Presumably both had burnt up in the spirit trap. He was horrified. Without these attributes of his power, the way back to his homeland was permanently barred.

Somehow he managed to find his way through the gloom back to the library.

On the surface of the Earth it was also dark. It was night. There was a light on in Michael's house, but he didn't go over to it. Unbeknownst to him, he had been wandering in the tunnels for two days. The week of the school trip was over and the holidays had begun.

Once again, he tried to transport himself into his refuge. But he couldn't manage it. Even with the greatest effort, he couldn't concentrate on his essential element in such a way that he could merge with the earth and achieve the breakthrough. He had been relying on the four mediating elements of human beings – fire, water, air, and earth – for too long. He had come to know and appreciate all four elements, but still he had not become a child of humankind. On the contrary: he had lost his spirituality. The return to his homeland was barred to him. He lacked the fifth element, which the initiates call Akasha. Only human beings had access to this all-encompassing fluid.

INCARNATION

Weary, Andy Mo lay down on the leather couch. He now knew who was holding his father captive. It was only a matter of time before they found him; he had escaped the criminal, but despite his success, he was desperate. The way things stood now, he wouldn't be able to save his father. The vial with the elixir was in the spirit realm, and he could no longer cross over. But without this magic potion, the king would not survive. Even if they could find him and free him, his time in the human realm would soon be up.

His friends still didn't know what his situation was. Somehow, he was ashamed to tell them. There he was, living among the humans to show them how to master the spiritual elements, and yet he couldn't even master his own spirit. He had permanently forgotten how to transport himself into his own world. He had known that this would happen, of course, but he hadn't expected it to happen so quickly.

He was overwhelmed with a deep sadness, and he didn't know

how to explain it to his friends. Because of him, Baphomet had brought misfortune upon their families. But instead of helping them, he couldn't even solve his own problems. They wanted to write a magic book for children, to explain to them how to harness the power of the spirit, but the spirit that governed the world was stronger. New obstacles which could not be mastered kept piling up. Not only was access to his spirit realm blocked, but his friends were not yet ready to enter the spiritual spheres. He had realised by now that acquiring magical abilities as a human takes more than a few months. What is child's play in the world of spirits seems almost impossible in the human realm.

Andy Mo tossed and turned restlessly on his makeshift bed. He lay on the large, old leather sofa and stared at the high windows, behind which the new day was slowly dawning. The remaining shadows were only grey, but although the night was over, he felt surrounded by darkness. Evil was pressing in on him from all sides. Hopelessness. Fear. And loneliness. How he wished he could pray to the God of humankind now. To Jesus Christ, or to his mother Mary, who, like the Egyptian goddess Isis, comforts all humans who turn to her in their distress. That, too, is a form of magic, Einstein had explained to them. And Miri Li also swears by this strange human magic. "Does it also help earth spirits?" Andy Mo wondered, thinking wistfully of his own mother, whom he would never see again. She had never made a distinction between him and the other gnome children; anyone who had worries came to her. After all, she was the Queen of the Gnomes alongside his father, King Andimo. In his desperation, he called upon both primal mothers at once:

"Isis and Maria, you know what I lack. Help me, I beg you – help me to fulfil my mission. It doesn't just concern me and my friends; the future of all humanity is at stake."

Suddenly a violent jolt shook his entire body. Confused, he sat up, thinking he had finally fallen asleep and it was all just a dream. But he was wide awake.

Then he thought of an earthquake. But everything was quiet. Nevertheless, he sensed that a terrible disaster had just occurred, or was about to happen. He felt threatened, yet he couldn't pinpoint the danger. It was four o'clock in the morning.

Leif hadn't been able to sleep that night, either. He had spent a long time reading, and had studied the 'Ritual of the Hermetic Four' from the Book of the Master [Emil Stejnar, *The Four Elements*, Stejnar Verlag, Vienna] in detail. Only now did he understand how amateurish the incantation at the cemetery had been, and what Andy Mo had been explaining back then. "With the formulas from this ritual, the evocation might have succeeded", he reflected. And he wondered if it could be used to summon nixies.

Like Andy Mo, he tossed and turned restlessly on his bed – and like Andy Mo, he was unhappy and felt lonely and abandoned. His thoughts were with the nixie Amue, whom he couldn't forget. It had been love at first sight. Ever since she had saved him from drowning in the lake three days earlier, there had been a constant, indescribable feeling pulsating within him like a second heartbeat – a hopeful yearning which never faded from his consciousness, like a melody you can't get out of your head. He still felt her presence, that magnetically cool and moist tingling warmth which had filled his whole body as she gently touched him and held his head above the water. But she was a nixie, a phantom – a spirit like Andy Mo.

"That's crazy", he thought. "You can't fall in love with spirits! Miri Li, on the other hand, is something tangible, something you can touch." He sensed that she did not feel indifferently towards him; but he also knew that Miri Li's feelings for Andy Mo were more than just friendly. The same perverse situation as his own, he pondered: a human child loves a spirit being. Have we all gone mad? An inner restlessness had seized him, and he knew that sleep was over for the night. Determined, he got dressed and went out into the street. The cold light of the early morning bathed the city in another phase of lonely abandon. No one was out at this hour. He was freezing.

Irritated, he went back into the house and rolled himself a joint. He had promised his friends he would quit smoking, and he'd sworn to himself never to touch the stuff again. He had a guilty conscience and knew what he was doing was uncaring. But he still let the poison into his bloodstream. After just two drags, all his worries had been forgotten. The disaster took its course. But only Baphomet knew that no power in the world would be able to correct it.

The drug's action addled him with hallucinations. He saw Amue within reach, stretching out her delicate arms towards him; he wanted to embrace her. But the phantom slipped away from him, moved farther away, waved sadly at him, and disappeared into the grey-green mist which arose and separated them once again.

"I'm coming, Amue, I'm coming", Leif moaned, and he spontaneously decided to drive to the lake.

His father was in New York that week. In the garage were two cars: an Audi A8 and the old automatic Golf which his mother had used in the past. Leif had driven it several times when his father was away and there had never been any problems.

When he started the Golf, the on-board computer signalled that he needed to refuel. So he went back again to get his debit card and put it in his hand-sewn, lined linen jacket along with his mobile phone. After this drop in temperature, there would definitely be a freezing cold wind by the lake. The casual jacket was custom-made; the last time he had worn it was when the nixie saved him from drowning. The fabric was still completely wrinkled, and the copper eyelets on the fashionable suede hem were now oxidised green. In the left inside pocket he found Andy Mo's crystal. It had saved his life back then. It was surely the power of Andy Mo which had called Amue to him in time.

Again, an uneasy feeling arose within him, but he suppressed the warning voice trying to make itself heard inside him. Determined, he put the magic stone in his trouser pocket, threw his jacket into the car, and drove off. He stopped at the Volksbank in Feldkellergasse to withdraw money from the ATM. It was a deserted area, and he left the engine running. When he returned to the car, he was grabbed from behind and brutally shoved onto the back seat. A second guy got behind the wheel and drove off. The person next to him – a lad about his age who wore his long hair in a ponytail, like he did – threatened him with a gun. Leif raised his hands, but the other lad thought he was fighting back and struck him on the temple with the gun, causing him to pass out.

When he regained consciousness, he had a hell of a headache. The heater wasn't working and he was cold. But he didn't move and only blinked cautiously through half-closed eyelids. He wanted to know who he was dealing with, but he didn't recognise the lads: he hadn't seen them in the old man's group, nor in the drug scene. So it was purely by chance that he was the victim they had been waiting for outside the bank. Meanwhile the lad next to him had put on his linen jacket, and was also in the process of taking his watch and the gold signet ring with his initials. When his accomplice saw this in the rear-view mirror, he became angry and hissed something in a foreign language. But the lad just laughed and put the ring on his finger. The wide gold band of the old Omega watch also fitted perfectly around his wrist. Naturally the money and his documents were also gone; only Andy Mo's magic stone, which was in his trouser pocket, had been overlooked. In the rear-view mirror, Leif recognised the installations and towers of the oil refinery. So they were driving on the eastern motorway towards the border. They wouldn't have got that far with the empty tank, so they had filled up while he was unconscious.

His mouth was completely dry, his temples ached, and he was thirsty and cold. Gradually he was able to think straight again.

Presumably they had taken him with them so he couldn't get the card blocked. This would give them the opportunity to withdraw from his account for a few days, even abroad. They hadn't even tied him up, so there was a chance to free himself. But the mobile phone was in his jacket.

"You usually only see this in the movies", Leif thought as he cautiously felt for Andy Mo's crystal. Once again, he desperately needed his help.

"Come on, Andy Mo, help me! I'm in danger!" he called out in his spirit, gripping the smooth angular stone in his hand. But the

329

lad next to him had noticed. Quick as a flash, he grabbed his arm and snatched away the magical instrument which was supposed to save him. At the same time he pointed the gun at him again.

"Don't move! You stay still, understand?"

"I understand", Leif said. "All right. But I'm freezing. Give me my jacket back." However, the other lad didn't respond. He just put the gun away and examined the crystal closely. Only when the driver shouted something at him in his own language did he gesture with his head to the old jacket he had presumably been wearing before taking Leif's designer jacket. It was lying between the seats; Leif pulled it out and slipped into it. It stank of sweat, but it was warm and comfortable. Then it happened, and very quickly. A wrong-way driver was approaching them in the morning fog. The guy at the wheel swore and swerved, but they were going too fast. The Golf clipped the oncoming vehicle, overturned, and instantly burst into flames. Leif, who had been ejected through the windscreen, lost consciousness for the second time that day. With his final thoughts, he was with Andy Mo. It was one second past four in the morning.

It was one second past four in the morning when Andy Mo suddenly grasped the situation. The pressure, the fear, the unknown threat which he couldn't place were gone in one fell swoop. Now he knew that Leif was in danger, not him. Leif needed his help. And he also immediately sensed where he was.

Despite his weakness, he was wide awake. All at once his energies returned. Within seconds he had located his friend, locked on to him, and transported himself close-by. Almost simultaneously, he landed next to the motorway where Leif's already severely injured body had crashed hard against the guardrail. His eyes were open, staring blankly into space. But he wasn't dead. As Andy Mo leant over him, he sensed that the injured boy was trying to tell him something.

"I'm going to die", Leif said without saying anything. He spoke with his silent gaze. Andy Mo looked into his eyes and grasped what he wanted to tell him. As if they were words, Leif continued speaking with his eyes. "I must leave so that you may come – only then can I help you. The One from the Shining Light told me. Take care of Miri Li." Then he lowered his eyelids as if to rest.

"He's dying," Andy Mo thought, "and I cannot help him." His next thought was the elixir. But that was in the spirit world. Unattainably far away. He was gripped by deep sorrow. He had come to help humans but had only brought calamity.

The two burning vehicles lay in the opposite lane. No car had passed by and stopped to call the rescue and fire brigade yet. There was little traffic at this hour. Andy Mo searched for a mobile phone in the old jacket Leif was wearing, but he couldn't find anything.

Desperate and shocked, he sat in front of the lifeless body and feverishly considered what he could do. He felt the spirit leave the battered body.

"You must not die," he said to him, "you must live." Systematically, he sensed his way through all the injured limbs and organs, transferring his entire strength to them. He touched every single cell of the body and filled it with his consciousness, with his spirit, with his life. Andy Mo concentrated with all his might and gave everything he had. He felt that this weakened him tremendously and that he was on the verge of losing his own life. But he was determined to make this sacrifice.

"Take my life, Leif – I give it to you. Just come back to your body and live!" Then his consciousness faded away, and he surrendered.

I AM

"I am Andy Mo", I said when I awoke. "I am an earth spirit; I am not from here. I come from another world."

I realised my mistake too late. I shouldn't have said that I was a spirit. But I was still dazed as a result of the injuries, and I didn't know where I was. They nodded gravely and exchanged meaningful glances. Presumably I had already spoken a lot of confused nonsense, because the next time I woke up I was in another room,

331

in a different bed. I had been transferred to the psychiatric ward of the hospital, as I learnt later.

I stared at the ceiling for hours. I was tormented by strange pains, and my body kept twitching and convulsing. But whenever I tried to move myself, I couldn't. I lay there limp and helpless, as if I were paralysed. I made several desperate attempts to transport myself to my refuge, but each time I remained lying like a lifeless stone. I had never been so dazed, so lonely, and so lost.

The memory of what had happened came like waves or flitting shadows and disappeared into nowhere again. I was unable to organise my thoughts. They obeyed me as little as my bodily limbs did. But I wasn't fully aware of that fact at the time. They tended to my head wound, hooked me up to devices, asked me questions, but I didn't understand a word and kept silent. Even my own spirit was alien to me, and I longed to fall back into a comfortable unconsciousness where there are no delirious fantasies to distress and disturb you. At some point I was transferred to a mental institution.

The journey didn't take long, but ever since then I feel as if I'm at the ends of the Earth. The windows are barred and the doors locked throughout the entire building. Initially I was together with other patients in a large room; then I was moved to a smaller room with green walls. There are no windows here.

There is no hope here, there is no love here, there is no life here; only madness and death. In the meantime I'm able to move, but only my body, not my spirit. No matter where I transport it, I remain lying like a stone. I sleep a lot and when I am awake, thoughts come like terrible demons. I chase them away. But one image keeps reappearing: a phantom of horror, the face with the black, pitiless eyes. It leans over me again and again. The memory of the diabolical visitor at Goldstein's villa who showed the video of his cruel experiments haunts me to the last corners of unconsciousness. Like bats, my thoughts flutter out of my head and circle me like vultures circling carrion. I can't distinguish reality from the world of dreams.

*

For a few days now I've been able to leave my bed. But it's strange. The ground is rippling with waves and I'm caught in the surge, swaying like a buoy in the sea. After a while, everything solidifies, and it's as if I'm fused with the spot where I'm currently standing and walking, while my shadow moves animatedly around. It's as if I'm stuck in a heavy mass which takes on the form of my body and moves with me as soon as I think: "I AM." No matter how I move, something moves with me. I stand behind myself, and it's not me but something else which walks and thinks and feels. And if I want to act consciously myself, the mass becomes incredibly heavy or collapses into an obstructive, lifeless heap which I must then penetrate again with my life, but I can't because I'm far too tired.

Nevertheless, it does not touch me. It is only my doughy shadow; what do I care what my shadow does? I live like a mirror image behind a glass wall from which I observe the world. Time and again it shatters into a heap of shards which I must put back together again, like a three-dimensional jigsaw puzzle.

*

In my dreams I sometimes look into a mirror: I stand in front of the mirror, and the mirror tears a hole in the wall.

A black hole into a world that is not there. And then Leif is standing in front of me.

*

I'm sitting here and writing all this down. They even encourage me to do so. They say it puts my mind in order. And they're right, because my memory is in fact gradually returning. But what they don't know is that I'm writing two different versions. One is for their psychoanalysis; the other notes which I hide in the bathroom behind the toilet cistern are for me. For my friends. Perhaps this secret report will reach one of them, or other people who will be alerted to the disaster by it. I myself will never be able to leave this infirmary. In the meantime I've seen through everything: the mirror is real and it's hanging in this room. I'm not crazy. And what I see in the mirror is myself. I am in Leif's body. When I tried to save his life and transferred my life force to him, he was already dead, and his empty body took over my spirit.

***

I have hands which hang off me like lumps of dough. I can only use them when I look at them. And my legs feel like rubber. While I used to concentrate on condensing myself, now I struggle to co-ordinate the movements I want to make. I'm as limp as a rag doll and I have no self-awareness. They think my clumsiness is due to the accident.

"It's a severe sensory neuropathy," diagnosed the neurologist, "but there's no disorder of the vestibular system."

The doctor was right. I just had to get used to being in a body, and I've learnt by now.

*

Baphomet has triumphed. Only now do I see through his diabolical plan. He watched me make friends, and he let our friendship flourish. He knew how it would turn out. Friendship, love, ideals – I fell into the trap all by myself. The human trap.

For a spirit, the human body is the safest prison in the world. No one comes out alive. And if the body, like mine, is in the secure ward of a psychiatric hospital, then there is no escape at all. I am doubly imprisoned.

I will never free my father. I will not change the world. I will never see my friends again. We wanted to write a Master Book for children to save people from evil. But who will believe a lunatic?! Whatever I say or write will remain a sick fantasy. That's why they allow me to write. And I write because it gives me hope and takes away my fear. Like Dr Stein from the Book of the Master – he was in a similar situation. Only instead of being in a hospital, he was in a prison. He managed to free himself, which I surely won't be able to do. I can only hope that my friends find me in time. Because no one can survive here for long.

*

The image of a merciless reality emerges ever more clearly from the fog of my fantasies. It's even worse than I first thought. It wasn't a phantom which was haunting me in my delirium: I am actually in the clinic of the sadistic doctor I saw at Goldstein's villa. He too wears the medallion with the balance scales. He shows up every evening to check on me, but it seems he hasn't yet devised a concept for the experiments he's going to perform on me. He thinks I have multiple personalities, that I'm schizophrenic. The penetrating gaze of his black eyes burns into my brain like a laser beam. But luckily he can't see through me. He has no idea that I know everything about him.

Sometimes he's accompanied by someone; at first I thought it was a man, but it's actually a woman. She's tall, thin, and wears her colourless hair so tightly drawn back and knotted that at first I thought she was bald. The ghostly white skin of her face hugs her skull so tightly that you would think it was a death's head, were it not for her protruding, hatchet-sharp nose. It dominates her whole face and lends her the appearance of a witch. Everything about her seems evil, stern, and pitiless. You get the feeling that the last vestiges of compassion have died within her. Even the skin on her long, thin fingers feels dry and lifeless, like parchment or snakeskin.

Like his, her eyes are deeply hidden in dark sockets. But they're as clear as crystal rather than black and burning; they are cold, icy cold, almost sightless, as if there's no one behind them to perceive anything. When she looks at you, the coldness is transmitted and makes your blood freeze in your veins. But it's not her malevolence which sends shivers down my spine, it's the utter emotional coldness. As soon as she comes to my bedside and begins her examinations, I freeze with fear.

Yesterday she was here again. Indifferent like an Egyptian mummy from antiquity, she was suddenly standing in front of my bed. She stared at me for a moment, then her gaze retreated back into her eye sockets. For a second, I experienced first-hand the evil which is born into the world through her.

Although she speaks very softly, her piercing voice slices through the air; as shrill as a cutting disc on rusty metal, it fills the room with penetrating echoes.

"He's not ready yet", she said, shining a small, bright lamp into my eyes. "But soon. We'll begin with the mental suggestor next week."

"How much Hypnotol should we give him?" the other person asked, jotting something down on the notes which still hang at the foot of my bed.

"Nothing!" she maliciously hissed, the ugly tone of her voice lingering in the room like a ghost. "He'll get HKX ninety-ten. I have something else planned for him. Are you sure he entered the country illegally? He speaks surprisingly good German for a foreigner!"

"The inspector assigned him to us as usual. He even had papers with him. His name's Hodapp or something similar – a dirty little thief who entered the country illegally. He was found lying injured on the motorway after a robbery. His accomplice and their victim Leif Andersson were burnt to death in the car. All three were identified from the items they had with them and the jewellery the victim was wearing. The case is closed; nobody's mourning this guy, he won't be missed by anyone."

Baphometa nodded.

"Then we'll dispose of him completely. Make a note of that."

So she was the boss, not him. Baphomet's beloved, it occurred to me – she might well look like that. Baphometa. That's why her gaze is so cold and empty and yet full of evil. It flows through her from another world and coagulates in her as diabolical life. A figure and a being designed from the Shadow. A human monster. I wonder if the doctor created her just as he created Adele, the champing, flesh-eating plant in Goldstein's panopticon, and Baphomet is directing her as his tool, lacking a will of her own?

Then they left and I was alone. The pressure that her presence always exerts on me slowly subsided, and I could relax.

And slowly I comprehend the grotesque situation. This Hodapp, the thief who had stolen from me – or rather from Leif – was dead. His master quickly fetched him away. He was burnt to death in the car accident with Leif's mobile phone, watch, and ring on him, so they mistook the thief for his victim. I remember the dirty jacket Leif was wearing when he was thrown out of the car. Obviously they not only took his jewellery but also his expensive jacket and swapped clothes. So then Leif – or rather me – had his jacket on, and Hodapp's papers were in that stinking jacket. Now they think I'm the illegal foreigner nobody is looking for, and they're not entirely wrong. No one's looking for me because they think Leif has been buried. I think I'm going crazy. Who am I now? Sometimes I grasp thoughts from Leif as if they were my own – after all, it's his brain I'm thinking with now. Then I imagine I'm not dead at all, and I feel like having a cigarette.

THE BODY IS A PRISON FOR A SPIRIT

I can't let myself fall to pieces. I must get out of here before they torture me to death and dispose of me. I have a mission to accomplish: I must finish writing our book. You don't die in the middle of the fifth chapter; the story must go on. I have to get out of this damned mental hospital and warn the friends about the school caretaker, and I must find the king and free him. Now there's another opportunity to get the elixir. Thanks to Leif's death we have an ally in the spirit world. As a human spirit, he can act differently from simple spirits. Maybe he can pass the vial over to us.

I still don't know who the bicycle in the secret passage belongs to. Even though the caretaker is clearly the culprit and is holding my father captive somewhere, I still have no idea what role Einstein is playing in this mystery play. The fact that he managed to gain our trust means nothing – even the stupidest monkey can play the role of a guru. He's highly intelligent, too. And what has Kathi's father got to do with all this?

I have to get out of here; but how? The doctor's secret private ward is so deeply hidden in the hospital that no one can uncover it. The old building is perfect for that. Nobody's looking for me up here in the attic. During the first three days when I was still downstairs with the others, I noticed that very few visitors came. The windows look out onto a park surrounded by a white wall, and behind the wall there's a church with a dome. Then I was taken away.

"Into the two-person operating theatre", the doctor had said to the nurse as they moved me here, giving me an injection. "This is to calm you down – you'll fall asleep in a minute."

But the stuff didn't work right away; I stayed awake, squinting through my eyelids. First we went up in a big lift from the official hospital ward. I couldn't see which floor the lift stopped at, but it was very quiet on that floor. There were no patients in sight, and very few staff members. The orderly pushed my bed through a long empty corridor, which branched out like a labyrinth in places until it abruptly stopped at a glass wall with the words: ACCESS FOR UNAUTHORISED PERSONNEL FORBIDDEN. He opened the sliding door with a magnetic card, placed my bed down and pressed the button on an intercom. "The patient for Operating Theatre Two is here", he said, looking at me. Then he made a note on the board by my bed and left me alone.

Above the next door it said 'OT', and above it a red light was flashing as a warning. I'd seen 'Emergency Room' on TV and knew only too well what was in store for me. Naturally I was scared because I thought I was going to be operated on. But slowly the drug began to take effect. I became sleepy and dozed off. Then someone came out, glanced at the board, and took me into the preparation room. Their face was unrecognisable because they were wearing a face mask like the ones doctors use during operations. But instead of preparing me for surgery, he lifted me onto a wheeled stretcher and immediately pushed me into Operating Theatre Two. It looked exactly like in the movies: gleaming lights on the ceiling, equipment, monitors, surgical instruments. It was like a torture chamber. The fear returned.

Out of the corner of my eye I could see the man opening a heavy green metal cupboard and folding up the shelves inside one after the other; suddenly the back wall also disappeared, revealing a passageway. Behind it was a storeroom which seemed to be serving as a wardrobe. He moved his foot a little to the side and pushed me in. As the door closed again behind us, he entered a code on his mobile phone, and suddenly the whole storeroom started moving with a gentle jolt. It was a disguised lift which was silently taking us upwards. It must have been the last floor, because the eerily empty, winding corridor through which he pushed me had no windows, and the light came down at an angle through old-fashioned skylights above me. The whole place looked like an attic, not a hospital. Through a simple wooden door we eventually reached the actual ward where I'm trapped now.

The furnishing is all ultra-modern. The rooms are bright but windowless. The whole thing reminds me of the hidden facility in Goldstein's villa and the horror prison of Yks. The same architect must have been at work here, except my dungeon is in an attic rather than a cellar. I realised immediately that no one would search for a hidden medical ward and a secret research laboratory here. They'll never find me. Those were my last thoughts before I fell asleep.

Only when I woke up again did I realise the full extent of the catastrophe. I'm in the room with the green walls where the little boy was lying. I'm alone. The other bed is unoccupied. There's a window in the ceiling – I only noticed it at night when the moon was shining through. It's not barred, but it's inaccessibly high. There's no way to get up there, and how would I get down from the roof? I can't fly now that I have this body.

In addition to the two figures from the Shadow Realm, there are also two strong orderlies with exotic appearances who take turns. Both seem absent-minded, moving like zombies and going about their tasks mechanically like robots. They're as expressionless as Baphometa and as silent as the grave. They say nothing and never answer my questions; perhaps they're mute or they don't understand what I'm saying. When I address them they seem frightened, which is the only emotion I can detect in them. I certainly can't expect any help from them. They bring the food and clean the room, the shower, and the toilet. Yesterday they both came together and changed my bed linen. They stuffed everything into a large green linen bag with a faded inscription on it, but I couldn't read it. It was probably the name of the laundry.

*

My memory is gradually returning. I must warn my friends. Who knows what else the school caretaker is up to? He managed to capture my father, and he almost killed me too. The whole school is undermined by evil, and the cellar with the alchemist's laboratory is a spiritual bomb which could explode at any time. They need to find out that the underground passage from Michael's house leads to the school, and they have to investigate it in the other two directions as well. Who owns the bicycle that was there? Who rides a bicycle in that tunnel, and where to? But they won't find the hidden spiral staircase which leads downwards: even I got lost in the confusing nooks and crannies of the basement. If they try to find it on their own, the school caretaker will make sure they disappear in his dungeon. But if they get the police involved, he'll be warned ahead of time. Officially, they have nothing on him.

*

I can't get out of this damn prison. I can't even leave my body.

*

I've realised that life in a human body of flesh and blood is completely different to life in the spiritual world. There is a significant difference between being a spirit and being a spirit trapped in a body.

*

In the meantime I have come to understand why it's so difficult for humans to gain magical abilities. It's a self-protection mechanism which prevents them from incurring karmic debts. The needs and emotions which you inherit with a human body constantly seduce and tempt you into impulsive actions. While life on the surface of the Earth was already full of temptations and dangers, in a human body you're even more strongly subject to the power of your desires. I almost killed the school caretaker in my rage, but if my thoughts still had their magical power, I would wilfully murder Baphometa. My impulses would turn me into a murderer.

*

For the first time in my gnome life, I'm casting a shadow. But although I now have a body, I feel disembodied. Am I still a spirit? Who am I? What part of me is spirit?

*

I feel as if I've been reduced to a programme on a hard drive, as if I'm running in sync with it. But it should be the other way round. I don't have a body with members and a brain; the brain has me. It thinks and wishes and wills, but where am I? I'm constantly lost in my thoughts, forgetting that I *am*. I must detach myself from this data and create a programme of my own, one which I can base myself upon. A programme of my own which says: I think. I feel. I will. A programme which knows: I am who I am, I am Andy Mo.

*

Now my bodily limbs obey me, allowing me to use them sensibly. But do I also control my spirit?

SPIRIT TIMES SPIRIT EQUALS HUMAN

I'm becoming increasingly aware of how quickly spiritual abilities atrophy when they aren't used. I haven't used many of my traits since I've been in the human realm. Talking on the phone instead of transmitting thoughts; asking directly instead of using clairvoyance; taking the bus instead of transporting myself to the desired place. Some things are more fun, some things are easier, and some things simply aren't done among humans. You don't spy on other people's thoughts and you don't turn up unannounced. When the spirit is in a human body, it has to train its spiritual muscles, just like an athlete, otherwise they atrophy. But I didn't know it could happen so quickly. Not only must I learn to better control my body, but I also have to become aware of my spirit again; I have to start from scratch. As a spirit, I was spirit and nothing else. As soon as I was in this human body, I began to identify with it and forgot who I really am. Now I understand the exercises from the Book of the Master which are dedicated to wakefulness. Just because you aren't asleep, it doesn't mean you are truly awake.

Consciousness means consciously BEING. But you only do that when you become aware that you *are*. It's not a spirit, a soul, or a body which is important, but the idea that I AM. As long as I think that and concentrate upon it, I am Andy Mo and cannot lose myself.

But I quickly forget that. In a human body, consciousness differs to the way it is in the environment of the spiritual world. You constantly identify with your body, sensations, and emotions, and you don't think of yourself as a spiritual being. You would have to practise from morning till night to be aware of your spirit in every moment. Who can do that?! After all, you're constantly being distracted. You incessantly hear and see things, or you have to do something so you go ahead and do it, be it automatically, out of habit, or as a reflex. You don't think about the fact that it's the spirit which wants, plans, and desires things, and the body is only the tool which follows the will of the spirit. In this way, consciousness atrophies and the power of the body grows along with its emotions, impulses, and drives. And because you do so much without thinking it over, the spectres of the psyche soon govern everything by themselves.

Since becoming a human being, I recognise increasingly clearly that it's not magical power which is important, but rather magical wakefulness concerning the idea: "I AM". Only with the realisation I AM can the spirit awaken, live, act, and be.

*

Now I'm experiencing first-hand in my own body what we previously only discussed theoretically. With Leif's body I also inherited the bodily instincts which ensure the body's survival, as well as the feelings awakened by those instincts, which I didn't know before. As a spirit, when I used to see chocolate pudding I thought it was a brown mass to eat. Now I get a craving for chocolate pudding as soon as I think of it. And when I think of the three centimetres of skin visible between Miri Li's jeans and the short top above her navel, my whole body starts to tingle, and those three centimetres become the most exciting centimetres in the world.

I've fallen into the human trap. Just like everyone else, I've been hooked. I swallowed one of the baits which the demons throw out to bind human souls to themselves; with love, desire, and passion, I guess anyone can be caught. But there's nothing bad that doesn't also have some good in it. I'm more than I used to be. Beyond the gross material world, the entire universe is open to me. I now have access to planes which aren't accessible to a simple spirit. I can transcend myself. If I overcome the resistance which opposes me, my possibilities are limitless. The things which take away my freedom simultaneously give me far greater freedom. I just have to seize the opportunities which present themselves.

And I will seize them. I know how to gain spiritual power in a human body: namely, by overcoming your urges. I'm not an earth spirit; now I am a human being. The fifth element has also been manifested within me, and with it I can simultaneously survey and experience the other four. I'm now able to balance my four elements so that they remain with me. When I was ready to sacrifice my life for Leif, I gained a new life in return. I'm still a spirit, but now I also possess a body. I have risen from the dead. Unknowingly, I realised the all-encompassing Christ principle which people do not understand. The sacrifice itself brings about multiplication.

*

That is the secret of the "Formula of Nothingness". That was the solution: I multiplied myself. Spirit times spirit equals human. Consciousness squared is the basis for a new reality. I'm now capable not only of thinking but also of observing myself thinking. I gain distance from myself without losing myself. I am free from everything which mediates my consciousness and thus binds my consciousness to itself, because – supported by the idea I AM – I can detach myself from myself and what I think. The thought I AM becomes a new spiritual mediator of consciousness. As long as I visualise my 'I', I cannot lose my consciousness. I am and remain a spiritual being, even if I am now more complex.

The sensational aspect of the Formula of Nothingness is the realisation that only a human being can solve the mystery of existence. Only from within a human body can a spirit gain distance from itself and from its thoughts and feelings, and can essentially reshape itself. As a spirit you're always stuck in your ideas, but as a human being you're free and can detach yourself from everything which binds you. The human brain is the most ingenious cosmic tool. I must explain this to my friends. This is the foundation for an entirely new magic.

LEARNING TO FLY

If I manage to separate myself from my body, then I can leave this hospital and warn my friends about the school caretaker. I can't get out of here with my body, but I can make it out as a spirit. There are no spirit traps set up here. I just need to learn to fly again.

But when you're in a human body, it's much more challenging than for a simple spirit. You can distance yourself from yourself, but it's difficult to get out of the body as long as it's alive. Only a few individuals are able to do this: those who are naturally talented and the so-called initiates. Humans call it an out-of-body experience. I found some books describing such experiences in Michael's library [Emil Stejnar, *Out-of-Body Experiences*, Stejnar Verlag, Vienna]. The Book of the Master also deals with this subject: it describes a special technique by which you use the dream world as a launchpad for your flights. Since I now dream when I sleep, it might work. It worked for Kathi; we discussed it extensively in our small circle. Kathi had already gained some experience:

"The decisive factor was a tip from the book *Creative Dreaming*", she revealed to us. "You prepare yourself for your dream journey before falling asleep. In your mind, you go to a place you know well and imagine yourself walking around the area or the rooms you're aiming at. You touch the objects, look around, and fall asleep with these imaginings already transporting your consciousness somewhere else. But then I ended up dreaming of something quite different", she recounted. "I didn't end up in Michael's library, which I had been concentrating on; instead, I was marvelling at a fairy-tale meadow of flowers, but I suddenly became aware that I was dreaming. It was a tremendously exhilarating feeling. And when I tried to fly, I rose into the air and soared away like a bird. Initially I was gliding through a beautiful landscape, then over dangerous precipices, ravines, and valleys, but I wasn't afraid."

Alas, then Kathi lost consciousness and fell asleep again. But at least it was an initial success. The others were enthusiastic and planned to try this method as well. I don't know how far they've come in the meantime. Now I'm performing these exercises myself, and I hope I'll soon be able to fly again.

Before, in the spirit world, I didn't need much sleep. And when I did sleep, it was like switching off and drifting away, like a relaxing meditation. In the human realm it's different; here consciousness constantly slips away. Since I've been in a human body, I actually fall asleep and lose track of reality in the dream world. I experience dreams as if they were reality. I now feel the same way humans do – I fall asleep and don't notice it. In my dreams I don't know that I'm asleep, and I don't think that I *am*. Life seems to continue on, and I don't notice that what I'm now perceiving are spiritual fantasies rather than my gross material surroundings.

As soon as I begin dreaming, I also forget that I am a spirit being. In truth, I even forget that fact while I am awake rather than sleeping. My body, the world, everything around me captures all of my attention. I think a hundred thousand things, but the thought 'I AM' does not cross my mind. And that is exactly what happens to me in my dreams.

Yet the dream realm forms the border to the true spirit world. Human dreams take place at the Borderlands of the spirit world and not only in the mind, where dream experiences are mirrored for the bodily senses. As an earth spirit I often encountered dreamers in the Borderlands, but they had no idea where they were. Now I feel the same way. I fall asleep and don't notice that I have. Now I'm a prisoner not only in my body but also in my dreams. If I were to recognise in the dream world that my body is asleep and that I'm travelling through spiritual realms as a spirit, the dream fantasies would not be able to bind me to them. I could consciously transport my spirit and leave the dream events, this body, and this infernal hospital.

-"If you realise in your dreams that you're dreaming, because you've become aware that your body is lying in a bed somewhere and is asleep, then you also become aware that you are a spirit being. Then you can move freely as a spirit and travel quite consciously and purposefully through your dreamscape", Kathi quoted a passage from the Book of the Master. "If you awaken in your dreams, you can fly wherever you wish. First through the world of your dreams, and then also through the gross material world and the other planes and spheres accessible to you, if you concentrate on it."-

Humans refer to this awakening as 'lucid dreaming'. That is, clear waking dreaming. The Book of the Master teaches a special dream training for this purpose. The aim is a 'magical awakening' during sleep without waking up in the body.

The exercises are simple. You just have to make sure that you're awake rather than asleep. During the day you remind yourself of this fact as often as possible. At the moment I'm reminding myself several times an hour that I'm on the physical plane and not in the dream world. I think to myself: "I am awake. I am a spirit, and I am living in this body." Then I try to float up to the ceiling, but since I'm in a body, I don't succeed. This way I know I'm in the gross material world.

I must do this so often that I remember this experience in my dreams. It's like brainwashing, because if I try to fly in my dream, I will be able to fly: I'll ascend to the ceiling and realise that I'm in the dream world. The dream will turn into a lucid dream, and I will magically awaken.

I can then take the opportunity to place myself in Miri Li's proximity. But so far I haven't succeeded. I'll continue to practise; I must mobilise my spiritual powers and regain my magical abilities.

*

The longing for Miri Li lends wings to my soul, but the certainty of my powerlessness paralyses my spiritual strength. I must learn to fly again. But reality is brutal and more powerful than dreams. The body hangs like lead on my limbs, even at night.

SPIRITUAL TRAINING – THE POWER OF IMAGINATION

Only now do I truly understand the words of the Book of the Master: "As a human being, you already carry all the power which the spirit needs within you. You need only draw it out of yourself."

As an earth spirit, I had no urges or impulses to struggle against. There was no resistance to overcome. The only danger for a spirit is excessively manifesting the qualities you possess. Frugality then becomes miserliness, or love of order becomes pedantry. I always had to keep that in mind and maintain balance.

But now things are different. I'm full of feelings, emotions, fears, and drives. I often feel tired and sluggish and would prefer not to move at all. And I'm constantly craving something: spaghetti, Wiener schnitzel, a real Viennese milk-cream strudel. They pamper me here with delicacies, as if I were in a five-star hotel. They measure my brain waves and blood values, look for hormones and other messenger substances, and then they let me starve for days, but show me the food and measure me again. It's frustrating. It's completely messing me up. But I control myself. The old witch is there every time, measuring, taking notes, and yesterday she said: "We're making progress; soon we'll be ready, then we'll use the mental suggestor." I don't know what that is, but it doesn't sound good.

But I know from the Book of the Master that all spiritual power resides in the body and can be gained through overcoming these impulses. Now this knowledge is serving me well. Whenever I notice that I'm letting myself go again, I pull myself together, fight against it, and consciously draw the energy of the bodily impulses into my own spirit. I am learning to be human without forgetting my spirit. It's not easy, but I'm making good progress. And something else has become clear to me since I became human. I now understand why humans can't perform magic. They lack the imaginative ability. They don't possess the necessary power of the imagination to shape the spirit. Yet only those who are capable of this can master the spirit and the spirits.

I'm now experiencing first-hand how difficult this is, and I realise why imagination exercises are so crucial. When you train your imagination, the organs necessary for spiritually seeing, hearing, smelling, and feeling are also formed. Thanks to these exercises I am slowly getting my spirit back under control.

The consciously reproduced ideas of sensory impressions – objects, colours, sounds, etc. – or of sensations such as smells, tastes, or hot and cold, are the first spiritual entities you can perceive when you're in a human body. When someone vividly imagines something that doesn't actually exist to the point of perceiving it internally, they behold a spiritual entity. Humans must learn this anew in every incarnation, and I've also needed to start all over again since inhabiting a body. I myself have been practising the exercises which I was explaining to my friends not long ago. I'm relearning how to observe and master my thoughts, and my next step is to condense the spirit with the power of my imagination.

In the spirit world this wasn't so difficult for me. As an earth spirit, I took the ethereal material of the earth and formed it with my imagination like clay or loam. It was my own element, and thoughts were my flesh and blood. But in a human body it's different. Here you must deal with four elements, and your concentration is hindered by the multitude of impressions and by the emotions and sensations which are constantly arising. In a body the soul is interposed, animating all impressions and filling them with its own impulses. An idea doesn't remain where it's placed like a stone, nor does it retain its form. That's why humans find it so difficult to concentrate. And now I'm also finding it difficult to condense an idea in such a way that I can transfer it to another consciousness. But I must relearn this, for only when I have mastered the spirit again is there a chance of escaping from here.

I have a plan, you see. The only thing which regularly leaves this room is the laundry bag. They take hygiene very seriously here, and they change all the bed covers and bathroom towels three times a week. The process is always the same. The heavily built orderlies who bring the food and do the cleaning place the bag next to the door and carry out their tasks in silence. While one mops the floor and changes the bedclothes, the other cleans the bathroom and toilet and changes the towels. Just like in a four-star hotel.

I could smuggle my secret notes out of this prison with the dirty laundry. I found an envelope and I put Michael's address on it. Someone in the laundry room will find the letter and forward it on. I can't escape from here alone. Only my friends can get me out of this madhouse. But I must get the cleaning lady to put the laundry bag in the bathroom instead of right next to the door. That's the only way I can get the diary out of its hiding place and place it in the bag without being seen. But neither of the cleaners are responding to my thought packets. My orders just glide straight through them. My imagination is too weak. They carry out their work mechanically and expressionlessly like robots, and sometimes I get the impression they don't even perceive me physically.

If I don't manage to carry out my plan soon, I will surely die. No one has ever survived the experiments they're conducting here. It's a race against time. I must learn to imagine again so that I can influence the cleaners.

I remember the day I was discussing these exercises with my friends. A sudden thunderstorm had driven us from the terrace. We were sitting in the library, drinking tea and snacking on vanilla crescent cookies, which Michael had baked using an old recipe of his grandmother. I couldn't eat them myself, but Yks was absolutely thrilled.

RECIPE

VANILLA CRESCENT COOKIES

Ingredients:
210 grams of cold butter
250 grams of flour mixed with 4 grams (= 1 pinch) of baking powder
70 grams of grated walnuts
70 grams of icing sugar

Knead everything together to form a smooth dough and let it rest in the fridge for about an hour. Roll the dough into small finger-thick rolls on your work surface, divide them into pieces about 6 cm long, then shape them into crescents. The dough must be cold so it can be shaped into rolls.

Place the crescent cookies on a baking tray lined with baking paper and bake at 180 degrees Celsius for approx. 20 minutes until they're light golden.

After baking, sprinkle them with a mixture of 100 grams of icing sugar and a packet of real (bourbon) vanilla sugar, or roll them in the mixture. The crescent cookies should still be warm.

We took the exercises for training our concentration and imaginative faculties from Franz Bardon's book *The Path of the True Adept*. He describes concentrating on objects and sensory perceptions, which you must imagine until you can actually perceive your imaginings. You can only master the spirit if you succeed in thinking of a smell, taste, feeling, colour, or sound in so concentrated a manner that you really see, hear, smell, feel, and taste what you're thinking of.

"What you create in the process is not just an image on the cerebral cortex, like any other normal idea or perception, but a replica of it", I explained to my friends. "It is in fact a spiritual entity which you have purposefully created with your concentration. Through these exercises, you not only learn to condense the spirit and form it into whatever you want, but you also automatically learn to see the spirit – that is, to perceive ethereal forms and to experience the spirit as it is. This is another prerequisite for conscious work with the spirit. For example, if you imagine the colour yellow and you actually succeed in seeing yellow before your inner eyes, then you have learnt to see spiritually, and if you imagine the sound of a church bell and then actually hear it ringing, you're perceiving spiritual sounds. If you achieve this, you'll soon be able to perceive the thoughts and imaginings of other people."

"I just can't manage it", Miri Li complained. "When I imagine the colour yellow or red or blue, I see grey or black, and it's no better with green. All I see are blurry shadows."

"It's the same for me", said Kathi. "I'm spiritually blind. But I do better with tones – I imagine myself playing the piano, and then I can actually hear the melody within me, as if I were really touching the keys."

I revealed a trick to the girls.

"When imagining yellow, think of a banana, and for red, think of a rose or a cherry. It's like with the piano: if you connect several reference points, it's easier to create a mental image. By recalling memories of your last holiday on a farm or by the sea, it's easier to conjure up the image of the smell of hay, the smell of a stable, or the taste of seawater."

"What's the purpose of all this?" asked Miri Li resignedly. "It's not as if I want to learn magic. My religion and my faith in God are enough for me."

"To train the willpower – specifically, for using it on the spiritual plane", I explained to her. "You humans don't seem to notice it, but the will expresses itself differently on each plane. On the gross material plane, it grants you the power to master your body and its urges. On the astral plane, which you experience in the human body as an apparent inner life in the form of your feelings, the will helps you to prevent your feelings, emotions, and affects from getting out of hand. And on the spiritual plane, the will manifests itself as the power of concentration and imagination. These are necessary to deal properly with spirit and the spirits – that is, with your own thoughts, ideas, and fantasies, as well as those of others. Only then are you able to communicate with spiritual beings. With a strong will you can attune yourself to spiritual entities in order to perceive them correctly, shape them, and shield yourself from unpleasant impressions, because you've gained mastery over them.

"When you die and must live without a body, it's crucial that you're able to arrange your surroundings as you wish. Here in the gross material world you need influence, power, and money to shape your life as you desire. On the ethereal planes, your capital is your willpower and imagination. And here, you can train them much better than you can without a body. There's more resistance to overcome, and it's precisely from that resistance that the power of the spirit arises. I only noticed this on the surface of the Earth."

At that time, I had no idea that it would be much more difficult in a human body than I thought. But I'm making progress. And I've confirmed something which Kathi had already recognised back then.

"It's easier when you're sick", she said. "Last week, when the meat poisoning from that stupid pizza almost finished me off, I experienced some very strange things in my delirious fantasies. A huge wardrobe suddenly appeared in my room, and an old man kept coming in and out. However, I was fully awake, and with my imagination, I managed to push the wardrobe out of the room. I hate wardrobes and dressers. Then the old man disappeared all by himself."

Christian had experienced something similar.

"You can also observe this when you're overtired or on the verge of being half asleep, like during a long train journey or on a plane", he said. "That's when thoughts immediately turn into real images. But I think there's a difference between purposefully and consciously imagining something and just letting your fantasies pass by."

"That's true", I agreed with him. "But in that detached state of consciousness you can also perceive your own imaginings more clearly. You can make good use of that for your practice, and beginners in particular can gain feedback and realise what it's really all about. Although Bardon writes that you mustn't fall asleep while practising, the Book of the Master recommends utilising the time before falling asleep as well. Surely it's better to train your imagination and fall asleep than not to practise at all."

Now I myself am in this situation. Like my friends, I'm stuck in a human body. I'm constantly tired because the experiments they perform on me are weakening me. But I practise anyway, and I fall asleep in the process. I make use of every free minute I have alone. I've become acquainted with new senses which weren't accessible to me as an earth spirit: now I can taste, smell, and experience lightness, warmth, pleasure, and pain.

*

Since I've been living in a human body, my old spirit life seems like that of a robot. What unimagined possibilities are open to human beings! What an abundance of impressions, feelings, sensations, and inspirations flow into me! As a spirit, my striving was always directed towards a single goal; now I'm pulled to and fro, yet I can decide what shapes my thinking, feeling, and willing.

*

Since I've possessed a body, I've developed new preferences. While this enriches my life, it becomes my undoing and torments me during the experiments they subject me to. At first they pampered me as if I were in a gourmet restaurant. They served me the most delicious things every day while they measured my brain waves and blood values, then they let me starve and only showed me pictures of the delicacies. That too was precisely measured and recorded. And now I'm only being punished. Every time I take some of the fragrant delights they serve me, I get a strong electric shock. It hurts like hell.

*

I'm no longer alone. Now the other bed is also occupied: his name is Milan, and he's a boy of my age. A pickpocket. He belonged to an organised gang, and he's been here for six weeks. No one misses Milan either, as he soberly remarked. Two other children are being held on this floor. They're both unconscious, and a third died yesterday. When Milan told me how it happened, my blood ran cold. I'm seized with horror whenever I recall the conversation, and mortal fear grips me as soon as one of the doctors enters the room.

"At the moment they're trying to figure out the process of dying", Milan had explained to me. "They want to record the fading of consciousness in order to unravel the mystery of life. In the meantime they manage ninety minutes."

"Ninety minutes of what?" I asked, but he remained silent and wouldn't tell me at first. Only when I insisted did he continue.

"Dead. He was dead for ninety minutes. Do you understand? Dead as a doornail, like completely gone. I managed fifty minutes. Most of them don't wake up after ten minutes. They extend the period each time, and eventually you stay over there. In the afterlife, I mean, if you believe in that."

I nodded.

"You'll get your turn too", he said pensively after a while. "So far, they've killed everyone that way. The longer you're a corpse, the more interesting you become to them. I don't know what they plan to do with me next, but when they pair up two people, usually one of them is going to have their turn. Still, I'd rather die here with you than alone on ice over in the operating theatre."

I looked at Milan questioningly.

"They cool you – or rather your blood – down to around ten or fifteen degrees, I think. It doesn't take long. At the same time they inject something into your veins. When your brain's cold enough, it no longer needs oxygen and shuts down. Brain death; no heartbeat; exodus. However, you remain intact for a while, and then they bring you back to life. Not everyone: some fall into a coma after being warmed up. They use a defibrillator at 30 degrees, and then the heart starts beating again. Sometimes they replace all your

355

blood with a special fluid. Then you survive up to five hours in the afterlife, but something goes wrong in your head. Apparently it's already working with pigs, though. They're conducting experiments with it in America: the old lady mentioned it the other day, and she's very proud that her research is further along than the others."

"You're well informed and speak perfect German", I noted. "Why did you end up on the streets?"

But Milan didn't want to talk about it.

"My father was a doctor, and I was an ass", was all he said. Then he turned on his side and fell asleep.

*

Time and again I look at the monitor next to Milan, and I feel relieved when his brain waves are still visible. They conduct various experiments on him, and I have to watch helplessly as they torture him. My own head is also wired up. They're measuring our frequencies and the hormones in our blood. "Fear acts on neurons like dopamine", she remarked yesterday. "We're on the trail of the true control centres of the emotions: a seemingly immaterial process in the cortex. The neural fields respond exactly like magnetic fields to the electric currents in a coil. The amygdala only serves as a transformer in this regard."

*

I'm still alive, thank God. They had taken me to the two-person operating theatre. There I was given an injection, but I didn't fall asleep. On the contrary: I became wide awake. I was trembling with fear. I knew my turn had come.

"The Romanians are out", Frankenstein said sadly. "The gang has been caught and taken to a shelter. We won't be receiving any more supplies."

"What about number 17?" asked Baphometa. "When do we get her?"

"I'll bring her up tomorrow, but we'll have to hurry. It's not a meningioma; it's a massive carcinoma affecting the orbitofrontal regions of both frontal lobes."

They were talking as if I wasn't present. I exist only as an experimental subject for them. While he was operating the equipment with an assistant who I couldn't recognise due to his face mask, she was intently watching the spikes and curves on the screens I was hooked up to. The blood they took from me ran through the heart-lung machine and came back chilled. But strangely enough, I didn't feel cold. Despite the icy chill, I soon felt pleasantly warm. I knew I was going to die, but suddenly it no longer affected me. I recognised the opportunity that was being offered to me and I wanted to use it. I concentrated on the formula: "I am a spirit, I am Andy Mo, I am", and hoped that I would succeed in retaining my consciousness.

"There!" she suddenly said excitedly. "The hippocampus is showing less neural activity than normal. A classic near-death experience. Give him the Haldal and put him back into the PET scanner."

And only then did I realise that I was observing the entire situation from above. I was floating above my body. While my head disappeared into the positron emission tomography scanner, I remained outside the tube like the others, and I was able to watch the whole process as a spectator. The curve on the green monitor turned into a flat line, and a steady tone announced my death. Baphometa seemed thrilled.

"Did you notice the transition? Fantastic! Bring him back. Ketamine anaesthesia might work on him too. It acts directly on the NMDA receptors – even if we lose him in the process, we'll make significant progress."

I'm still alive, but I won't be for long. I missed my chance. As I was hovering over my body, I intended to transport myself to Michael's house. But I waited too long, and when my heart started beating again, something held me back. The fact that I could fly again had confused me. I don't know if I'll be able to do it again, or what it will be like when I'm finally dead. My spiritual muscles are still too weak. I'm curious about how I'm going to be leaving this prison.

*

Yesterday they came for Milan, but they didn't bring him back. I don't have much time left. May God grant that someone will find these notes and send them to my friends.

CONCERNING THE BEYOND AND LIFE AFTER DEATH

I often think about Leif. I wonder where he is right now and how he's doing. When I tried to contact him last night, I almost succeeded. I dreamt of him. I could observe him from a distance. At first I saw him together with Amue in emerald green, crystal clear water. She was showing him how to move through her element. Immediately afterwards, the two of them were walking through the rocky desert in the Borderlands, and then he was the one who was supporting her and taking the lead. You could see he was in his element. That surprised me, because normally it takes much longer for the deceased to orient themselves in this in-between world, where the old life is extinguished and the new one is still shapeless, and to find their way into their soul garden. Most wander aimlessly, unaware that they have died.

Leif didn't notice me, and neither did Amue when I waved to her. But that doesn't surprise me. Space and time merge together in the world of dreams. What I was able to observe was probably already in the past for them. Nevertheless, I'm happy about what I saw, because the fact that Leif moved so confidently in the intermediate realm suggests he has assimilated parts of my being. When I transferred my life force to him, our spirits merged. In the process, parts of me – i.e. ideas, experiences, and abilities from my gnome life – blended into his consciousness. Just as I use his human body here, spiritual molecules of mine mediate him over there.

Now Leif is evidently experiencing an introduction to the four elements. And he's taking Amue with him – just like Tamino takes Pamina and Papageno takes Papagena in the wonderful Masonic opera *The Magic Flute*, it occurs to me. The Freemasons symbolically lead newly admitted members through the four elements, and with this ritual they aim to make them aware that they're more than just a body of skin, flesh, and bones. The confrontation with fire, water, air, and earth is intended to make them aware of the limbs of their true being, their ethereal body, which consists of thinking, feeling, willing, and consciousness in accordance with the four primal substances.

Belatedly, Leif is now experiencing an authentic initiation, up close and personal. Now he is truly learning the power and force of the four foundations of life, the four limbs of self-awareness, and the four pillars of creation. And he is meeting the beings behind them. He has already acquired theoretical knowledge from the books of Franz Bardon and Emil Stejnar, which we discussed for hours in our discussion groups. I'm reassured by the fact that components of my being are now helping him on his real journey through the four elements. Just as I am currently using his body, so he can benefit from my experiences and abilities, and thus navigate the spirit realm much better than ordinary humans. He is living with elementals from me – just like Papageno the bird catcher, I think to myself. Don't humans also catch their thoughts as if they were colourful birds?

*

I was interrupted while writing. What I experienced makes my blood run cold, even without the refrigeration. Now I know what Milan didn't want to tell me when I asked him why nobody cries out for help.

"Why isn't anyone screaming for help?", I had asked Milan.

"After all, this is a hospital in the middle of Vienna." But he had only laughed sarcastically.

"We're in the loony bin, don't forget that. There's always someone yelling in this building, isn't there? And if you get agitated up here, they'll inject you into a coma and use you for an experiment which I don't want to experience. You won't have any air, so you won't be able to scream anymore." Then Milan had fallen silent, and he said nothing more despite my urging.

Now I know what he meant. What I saw really can't be described in words – it was a horrific event which surpasses any horror film. A doctor or nurse had unexpectedly appeared, again wearing a face mask so I couldn't see his face. He gave me an injection and shoved me, along with my bed, into the one-person operating theatre. Usually they conduct experiments in the two-person operating theatre in the afternoon, but this time they had taken me in the middle of the night. Next to the MRI in the operating theatre there was a PET, which is also a tube which they slide you into, only smaller and less noisy. These tomographs allow examination of the inner workings of the body, similar to X-ray machines. Baphometa is studying the brain with them. Since different aspects of life are controlled by different regions of the brain, the screen displays which impressions are currently being processed and what's likely to be happening in consciousness: whether the person is experiencing pleasure or pain, whether they're tracking something acoustically or visually, which body organs they're currently moving or want to move, and so forth. The corresponding brain region requires more oxygen to work, and thus it receives a slightly higher blood supply. By preparing the blood with an isotope marker, they can make the increased blood flow visible on a monitor. The results from this tomograph are far more revealing than those from an EEG, which they use to measure our brain waves almost all day long. That's roughly how Milan explained it to me; he had been here for a while and knew his stuff.

"Look at this!" shrieked Baphometa, staring at the monitor without paying any attention to my arrival. "It's still showing a reaction. Just one more minute and we'll have a breakthrough."

While the doctor who had pushed me into the operating theatre inserted and secured a needle at the crook of my arm, I could watch the screen. It showed a brain with colourful flecks.

"Give it light now!" commanded the witch; Frankenstein, who was operating the equipment, pressed some buttons and flipped a small lever. Almost simultaneously the image changed. Apparently the poor devil in the tube had reacted again. Then she demanded level two, and then level three, and each time the patterns of activity on the screened brain images changed. "It's responding, it can see!" Baphometa exclaimed excitedly. "Now some sound, and then pain. Start again at stage one."

Meanwhile the drug they had given me began to take effect. I felt groggy, then I fell asleep. Not fully asleep, though; I dipped only briefly into the world of dreams, landing in a swamp which threatened to swallow me up, but then I remembered my training, attempted to fly, and succeeded. I realised that I was dreaming, so I was spiritually awake, but once again I missed the opportunity to visit my friends. Instead of transporting myself near Miri Li as I had planned, I thought of the patient in the tube undergoing the experiments. I wanted to know if it was Milan or some other boy whose brain they were about to stimulate – not with light and sound, but with pain, as they had announced. These thoughts promptly drew me back into the operating theatre. I hovered over my body, flew slowly up to the ceiling, and looked down at the apparatus in which my fellow sufferer lay.

What I saw then I will never forget for all eternity. Now I understood why she had said 'it' rather than 'he' or 'she'. Because what they slid out of the tube beneath me was not a boy, nor was it Milan or any other captive patient. What emerged from the tomograph was a head. A living head without a torso or limbs, its eyes peeled wide open in horror; no, not peeled – the eyelids had been fixed with adhesive tape to prevent them from closing. The silent gaze was one endless, soundless scream. It was ghostly. Two tubes, pulsating with blood, led from the neck to a device – probably a heart-lung machine – which kept 'it', the brain, alive. Most grotesque of all, the head was wearing headphones and had long hair; perhaps it had belonged to a girl. I wanted to scream, and I probably did. Then I lost consciousness completely, and only came to again in my room. Thankfully, I was unaware of what they had done to me. But I now know how I will end up if my friends don't find me.

*

Now I'm continuing to write my notes. It's the only way to calm my agitated emotions. My senses, too, are realigned by thoughts of my friends, of the power of the spirit we discussed, and of the time when the world was still congenial for me. I immerse myself in the memories as if they were reality, leaving behind the terrible place I am actually in.

We were speaking about life after death, the beyond, and the spirit realm. We were sitting on the terrace at Michael's, and I cited the Book of the Master:

"Just as a new-born infant must learn to navigate the physical world, so it takes some time after death to orient yourself and move around on the spiritual planes." I didn't know at the time just how difficult this was for humans to grasp. They believe that beyond the gross material world you can fly freely through all the planes and spheres as you please. But the beyond is just as infinite as the gross material world, and much more complex. Finding your way around in the realm of the spirit is far more challenging than here.

I remember trying to explain this to Michael back when he asked me to visit his deceased mother and tell her that he was doing well. I would gladly have complied with his request, but the realm of spirits is not the same world where human spirits end up after discarding their bodies. Every spirit is bound to the location corresponding to its nature. In the gross material world, you also don't have access to every building. And if you travel to the Arctic, you need to dress accordingly if you don't want to freeze to death. People living here in Europe are far away from Australia and don't see what's happening in that part of the world. And those who reside in the realms of the elemental spirits don't know what's happening in the spheres of the planetary spirits.

"Just as you can't move away from the Earth without a spaceship", I said, "so you also need something on the spiritual planes to carry you if you wish to go somewhere else. It's not as simple as in the internet game 'Second Life' where you can choose a body and fly anywhere with it. What is close to you here because it's the place where you're currently residing is close to you in the beyond because it corresponds to your personal nature and character. On the ethereal planes it's personal qualities, inclinations, and interests which carry a spirit into the region corresponding to its disposition. What you don't already have within yourself seems infinitely distant. This is true of all spiritual beings, including angels, gods, and demons, not just the spirits of people who have died."

"But you told us that a spirit can transport itself anywhere with the power of thought", said Leif. "Doesn't that apply to us after death?"

"It does, but you must learn how to do it first. Your spirit will only fly if you can imagine it. And even then, it's not certain that you'll land where you wish to, because you must have an idea of your destination within you as well, otherwise you won't arrive there. That's why the ability to imagine is so important. If you can't identify with the place you want to reach, you won't get there. Initially you'll always remain in your own world. Your thoughts and emotions form a landscape from which it's difficult to remove yourself.

"An earth spirit is incapable of flying through the realm of air spirits because the properties of its element are heavy, dense, and impenetrable. And an air spirit can't gain a foothold in the element of earth because its entire being is loose, light, and fleeting. Because of their hot temper, fire spirits remain bound to the fire and to regions where their energy and passion can run riot, while sensitive water spirits stay in the depths of the seas and in the regions where deep emotions determine the landscape.

"Human spirits could experience all four realms, but since they're used to experiencing everything from the point of view of their thoughts and feelings, without magical training they remain trapped in their own imaginary world."

Leif understood what I meant and nodded.

"In fact it's the same now. No matter where you are and what you perceive, you'll only ever grasp it in the form of your own imaginings. Everything you hear or see or feel of your surroundings is the idea in your head of what you perceive, not the actual object in front of you. If the image of that tree over there didn't arise in my brain, I wouldn't be able to see it."

"Exactly. The Indians call this phenomenon *maya*. By this they don't mean that the material world is an illusion, as some claim on the basis of false translations; rather, they mean it can only be perceived in the form of imagining, i.e. spiritual images. Consciousness remains bound to the spirit even in the material world, and thus nothing changes in your world of thoughts even after death. It remains intact. Stejnar calls this inverted inner world the personal soul garden. It's the space in which all the thoughts, desires, and ideas which you've carried within you during your life present themselves to you as a living environment. What currently takes place in your mind will then happen in your soul garden, and you'll be standing right in the midst of it.

"Consciousness of yourself – that is, the thought 'I AM' – is the fifth element which permeates your entire soul garden and enables you to observe yourself. Just as an infant looks at its hands without realising they are parts of itself, so in the beyond your components of being – your thoughts, feelings, and uncontrolled impulses – confront you as strange beings and lead you to believe they're demons and angels."

"I still don't quite understand that", Michael said. "I thought when you die you wake up in the afterlife and are welcomed by those who passed away before you. But now you're telling us that even angels and demons are just imaginings."

"No, these beings really exist, and of course the spirits of the departed do as well, and they can also appear to you. However, you won't always perceive them. You must first awaken if you wish to communicate with them properly. The world in your soul garden is almost the same as the one in which you find yourself when you're asleep. There, too, the sensory organs of your body are deactivated and you don't notice what's happening around you. You're unaware that you're dreaming and imagining everything, and you believe you're in the real world. You consist solely of thoughts and feelings, and you experience your fantasies as if they were reality. A mentally disturbed person also believes their hallucinations are the true reality.

"What initially confronts you in your soul garden are also mere imaginings. They're images of landscapes, beings, people, and situations which form apparently genuine realities from the impulses you have within you, just like in your dreams. They are thoughts and feelings from within you – that is, parts of yourself rather than alien entities from another world."

"You mean you see yourself as in a mirror, or let's say like in the fragments of a broken mirror?" But I shook my head.

"Since they're your own imaginings, they aren't lifeless mirror images, but the same little spirits which already have a life of their own within you, and which you must constantly struggle against. Consider what your spirit consists of. What remains of you when you die? What is the foundation of your existence?"

"My consciousness, of course – and above all, the idea 'I AM'. When I think: "I am", then I feel as if I am grasping myself. So I am what I think. But I am also what I feel and want. So I consist of my thoughts, my feelings, and what I desire. But I'm more than that. I also consist of the ability to deal with these thoughts, feelings, and desires. Essentially I consist of my qualities, that is, my character."

"Correct", I confirmed. "Depending on your character, you'll harbour different thoughts, feelings, and desires, and conversely, your thoughts and desires will influence your character. If you don't master your thoughts and feelings, they master you. That's something you don't notice in normal life. Then these components of your being function like an engine which drives you onward and enables you to act, or like a boat preventing you from sinking into the sea of unconsciousness. There is pure consciousness, but without the contents of consciousness it doesn't recognise its own existence.

"You are more than your thoughts and feelings, but without your thoughts and feelings no desire or will would arise, and your 'I'-consciousness would fade away. Without thinking, feeling, and wanting, you no longer notice your own existence.

"Currently the spiritual components of your being are within your body, together with your consciousness. But if your body is deactivated – when you're asleep, for example – then you experience the things taking place within you as if they were around you, i.e. outside of you in the form of a dreamscape. It's the same after death. Most people don't even notice that they've died. When you dream, you also don't think about the fact that your body is lying in bed and you're only dreaming everything. You don't even realise that you've fallen asleep. You must first learn to awaken in a dream, and it's the same in your soul garden. Only when you're aware of your situation can you reassemble the spiritual components of your being and form an ethereal body from them – the mystics call it the light body. With it you can explore the spiritual realms which lie beyond your soul garden."

"Then the soul garden is something like the antechamber to the beyond", Leif remarked, and I nodded.

"First you look into the room – that is, into yourself – rather than looking out of the window."

"Okay. But how do I awaken, how do I shape my soul garden, how do I keep the spiritual components of my being together after I die?"

"The same way you do in life: with the power of your will and imagination. If you're able to consciously observe and control your thoughts and desires, and you don't constantly lose yourself in your fantasies or get tossed around by unrealistic hopes or unfounded fears, then you possess precisely the same ability which shapes the spirit into true realities in the ethereal worlds. Your wish-laden thoughts move you, prompt you to act, and shape your life. It's no different without a body."

"In fact we're already shaping our personal afterlife, our inner world", Michael commented. "We already live almost exclusively in our own world. After all, it's our thoughts and feelings which determine our mood and well-being. Why should that be any different after death? You shouldn't assume that when you die, you're rid of your fears or your selfish qualities and rise up as an angel. These impulses will still be stirring within you. And if what you have within yourself appears to you as external reality in the spiritual realm, just as it does in dreams, then it's better to have positive rather than negative thoughts and feelings within yourself."

"You've hit the nail right on the head", I said. "It pays to be good. As personal qualities, compassion and the desire to help others are just as much spiritual components of your being which mediate consciousness as selfishness and ruthlessness. If someone delights in intimidating other people, then there's something within that person which will frighten them as soon as it confronts them as a spirit in their soul garden. Forbearance, patience, and compassion will manifest as benevolent angels."

"If that's true and this soul garden really exists, then calls for virtuous and ethical behaviour aren't just judgmental moralising – they're a sensible suggestion you should follow", said Leif. "So saying 'thou shalt not' and 'thou wilt not' because otherwise you'll end up in hell isn't a threat: it's a statement. If it is indeed your character which determines the place where you end up after death, I'd prefer to consist of noble spiritual components of being. While Miri Li is happy giving a homeless person a euro from her pocket money, my father takes pleasure in swindling people. There doesn't even have to be a lot of money at stake. He's already satisfied if he can simply snatch a parking space from under someone's nose. And if it's your own being which is the first thing to confront you after your death, visibly manifesting as your surroundings, then I'd rather have the selfless spiritual components of Miri Li's being. They're more likely to manifest themselves as a peaceful landscape and a good fairy than my father's egoistic impulses. He'll never find a parking spot in his afterlife, and he'll constantly have enemies – a nightmare if it really works out that way."

"That reminds me of a Chinese proverb", Michael remarked. "Miri Li quoted it the other day: 'What you give away in life, you get back in the afterlife.'"

Since that conversation, a change had taken place in Leif. He had become thoughtful, quieter, and more helpful. And now we're both benefiting from it. Although we seem to be trapped in each other's worlds, it's precisely the spiritual components of being we're bound to which can free us from the world we find ourselves in. As a human, I don't know if I will succeed in learning to fly again. Nevertheless, I have made progress. And like Leif, I will not give up. I will persevere; it's not too late yet.

THE SECRET SOCIETY OF 'THE SCALES'

Slowly Michael let the last page of Andy Mo's diary fall. No one said a word. It was like being at a funeral. The brown envelope with the dreadful contents had arrived in the post. He had read it aloud, and the others had listened in silence.

"He's stuck in the body of Leif", Yks croaked, raising his wings in bewilderment. "That's completely perverse. Now I understand why I couldn't find him. It's not the fault of the beer – I was looking for Andy Mo, not Leif. We all thought he had died in the accident. I was convinced the boy was dead."

"Strictly speaking, he is", Michael said. "But his body is now animated by Andy Mo."

"Assuming he's still alive", Kathi pointed out. "We don't know when he wrote the last entry. It's a diary, but it doesn't have any dates. Maybe they've already experimented him to death."

Michael rummaged through a pile of newspapers and retrieved a calendar.

"The accident happened exactly four weeks ago. He can't be killed off that quickly. But why the hell doesn't he write where this damn hospital is?"

"He doesn't know. You just read it out – the hospital room where he's being held has no windows and is always locked. He was injured, weakened, and unconscious. But the worst thing is that he's lost his magical abilities since he's been stuck in a human body. He can't get out of there on his own."

"I think we have a good chance of rescuing him. It can't be that hard to find a hospital that size. We'll just have to tackle it one hospital at a time. His description clearly indicates that there's a regular hospital in the lower section."

Suddenly Kathi jumped to her feet.

"Miri Li!" she cried. "Miri Li is in danger! Andy Mo writes that the culprit at school is the caretaker. He's holding the Gnome King prisoner because he wants to get the recipe for the Philosophers' Stone from him. If I understand correctly, he also had Andy Mo in his clutches, but he managed to escape."

"That's right", Michael said. "But what does that have to do with Miri Li?"

"Quasi made advances on Miri Li. It seems he learnt from Andy Mo that the pair liked each other, although you didn't have to be much of a psychic to notice that. He visited her restaurant yesterday, ordered spaghetti, then started chatting her up and trying to gain information. Then he told her he dabbles in divination and offered to read her cards. 'You've got a friend who has disappeared', he announced. 'He comes from far away. Now he is in great danger.' Of course Miri Li was taken aback and wanted to know more. He pretended he needed more tranquil surroundings as he couldn't concentrate in the restaurant, so she should come to his place. But she wasn't allowed to tell anyone – foreign thoughts would disrupt the process and they had to be alone. She told me, of course. She knew he was one of the suspects. We thought we'd both go to his place and sound him out; after all, it worked with Goldstein. But I haven't seen her since we spoke."

They immediately tried to reach Miri Li, but she didn't answer. She wasn't with her parents at the restaurant either. Her mother had thought she was with Kathi, and she was worried to find out this wasn't the case.

"Why does she refuse to use a mobile phone?" grumbled Michael, throwing his Nokia on the table. "It could save her life now."

"She doesn't want to be like everyone else and buy everything on offer", Yks said. "And I think she's right. I'll try to locate her, just keep quiet for five minutes."

But even after ten minutes he had found no trace of her.

"Damn beer", he whined. "I've lost all my spiritual faculties. This is so embarrassing. My honour, my dignity, and my power are all gone. Never again! That's a sacred oath. I'm not drinking another drop of that stuff." The raven was utterly remorseful and retreated to a corner in shame.

"Come here, you twerp", Christian scolded. "We need you now. We need to figure out how to proceed. We have two problems to solve: we not only have to find Andy Mo's hospital, but we must also find Miri Li. Either we do it ourselves or we go to the police."

"The police are no use", Michael asserted. "If we show them the diary of a deranged earth spirit stuck in the body of a deceased boy being tortured in a private hospital for experimental purposes, they'll lock us up in an asylum too. But now that we know Quasi is the evildoer, we could confide in Kathi's father and Einstein."

Kathi shook her head.

"I'm afraid that's not possible. There was a medallion with the sign of the scales on my father's desk; I only discovered it yesterday. He was born in early October, but it looks exactly like the piece of jewellery we found on the dead man in the basement. The stars are set with diamonds."

"That's mind-blowing!" said Michael. "And what about Einstein?"

"The bicycle. Andy Mo writes that there was a bicycle in the secret passageway beneath the school. Which one of us rides a bike?"

No one said a word. The worry and fear became almost palpable.

Apparently the whole school was in fact a secret centre of hidden powers. Even the raven was visibly affected and slumped his shoulders even more.

"We have two options. Either we simply confront the caretaker, tell him straight to his face what we know about him, and threaten him with the police for kidnapping, or we take the back entrance through the tunnel and search the basement ourselves."

"None of us can walk through walls", Kathi reminded the friends. "Remember the iron doors, the wall, and the collapsed area. Digging through that would take too much time. I suggest we take the way through the school, but without informing my father or the caretaker. I'll get the two master keys: they'll get us in everywhere, including the labs in the renovated wing. I don't know about the lower part of the basement. I don't know it and I've never been down there. I hope we can find the hidden spiral staircase Andy Mo mentions, as well as the alchemist's secret laboratory. The caretaker's official room is on the ground floor right next to the main entrance of the school. We have to be careful not to be noticed by him."

Michael nodded.

"It's best if we wait until it's dark. I'll take my walkie-talkie and my father's GPS – it's a custom-made device for cave explorers. If we get lost, it will help us find our way back. But before that, I'll make us a quark pancake to strengthen us."

"And in the meantime, I'll look up the addresses of all the hospitals, clinics, and asylums in Vienna", said Christian. "After all, according to his description, the lower wing is quite normal. Then we'll inspect each building to see if it could be Andy Mo's prison."

First he looked in the phone book. There were 48 entries in all.

"We'll never manage that", Yks said. "How are we supposed to inspect them all?"

But Christian was confident.

"We can rule out the big hospitals in the municipality of Vienna. According to Andy Mo's description, it's more likely to be a small private hospital. It's located in a park and surrounded by a whitewashed wall. And behind that wall there's a church with a dome.

That much is clear from the diary."

"That information changes the whole picture", Yks agreed, taking out the city map. He had a phenomenal sense for streets and buildings. To him, this map was like Google Earth. He was used to looking at the world from a bird's eye view; while the others were munching on the delicious quark pancakes, he managed to narrow down the number of hospitals in question to four on the basis of the criteria. He pecked a hole in the paper to mark each one and was mighty proud of his work. Then he also treated himself to a portion of the fragrant dessert.

RECIPE

QUARK PANCAKE

Ingredients:
250 grams of quark
2 packets of real vanilla sugar
1 egg
1 tablespoon of icing sugar
a little grated lemon zest (about a quarter of an unsprayed lemon)
3 tablespoons of flour
a pinch of salt
2 tablespoons of butter to grease the pan

Preparation:
Mix all the ingredients with a hand mixer, starting with the egg, vanilla sugar, icing sugar, salt, and lemon zest, then adding the flour and quark. Mix everything well and spread the mixture into a cold pan thickly greased with butter. Place it on the hot hob and flip the mixture when the underside is brown. Add a little more butter if necessary. When both sides are crispy brown, tear into small pieces with two forks, sprinkle with sugar, and serve with compote or fruit salad.

Michael served it with homemade stewed plums.

STEWED PLUMS

Cover 200 grams of seedless prunes and 4 tablespoons of sugar with water and soak for a few hours, if possible. Bring everything to the boil and simmer gently until the plums are soft. Then roughly blend the plums with a hand blender. (Naturally you can also make this with fresh plums. You can add a slice of lemon, a clove, and a small piece of cinnamon bark to the plums; tie the spices in a small linen bag or fish them out before blending!).

After the meal, the raven summed things up: "The quark pancake was majestic. We have been revivified. Andy Mo is alive, I can feel it, and we'll soon find the hospital where he's being held. Despite all the tragedy, we have made good progress. Now that we know the school caretaker is holding the king captive, it's only a matter of time before we free him too. Miri Li can't be far away either. We'll take care of that guy. The banker extended the loan, thanks to Andy Mo. Even Leif's death wasn't a meaningless sacrifice, as it gave Andy Mo the opportunity to incarnate in a human body and solve the riddle of the Formula of Nothingness. You real humans would probably have needed another two thousand years to do that, and in the meantime the whole of Creation would have gone down the drain. It's written somewhere that the Creator is asleep, which explains all the misery in this world and compels us to take action. So let's act."

Kathi looked at the clock.

"It's seven now. Let's say nine: I'll let you in through the back entrance then. In the meantime, I'll look around intently to see if I can spot anything suspicious. Maybe I'll find plans of the old wing of the school; the ones from the renovation are in the office, in any case."

"Watch yourself", Michael warned. "The school caretaker is a dangerous criminal and completely unpredictable. He must not suspect that we know his secret. Your father mustn't suspect anything either; we don't know to what extent he's in cahoots with the caretaker or why."

Two hours later Michael and Christian were standing outside the school, and Kathi let them in.

"There's fewer and fewer of us", grumbled the raven as he sat perched on Michael's shoulder. "Have you noticed that? It's like the story of the ten little Indians."

Kathi put a finger to her lips.

"Shh!" she warned, "I don't know where the school caretaker is. An hour ago there was a light on in his room. Now it's dark – he never goes to bed that early. I didn't notice him leave his quarters. He must be somewhere nearby."

They crept cautiously through the assembly hall and disappeared into the corridor leading to the modern research wing.

"Now we have to look for the staircase; even Andy Mo couldn't find it again right away. But I also don't know of any secret descent which leads even deeper into the basement."

"He mentioned a floor slab at the top of the spiral staircase", Christian recalled, shining a light on the tiles. But there was no slab. Then Yks noticed a cool draft and traced it to its source. Sure enough, behind a partially shifted metal shelf they discovered a hidden door that was slightly ajar.

"Someone was in a hurry and didn't close it behind them", Michael noted with satisfaction.

"Or they didn't expect anyone to follow them", Kathi said. "After all, so far they have remained undetected. No wonder they feel safe."

Rather than turning on the lights, they illuminated the corridor with their torches. And then Kathi also spotted the heavy floor slab at the end of the passageway; it hadn't been pushed all the way back over the opening. Through the gap yawned a dark hole leading into the old basement wing. When they pushed the stone fully aside, they were standing in front of the spiral staircase they were looking for. Something gleamed in the light of the torches: Miri Li's student ID was lying on the worn granite steps.

"We're on the right track", Michael said, leading the way. "Now we have to be careful."

The small wooden door at the landing of the stairs was also unlocked. They followed the narrow passageway along, peered into all the alcoves and rooms, and suddenly found themselves standing in front of the alchemist's laboratory. But it was empty. There was no sign of Miri Li. Yks tried to tune in to her presence, but he couldn't locate her anywhere, despite his utmost concentration. After ten minutes, he shook his head.

"He's taken her somewhere else", Kathi sighed in disappointment. "She can't be upstairs; I've searched the whole school for her. Even the attic. And she's not down here either. We'll have to keep searching for her outside in the catacombs."

She shivered at the thought of going into the dangerous tunnels for the third time. But it was the only chance of finding Miri Li. She bravely returned to the stairs, and the others followed her. Even the raven was quiet and didn't make any jokes for once. Michael switched on the GPS device, but it didn't work.

"We're too deep; I was afraid this would happen. The building above us has too much mass. But maybe it will work outside in the tunnels."

"If we manage to get out", Christian said. "I saw a massive iron door at the bottom of the stairs."

But to their surprise, that wasn't locked either. It moved silently on freshly greased hinges. They made their way into the underground passage without any problems. The bicycle which Andy Mo had mentioned in his diary was still leaning against the wall.

"That's not Einstein's bike", Kathi noticed immediately. "He only rides a ten-speed – he has a problem with his knee." Then she tried to see if the school's master key would fit the iron door, but it didn't. Although this would be detrimental to their progress, she was relieved.

"That means my father doesn't know about this hidden wing in the basement. This secret exit wasn't officially built with his knowledge, otherwise building regulations stipulate the key would have to fit. So it's clear the caretaker is working alone."

"Now we just have to find him", Michael said. "Then we'll have Miri Li too." He shone the laser flashlight down the corridor in both directions and compared their location with the map Andy Mo had completed. "Left leads to my house, and according to Andy Mo's description, only an earth spirit can get through there. We either have to go straight ahead or through the narrow side passage leading from the junction he marked down on the way here."

They opted for the wider tunnel. The passageway wasn't in good condition. Only some of the walls were still covered with bricks, the clay floor wasn't always dry and firm, and in some places the brickwork was crumbling. Nevertheless, they made good progress. Once, when the passageway led steeply upwards, even the GPS navigator came to life.

"What if he took Miri Li in the opposite direction, and then he comes back and locks the gate?" Kathi mused. "Then we'll be trapped down here."

Michael stopped.

"She's right. We have to split up, and someone must stay in the building. It would be best if Kathi did that; after all, she's at home there."

But Kathi was afraid to go back alone. Christian offered to stay with her, and Michael continued along the path alone with the raven. Since the GPS wasn't working, he oriented himself with the compass and marked the positions on the city map every five hundred steps. The corridor led westward. Yks had a small torch strapped around his belly and kept flying ahead to reconnoitre the situation. They kept in constant voice contact with the other two via the walkie-talkie.

"I think we should have searched in the other direction", Michael said. "I don't see any tyre tracks from the bike anywhere. You should be able to make out prints in the muddy places. It's reasonable to assume he's using the bike; he's probably shuttling back and forth between Andy Mo's father's prison and has now taken Miri Li there too."

After a few minutes his hunch was confirmed.

"That's right, there are clear tyre marks here in the left tunnel. Come back, we'll go in the other direction."

But as Michael stopped to turn, the raven came flying back excitedly.

"The end of the passageway is just around the corner. It's walled up: no passage, no door, no iron gate. But there's something behind it, all the same. I can sense it; this place isn't entirely safe. It's making my feathers stand on end."

Michael also had an uneasy feeling as he examined the dead-end more closely. And then he discovered a niche with a narrow hole which he could actually squeeze through. Behind it there was a narrow staircase leading upwards, but the way was eventually blocked by a rotten wooden door. The whole thing resembled the school entrance, except that everything was in a completely dilapidated state.

"Nobody has come through here for decades", Michael observed. "They can't be here. We're turning back."

But Yks wouldn't give up.

"We have to try – there's something there, though I can't analyse it precisely. It's not an amusement park up there, that's for sure."

Michael spread out the city map and examined his notes to mark the spot.

"According to my calculations, this is where we are", he said, intending to mark down the end of the tunnel on the map. But there was already a mark there. A hole. Yks had noted the presence of a hospital at that location.

"That can't be a coincidence. Our uneasy feeling, a hospital, and this secret connecting passage. I think we've got Andy Mo. Let's get out of here, we'll check it out from above."

After half an hour they were back at their starting point, where Kathi and Christian were impatiently awaiting their arrival. They were freezing, thirsty, and tired. But the news had given them courage and hope. Even if they hadn't found Miri Li yet, they were probably on Andy Mo's trail.

"He didn't take her to that hospital", Christian said. "Miri Li must be somewhere else. But I'm afraid it's too late now to investigate the other corridor as well; we were lucky he didn't come back before us. Who knows how he'll react if he feels trapped."

"We still have to risk it", Kathi insisted. "When I imagine her lying somewhere, alone, tied up, I can't even bear to think about it."

But then the situation changed.

"Be quiet!" Yks said. "There's something there: I can sense Miri Li, I'm suddenly able to locate her." The others stared at him inquiringly.

"She's close by. She's on the premises; she must be in the school. Did you really search all the rooms?"

Kathi slapped her forehead with her hand.

"Not all of them", she answered. "I wasn't in his official quarters. I couldn't go in there while he was in the building, could I? And then I forgot about it."

"None of us thought of it", Michael said. "Yet it's the most obvious hiding place. No one would think to look for her there."

They hurried up the spiral staircase, through the corridors leading back into the assembly hall, and a few minutes later Kathi unlocked the school caretaker's quarters with the master key. A faint moan came from the back. Then they found Miri Li – she was lying bound and gagged on the bathroom floor. In a few moments they freed her. She was unharmed.

"He gave me something to drink, then I fell asleep", Miri Li explained, and she began to cry with joy. She was still quite confused. "First he took me to the basement. When I realised what was going on, I managed to break free and escape from him. But he caught me and locked me in here. He said he knows where Andy Mo is now, and as soon as he finds out he has me captive, he'll surely get him the stone. Then he made me drink something and I fell asleep."

"Let's get out of here before he comes back", Michael said. But it was too late. Before they could leave the room, they heard a firm voice behind them.

"What's going on? What are you doing in here? Where's Gruber?"

It was the headmaster. For the first time they realised Quasi had a real name.

They were simultaneously startled and relieved that it was Kathi's father rather than the caretaker.

"Gruber's not here", said Kathi, who was the first to recover from the fright. "He locked Miri Li in here. We just freed her."

The headmaster looked at his daughter and then at Miri Li in alarm. "What did he want from you? Did he do anything to you? Did something happen to you?"

Miri Li shook her head.

"It's all right. Please don't tell my parents, it would worry them unnecessarily. They're thinking about the mafia, but this is something else."

"I believe you owe me an explanation. I suggest we go to my office – or to the kitchen, you look like you could use a pick-me-up."

Shortly afterwards they were sitting comfortably at the kitchen table with cheese toast, milk, and hot tea. Miri Li had recovered quickly after the adventure. The headmaster had notified her parents and said she had been accidentally locked in the gym locker room. The raven remained in the background, winking at Kathi.

"Before I tell you everything, I have a question for you", Kathi said, looking at her father. "What does the medallion on your desk mean?"

"That belongs to Gruber. I found it on the stairs and haven't had a chance to give it to him yet." Then he became serious. "What do you know about this piece of jewellery? Why are you asking about it?"

Kathi felt a weight lifted off her chest.

"It's not just the school caretaker who wears this pendant. We also saw Goldstein wearing it, and another criminal as well. We suspect there's a secret organisation behind it. Thank God you're not part of it." And then she recounted the whole story to him. Only she didn't tell him about Andy Mo, nor about Leif and the hospital. If she did, her father would have to inform the police immediately, and that would put Andy Mo's life in even greater danger. And how were they supposed to explain that Leif had still died, and that an earth spirit was currently living in his body? They had to free him alone.

Her father listened in silence and asked no questions. Then he said:

"Gruber won't show up again; he surely understands that his double life has been exposed. I don't think he'll show his face around here anymore. We'll report his disappearance but won't file any charges against him. That would only cause a scandal and alert the other criminals; we don't know who else belongs to Goldstein's secret society. A school with an alchemist's laboratory in the basement, a headmaster who talks to a raven, and a philosophy professor who deals with magic and believes in spirits: imagine the reports in the newspapers! Yet we knew nothing about any of this. Einstein suspected that something was amiss, but we discovered Goldstein's machinations too late.

"It all started with the school renovation. A box with some old manuscripts was found during the construction work, which Goldstein generously financed. The medallions were also lying among them. They were alchemical writings from a Lodge called 'Bon Pasteur', and their secret sign was the constellation of Libra, the symbol of balance and harmony. Goldstein liked the idea and revived the old order. Thus, as so often happens, good was taken over by minions of evil. He probably didn't know about the alchemical lab in the basement. I think Gruber only discovered that later and kept it to himself."

"Are you also a member of this Lodge?" asked Kathi, but the headmaster shook his head.

"I don't belong to any secret society. Nor does Einstein. However, for centuries there has been a spiritual community which I profess to belong to. Everyone who stands up for truth, justice, and compassion belongs to this circle and is involved in this community, even if they know nothing about it. We don't recognise each other by any signs, but rather by the ethos which shapes our actions. Everyone follows their own path. But it can transpire that two or more of us meet one another and align our goals together for a certain period of time. That's what has happened in our case.

"In the past, certain cults, orders, and organisations provided a spiritual environment for individuals involved in politics, business, science, and culture. The Templars built bridges between Muslims and Christianity; the Rosicrucians attempted reform and preserved the traditional body of knowledge; the Illuminati restrained the degenerate nobility; Freemasonry enlightened and paved the way for a new age of science. Later, inconspicuous associations such as the Club of Rome or the Red Cross provided a field of activity through which individuals could influence world events. But the powers which represent the principle of destruction are stronger and immediately infiltrate every idealistic association. Major global institutions such as the UN, the World Bank, and the World Trade Organisation together with their committees have long since become nothing more than tools of the Shadow. Evil has always excelled in camouflaging itself. It always nests where you least expect it."

The headmaster's calm, pleasant voice captivated them all.

"Today, there is no institution left which serves the good. It's exclusively corrupt and criminal individuals who occupy positions in the parliaments and on the boards of directors and supervisory boards of banks, insurance companies, media corporations, and other firms. The various ideological, religious, and cultural groups are also permeated with stupidity, corruption, and thirst for power. Today, only the individual can be a beacon of light in the shadow of the madness which rules the world. Each person is a solitary fighter and should not expect any support. Those who stand up for truth, justice, and compassion receive no recognition or reward. Only rarely can one of them help another, because as soon as a network becomes visible, it casts a shadow and is immediately infiltrated by the powers of the Shadow. For this reason never more than three people, or at most seven, should join forces. Ideally, you should be alone. Great things have always been brought into being by a single individual.

"However, even the individual must not make themselves conspicuous by behaving in a militant or fanatical manner. Civil courage, yes – but not martyrdom. Those who occupy higher positions must be all the more inconspicuous and modest. The true greats are always standing in the second or third rank. Only the foolish or those burdened with complexes push their way to the front. Among us, there is no minister, no pope, no president. Those who serve the good remain unrecognised; only puppets stand in the limelight. The real leaders appear and disappear. Their traces are myths, their legacy a better world."

Kathi's father had been pacing back and forth while he spoke. Suddenly he stopped and stared at the map of Vienna which Michael had placed beside him.

"What is this? What do these markings mean? That's most intriguing", he said, placing the city map on the table and leaning over it with interest.

Kathi explained it to him.

"Here is Michael's house. There's Goldstein's villa. And there's the end of the tunnel which leads west from the school. The fourth asterisk is us; that's the school, the place where we are right now." And then she too realised what her father had noticed.

"Libra!" she exclaimed in surprise. "Together with the markings of Baumann's antique shop and Miri Li's house, it forms the constellation of Libra. That's amazing, totally crazy – it can't be a coincidence!"

The others approached and looked curiously at the map.

"Indeed, the constellation of Libra", confirmed the raven, shaking his head in disbelief.

"Now I understand why Goldstein was so interested in these properties", said Kathi's father. "They belong together. They form a symbol. They were built by the Lodge. He realised that and hoped to find the missing manuscripts in one of the buildings – hence his generous donation to rebuild the basement of our school. Then he clandestinely applied pressure to the fathers of Christian and Michael. And it also explains the origin of this Lodge, whose members were dedicated to the symbol of the scales. Its foundation coincides with the time when these buildings were erected. Without exception, they're the villas or small chateaus of wealthy, influential people. They were deliberately built in these locations to create a great Kyilkhor in the landscape."

The headmaster wanted to explain what a Kyilkhor was, but Kathi gestured to him that it wasn't necessary.

"We've read about it in Bardon and Stejnar. In magic, oversized symbols like these are used to draw down the corresponding power and force, which is meant to condense and develop in the small medallion with the same symbol and thus serve the individual. The geoglyphs in Peru had the same function."

"You're surprisingly knowledgeable", marvelled the headmaster. "But I'm sure you're right. It was likely intended as a counterbalance to the Gothic cathedrals built in France in the twelfth century, which were arranged according to the constellation of Virgo. Austria and especially Vienna fully resonate with the qualities associated with Libra, so they erected a shadow network here and chose Libra as their symbol."

"But the scales are a symbol of harmony and peace", Kathi said. "They represent balance, equilibrium, and love. That doesn't contradict the Christian values of the Church, does it?"

Her father nodded.

"The scales enable the establishment of balance and thus the recovery of values before they degenerate. It promotes the side which is neglected. The balance which the scales symbolise as the foundation for peace is harmonious equilibrium. Nevertheless, the goal is not static, but living movement, as something new is always added. For the Shadow it is the opposite. But he does not recognise this fact. His striving is for exaggeration or understatement. In this way, he denigrates even the noblest aspirations and qualities. He always sees only one side and wants to strengthen it to the point of degeneration. Therefore the principle of balance for him is not harmony and justice, but stagnation and death; it becomes another means of suppressing the development of humankind. And that's why he also supported the ideals of Libra, regardless of which way the scales lean."

The headmaster glanced at his watch. "It's getting late. You're on holiday, but I have to go to a congress tomorrow – I'll treat you to a taxi now. We'll keep this business about Gruber to ourselves for the time being."

THE RESCUE MISSION

The next day the sun was shining brightly. They sat on Michael's terrace for brunch and discussed their next steps. The experiences of the previous night had shaken each and every one of them.

"It was really great how your father reacted", Miri Li said to Kathi, helping herself to some of the chocolate. "He was totally cool about taking our side and trusting us, and he spared me an embarrassing conversation at the police station. I actually feel sorry for Quasi. He didn't do anything to me."

"Don't forget that he's holding Andy Mo's father captive", Kathi reminded her. "Incidentally, he must have returned during the night after all. His things have disappeared from his quarters. Now we can't learn from him where he's holding the king."

"In any case, we have to free Andy Mo first", Michael decided. "Maybe he knows more by now. I'm convinced we've found the hospital; the only question is how to get him out of there. Yks and Christian have already gone there and are scouting the building."

A helicopter rumbled overhead, but it turned out to be the raven. He was trembling all over.

"I've been there, I've seen her – she really is an infernal woman. Poor Andy Mo, I wouldn't want to spend one minute in that hospital. Just seeing her is enough to kill you."

"He probably means Baphometa", Kathi said, offering the shocked professor a cheese toast. But he couldn't bring himself to take a bite.

"The research lab is in the attic. Andy Mo is alive; I could sense him clearly, and I was even able to locate the room where they locked him up. However, he didn't perceive my thoughts. It's terrible: he's turned into a completely normal human. But maybe he's just weakened or ill. And there's another problem – the skylights don't open, not even from the inside. I examined them. This isn't a dusty attic; everything is very modern, air conditioning and all. But we can only get him out from up there. We'll never get to him through the building."

Then Christian arrived too. He had heard the raven's last sentence.

"Yks is right. There are alarms and surveillance monitors everywhere. The floor below the attic is disguised as a secure unit and is off-limits to visitors. The whole thing is like a maximum-security wing in a prison. Only the two lower floors and the ground floor operate normally; I couldn't even get to the second floor. A nurse immediately ran after me and brought me back. There's a wall surrounding the premises, and the gates have double electronic security. There's a guard sitting at the entrance, and every visitor is asked which patient they're visiting. Luckily I overheard someone in front of me saying "Dr Schober", so I said "Dr Schober", and he looked in a list and let me pass too. A second guard is sitting inside the building behind the entrance. We can't get in the normal way, and we won't be able to get out that way later with Andy Mo either."

"We'll have to free him via the roof", Michael said. "And since we can't fly, we'll climb. Leif was a mountaineer, and Andy Mo can do that now, too. If Yks can manage to get a rope up to the roof, he can use it to abseil down."

Christian nodded.

"But how do we get in? Into the hospital grounds, I mean. Even the wall is secured. Yks might manage to hoist one end of the rope up to the roof, but we'll have to carry it to the wall of the building. And how will Andy Mo get out of the gardens?"

"We'll try the connecting tunnel. The wooden door at the end of the ascent was rotten; we'll pry that open with a crowbar. I suspect it's the same structural layout as in the school. You'll come out somewhere inside the building."

"I'm not so sure about that", Yks said. "I saw brick walls in the hospital gardens – the remnants of a Romanesque ruin, converted into a flower-decked pavilion. I suspect the passageway ends beneath that structure."

"That would be even better", Christian remarked. "But we don't have time to investigate that; we must free Andy Mo from his prison immediately. His life is in danger. What about the iron door at the school, Kathi? What if Quasi has locked that in the meantime?"

"My father hired a locksmith to change the lock. That was done this morning, so now the master key fits. We can leave right away."

But the raven put a check on proceedings.

"We'll have to wait until it's dark. I didn't tell you because I didn't want to worry you, but Frankenstein saw me twice outside the window and watched me attentively. He knows me from Goldstein's panopticon. I fear he's suspicious. He immediately thought of Goldstein, a shotgun, and the police, in exactly that order."

"Will the problems never end?" groaned Miri Li. "What if he shuts the place down and moves Andy Mo – or even kills him to get rid of the witness?"

Suddenly Kathi was having second thoughts as well.

"It would already be a disaster if he puts him back into a deep sleep. He wouldn't be able to escape then. I wonder if we shouldn't get the police involved?"

Michael shook his head.

"Not until Andy Mo is out. By the time they get to the building and find him, Frankenstein will have killed him and taken him away. They won't storm in right away – they'll start an investigation first, and by the time they've explored everything it'll be too late."

The raven nodded.

"He'll be completely disposed of, just as the fine lady ordered. I'm sure they won't find the slightest trace of him, whatever that might be. We shouldn't waste any time. If we break down the rotten door during the day, the noise won't attract as much attention as at night, when every sound can be heard twice as far away."

"He's right", Michael said, standing up. "We must be prepared for anything. We don't even know if the passageway really ends at the building in the hospital gardens, or whether it leads to the basement of the building after all. I'll go and get some ropes – my father has enough equipment. I'll also take a seat harness in case Andy Mo is too weak; then we can lower him down on the rope. So you'll all have to come with me. I definitely need to get on the roof because of the window."

"We'll need a rope ladder as well", the raven added. "The window is in the ceiling, and the old attic is at least three metres high."

While Michael gathered the equipment, the girls packed sandwiches and drinks.

"We'll get hungry", Kathi remarked. "And who knows when Andy Mo last ate."

Miri Li was silent and looked glum.

"What's wrong with you?" asked Christian. "You haven't said ten words all day."

"Man, you just don't get it", said Michael. "First she has her eyes set on Leif, then Andy Mo turns her head, and now she's got both of them in a double package."

"God, you're both idiots!" Kathi rebuked them. But Miri Li dismissed her with a wave.

"Leave them alone – after all, they're right. I guess we're all a bit overexcited. Even I don't know what's wrong with me. When's your father coming back?"

"Not until tomorrow. At least we'll be undisturbed in the school building."

Two hours later they were back in the tunnel. The bicycle was gone.

"That means Quasi is still hanging around down here", Christian stated soberly. "But we'll have to live with that. Once we free Andy Mo, it will be a matter for the police."

"Maybe my father took it, or perhaps the locksmith", Kathi tried to reassure them. But she didn't sound convincing. They continued through the tunnel in silence. Everyone was lost in their own thoughts. When they reached their destination, they were confronted with a new problem.

At first everything went smoothly. They squeezed through the gap in the wall, found the stairway, and broke open the rotten wooden door without any problems. But then there was no way forward. The passageway behind it had been cemented over.

Exhausted and desperate, they squatted on the dusty floor. Kathi lit two candles and fetched drinks from her rucksack, but no one wanted to eat anything. They were downcast and silent; only the candles flickered restlessly, casting ghostly shadows on the wall.

"There's a draught here", Yks remarked. "That shouldn't be the case. There must be another passage here somewhere." Using his sensitive feathers, he traced the draught and followed it along. Then he found the source.

"Come here, look at this! There's a passageway we missed."

Immediately life returned to the group. They followed the passage, and after about twenty metres they reached another alcove. There were white letters on the wall – 'EE' – and a thick arrow pointing upwards.

"This is an air-raid shelter from the Second World War", Kathi explained. "'EE' stands for 'emergency exit'. I bet there's an exit up there beyond the arrow. Even the iron ladder is still here."

Yks flew up, disappeared, and quickly returned.

"You're right. There's a gap just below the ceiling, wide enough for all of you to squeeze through. The pavilion is on the other side."

"Now I need some refreshments", Michael said with relief, and the others also hungrily ate the food they'd brought. Then it was time. They climbed out of the basement and found themselves between the flower-decked walls in the hospital gardens. In the meantime the weather had changed: it was cloudy, pitch black, and a gusty wind was blowing. The lightning from a thunderstorm flashed in the distance, and the rumble of thunder grew ominously closer.

"If the ropes get wet, I won't be able to lift them", Yks feared. "They're old and they'll soak up water."

Michael agreed with him.

"We'll have to hurry. Go and check if Andy Mo is awake or asleep. We still don't know if he's capable of abseiling down on his own."

But when Yks returned, he looked distressed.

"He's awake, he's thinking, but he obviously can't move. I know exactly where he is. But when I knocked on the window, he didn't react. Since it's dark in the room, I couldn't see anything else. I think we should take the second rope up to the roof as well."

"I don't have a good feeling about this", Kathi said gloomily, looking towards the large building. Amid the sheet lightning the hospital looked archaic and menacing, like a haunted castle from an English horror film. Lights were still on behind some of the windows on the lower floors. Through the glass wall of the entrance, the night guard could be seen sitting in front of a television.

Michael resolutely grabbed the rope and slung the climbing gear over his shoulder. He paused for a moment, listening, then ducked down and ran in the shadows of the trees towards the building. Yks and the others hurried after him. With a few movements, he unwound the rope, expertly knotted a loop in one end, and nodded briefly to the raven. The raven grabbed the rope and took off. But to their dismay, he couldn't ascend. With each metre he got slower and slower, and halfway up he tilted to the side like a kite in the wind and plummeted down. Miri Li moaned and buried her face in her hands. Kathi also began to cry silently. The whole plan was going wrong.

Yks was completely out of breath, and he propped himself up in a daze with his two wings. Behind him stood his friends, pressed against the wall of the building and unsure of how to proceed.

"We'll have to go about this differently", he gasped. "I think I know a way to do it. Follow me behind the building."

Looking up at the façade at the back of the building, they understood what he meant. There was a balcony on each floor. Yks wanted to try it in stages: he though it should work that way, and in fact it did. He flew with the end of the rope up to the first balcony and hooked the loop on a spiral in the iron railings. Then he beckoned to Michael to follow him. Michael managed to pull himself up and was soon standing next to him. Now Yks flew with the rope to the next floor, and Michael climbed up behind him again. After five minutes they had already reached the balcony on the third floor. Up until that point, everything remained quiet in the building. Most of the windows and doors had been closed due to the approaching thunderstorm. For the last stretch beyond the roof, Yks circled the rope around the chimney and threw it to Michael, who threaded the other end through the loop and pulled it back up until the rope was secure. The end was now hanging down to the ground again. Then Michael also climbed onto the ledge. Yks showed him the skylight of Andy Mo's room; in order to do this, they had to climb three metres across the steep roof onto the narrow side of the building. It was perilous for Michael, but he managed this last obstacle as well. As expected, the window couldn't be opened. Michael took the crowbar out of his backpack and looked for a suitable spot to start prying.

"It'll make a hell of a noise", he warned. "But it has to succeed the first time. One noise doesn't get noticed, as every burglar knows. Nobody cares about it. It's only the second time that people get suspicious and react with alarm." He carefully slid the tip of the iron between the sheet metal and the wood and applied some pressure. The frame came loose with a bursting noise, reverberating like a gunshot with an echo that seemed to linger endlessly over the abyss. "You can hear that all over the world", Michael thought, but in fact there was no reaction. Relieved, he lifted the window from its frame, attached the rope ladder to an iron strut, and climbed down into the room.

Andy Mo was lying in bed. Yks was already with him, examining the restraints that held him. They were the cuffs usually used to restrain agitated patients in psychiatric hospitals. With a few quick motions Michael had freed him.

"Are you able to abseil down the roof?" asked Michael, and Andy Mo nodded. Then everything proceeded very rapidly.

They climbed back onto the roof without any problems, and Michael helped his friend to the dangling rope. He was visibly weakened, but somehow he managed the difficult balancing act over the loose and slippery tiles. It had started to rain.

But then it happened: part of the roof cladding came loose and crashed down with a loud noise. A scream came from below; obviously someone had been hit by some of the debris.

"Go!" Michael shouted, tapping Andy Mo vigorously on the shoulder. Andy Mo resolutely grabbed the rope and disappeared into the darkness. Shortly afterwards, the okay came from below and Michael rappelled down as well.

"Leave everything behind and escape!" he shouted down, throwing caution to the wind. He knew it was only a matter of time before they were discovered. Then the first spotlights were turned on. Windows were opened, excited voices called out to each other, and an alarm system emitted its penetrating siren wail into the night. Michael jumped; he only had three metres to go. He skilfully rolled and ran after the others.

Somewhere dogs were barking, and his left foot hurt like hell, but he made it to the pavilion and was able to disappear under the wall just in time.

The silence of the basement surrounded them like a protective wall. The barking of the dogs grew quieter – they had run in the opposite direction and were biting at the rope hanging from the wall of the building.

"That was close", Michael gasped, finally hugging his rescued friend. "Welcome to the club!"

"You greeted me like this once before", Andy Mo recalled, touched. "You have brought me into your world for a second time."

"Now it's your world too", said Miri Li, nestling tenderly against his side. "You're no longer the same as you were: you're not Leif, but you're not Andy Mo anymore either."

Leif did indeed look different somehow. They had shaved his hair to three millimetres, but his facial features had changed as well. He had matured during his days of captivity, and his appearance was now marked by the spirit of Andy Mo.

"We need to get out of here as soon as possible", Michael said. "But first I must have a drink."

Only now did they notice that he was injured and limping. Miri

Li examined his foot; fortunately it wasn't broken, and she tied her scarf around the swollen ankle. Meanwhile Kathi found the backpack with the provisions they had left behind. Andy Mo drank greedily from the bottle as well. Then they began their return journey. Due to Michael's injury and Andy Mo's weakened condition, their progress was slow, but the fear of the dogs drove them onwards. They eventually made it after an hour, and were standing in the assembly hall, relieved.

Once again Kathi's father surprised them. He had just gotten out of the taxi that had brought him from the airport when they emerged from the basement. Shaking his head, he examined the small, sweaty, exhausted group.

"I have boundless faith in my daughter – but was that really necessary? The passageway is at risk of collapsing, and maybe Gruber is still lurking around down there. Who were you searching for and rescuing this time?" Then he recognised Leif.

"Leif Andersson. You're Leif Andersson, aren't you? Where did you come from? You're real, not a ghost. Ghosts wear nightgowns, not pyjamas." Until now, no one had noticed that Andy Mo was still wearing hospital clothes. The headmaster embraced his student; everyone had believed he was dead. "Now I can't wait to hear how you explain all this. Best we sit down in the kitchen again."

This time they told him about everything – except for Andy Mo, who they kept silent about. Nor did they say anything about his missing father. That, they had decided, should remain their secret. The ability to remain silent is a fundamental requirement of magic. It would only cause further confusion. Besides, their adventure wasn't over yet. The most important task – the liberation of the Gnome King – still lay ahead of them.

It was a long night. When the headmaster learnt that there were other children locked up in the hospital who were probably still alive, he immediately informed the police. Just one hour later, the entire hospital was searched and the other victims were also freed. Two nurses and a doctor were temporarily detained for questioning.

Frankenstein and Baphometa had managed to escape; however, the superintendent who had been providing them with helpless patients was identified, and he immediately confessed.

The next day there was a lot of bureaucratic paperwork to take care of. Since Leif had been declared dead, Andy Mo had to apply for new papers. He was also given a completely new set of clothes. Leif's father had sold his house in the meantime and had moved to the Emirates, which suited Andy Mo very well. He was glad to be on his own and start afresh. He had moved in with Michael and quickly adapted to life in freedom. Although he still perceived the human body as a kind of prison, he also learnt to appreciate the beautiful aspects which life now offered him. His magical abilities weren't entirely lost to him, although he had to regain them, and he was determined to conscientiously carry out the exercises. He was concerned with spiritual strength rather than magical power. He was aware that the very body which restricted and hindered his freedom of movement, with its needs, impulses, and desires, provided him with the energy for his spirit and soul. Now he could evolve much more rapidly and successfully than when he had only possessed a spiritual body. As a human being, the entire universe and all the spheres and planes were open to him. By contrast, the life of spirits was limited to only one plane at a time. And they didn't possess the yearnings and impulses of the soul to incarnate in a material body.

In the evening they sat around the fireplace, tired but relieved. The storm had passed, but it was a little chilly for that time of year. They told Andy Mo how they had found him and showed him the city map.

"If you hadn't marked down our addresses beforehand, I doubt we would have ever figured it out", Kathi explained, taking the medallion and the drawing out of the chest. Then they told him what they had learnt about the secret society of the scales.

Andy Mo listened attentively and compared the arrangements of the stars with interest.

"No wonder my father noticed the reactivation of this cosmic network. His fundamental aspirations were directed towards alchemy, and that's the area under his jurisdiction on this planet." Suddenly he hesitated.

"Look at this: there's a third-order star missing." He fumbled for a pen and marked the relevant spot on the map. "There! There should be something else there."

Everyone stared at the map, but there was nothing there, just an empty field. There was no building, no villa – not even a garden shed. Yks also came flying up curiously.

"That's at the rise where you marked down a junction in the secret passageway to the school, isn't it? That could be where Gruber is holding your father captive. I think we've found him. Where else could he be? The bicycle tracks led off to the left."

"You're right, the tyre prints went in that direction", Kathi said. "So we have to go back to the catacombs. But how are we going to explain this to my father? We mustn't overwhelm him with troubles."

The raven nodded.

"Besides, it's too dangerous. If the school caretaker is still down there, he'll just be waiting for us to arrive. Tomorrow I'll take a look at it from above. After all, what's the point of being able to fly?"

The others were confident, but Andy Mo remained silent.

"What good is it if we find the king? I can't get to the elixir. And I haven't the faintest idea how to bring it to the human realm."

But Miri Li had an idea.

"What if we summon the old tree spirit Krux and ask him to pass the vial over to us?"

Andy Mo shook his head in resignation.

"I've tried that already. I even managed to reach him last night, but neither he nor I managed to cross the barrier separating our worlds. Only our thoughts met."

"Then Leif will have to try", Miri Li insisted. "Perhaps he will succeed where nature spirits fail. As a human spirit, he has options available in the afterlife which they don't have."

Andy Mo thought of Leif's last words: "I must leave so that you may come – only then can I help you. The One from the Shining Light told me. Take care of Miri Li."

He stroked his girlfriend's hair tenderly.

"Perhaps you're right. Before he died, he actually hinted in that direction. If his fate was meant to unfold this way, his premature death would suddenly take on meaning." Andy Mo separated from Miri Li and stood up. "Let's summon Leif. We'll do it right now. Outside, on my boulder, where you also summoned me into this world."

Nature had calmed down completely. It had suddenly become warmer. Summer had reasserted itself. The sun was low on the horizon, illuminating the scene in a surreal and mystical way, rather like a theatre stage. Andy Mo made no grand pronouncements. He celebrated the 'Ritual of the Hermetic Four' [Emil Stejnar, *The Four Elements: The Secret Key to Spiritual Power*, Stejnar Verlag, Vienna] and recited the ancient formula of evocation which unites the living with the dead:

"Let us think of the Eternal East, and of those who have gone ahead of us. Let us think of Leif Andersson. Let us consecrate to him a few heartbeats of silent remembrance."

They formed the living magical chain which connects humans and spirits. Grasping each other's hands, they closed the circle. Thus they stood around the boulder, lost in thought. Each person dwelt on their personal memories, and through the power of thought became connected to their departed friend. A solemn and reverent atmosphere spread, creating a mental field around them which encompassed all planes, including Leif and the afterlife.

And then they saw him. Leif had manifested himself. He was bathed in a radiant light which seemed to blend with the light of the setting sun. He emanated contentment and a confidence which was soothingly transmitted like light and warmth to his friends. He didn't utter a word, yet everyone felt personally addressed. A glowing light also seemed to emanate from Andy Mo, detaching itself from him and connecting with the apparition. It was like an intimate embrace of spirits. The whole experience lasted a moment or an eternity. Just as the figure from the afterlife disappeared, the sun also set; its last rays were reflected in the red tincture of the vial which now lay where Leif had just been standing.

They were all stunned. The encounter had made a deep impression on them. Andy Mo released the spell by uttering the second part of the formula:

"We release our hands, but the chain remains closed. Let us go forth and bring peace." Then he took the elixir. He knew it would save the Gnome King's life.

*

When they met the next day at Michael's for a late breakfast, Yks was already on his way.

"He flew to the location marked on the map just after sunrise", Andy Mo said, keeping an eye out for his feathered friend. "He should have arrived back by now – I don't understand what's taking him so long."

Michael was also looking impatiently at his watch and kept staring at the sky. No one felt like eating anything: they were all worried about the bird, and they feared something bad had happened to him.

"We should call a taxi and go check on him", Miri Li suggested. "If the king really is being held captive at that location, the school caretaker will also be lurking around there. Perhaps he surprised Yks and captured him. It's reasonable to assume that he, too, knows the secret of the source of Goldstein's money."

But then the missing bird finally turned up and landed expertly on the toaster. Fortunately it wasn't switched on. His black feathers usually gleamed immaculately, but now they were dusty and dishevelled. That didn't seem to bother him at all, however.

"He is indeed there – I have found the king, he is alive!" The proud raven hopped excitedly back and forth on the table. "I should have realised earlier: Dr Stein's house used to stand on that land. He was friends with thingamajig who wrote the Book of the Master; I was acquainted with both of them, but you know that. How could I forget! The beer has been clouding my mind. The villa was originally part of the alchemists' network, but it burnt down. There were newspaper reports about it. The alchemical laboratory in the cellar apparently remained intact, and later it was put to use by the school caretaker. Then he hid the unconscious Gnome King in that magical location. The left side passage under the school leads directly there. It's said that the ruins from the fire are haunted, and no one has dared to go there for decades: the *Kronen Zeitung* reported that as well. He's lying in the buried cellar. I managed to squeeze through a small opening – you won't be able to get through there, but there's a second exit which leads to the ruins of the gatehouse. I'll lead you there." Yks spoke rapidly, and the words bubbled out of him as soon as he'd thought of them, but they got the idea.

"Thank God, we've reached our destination", Michael said, setting aside the slice of bread he was about to put in the toaster. There was no more thought of eating now. Christian also pushed his plate away and stood up.

"We must free the king as soon as possible. What about the spirit trap? Did you notice anything?"

"There was nothing there", said Yks. "I couldn't have got through to the king otherwise. It was deactivated."

"I'm sure it was", Andy Mo said, nodding. "When I escaped from Gruber, he wanted me to find my father so he could recapture me and blackmail me. He's lurking in the passageway now, waiting for me to come."

"Then we'll just take the path from above rather than through the tunnel", Michael decided, and he phoned for a taxi. "Yks, lead us to the gatehouse and show us the way."

And then everything proceeded very smoothly and rapidly.

FAREWELL

Andy Mo lovingly stroked his father's temples and moistened them with the elixir. It took a long time, but eventually his frail body revived and colour returned to his pale, wrinkled face.

"Here you are at last, my son. You have found your way to your father. And you have put yourself in great danger to do so." The old man sat up with difficulty and embraced him warmly. "Can you forgive me for having you killed? I knew what Baphomet was up to, and I knew he would lure you into the human trap. But I also knew you would master your task.

"You were a simple spirit, you died, and you arose as a Son of Man. Because you were strong and willing to sacrifice yourself, you overcame the four elements and absorbed them within you. And you were also able to manifest the fifth element within yourself. You have passed all the trials and you now possess a body, a soul, and a spirit.

"Only those who surrender will live, and only those who recognise that they *are* need not die. Walk your path consciously.

"Now true life begins for you. You have succeeded in fathoming the Formula of Nothingness. It is a new cornerstone of thought which will change the world. Write your book together and place the formula at its end.

"But there is still much work to be done.

"Creation is not yet complete. The ONE, the great architect of all worlds, has placed his work in the hands of human beings. You are one of them. It is up to you to shape this planet and its spiritual spheres in such a way that paradise emerges – a paradise which has hitherto perished repeatedly through the actions of the OTHER."

The king fell silent for a long time. Andy Mo was shaken, and the friends standing around the old man's simple confines sank to their knees. They all felt personally addressed, and they sensed they had just received a sacred consecration. The dilapidated laboratory was filled with an unearthly light. The grey walls receded and transformed themselves into a magnificent cathedral whose dimensions were lost in infinity. The celestial sounds of the music of the spheres filled the sacred space.

"I am going to your mother now, my son. I thank you all. May God bless you and your friends. May God bless all the beings of this wonderful world."

Then the Gnome King dissolved and disappeared.

SHAPING THIS WORLD AND THE NEXT WITH THE FORMULA OF NOTHINGNESS

The experience had made a lasting impression on everyone, each in their own special way. And they had all become more serious. No one was the same as before. The world looked different to them. They had gained insight into the workings of the powers, and they knew that the danger to humanity had not yet been averted.

But their problems were solved for the time being. The king had been saved and returned to his kingdom in good health, and Michael's father was on his way back home as well. He would never have to dig for treasure in dangerous ravines again. The emerald he had found with Andy Mo's help was priceless. He hadn't revealed the stone's hiding place to the bandits who had kidnapped and held him captive for weeks. When he weakened, developed a fever, and fainted from the torture, they thought he was dead and had left him lying there.

Christian's father was back in business and was expanding his antiquarian bookshop. Christian hoped to take over the business one day. He had re-established contact with Gloria Ogris, the pretty girl who had obtained the Master Books for them – and she had not only awakened his love for her, but also his passion for dealing with old books. They had allowed Mr Büchli to see the documents he had been searching for, and he promised to introduce Christian to the business.

Miri Li's parents were also able to keep and continue running their establishments. The fire damage to their home was covered by the insurance company, and the reconstruction was in full swing.

Kathi had devoted herself entirely to astrology. She studied all the relevant books she could find and was determined to become an astrological life advisor. Michael, who was fascinated by thought magic, wanted to study neurology and investigate this phenomenon scientifically.

Andy Mo was happy as well. For him, being human was as impressive as magic was for his friends. He had quickly settled into his new life as Leif Andersson. His features had changed a little, and his friends saw him as Andy Mo rather than Leif. Miri Li also accepted him as he was. She represented more of the mystical side within the group, and she provided balance when there were discussions.

So everyone had found their focus. Their meetings at Michael's place continued. The book they were working on was almost finished, but they sensed that evil still prevailed in the world. Goldstein remained missing, supposedly in hiding somewhere in the Caribbean. The sadistic doctor and his female partner from the clinic had also managed to evade arrest, and they were still being sought. Only Quasi, the school caretaker, was dead. He had hanged himself in an alcove of the tunnel.

They sat quietly around the large table in the library, lost in thought. Their problems had been solved. "In fact, we could be satisfied with what we've achieved", Kathi said, breaking the silence that had crept into the room like an unwelcome visitor. "But I still don't have a good feeling. It's as if evil is lurking in a dark corner, waiting for us to make a mistake."

Miri Li nodded, agreeing with her.

"I feel the same way. I know the Shadow is still hanging over us. Our story is not yet complete. We should hurry before it's too late."

"Don't be so pessimistic", Michael scolded, nudging the raven who, like the others, was brooding quietly. "All we have to do is present and explain the Formula of Nothingness which Andy Mo found – or rather invented. Then his mission will be accomplished, and our Master Book for children will be ready." He stood up and wrote the formula on the blackboard where they made notes during their discussions:

BEING IS CONSCIOUS EXISTENCE SQUARED PLUS THE POWER OF IMAGINATION TIMES FAITH AND LOVE

"Andy Mo has solved the riddle: only in a human body is a spirit capable of gaining distance from itself – that is, from its thoughts, feelings, and impulses of the will – in order to recognise and reshape itself. The Formula of Nothingness is not a magical formula, but a key which opens up access to the spiritual worlds. The insights which can be derived from this formula are truly sensational. They will change the world and human consciousness. From this, it further follows:

CONSCIOUSNESS MANIFESTS ITSELF AS SPIRITUAL REALITY AND IS A LIVING MIRROR OF EXISTENCE

"Actually, every reader should explore this for themselves", Andy Mo reflected. "Pondering this formula has brought me many insights which I would never have encountered otherwise. More important than understanding the formula is contemplating it – that is, contemplating yourself and your spiritual essence. Seeking to fathom who you are. For instance, readers should ask themselves: where does the will fit into this formula? And when they reflect upon it, they will understand that it manifests itself in the concentrated power of imagination. They should ask themselves what is meant by love, and recognise all those things connected with the mystery of emotions which concentrate the power of desire, namely devotion, affection, longing, connectedness, openness, and much more. They should realise that faith acts like a light which illuminates everything equally, even those things which do not exist, and thus it brings them into view as existent."

The others agreed with him. But they still had unanswered questions of their own. They wanted to discuss them and make an official transcript, and Andy Mo eventually agreed to the plan. Christian immediately brought up the first ambiguity.

"What does 'consciousness squared' mean? Three times three is nine, sure. But Christian times Christian is what? How can you multiply yourself with yourself? Can you explain that to us?"

"I'll try", Andy Mo said. "Listen carefully. First I was an earth spirit, and now I'm a human. Although I am still who I am, I am more now than I was before."

Christian looked at him with wide eyes.

"So you want me to slip inside an earth spirit, or into a bird like Yks?"

"No need for that", exclaimed Yks, laughing. "Human spirits already possess two bodies: an ethereal one of spirit and soul, and a gross material one of flesh and life. This allows them to adopt more than one point of view. That's why they can indeed multiply themselves with themselves.

"Think about it: when you're thinking, even though your spirit is in a body, it's also in the spirit world. You just have to become aware of it. That's what the Master Books describe as 'awakening'. When you observe yourself thinking and you become aware that you're observing yourself, you're essentially able to step outside yourself, and then you realise that you can detach yourself from yourself. You can in fact multiply yourself. It doesn't matter if you use your cerebral cortex as a display for this realisation, just as you do with all your other thoughts; if you visualise it often enough, this idea – which is an elemental, i.e. a spiritual structure – becomes a new mediator of consciousness for you. You can also reach other planes with it, such as your soul garden or the world of spirits – what people call the beyond or the astral plane." Yks closed his eyes briefly, then continued.

"Andy Mo figured it out because he was inspired by Einstein's formula. The Magic and Mysticism of the Third Millennium should not settle for the knowledge of the old wizards from the Middle Ages. Today, students of magic can also learn from the initiates of modern science. One spirit squared means multiplication with yourself. That's exactly what Andy Mo did. He was a simple earth spirit, and now he's human. A being with a spirit and a body. Hence he is present on two planes at the same time. That's how you already were when you were born; you just need to become aware of it. Consciousness requires the possibility of a projection surface and memory storage. Whoever understands this fact is on the trail of the secret."

"Let's write that down", Kathi said. "And what you mentioned earlier would be a good title for our book:

MAGIC AND MYSTIC OF THE THIRD MILLENNIUM ANDY MO – THE SON OF THE GNOME KING IN THE HUMAN REALM

She also noted this down in her notebook. Then the raven continued.

"The formula reveals another secret. It says something truly sensational concerning the spiritual planes: namely, that they are constantly changing. The so-called beyond takes shape according to the ideas which people form in their consciousness. Depending on what people believe, the spiritual landscape reshapes itself and becomes an ethereal reality."

"But that only applies to the observer who believes their imaginings are real, doesn't it?" asked Christian. "Maya, hallucinations, dream worlds – everyone only sees what they want to see or what affects them emotionally, even in the gross material world. Psychology has long since proved that."

But Yks disagreed. "If enough human minds think the same thing, then the whole spiritual world actually deforms. I have been able to trace this myself. Just as the cities in the gross material world were completely remodelled by people over time and look completely different today than they did a thousand years ago, the landscapes of the subtle spheres also changed. I remember exactly the afterlife of the ancient Egyptians. It looked different then than the one the believers there experience today. It is no longer the same. And for Christians, heaven and hell are different than for Muslims. That proves that people build their own afterlife. The formula is correct. The deceased end up where they hope or fear they will be after death.

"And I can assure you, it's a very real world, not the fantasy of an individual. I'm not the only one to assert this; famous seers also report being able to visit the human afterlife. One from ancient Greece – I believe its related by Homer – reports a visit to his deceased mother and says afterwards: 'Better a beggar in this world than a king in Hades.' I believe he would see it differently today."

Andy Mo nodded.

"As an earth spirit, I had no access to the human realm of the dead. I only saw those who were lost in the Borderlands. But I was reading a book about different conceptions of the afterlife which were subsequently confirmed by seers who claimed they had been there. It's not just Christians who are promised a hell of wailing and gnashing of teeth: the sinners of other religions were also threatened with such abodes of horror. "Only the offences for which a poor soul was banished there were evaluated differently depending on their religion and culture. For example, while murder meant a one-way ticket to eternal damnation for a Christian, it was the opposite among the indigenous people of the islands of Fiji: in their belief system, those men who had killed at least one person and consumed their flesh were the ones who went to heaven. In ancient Iran, women who did not submit to their husbands were punished with hell. For Muslims, too, a woman preparing a meal during her period was enough for her soul to be doomed to darkness.

If you study the various conceptions of the afterlife which people have held over the centuries, you'll realise that the seers always saw exactly what corresponded to their tradition and era, and what was then taught by the priests and philosophers. From the Pyramid

Texts to the near-death experiences of the present day, those who have caught a glimpse of the other side report exactly what is being taught at the time."

"What kind of experiences are these?" the raven wanted to know. "I haven't heard anything about them."

"Those are the reports from people who died in an accident or during an operation, and who were brought back to life by the doctors", Michael explained. "I found some interesting books in the library. The amazing thing is that all the accounts from these people who almost died coincide with one another. They speak of a dark tunnel through which you pass into a radiant world of light and peace, of flowering meadows, and of beings of light who receive the deceased but send them back again."

"Unless we accuse the seers of making everything up," Andy Mo continued, "it confirms that the thoughts and imaginings of the living shape the worlds in which the dead find themselves. Naturally this makes beliefs much more important than you might think. Indeed, it would mean that even the people alive today contribute to shaping heaven and hell. The deceased merely reproduce it with their beliefs.

"Humans beings have the ability to imagine anything. Akasha, the living hard drive of the universe, is infinitely large and holds enough space for every thought that can ever be thought. And by imagining something, a living person changes the ethereal reality (which, as we know, consists not of matter but of ideas).

"It's clear that people initially prepare the conditions of existence in the gross material world in their thoughts; they think something up, make inventions, work out plans, and thus they improve the world. The Earth looks different today than it did two thousand years ago. Why shouldn't we be able to reshape the spiritual realms with our ideas as well? If the spiritual world consists of thought forms which are animated by emotions, it's quite clear that we also alter the hereafter with our thoughts and feelings. In the afterlife, spiritual power has a direct effect on spiritual substance. If Einstein is correct, then energy and mass are like two sides of the same coin on the ethereal plane as well, and imagination and existence must automatically manifest themselves from within themselves.

"A world consisting of thought-forms will naturally shape itself from thoughts, and it can also be reshaped by the power of thoughts. That is the secret of the Formula of Nothingness."

"That means", Christian noted, "that people think and believe things, and if enough people think and believe the same thing, then not only the individual's soul garden but the entire hereafter forms itself according to that image. Then, when we die, we actually experience what we imagined when we were alive. That would further imply that not only the afterlife but also the beings which inhabit it can be reshaped by human thought. The gods and demons would then be nourished by our fantasies and depend on us believing in them. The more people worship or fear them, the more powerful they become. No wonder they incite people to fight against each other in religious wars; that way they can eliminate the competitive thinkers."

"Does that mean that God, the ONE, is also just a figment of human imagination?" asked Kathi.

"No", said Andy Mo. "On the contrary. The very Formula of Nothingness proves his existence. The ONE, the great architect of all worlds, existed before the visible, gross material universe came into being. Someone must have thought up the whole thing. But presumably he had a host of attendant spirits who served as executive 'organs' and helped to bring it all about.

"The fact that Creation is the way it is, and that there are human beings who recognise everything and are even involved in shaping it all – that is more than a miracle. It could never have come into being on its own. It's the mightiest animation of light and shadow – four-dimensional, infinite – and every pixel is filled with consciousness and life. And where the pixels arrange themselves correctly in relation to each other, the bits and bytes can become independent and lead a life of their own as spirits. The fact that the billions of atoms which comprise you have arranged themselves in such a way as to become you cannot be a coincidence. Let a game designer try to replicate that. Even if that were to become possible one day, they would still have to resort to molecules, atoms, and quanta whose substance and quality were created billions of years ago by the ONE rather than by them. Keep on believing in your God so that he remains within reach for you and for us."

"In that case I'm reassured", said Kathi. "I suggest we go over what we've discussed and decide which parts we're going to write down in our book."

They discussed matters enthusiastically. Kathi took notes, and then she read aloud:

THOUGHTS ALTER DESTINY
AND CAN ALSO SHAPE THE AFTERLIFE

"People not only build their material surroundings in accordance with their ideas, but they also alter the spheres of the spiritual world with their thought-images. Not only this world, but also the hereafter is formed by thoughts and is subject to constant change. But people are unaware of the power which lies in their imaginations. They only understand that they must first plan something before they can realise it in *this* world. They draw up plans and follow them to build their houses, machines, and computers, but they don't realise that they're also shaping their afterlife with their thoughts.

"At the very beginning stands the fairy tale, the dream, the fantasy. The space age was prepared by Perry Rhodan: first in readers' imaginations, then in visible images as Star Wars, and today humans are actually building laser cannons capable of knocking rockets out of the sky. And they really are beginning to conquer the realm of outer space.

"Similarly, the teachings of the religions have shaped the landscape images of the spiritual worlds, and they continue to do so. Threatened punishments of hell for trivial offences instil fear in the faithful, debasing them to the level of servants of a God on whose benevolence they feel dependent. The Muslim belief in the dubious pleasures of a dubious paradise, where even suicide bombers end up; the indistinct purgatory and Last Judgement of the Christians; the Buddhist teachings of purifying reincarnation in a world of suffering – none of these are any consolation. Instead, the fear of punishment in hell for sinners is imprinted all the more deeply. These aren't worlds you would want to wake up in after death. It's better to imagine your own soul garden, which you design with your thoughts while you're still alive, and where you then shape the landscapes of the spiritual worlds together with other people, just as you do now in the Earthly realm."

Kathi paused and asked: "Is that okay?"

"You've summed it up perfectly", praised Andy Mo, and the others rapped their knuckles on the table in appreciation. "I'm convinced our book will finally lend humans the knowledge they need to harness the power of their spirits consciously and correctly. It will inspire readers to purposefully shape their own destinies with their thoughts and to conquer the spiritual realms, creating positive, consciousness-mediating worlds rather than heaven and hell.

"Just think, it was Harry Potter rather than the medieval wizards who truly ushered in the age of magic. Once more, children are growing up with an understanding of spiritual beings and spiritual realms. Humans will reconnect with their spirit and shape the spiritual planes with light. Our book explains how and why in a way which children will also understand, so helping them to handle the power of the spirit correctly.

Belief in the punishments of hell will give way to belief in the power and strength of thoughts to shape a luminous afterlife. Thus the fear and terror of death will vanish. Humans will build their own paradise and then determine for themselves how they wish to live in this world and the hereafter. They will no longer need the gross material worlds. They will stand above the demons and gods, creating their own spiritual world in the eternal realm of the ONE."

Kathi nodded. "I've divided the formula into five points:

1. Every thought changes spiritual reality – for other people as well. The planes and spheres of the gods, spirits, and demons are also shaped by people's thinking.
2. The power of the imagination is thus the most potent magical tool in the universe.
3. Faith is the illuminating light.
4. Love, affection, and sympathy are the most powerful forces, because they direct attention and thus consciousness towards the goal you're striving for.
5. The limitations which seem to exist are in fact set by humans with their beliefs about themselves and the hereafter. That's why the gods are always inventing new afterlife concepts, religions, and esoteric traditions to bind the living to themselves through their beliefs and ideas.

The secret of the formula is that it illuminates the freedom of the human spirit. It explains that people shape not only their personal realm of consciousness – the so-called soul garden – with their thoughts and feelings, but also the realms of gods and demons and the infinite void of nothingness beyond the soul garden. It proves that they can free themselves from dependence on the gods by adopting different ideas about the spiritual realms and beings."

Michael interrupted her.

"Do you really think children can follow us? We had Andy Mo and Einstein as teachers, and we read the books by Bardon and Stejnar. Our readers won't be so well prepared. They won't understand."

But Kathi had no concerns.

"Even though we're writing the book for children, adults will read it too. And the children will grow older. The book will accompany them; they'll read it several times and understand it better each time."

Andy Mo agreed with Kathi.

"You don't have to grasp everything immediately. The main thing is that the spiritual seeds have been planted in the readers' consciousness. Eventually they will sprout and become opinions and insights.

"I also didn't understand the secret of the four elements until I became a human being and could also grasp Akasha, the fifth element. Only now have I fathomed the anatomy of the five organs (that is, the five elements which mediate consciousness), and I have made them the foundation of my spiritual training. It was only with this key that I cracked the Formula of Nothingness. I even put together a special exercise programme for it."

After Andy Mo had revealed his personal spiritual training to the friends, they decided to include these instructions in the book as well. Once again, Kathi summarised everything in five points and read it out:

1. "Your imagination is the spiritual organ with which your spirit shapes the world of spirits. Consciously create a spiritual world in your thoughts which gives you and all beings freedom and peace. In the infinite, there are no limits. Even the Earthly tides which shape your destiny must follow the spiritual images. Only doubt, fear, and prejudice can hinder you. **Train the power of concentration of your thinking.** Master your body. Refine your soul. Train your spirit. Be aware that you *are*.

2. "Your willpower is the spiritual organ with which your spirit controls the world of spirits. It grows with every act of self-mastery. Master your bodily urges, your emotions, and your desires. **Master yourself.** Consciously train the power of your will every day. Master your body. Refine your soul. Train your spirit. Be aware that you *are*.

3. "Your compassion is the spiritual organ which opens up the essence of all other beings to your spirit and opens gates which would otherwise remain closed. Egoism narrows. Love, empathy, and compassion expand you. **Refine your Self.** Truth, justice, and compassion are the purified qualities of the spirit which

lead you to higher worlds. Master your body. Refine your soul. Train your spirit. Be aware that you *are*.

4. "Your faith is the spiritual organ which – by virtue of conviction – makes the world of the spirit visible. Your faith is the light of the spirit. What you believe to be true becomes illuminated and existent for you, even that which is false or does not exist at all. **Therefore, examine your opinions, ideas, and thoughts.** And illuminate what you're wishing with your firm conviction. Master your body. Refine your soul. Train your spirit. Be aware that you *are*.

5. "Your consciousness is the spiritual organ upon which your entire existence is based. But only in 'magical wakefulness' are you SELF conscious. **Observe yourself while thinking, feeling, and willing, and recognise yourself as the observer of your being.** Recognise your spiritual being, recognise who you are, recognise yourself, and awaken! You are a spirit which is in a body. This thought forms a body of light which carries you through the spirit worlds. As often as possible, think: 'I AM', and in this way awaken your true spiritual being. Awaken. Master your body. Refine your soul. Train your spirit. Be aware that you *are*.

"Everything in the world begins with a thought, so always consider what kind of spirit is near you and is inspiring you to think what you are thinking. Is it one of the Shadow Princes or an angel of light? And if you then decide to wish for something or not to wish for something, to say or not to say, to do or not to do, only act after you have made yourself aware that YOU are the one who is deciding and YOU are the one who truly wants it.

"You can always say YES or NO to what you think, do, or want.

"Be aware that after reading this book you are an initiate. Your thinking and your faith will be crucial in breaking the power of evil which currently dominates the world. Be aware that you are a spirit in a body, and train your spiritual muscles so that – like a spirit – you can live in accordance with your will even without your body, relying only on the spirit of your invisible 'I'."

Andy Mo had been listening attentively and nodded.

"That's good", he said. "Everyone can relate to that. We will conclude our book with this explanation of the Formula of Nothingness. I'm convinced this text will change the thinking of our readers – and with thinking, as we now know, the whole world changes."

EPILOGUE

Shadow Princes. Silently they stand around the square of light and shadow, observing the events in the world. Untouched and immovable, congealed pillars of nothingness, lost in the infinite darkness they mediate. Their temple is the stagnant emptiness of space. Hidden in darkness yet omnipresent, Baphomet and the princes fill time and space, bridging infinity with their vacuum.

The Gnome King has outwitted us, he thinks. First he lured his son into the human realm, and then he sacrificed his life. The spirit from the earth has become human and uncovered the formula. The battle is lost, but the fight will continue. As long as there is light, the Shadow will not fade.

They think they have won, he thinks, but their success is already part of his new plan. We turn children into youths and make them mature faster. Children grow older too. Their all-encompassing ideals become ingrained opinions and personal goals. And their desires and hopes become urges, impulses, and needs which absorb them into his Shadow after all. Love, money, and power – he knows, he only has to wait until they cultivate his fields all by themselves. They will serve him without even realising it. Now that they know the laws of magic, they will serve him even more so than before, when they were still relying on the charity of the gods. No one will follow the path revealed to them to the very end. They will begin magical experiments prematurely and without the proper preparation. After limited initial successes, failures will arise. They will seek shortcuts. They will look for simpler methods, and they will study books written by his minions which promise more. Then they will turn to him and work in his Shadow. They will have long since turned their backs on the light.

Magic, the mysterious enchantment of spiritual laws. First it fascinates, then it arouses a thirst to explore, and eventually the desire for magic becomes an addiction and a delusion. Once someone has experienced the power of the spirit in the Earthly realm, they cannot forget it. The bite of the green serpent holds everybody eternally in its thrall. Whether they are driven by pious ideals or pure egoism, whether it is love, power, or vanity which urges them on to perform the rites, they can no longer break free.

And yet, he also knows this: as long as there is even one among them who fights for justice, truth, and compassion, the threat to his Shadow Realm is not averted. Even if only one of them spreads light and love and thus casts no shadow themselves, the world remains sufficiently illumined for a second person, and then the next, to follow the path of the ONE.

He knows that the danger to his realm has not been banished.

THE END

THE BOOKS OF MAGIC AND MYSTICISM OF THE THIRD MILLENNIUM

Magic is the science of working with the spirit and the art of shaping the self. The term spirit refers to the ethereal, highly animate forms of thoughts and ideas: the inner images that awaken feelings and emotions, which can then either stimulate and move or restrain a person.

A common misconception among people involved with the esoteric is to see the spirit as a nebulous, immaterial web of light. Spirit particles do not clump together to form earth, water, fire, or air; rather, they appear in four different states of aggregation and are subject to laws that give them order, just like compact atoms and molecules. Using concentration and imagination, the spirit can be formed into images and fantasies. In this process it is possible to observe how the mental images, ideas, and feelings combine to form mental complexes which, if left unchecked, develop a life of their own within consciousness, which can in certain circumstances rob the person of their freedom. Not only in the form of fantasies, obsessive thoughts, or other psychic complexes, but also the mental image of the cake or the beer which draws us to the fridge, and which doesn't just move us internally but takes hold of the whole body.

One of the most important findings of modern spiritual research is the realisation that thoughts, ideas, and feelings on which the consciousness of a person relies are the ethereal cells of being of the spiritual and soul body, and that also the spirit of gods, attendant spirits, and demons are made of such cells of being. Thoughts and feelings are the living flesh of the spirit and the spirits. This means that we know what binds the beings of the ethereal planes to the beings of the earthly realm, and we also know the mental messengers.

Magic and Mysticism of the Third Millennium teaches how to control your personal spiritual cells of being, which in contrast to the gross material body cells act as if they were small spirits, and how you can thereby control the influence of the gods and demons which sway people and earthly events via these shared cells of being. Thanks to new discoveries in astrological research, we also know the tides of power of the attendant spirits and demons and the time in which we ourselves are powerful. Astrology describes not only the qualities of the cells of being, but also the anatomy and physiology of the ethereal body, and has cracked the genetic code of spirit and soul. With this knowledge, everyone can shape themselves and their lives.

There are insights that can only be truly experienced and grasped after focused training of the spirit and human maturity. For this reason, the traditions have always made their body of ideas accessible only to a group of select, powerful, and suitably prepared students. But the spirit of the times that today determines the thoughts, feelings, and actions of so many people is degenerate. The intended development for the perfection of the beings on this planet is being increasingly hindered by negative powers. It is essential that people learn more about the connections and interplay that exists between the ethereal worlds and the physical world. Nobody needs to be shocked by this any longer, because *Magic and Mysticism of the Third Millennium* also describes how to oppose the powers.

Thus, following Franz Bardon, Emil Stejnar has now also brought to the public the secret instructions of Gnostic Hermetics, as well as the latest research results of this magical tradition, in the form of the 13 volumes of *Magic and Mysticism of the Third Millennium*. With its publication, the era of secret-keepers and secret societies has finally finished. Knowledge that has never been published before is now accessible, and the hidden connections between the spiritual spheres and the world of humanity are revealed.

The books of *Magic and Mysticism of the Third Millennium* contain no new global conspiracy theories, but instead uncover what was previously unknown: namely, that the real rulers of this planet are not to be found on the political stage or among secret societies, but instead are to be sought on the ethereal planes. They are powers from the realm of the spiritual worlds that inspire people to do their will and thus determine the fate of humanity.

The books of *Magic and Mysticism of the Third Millennium* not only describe these powers – they also show a way to shape your 'I', to awaken, and to free yourself from their sphere of influence. Just like the natural sciences and the world of technology, the science of spirituality and the soul has also developed further. New discoveries have been made and valuable insights have been gained; we are not simply on the trail of the secrets of the gods and demons, but also of the mystery of consciousness and its media.

The important thing about the new discoveries and exercises is not that we acquire magical powers, but that we are transformed in such a way that we no longer even need them. To the same degree that the abilities to work magic grow, the desire to use such abilities lessens. This is a mystery that is experienced by everyone who actually follows the path shown. It is therefore not just a question of magic and mysticism. The modern science of the spirit also offers a valuable aid to living in ordinary life. It is not spirits that are conjured up, it is the power and energy of your own spirit that is awoken. The goal is not to use magic to rule over the world and the spirits; rather, it is to transform yourself in such a way that the world and the spirits can no longer rule you.

The reader who follows the instructions and advice will become a master and priest of secret knowledge, and will have nothing more to learn from any manuscript, guru, or order. The reader will themselves be capable of showing the path to other people as a spiritual guide.

The books of *Magic and Mysticism of the Third Millennium* consist of 13 volumes. They provide an accurate, comprehensive introduction to the entire range of the esoteric and they are a unique course of instruction in magic and schooling in life. Emil Stejnar has, with his work, brought the magic and mysticism of the medieval world of miracles into the modern world of science.

BOOK 1: THE BOOK OF THE MASTER AND HIS HEIRS
A Masonic Initiation Novel.

The author narrates the adventures, in part based on fact, of two incarnations of an initiate and the path that must be travelled by everyone who, like this master, follows the secret instructions:

In a Viennese lodge of the Freemasons, a doctor named Michael Stein is elevated to the level of master. During the secret ritual he experiences a so-called soul journey and is transported to the 13th century. There he is a monk and is initiated into the mysteries of the Templars. And he is investigating the secret of Baphomet. Because of his great success in healing, he is accused of witchcraft, and a fire is set to execute him at the stake. But instead of dying in the flames, the monk awakens in the lodge temple, in the body of Michael Stein. He is shocked to realise that his past has caught up with him. He remembers his mission: it is up to him to save humanity and to vanquish Baphomet and his earthly agents. He must once again find the chest containing the objects of power and *The Book of the Master*, which he hid in a cave before his death.

Maria, the fifteen-year-old daughter of his shady lodge brother, Brandström, accompanies him on his exciting quest. Along the way he introduces her – and along with her the reader – to the secrets of magic and mysticism. A tender, millennia-old love binds the two, but they have no idea of the danger they are in. The earthly representatives of evil, the Brethren of the Shadow, are also searching for the chest and will mercilessly hunt the pair down.

The responses of readers confirm that *The Book of the Master* is far more than a fantasy novel. Higher learning is revealed and explained in a way that is easy to understand. The images of mysterious, fantastic scenes, conveyed by the magic of the writing alone, has left many readers with such a lasting impression that it has transformed their entire lives. What otherwise can only be achieved by special initiation rituals, is achieved by the mystery of the story and draws the reader into its mysteries. The reader actually experiences an initiation first-hand – a ceremony which alters consciousness, transforms the personality, and sets the rest of the person's life on a new track. It can therefore be said, without exaggeration, that this book is a magical text that contains within it a spiritual power with exceptional effects. By reading it, readers themselves becomes an 'heir' of *The Book of the Master*, and an initiate of the mysterious Gnostic-Hermetic tradition.

From the contents:
- The mystery of spirit and soul.
- The personal soul garden where you awaken after death.
- Who are the true directors of events on this planet?
- Baphomet, the Lord of the World and the Princes of Power.
- The secret superiors of this life and the afterlife.
- How to free yourself from their power.

BOOK 2: SPIRITUAL EXERCISES FOR FREEMASONS
Instructions and Lodge Speeches.

You have surely asked yourself: who really determines the fate of the world? Where do the powerful get their authority from? Who protects them, who supports them, who gives them their power? Why do some people always succeed, while others struggle and toil and still get nowhere? Is this for real?

The answer is: yes. There are in actuality mechanisms of power that do not recognise good or evil, but follow spiritual laws. Those who know these laws can use the powers for their own purposes. For millennia, initiates, orders, and lodges have been cultivating this knowledge and passing it on to suitable people. It is not only the Freemasons – the Catholic Church also has its esotericism and the key to the mysteries of magic and mysticism.

But the time of secrets is over. Thanks to *Spiritual Exercises for Freemasons*, every reader can awaken the power and energy of the spirit within them and use it. Everyone now has access to the mysteries that teach the method of control of the four elements and how to approach the power of the gods. After Franz Bardon demonstrated this in his work *The Path of the True Adept*, Stejnar's book will illuminate this path and provide strength on the journey to an awakened SELF.

From the contents:
- Religious exercises for Freemasons.
- Ritual magic in the Lodge Temple.
- The magical research lodge 'Esoteric Circle'.
- The journey through the elements of fire, water, air, and earth.
- How to awaken the power and energy of the elements within you.
- The mysteries of the four elements.
- The cybernetics of consciousness.
- The secret power of Christian mysticism.

- The magic teachings of the Jesuits.
- How to control yourself and others.
- How extraordinary gifts are developed.
- How extraordinary abilities are developed.
- How to achieve an inner balance.
- The secret of success.
- The basics of the Gnostic-Hermetic tradition.
- Magic and Mysticism of the Third Millennium.
- Work with the spirit: 60 years of practical experience with magic.

What has hitherto reached the public concerning Freemasons are conspiracy theories and rumours that have nothing to do with reality. The true secret of Freemasonry is known only to a few: it is the practice of magic and mysticism, which is contained within ritual and the correct use of symbols. This book gives the first insight into the hidden side of the lodge and religious orders. Stejnar also describes the spirit that moves people in the temple.

The spiritual organs and the cybernetics of spirit and soul: fire, water, air, and earth – thinking, feeling, willing, and consciousness. These are the four elements of life and the four energetic limbs of human existence. The Freemasons learn how to control the four elements, which in their interplay form the basis of consciousness, thanks to a special spiritual education. By assigning every one of these elements the same significance, a fifth element is discovered: the awoken I-SELF. From this point of view, the Freemason not only controls themselves, they also master every other power, being, and spirit. The mason is not nailed to a cross, but instead supported by four beams.

The lost word and the lost symbol: Dan Brown in his book about the Freemasons only hints at 'The Lost Symbol', but it is revealed and described by Stejnar: as the mystery of the lost word and the secret of the pyramid's apex. Stejnar explains how the five points of a pyramid are linked in the form of a pentacle, and thus awaken the 'five points of mastery'.

The magic and mysticism of the Christian tradition: it is little known that the Christian Church, which officially condemns and demonizes any form of magic, also follows the tradition of magical exercises and practices. The exercises of the Jesuits are nothing other than the training of spirit and soul which is also taught within the tradition of Hermetics.

Lodge speeches: secret instructions, directions, and practices which have hitherto been reserved for only a few initiates are for the first time also made accessible to outsiders.

BOOK 3: THE FOUR ELEMENTS
The Secret Key to Spiritual Power.

Spirit and soul are not a nebulous web of light; rather, they consist of limbs, organs, and spiritual cells of being just as the earthly body does. These cells of being of the spirit are themselves small spirits that must be mastered in order to master the world of the spirit and spirits. Only those who have mastered their own spirit, thoughts, feelings, and emotions – in other words, the spirit beings which comprise us – also master the spirits of gods, attendant spirits, and demons.

Gnostic Hermetics describes how to gain the energy for this purpose. There are various techniques that are used to transform drives and emotions into pure spirit power, and to expand consciousness to such an extent that it is elevated above all visible and invisible barriers and is even not lost in death. Gnostic Hermetics shows you how to transform your weaknesses into strengths.

The true goal, however, is not to master the world or the spirits using magical power, but rather to transform yourself so that the world and the spirits cannot master you anymore. This is also achieved by special spirit and soul teachings. Thus the Gnostic-Hermetic student does not withdraw for hours at a time to brood or to meditate; instead, they use everyday life very consciously to train their spirit. It is not trance but wakefulness that is striven for.

From the contents:
- How to shape your immortal light body.
- How to master the spiritual powers.
- Magic in everyday life: the magic of thought, wishes, and curses, and the fear of 'dark' magic.
- The magic of helpful spirits: the Kyilkhor and the spirit in the bottle.
- Alchemy: the secret practice of alchemical transformation.
- How to earn gold in this world for the afterlife.
- The magic of books and word magic: using language magically. Every word is an effective being.
- The Kabbalah: the magical formula for practice, according to Franz Bardon.
- Lodge magic: THE RITUAL OF THE HERMETIC FOUR. This ritual lends access to the power and energy of the four elements. With this, seekers who do not wish to be bound by oaths also have access to a ritual magic that until now was reserved only for members of lodges and orders. The ritual is not intended just for temple work in a lodge. It is also possible to work alone with it to achieve inner elementary balance.
- Mysticism: the 'Ritual of the Monastery Gate' opens up to everyone the portal to an inner monastery which they can enter and leave at any time, and which binds them in the spirit of the international community of all brothers and sisters living in monastic seclusion without having to renounce the world.
- After death: you do not awaken in an 'afterlife', but first in a very personal 'soul garden' where the inner being, thoughts, and feelings become the environment. Only those who are prepared for this can preserve their consciousness.
- School for priests and counselling: this book also enables the reader to help others with the power of their spirit. This knowledge was originally only for priests and initiates to train their successors. Those who follow the path are given the ability to show seekers the way to the light and to themselves.

BOOK 4: OUT-OF-BODY EXPERIENCES
Learning to Live without Your Body.

It's one of the most impressive experiences in life, and one of the highlights of the Hermetic journey: to experience yourself outside your body. Even the most sublime spiritual knowledge remains mere theory as long as you have not felt your own spiritual existence first-hand. Thus in the old temple schools, this experience was one of the first lessons that was taught to the neophyte during their initiation.

Magic and Mysticism of the Third Millennium again follows this old tradition and initiates students into the secrets of the astral travellers. An entirely new technique has been developed which allows everyone to leave their body very rapidly. From the moment of the preparatory exercises and first attempts to travel, you gain an insight into a completely new existence, and ethereal cells of being are created that are indispensable not only for consciousness in the out-of-body state, but also for conscious living after death.

From the contents:
- The twelve steps that elevate the consciousness and free it from the body:
- Wakefulness in daily life, wakefulness in dreams
- The dream body as vessel of consciousness
- How to train dream consciousness
- Falling asleep correctly
- How we learn to awake within dreams
- Lucid dreaming as a launching pad for mental travel
- Flying dreams as an aid to starting
- The secret of flying carpets
- In the borderlands of dreams – in unfamiliar soul gardens
- How everyone can leave their body
- The dream world as a location for encounters with death

Before now we sank within our body, went into a trance, and expected our consciousness to rise up out of it. As a rule this doesn't actually work. It's as if an astronaut sets out for the moon in a car from right outside their house.

Future space flights will start from orbit around the Earth, and the best launching pad for astral travel is to be found on the dream plane. As soon as you awaken into a lucid dream, you can cast off your body.

Research focused on the spirit has shown that it is not trance but wakefulness that is required for astral travel. The best conditions for this are to be found in the world of dreams, because the ethereal is already somewhat detached from gross matter and we can leave the body more easily. It's much simpler to do this from a waking dream than from the reduced state of consciousness of a trance. It is possible to learn lucid dreaming. There is a simple technique that allows this ability to be developed.

The dream world is also a place where it is possible to encounter the dead. But leaving the body does not necessarily mean entering another world. The state of consciousness in which we find ourselves allows what we are experiencing at that moment to appear as absolute reality, but not everything actually does correspond to reality. In the landscape under observation, fantasies can intrude – ours, as well as those of other living people and the dead. For this, too, there is a guide to better orient yourself in these convoluted worlds and to correctly grasp the special symbolism used by the spirit between the planes. Those who grasp their situation and understand the symbolic language gain better insights into other planes via their dreams than through incantations, messages from a medium, or experiments in trance.

BOOK 5: ASTROLOGY
Navigation for the Journey of Life,
Genetic Code of Spirit and Soul.

Emil Stejnar was an astrological life coach for five decades. In this book he not only describes the approach to classical astrology, but also reveals completely new insights and perspectives.

- A horoscope describes the anatomy and physiology of the spirit and soul. The planets correspond to the spiritual organs that enable consciousness, and their positions at the moment of birth determine their functionality and quality: the Sun is the organ for self-awareness, the Moon for your emotional life, Mercury for thinking, Venus for love, Mars for your driving force, Jupiter for your sense of justice, and Saturn for discipline. With Uranus, Neptune, and Pluto you gaze beyond the horizon of your consciousness. The disposition of your character and personal being arises from the interaction of the organs.
- On the basis of the ever-shifting planetary positions, an astrological forecast calculates when specific organs will be particularly activated or impaired, and when they will function well or less well.
- Mundane astrology investigates the spirit of the times, which acts as a guiding current or trend to determine popular consciousness and world events.

Through the practice of astrology you can come to know yourself, your fellow humans, and the tides of the cosmos, and you can utilise the operative powers to shape yourself and take action successfully.

Of all the philosophical, religious, and occult traditions, astrology is the only spiritual science that can be used to prove that the spirit and the spiritual powers (energies or gods) actually exist. Astrology is an empirical science based upon the observation of cosmic changes and their effects on consciousness.

With this book, even a layperson can rapidly learn the basic rules of astrology. The beginner will be astounded at how easy it is to understand a horoscope, and experienced astrologers will discover new possibilities for their astrological analyses with the original insights presented here.

Astrology is not about asking what fate will bring; rather, it is about knowing when to act so that your plans succeed and the things you fear don't come to pass.

BOOK 6: THE ADEPT FRANZ BARDON
Who Was He, What Did He Teach, Where Does His Path Lead?

Franz Bardon was certainly the most important personality in the world of Hermetics. With his works, he left his mark on spiritual research for the next century and created the basis for *Magic and Mysticism of the Third Millennium.*

The actual goal of the journey that he describes is not to gain magical power; rather, it is the perfection of spirit and soul. It is about more spiritual energy, so you can consciously shape life, both in this world and in the afterlife. Not all 'true adepts' conjure spirits and perform miracles. Every personality that does something exceptional for humanity, every exceptional artist, doctor, or scientist, everyone who selflessly strives for freedom, peace, and progress can become a higher initiate. Magic is a high-performance sport that requires full attention and the whole of the personality. What Bardon describes cannot be pursued part-time like a hobby. Those who take on an important mission happily forego the memory of their magical abilities so that they can fully dedicate themselves to their concrete earthly duties.

Those who don't engage with magic can also shape their life, spirit, and soul for the better, according to Franz Bardon's instructions. If you integrate his directions into everyday life, as Stejnar explains in his book, you will see the path that Bardon describes leads to practical help with life.

Stejnar's book is a guide to Bardon's *The Path of the True Adept*. He answers recurring questions, the path is illuminated, and ambiguities about Franz Bardon are clarified. Nobody becomes an adept in a year. Some practitioners who don't bear this in mind believe they are doing something wrong, doubt themselves or doubt Franz Bardon, and stop practising. This is a shame, but it's understandable, because unfortunately the path is not as easy to master as Franz Bardon promises. But this is no reason to give up. Stejnar describes tried and tested techniques that can be used to overcome these obstacles.

From the contents:
- Franz Bardon: who was he, what were his teachings, what is the destination of his path?
- Was Franz Bardon really an adept?
- Excerpts from letters written by Franz Bardon's widow.
- Letters by Franz Bardon.
- That was Franz Bardon: stories from people of his time.
- Is what's written in FRABATO true?
- Did the FOGC lodge exist and who is Baphomet?
- How does it work with Bardon's attendant spirits and Abramelin magic?
- Is it possible to work magic by following Franz Bardon's instructions?
- What am I doing wrong if it doesn't work?
- How do you create the path that Franz Bardon describes?
- Bardon and the demons, the Freemasons, and alchemy.
- Personal letters to friends about Bardon's magic and mysticism.
- Experiences from personal practice and advice for the path.
- Sättler, Quintscher, Bardon, Stejnar.
- The secret of the fourth tarot card.
- The mystery of tarot card 0
- The pyramid and the pentagram

With this book, the reader receives something very special. A unique icon: THE SUN OF FRABATO. It is an image given by Franz Bardon to his students and patients as a very personal amulet, thus including them within his power. This image represents Bardon's main ideas as a four-colour Kyilkhor: Divinity reveals itself as a radiant sun. The sun breaks through the clouds. The light defeats the darkness.

Bardon also makes this mystery his personal logo and uses the symbol of the sun in connection with the word FRABATO for magical purposes. This Kyilkhor, which is saturated by positive energies, has never before been published, and after Bardon's death was only available to a few friends; with the approval of Franz Bardon's daughter, it is presented at the front of this book. It will act like a window into his worlds and illuminate the path to the true adept for its readers, and it will give strength on this journey to an awoken SELF.

Book 7: THE BOOK OF GUARDIAN ANGELS
How to Make Contact with Higher Beings.

For over 40 years, Stejnar's *The Book of Guardian Angels* has been one of the most sought-after and popular works of the literature about angels. People have known for millennia that there are angels. The religions teach about them, Franz Bardon describes them, but Stejnar's *The Book of Guardian Angels* has made them accessible to all. What in earlier times was only possible for priests and initiates is now possible for all who follow his instructions. For the new edition, the author has expanded his book with several new chapters and enriched it with new, important experiences from his magical practice.

For every area of life there is a responsible angel. Stejnar reveals how to ask for an angel's help and which angel to turn to when you have a problem. A simple method makes it possible to make contact with the desired angel, even without magical evocation.

From his decades of practice as an astrological life advisor, Stejnar knows about people's worries and speaks in *The Book of Guardian Angels* about the most common problems. He describes his experience in dealing with invisible intelligences in the form of concrete case studies, where he was able to help through an amulet with the seal of an angel. Excerpts from letters of thanks are evidence of the beneficial effects of the ethereal beings.

Personal teachings from individual angels supplement the descriptions of their activities. In this way, everyone can correctly shape their own life for themselves. This conscious collaboration between the guardian angels and humans enables the best possible help. Anyone can immediately follow the teachings and advice from the angels presented here. For all of life's problems, a solution is given from the perspective of beings from the beyond who have a greater overview from their plane than human beings.

In this way Stejnar has created a completely new book of help for life. The laws of success and earthly happiness, from the perspective of the angels, allow many things to be seen in a new light.

A path is shown that leads to the realm of the spirit. Without religious dogma, and without magical conjuring rituals, comfort and aid can be found in communion with guardian angels. For the following life problems, you can find the responsible angels, their names, seals, and special teachings:

- Health, illness, nervous crises, protection from accidents, infertility,
- Happiness in love, love troubles, loneliness, beauty, comfort,
- Happiness, success, money, career,
- Education, exams, self-confidence,
- Marriage, faithfulness, children, family, divorce, sex,
- Justice, law, enemies, fateful events, protection,
- Vitality, youth, sport, willpower,
- Mediumistic abilities, magic, magical persecution, religion, astrology,
- Black magic, the afterlife and death, earth rays, demons,
- Alcohol, drugs, and diet problems.

Emil Stejnar's *Book of Guardian Angels* bridges the gap between science and religion, between magic and mysticism, between this world and the afterlife. Those who follow the simple instructions are granted access to the spiritual world. Thousands of people have already been impressed by the miraculous help of the angels.

The Book of Guardian Angels is not an ordinary book. It is a real help in life and often works miracles for readers. The valuable advice that has been provided by heavenly helpers makes this unusual book of life-help a source of wisdom and comfort, and even lends hope and confidence in hopeless situations.

BOOK 8: THE THEBAN CALENDAR
The 360 Principals of the Earth Belt Zone and the Tides of Their Power. The World of Demons, Gods, and Spirits.

In his book *The Practice of Magical Evocation*, Franz Bardon describes the 360 intelligences of the Earth Belt Zone. Anyone who wants to contact an angelic being from the Earth Belt Zone will find a valuable aid in *The Theban Calendar*. Once per day, every intelligence is very near to your current location. If you consciously await the being at that time and approach it in your spirit, it's impossible to fail. In order to do this, you must know in advance when the time of their proximity is approaching.

The Theban Calendar is a perpetual calendar. For every day of the year you can look up which time a desired principal is easiest to reach. Like the visible sun that rises every morning in the East, the invisible hierarchy of 360 attendant spirits also travels once daily around the Earth. Every four minutes, a new degree rises above the ecliptic, and for every degree there is a spiritual intelligence as 'principal' of this cosmic location. Every principal that is in the process of rising is especially close to earthly events and, in the hour of its rising, is especially powerful in action. At this time the presence of the angel is more powerfully felt than at other times, and you can make contact more easily than if you turn to the angel from the other side of the planet.

In order to avoid complicated calculations, priests and magicians of ancient times used what is called *The Theban Calendar*. Emil Stejnar was given the opportunity to inspect and make notes on this calendar, which Quintscher published for his magical research lodge during his lifetime, and which Franz Bardon also used. During this process some errors in the original became apparent. Stejnar therefore calculated the entire calendar anew, and expanded it with comments, advice, and important directions from his own practice, publishing this in the form of *The Theban Calendar*.

The mystical invocation and the correct point in time. In these notes the practice of mystical evocation is also described. This is a technique that is known to only a few initiates. With this method, you can use, even without magical evocation, the positive characteristics of each principal, and the special qualities of a certain plane.

It isn't necessary to summon a principal to the earthly world; instead, use meditative attention to transfer yourself at the correct time into the being's presence and identify yourself with its being. You use the tides of power and you avail yourself of the living cells of being that prevail at that moment due to the proximity of an intelligence. Those who consciously dive into the aura of a being at the right time can profit from their proximity and thus change their being positively.

The Theban Calendar lists the names of all 360 attendant spirits, and there is an index for the most important requests that allows you to swiftly find the principal you seek. Those who urgently need the help or inspiration of a principal will reach them most reliably at the time of their proximity. Those who wish to charge a seal, an amulet, or a magical gesture can do this more easily at the time of the being's proximity than if they have to summon the being first.

From the contents:
- The 360 principals and the tides of their power.
- Jesus and the attendant spirits, a Gnostic work as the key to Hermetics.
- The practice of mystical evocation.
- How to avoid an undesired pact.
- Concerning the right time. Using the astrological tides.
- Tips for practice.
- The three great mysteries of spiritual power.
- Index of the characteristics and realms of the attendant spirits.
- Gods, attendant spirits, and demons and the correct names of power.
- The names of the 360 attendant spirits of the various traditions.

Warning!
Stejnar also points out the dangers associated with contact with the attendant spirits. Every evocation or invocation of a power that you have not mastered has consequences and repercussions. Many beginners, but also advanced magicians who overestimate their own power, eventually become impoverished, sickened, or insane.

BOOK 9: DIET-YOGA
How to Beat the Yo-Yo Effect. How to Stop Smoking.
How to Turn Your Weaknesses into Willpower.

Some people have an aura which is instantly impressive. You can really feel that they not only want what they want, but also do what they want, and that they are a self-determined personality. Where do they get this power from?

The answer is simple: they turn their weaknesses into strengths. Smoking, snacks, alcohol, food, mobile phones, and the internet are all urges in the form of habits, needs, and desires that resist the mind and the will, and take spiritual energy from you the moment you satisfy them. Conversely, you gain energy from these schemata by determinedly refusing to follow them and putting them in their place. This is a fact and a cosmic law: **eat or be eaten**. Every time you determinedly refuse, it strengthens your spirit. This isn't about asceticism, it is mental fitness training.

Diet-Yoga does not move your body, it moves your spirit. Diet-Yoga is not a new, mystical fad or some banal weight-loss or smoking-cessation plan: it is ancient wisdom.

The adepts of Ancient Egypt used the secret knowledge of the power of the spirit over the urges of the body. They understood that physical drives contain the same power as the power of the will, and they represented this knowledge in the form of the Sphinx.

The Secret of the Sphinx. The Sphinx has the body of a lion and the head of a mighty pharaoh. It is the symbol for the nature of the human being in its entirety: within humans, the irrepressible power of the lion is combined with the directing power of human reason. An animal driving force and discerning understanding form a living unity. The head determines in which direction the energy flows. The head is where the lever is pulled.

The resolute decision to go without something automatically and effortlessly transforms the driving force of craving into pure will. In contrast the convulsive suppression of desires and cravings,

Diet-Yoga doesn't require any energy to be expended; instead, the lever is simply pulled.

It is the decision that shifts the lever. The decision is an expression of the will. The decision determines if the human or the animal acts: reason instead of cigarettes, feelings of self-worth rather than chocolate. Freedom rather than being a slave to your desires. The conscious direction of drives by the mind is what separates humans from animals. When a decision is made, this determination sends flows of the animal power of the lion into the decisive power of the will, and immediately places it under the control of the spirit – for a period you decide. This all works because of the **zero time effect.**

It is the time factor that causes the lever to snap into place. The time factor is now! The immediate NOW. The zero time effect is based on this lightning-fast spark of timeless NOW. The spontaneous decision that from NOW until tonight there will be no smoking, or no snacking, or no eating – this is what blindsides the drives and surprises the self. There is no time for the lion to resist. Diet-Yoga uses this surprise effect for self-determination.

If you don't act on the instant, that instant, then the lever does not lock in. If, for example, you decide to give up smoking for New Year, or to start fasting tomorrow, or not to snack this evening, then the craving – in other words, the lion – has enough time to use its animal energy complexes against you and the good intentions then disappear.
- It doesn't depend on strong willpower, it depends on the decision: "I will!"
- Physical urges, passions, cravings, and desires contain the same energy as willpower does.
- Everyone can decide for themselves what they use these energies for: for their cravings or for their strength of purpose, which says no and stands against the undesirable drives.

A spontaneous decision unleashes the zero time effect and sets the course for the assertion of the will. The sphinx phenomenon is based on this psycho-physical mechanism which can be activated over and over again.

It is astonishing how easy it is to override and suppress the desire to eat or smoke using the power of surprise. If the lion realises that it will definitely not receive anything for the next few hours, it withdraws and the craving doesn't even arise.

If you are overweight and want to lose weight, and have tried many times without success, then you should read this book.

If you want to stop smoking, but have never managed it, or if you are frightened of eating more if you don't smoke, then you should read this book.

If you are tired of being a slave to cravings and want to decide for yourself for once, then you should read this book.

The secret of the yo-yo short diet:
- The thermostat weight and confusion tactics.
- Economy mode, delay mechanism, and the habituation factor.
- Desired weight, alarm weight, and maximum weight.

How to beat the addiction to smoking:
- Sudden quitting using the surprise effect.
- Quitting in stages as a spiritual sport.
- 20 tips to quit smoking more easily.

How to turn your weaknesses into willpower:
- The sphinx phenomenon.
- The zero time effect.
- Working with the Hypnodisc.

The Hypnodisc accompanies this book. This pulsing mandala can be used to put you in an altered state of consciousness in which you are able to programme the subconscious and rob food, snacking, drinking, and smoking of importance.

BOOK 10: ANDY MO
The Son of the Gnome King in the Human Realm.

A boy finds *The Book of the Master* in the cellar of his parent's house and a new generation takes up the magical legacy. Those who have read *The Book of the Master and his Heirs* will read the sequel to this story with great pleasure, and will be initiated even more deeply into the secrets of the mysterious world of spirits and the power of the human spirit.

Andy Mo is a young earth spirit who ventures into the world of humans to search there for his lost father, Andimo the Gnome King. Baphomet, the Lord of the World, is holding him captive somewhere. The Prince of Shadows wants to prevent the old king from finding the document with the 'Formula of Nothingness' and revealing the last great secret to humanity – namely, how to be free forevermore from the domain of evil and the ruling powers. Andy Mo doesn't have much time to complete his mission, because when a spirit spends too much time on the surface of the earth he can never return to his spiritual home. Luckily, he finds friends among humans of the same age who believe in spirits, and who can therefore see him. They help him search for his father. In return, he helps them with his magic powers, and gradually initiates them into the secrets of magic and mysticism. In the process, they come across the trail of Dr Stein and the books of mastery he has written. The clever raven Yks is also with them, of course. Andy Mo soon realises that people don't need any magic or any spirits to conjure things up. Those who practice the rules of positive thinking are already magicians who can shape their future in mysterious ways according to their imagination. Every thought can serve as a helpful spirit . Thoughts can also be revealed as demons. That's why it's important that people master their thoughts, and that is precisely the purpose of magical training.

Andy Mo is invisible to most people, so there are constantly surprising and funny situations when he uses his magical abilities to defend weaker people. But magic doesn't always help. The earthly agents of Baphomet seem to be sincere, but in reality they are criminals who do not spare his friends or their families. It's a race against time and a battle against the powers of darkness. Will Andy Mo and his friends manage to find the Gnome King and free him? Can he fulfil his mission to enlighten people, or will evil triumph in the end? The pressure of the shadow on the children becomes ever greater. When Andy Mo falls in love with a girl from the group, Miri Li, and wants to stay with the humans, it looks like Baphomet has won. Problems arise; the whole world seems to be in a conspiracy against the friendly earth spirit and his friends.

Suspense is guaranteed until the very last page. At the same time, all you need to know about the spirit and the spiritual mechanisms which determine how people live and die is explained in an easy-to-understand way. The secret of the 'Formula of Nothingness' is revealed for the first time. With this surprising new knowledge of the power of the spirit, the foundation is laid for the *Magic and Mysticism of the Third Millennium*. This brings a new age for humanity.

Originally Andy Mo was supposed to initiate children and young people into the world of magic and mysticism. But it came about that even experienced esoteric practitioners could learn a great deal from Andy Mo. He explains how magic functions in practice, but also how without magic, with only the power of thought, life can be 'magically' altered in miraculous ways. Working with your spirit and with spirits is actually possible.

Twelve years after publishing the tenth volume, Emil Stejnar decided to publish the last three books as well, which he had previously revealed only to his close friends due to their explosive content. The sensational information and provocative ideas might shock many readers or horrify them, but will also incite them to think, and that is the first step on the path to an awoken SELF.

They concern 'dear' God and the question of what importance humanity has for the gods, attendant spirits, and demons. And they are about freedom, awakening, and the birth of the 'I AM'.

They concern the realisation that people, both the most powerful and most powerless of them, are unknowing playthings of the gods in a strategy game. They are about the techniques that make it possible for us to free ourselves, awaken, and jump off this board game.

The instructions in the 11th and 12th books lead to the goal of every Hermetic exercise – but also to the beginning – because those awakened gain the spiritual education of a com-pletely new appreciation. Those who have awoken see themselves and their lives, as well as death and the afterlife, from a new perspective. Nothing is as it was before. The new perspective is experienced by consciousness as a rebirth. In the 13th book, the mystery of the serpent and the true meaning of sex magic is revealed.

BOOK 11: AT THE PORTAL TO THE FINAL LANTERN
A Novel of Initiation.

Not just the title, but this entire book might have been inspired by Gustav Meyrink. Stejnar makes skilful use of Meyrink's mastery of words and brings his spirit back to life. He weaves together both well-known and unknown quotations from the author into his story, until he merges with him to form a unity. What Meyrink began, Stejnar completes with this book. Readers will find themselves and awaken.

Annika, a young scientist, has been kidnapped. Her fiancé, Professor Berg, who is desperately searching for her, is also in mortal danger. The data for an epoch-making discovery is at stake. A fanatical, merciless cult intends to prevent humanity from taking this step at any price, and it will not stop at torture and murder. A powerful, unscrupulous company is also chasing the secret. It's a race against time. The trail leads to Prague, where Professor Berg mysteriously awakens after an accident in a strange house.

Awakening is the central concern of every initiation and spiritual training. This special state of consciousness, in which we grasp that we exist, is the basis of every self-determined personality and the first goal of every occult tradition. As long as a person is not awakened, engaging with magic and mysticism doesn't make much sense. Only an awakened spirit is able to free itself from the powers that the person is dependent on because they support them.

"Most people believe that 'being awake' is about opening your senses and your eyes and keeping your body up during the night. One of the things people are most convinced of is that we are awake; however, in reality we are caught in a net that we ourselves weave out of thoughts and feelings, the phantasms woven from dreams. The person remains a dreamer."

Gustav Meyrink wrote about, understood, revealed, and described the mysticism of being awake like no other spiritual researcher.

We are trapped in a body, deadened by its urges and hypnotised by its brain functions. We believe we are awake, but in truth we are directed by thoughts, and they trap us in the mental treadmill of the everyday in the anteroom of consciousness.

In this exciting thriller, the 'awakening' is illuminated from comprehensible perspectives and described in different ways so that what is presented actually gives you access to this mystery.

The suggestive imagery, woven through with the words of Gustav Meyrink, draws the reader – without them realising or being able to do anything about it – deeper and deeper into the world of the protagonist. A world in which illusion and reality can no longer be distinguished. Eventually we start to question whether we are moving through the world of the living, the dreamers, or the dead.

It is an enormously perplexing experience when, while reading a chapter, you are no longer sure if you are awake or dreaming. But it is precisely this Kafkaesque confusion that, in the end, effects the awakening that, in the same way as initiation, leads to a new knowledge of the self. In reading, a mechanism is set in motion that alters consciousness and lends the knowledge that you have of yourself an entirely new quality.

Once again, Stejnar shows that esotericism can be intelligent, insightful, and unusually helpful for life (and death).

Everyone who knows the work of Stejnar and Meyrink should read this book.

BOOK 12: DREAMING CAN BE DANGEROUS
Mystical Tales, Exciting Short Stories, Mysterious Sketches.

Mysticism and unusual tales about subjects as diverse as love, illusion, desire, bloodlust, and death. Dream or reality, that's the question, and the answer will always come as a surprise. Every one of the exciting and entertaining episodes herein contains a serious idea which invites consideration and analysis.

It concerns the abyss, both in this life and in the afterlife, into which we can fall. It's about dreams in which we know we are dreaming, and it's about reality in which, even though we are convinced we are awake, we are actually sleep. And it is about an awakening, about being awake and the rebirth of the SELF.

Even if many tales leave the impression that the author is making fun of God, the world, and esoterica, as soon as you also read the 'Notes on the Stories' you begin to understand more clearly. Slanted representations of the world are adjusted and corrected. Beliefs are thrown into question and new ways of seeing illuminate what had until now remained in darkness.

These revolutionary ideas about the mysticism of consciousness, about the world of dreams, about beings that are gods and spirits and their hidden influence on humanity, come together to create an entirely new image of the world.

Gods are dethroned, temple columns topple, mosques and cathedrals are stormed. A new, more powerful, indestructible cathedral is built from spirit and the thought 'I AM'. Those who awaken in this personal refuge have understood the mystery of consciousness. At any time they can be the self-knowing observers of their thoughts, the self-knowing observer of their feelings, the self-knowing observer of their being and their creator.

To the question of what he felt was the most important aspect of magic and mysticism, the shaman Don Eduardo, who is called the magician of the four winds, answered "humour". Meyrink too often used satire to effectively convey his magical and mystical experiences. Emil Stejnar has also now discovered this, and the most recent discoveries of spiritual investigation are couched in entertaining stories. So don't take what happens as seriously as they should really be taken. But stay alert and awake! This is because tales carry you away to another world. And to be in the world of dreams and dreamers can be dangerous.

BOOK 13: GNOSIS TANTRA KABBALAH
The serpent, the power, and the force

There are thousands of treatises on Gnosis, Tantra, and Kabbalah. All merely theory. Now, at last, the practice is explained in a way that is easy to understand, and it is proven that the different methods of the different traditions are based on the same spiritual foundations and insights.

- **3 traditions, 2 paths, 1 goal.** All three systems are explicable in terms of the mystery of the serpent.
- **Kundalini Shakti – the serpent** of the Tantrists – is the serpent of the Gnostics – is the serpent of the Kabbalists – is the manifestation of the power that brings something into being: an image, a thought, a feeling, a decision.
- **The serpent is the power of imagination,** the power of conception, the creative power of thought with which every action begins. It is also the manifestation of the power with which one conquers unwanted ideas and impulses. It is power and force at the same time.
- **This is how you get a grip on the serpent.** In the beginning is always the word – that is, the thought. A thought can seduce, fertilise, or oppose the power of an unwanted thought.
- **Tantra, yoga, and sex magic.**
- **Gnosis means knowledge.** It does not concern knowledge of facts, but rather knowledge of yourself. Not who I am, or what I am, or how I am – it concerns the realisation: "I AM" as the

centre and bearer of consciousness. Around this centre, those who are awakened arrange their subtle organs and limbs.
- **The God who can recycle himself.**
- **The flesh of spirit and soul.**
- Franz Bardon describes **the frequencies of the cosmic language** with which Kabbalists shape themselves and work magic as the effective power of colour, sound, sensation, and quality. These powers are linked to letters, which serve as containers and building blocks.
- **The astrological code** as the key to understanding Bardon's system of Kabbalah.

THE BOOKS OF *MAGIC & MYSTICISM OF THE THIRD MILLENNIUM* IN 13 VOLUMES:

Book 1: THE BOOK OF THE MASTER AND HIS HEIRS. An exciting novel of initiation from the world of magic, Freemasonry, and the afterlife.
ISBN 978-3-900721-24-4, ISBN 978-3-900721-25-1

Book 2: SPIRITUAL EXERCISES FOR FREEMASONS. Instructions and lodge speeches about magic and mysticism. An insight into the true essence of the Freemasonic tradition and the secret magic of Christian mysticism.
ISBN 978-3-900721-02-2, ISBN 978-3-900721-06-0

Book 3: THE FOUR ELEMENTS. The secret key to spiritual magic. How to shape your immortal light body and how to master the spiritual powers.
ISBN 978-3-900721-22-0, ISBN 978-3-900721-09-1

Book 4: OUT-OF-BODY EXPERIENCES. Learning to live without your body.
ISBN 978-3-900721-23-7, ISBN 978-3-900721-26-8

Book 5: ASTROLOGY. Navigation for the journey of life. Genetic code of spirit and soul. *ISBN 978-3-900721-11-4, ISBN 978-3-900721-12-1*

Book 6: THE ADEPT FRANZ BARDON. Who Was He, What Did He Teach, Where Does His Path Lead?
ISBN 978-3-900721-15-2, ISBN 978-3-900721-16-9

Book 7: THE BOOK OF GUARDIAN ANGELS. How do I make contact with higher beings? The attendant spirits of the Earth Belt Zone, their effects, and what you must do to get them to help you to ease your destiny.
ISBN 978-3-900721-19-0, ISBN 978-3-900721-05-3, ISBN 978-3-900721-04-6

Book 8: THE THEBAN CALENDAR. The 360 principals of the Earth Belt Zone and the tides of their power. The world of demons, gods, and spirits.
ISBN 978-3-900721-20-6, ISBN 978-3-900721-21-3

Book 9: DIET-YOGA. How to beat the yo-yo effect. How to stop smoking. How to turn your weaknesses into willpower.
ISBN 978-3-900721-07-7, ISBN 978-3-900721-10-7

Book 10: ANDY MO. The Son of the Gnome King in the Human Realm. A fantasy novel but also excitingly real. An induction into the world of magic and mysticism. For children and adults. *ISBN 978-3-900721-17-6, ISBN 978-3-900721-27-5*

Book 11: AT THE PORTAL TO THE FINAL LANTERN. An incredibly exciting thriller about hidden powers that control world events, the consciousnesses of the living and the dead, and how we awaken and free ourselves from this spiritual net.
ISBN 978-3-900721-00-8, ISBN 978-3-900721-08-4

Book 12: DREAMING CAN BE DANGEROUS. Unusual, exciting, and provocative tales about the mystery of being awake, death, and the abyss we can fall into, both in this world and in the afterlife. Finding yourself and awakening are the greatest goals of the Hermetic path. How we manage to achieve this is revealed in these last two books.
ISBN 978-3-900721-01-5, ISBN 978-3-900721-03-9, ISBN 978-3-900721-28-2

Book 13: GNOSIS TANTRA KABBALAH. The serpent, the power, and the force.
ISBN 978-3-900721-13-8, ISBN 978-3-900721-14-5

WWW.STEJNAR-VERLAG.COM

Emil Stejnar

Born in 1939 in Vienna (Austria), Stejnar has been engaged in magic and mysticism since his early youth. Through numerous publications and media appearances he became well known at home and abroad. Next to running his own jewellery store, for twenty years he directed the Institute for Scientific Destiny Research, and is the founder of Gnostic Hermetics, which carries the old Traditions forward into the third millennium.

He is particularly concerned with Freemasonry and Astrology, as this is where he found the interface that links the world of the spirit with the world of matter, and thus the world of esotericism with the world of science.

Stejnar is reckoned to be the successor of the famous magician Franz Bardon, and he is mentioned in the preface of the new edition of George R. S. Mead's work on Gnosis, *Fragments of a Faith Forgotten*, as the last major Gnostic next to great minds such as C. G. Jung, Mozart, Hegel, Nietzsche, Rilke, and Kafka, and next to adepts such as Jakob Böhme, Papus, Eliphas Levi, and Aleister Crowley.